A Time to Bloom

Books by Lauraine Snelling

Leah's Garden • 2

A Time to Bloom

LAURAINE SNELLING

with Kiersti Giron

BETHANYHOUSE

a division of Baker Publishing Group
Minneapolis, Minnesota

© 2022 by Lauraine Snelling

Published by Bethany House Publishers
11400 Hampshire Avenue South
Minneapolis, Minnesota 55438
www.bethanyhouse.com

Bethany House Publishers is a division of
Baker Publishing Group, Grand Rapids, Michigan

Printed in the United States of America

Library of Congress Cataloging-in-Publication Data
Names: Snelling, Lauraine, author.
Title: A time to bloom / Lauraine Snelling ; with Kiersti Giron.
Description: Minneapolis, Minnesota : Bethany House Publishers, a division
  of Baker Publishing Group, [2022] | Series: Leah's garden ; 2
Identifiers: LCCN 2021057108 | ISBN 9780764235726 (trade paper) | ISBN
  9780764235733 (cloth) | ISBN 9780764235740 (large print) | ISBN
  9781493437245 (ebook)
Subjects: LCGFT: Novels.
Classification: LCC PS3569.N39 T56 2022 | DDC 813/.54—dc23/eng/20211129
LC record available at https://lccn.loc.gov/2021057108

Scripture quotations are from the King James Version of the Bible.

Cover design by Dan Thornberg, Design Source Creative Services

Author is represented by Books & Such Literary Agency.

Baker Publishing Group publications use paper produced from sustainable forestry practices and post-consumer waste whenever possible.

22 23 24 25 26 27 28   7 6 5 4 3 2 1

To Wendy Lawton.

Wendy is one of the most creative
people I know, in so many ways.
Her marvelous business sense is put
to good use as an agent,
where she blesses us all through her skills
and encouragement.

Delphinium

Derived from the Greek word *delphis*,
meaning *dolphin*, since the flowers
are shaped like dolphins.

They symbolize an open heart
and ardent attachment
and convey a feeling of light and levity.

1

Has it been an entire year? Delphinium Nielsen thought in surprise.

She and her three sisters were gathered around the table in their sod house. She said aloud, "We've been here in Nebraska for a whole year, and I think we need to celebrate. After all, we've accomplished a great deal."

She waved to include the addition to the house and their section of land that would one day become Leah's Garden. They already had the sign up at the end of their lane. The garden would be a dedication to their mother, who dreamed of having a nursery of plants, flowers, bushes, trees of the flowering and shade kinds, and also fruit and nut trees. Her dream had been in Ohio, but then the war got in the way, and both of their parents passed on to their heavenly reward.

"I agree." Larkspur, the eldest, nodded.

"So what are you thinking?" Forsythia, the first of them married and the third in line, asked.

Del shrugged. "I don't know. The words just popped out of

7

my mouth. I guess a party for all of our friends here in Salton. I could invite the families of my students too."

Excitement pricked at the thought of seeing her beloved schoolchildren again. She needed to start planning for the fall term soon. With all the new families in town, she could have a much fuller classroom. Hopefully in an actual school building this year instead of the church, where they'd been meeting since the tornado last fall.

"We could ask people to bring their own chairs or benches." Lilac, the youngest, held Mikael, the baby they had adopted on their trip west, along with Robbie and Sofie, who were playing with their carved animals outside. Forsythia had promised both of the two mothers who died on the trail that she would take care of their children. When she married Dr. Adam Brownsville, they had a ready-made family.

"We'd have to." Del paused. "You know, there's a town meeting coming up. We could issue the invitation there."

"Why not at church tomorrow?" Lilac watched Mikael as he woke and grinned up at her. She kissed his forehead. "You are such a good baby." Her words earned her another grin.

"True, but I also need to ask around about more important things." Lark sighed. "I need to find a bull for Buttercup. She should have been bred several months ago."

Robbie had decided that the little heifer born to Buttercup was his. He named her Clover, and she followed him around like a dog. Right now she was lying in the shade of the house, chewing her cud while the children played.

"Doesn't the Weber family north of town have one?" Forsythia asked.

"I'll find out." Lark looked up. "Just think, with a roof from this side of the house, we could have shade outside for gatherings like this. Our trees can't grow fast enough. When I think of home, I covet the trees."

The cottonwood they'd dug up at the creek bed and planted off the corner of the house last fall had made it through the winter and leafed out, but it couldn't be called a shade tree yet.

"There aren't many around here, that's for sure." Del dug a sheet of paper out of the cabinet Jesse, Adam's nephew, had made for them. He had even carved the handles for the doors. She sat back down at the table. "All right, let's plan this event. A week or two from this Saturday?"

"No, let's do as Lilac suggested and have Reverend Pritchard announce it in church tomorrow for next Saturday. Why put it off?" Lark asked.

They all shrugged, so Del wrote that on the paper. "We'll have a potluck supper and music for singing and dancing after."

"If there's to be dancing, we need to firm up some dirt," Lark said. "We've not had that many people out here at one time before."

"I know. A real celebration." Del beamed.

"I thought we had a fine celebration after our wedding," Forsythia said. "That was only a few weeks ago."

"We did, but no potluck or dancing. And besides, that was in town," Del said. "This will be right here."

Sofie came in from outside. "Mama, Robbie growled at me."

Forsythia rolled her eyes. "You go tell Robbie that Mama said to play nice." She paused. "Wait. What did you do that made him growl?"

They all knew that Robbie was infinitely patient with Sofie.

"I smashed his fence."

"And why did you smash his fence?"

"Because." The little girl studied her bare feet on the finished dirt floor, her light blond hair in two braids.

"Because why?"

Del pushed her laughter down. Forsythia was so patient with the little ones.

"'Cause he said my cow couldn't come in his pasture."

"And why was that?"

"'Cause there was no gate, so I smashed the fence to make a gate." She pulled her shoulders up to her ears. "And now my cow can go in his pasture."

"Makes perfect sense to me," Del muttered. Lilac nearly burst trying not to laugh.

Forsythia sent a pleading look to the others, then shook her head. "Big help you are."

Del pushed back her bench seat and took the tin they used for cookies down off a shelf. She handed two to Sofie. "You take these and give one to Robbie. That'll make him stop growling."

As the little girl happily trotted outside, the four sisters looked at one another and let the laughter roll.

"You've got to admit, she thought it through before smashing the fence. That'll teach him to build gates." Lark reached for a cookie and passed on the tin.

"As Ma would have said, there's a life lesson here: Always build gates. First is probably best." Del nodded. "Our mother was a very wise woman." She hoped to pass along some of that wisdom to her students, since she doubted she'd ever have a family of her own.

"She would have so enjoyed these little ones. Sometimes I miss her so much I hurt all over." Lilac looked down at the year-old boy starting to wiggle in her arms. "We need to remember to tell Jesse about the fence smashing."

Adam and Jesse were spending every spare minute trying to complete the four upstairs bedrooms in Adam's house. He was already muttering that they should have made the house larger. Forsythia suggested the answer was to move his office and treatment rooms to a separate building or off one side of the house. Ideally, they could add a room or two for patients who needed more extensive care.

"Any more planning we need to do for the party?" Forsythia asked.

"Not that I can think of, except what food we want to fix," Del said. "Folks will bring the rest. What else needs to be done here, besides creating a place to dance?"

"Pray for rain. Carrying buckets to water the garden is a real backbreaker. I should ask Jesse if he could fashion me a yoke to carry two buckets, like I've seen in pictures." Lark looked to Lilac. "Could you draw a diagram?"

Lilac thought a bit. "I've seen pictures like that. It might be faster than hauling buckets in the wagon. What about the barrel that was on the wagon we came west in?"

"Too big for the wagon we have now. We'll use that to collect rainwater as soon as we have a shingled roof on some building." Lark thought a moment. "Remember using water from the rain barrel to wash our hair?"

"Or dancing in the rain to do the same."

"Next rain here, we can do that again. It should be warm enough by now. I need to hitch the oxen and plow another section for seeding more grain. If it stays dry, we can start scything the hayfield. Then move the grazers over. An article I read in the farming magazine talked about alternating pastures. It means more fencing, but everything not planted can be hayed." Lark rubbed her forehead. "Isn't that the way of farming? We need rain for the growing things, and yet to get the hay down and stacked, we need sun."

"While you're plowing, I need to start hoeing so the weeds don't get ahead of us. I think we have enough leaf lettuce for supper tonight. And the peas will be ready to pick any day now." Del pushed back from the table. "It must be close to dinnertime too."

"I'm hungry, Ma," Robbie announced from the doorway.

"We'll have bread and jam in just a bit." Del pulled the long knife from its slot in a wooden knife holder, something else

Jesse had carved for them. He spent many of the long winter evenings carving utensils and building furniture. Adam helped whenever he could.

There was so much to do, getting a new farm up and running, a new home, a new life. School planning on top of it all. And now she'd added preparing for a party to the list.

That Sunday at church, Rev. Pritchard announced the invitation for the gathering the following Saturday. "To think the Nielsen sisters have been here for a full year. They promised the evening would include singing and dancing, so bring whatever you would like for the potluck supper and musical instruments besides. Extra chairs or benches if you can." He nodded to Henry Caldwell, the attorney. "You have an announcement?"

Caldwell stood. "We have scheduled a town meeting for a week from Monday. There are many exciting things on the horizon, and we want to make everyone aware of the possibilities. I know we've been talking about when the train will be running on those tracks out there. It turns out the railroad company has designated Salton to be a water stop. They will start constructing the water tanks and towers soon, but drilling the well comes first. We hired a dowser, and he's certain there is plenty of water. It just depends on how deep they will have to drill."

"Any more announcements?" the young pastor asked, then nodded. "We will continue with our closing hymn, 'Blest Be the Tie That Binds.'"

He nodded to Mrs. Caldwell, the attorney's wife, who sat at the piano. Forsythia lifted her violin, and Lark was ready on the guitar. They joined in at the opening bars.

Del tapped her foot as they all sang, "'. . . binds our hearts in Christian love.'" It was a blessing to have moved close enough to a town that already had a church and a school, and now a doctor. With the railroad investing in the town, all manner of changes would come. *Lord, show us your way.* She scanned the congregation, counting the heads of school-age boys and girls. She'd found a joy in teaching that she'd never imagined, a chance to make a difference in the lives of not just children but also their families. Yet the new building the town had promised was not yet begun. Worry pinched her middle. She needed to speak to someone about that. Again.

They finished the fourth verse, and the musicians continued to play softly as Rev. Pritchard raised his arms and, with a glorious smile, pronounced the ancient words: "And now, the Lord bless us and keep us, the Lord lift up His countenance upon us and give us His peace. Amen." Smiling, he made his way to the front door to greet all the congregation.

At Forsythia's nod, Robbie and Sofie followed the older children outside to play. Mikael woke and stretched in Forsythia's arms, his contagious smile evoking returning smiles from the adults around him.

"Oh, Forsythia, he is such a charmer." Rachel Armstead wiggled her eyebrows, making Mikael chortle. "Is he walking yet?"

"Oh, so close. I figure any day now, he'll make the decision and run to catch up to the other two. As it is now, he can crawl mighty fast."

"Do you have something special you would like us to bring to the party? I have a whole ham I can hardly get in the oven, but it should go a long way to feeding everyone."

"Oh, that would be marvelous. I'll tell Lark."

"You'll tell Lark what?"

Forsythia turned to grin at their oldest sister, who was reaching for Mikael as he reached for her.

"Hey, big boy." Lark bounced him in her arms, making him giggle. She smiled and nodded to Rachel. "A big ham like that would be perfect. We have a couple of young roosters I figured would bake up real well too. If you have any sawhorses so we can make tables, we'd be obliged."

"I'll ask Pa if he will bring benches and such." A cloud passed over Rachel's face. *If they come* was the unspoken addition. Her mother, Mrs. Jorgensen, was still having trouble with the new doctor, even though he had saved her grandson's snakebit leg and life. She referred to that as an accidental good thing. Trust came hard for her after a charlatan doctor failed to help her other daughter.

"I'd hate for them to miss out on such a good time," Del said. Rachel nodded. "Me too."

As Rachel Armstead left, Beatrice Caldwell, Henry's wife, joined them. "I so enjoy playing with you two. It's a shame we can't bring the piano out to your place."

"Why can't we?" Lark and Forsythia grinned and nodded at the same time. "If Reverend Pritchard agrees, the men could push it up on a wagon, and you could play it right from the wagon bed. That'd make it easy to return to the church."

"I wonder who else plays instruments," Beatrice said.

"I think Anthony Armstead plays the concertina, which is good for dancing. Lark plays anything, and Lilac is great on a drum. At home we had an old washtub that Pa made into a bass fiddle with a rope and a pitchfork. But washtubs are too precious out here to drill a hole in one." Forsythia glanced over at the men gathered together nearby.

Discussing "important" business, no doubt. Why was it that whenever decisions were made that affected the whole town, the men tacitly decided to leave the women out of it?

Del raised her eyebrows with a slight nod to Lark. She tipped her head at the men, and Lark gave an answering lift of her brows, then nodded in return. Good thing they had perfected silent communication over the years.

Passing Mikael to Lilac, Lark ambled over to stand just outside of the circle. Maybelle Young, the banker's wife, also stood nearby, trying to act disinterested and failing miserably.

Del rolled her lips together to keep from chuckling. If anyone could find out what the men were up to, it was Lark.

She glanced over the rest of the gathering. She should talk to some of her students' mothers about the next term. She'd had concerns at the end of last term that some of the older children might not come back, kept home to help with farming instead. Building up the land was important, but so was education, or the next generation wouldn't be equipped to steward this soon-to-be state into the future. Now that she'd had a break since the end of spring term, new ideas for the coming school year popped up in her mind every day. With a larger group, she wanted some of the older children to help teach the younger—after all, the best way to truly learn something was to teach it. And she could bring in more of her sisters' talents this year to expand the curriculum—music, art, even botany.

Rev. Pritchard approached the circle of sisters, beaming. "We sure are looking forward to that shindig at your place, ladies."

"Thank you for announcing it this morning." Lilac shifted Mikael on her hip. "You should bring one of your instruments and join in the music."

"Perhaps I will."

"Reverend, have you heard any more about when we might be able to start the school building?" Del asked. "I'd really rather not crowd your space in the church for the new term."

"I haven't." He hesitated. "The focus has been on the railroad since we learned Salton would be a water stop. I'll talk to some of the men, though."

"Maybe we could go talk with them right now." Del peered around him at the circle of menfolk.

"I don't think this is the time." Rev. Pritchard shook his head with an indulgent smile.

When will it be the time? Del swallowed back the retort. The pastor meant well. He always did. Yet shouldn't her input matter, as the sole teacher of Salton's young people?

Del noticed the Weber family passing by. They had six children. At least she could talk to Mrs. Weber. "Excuse me."

But the Webers had reached their wagon by the time Del caught up, Mrs. Weber wrestling a crying toddler. Del stopped and glanced around. The gathering was dispersing, wagons heading in all directions. Disappointment sagged her shoulders. She had waited too long. She'd have to talk to parents at the party.

"What did you learn, Lark?" Del asked from the driver's seat on the way home.

"They've settled on a location for the water towers and train station. The railroad already owns that land, so they'll be paying for the construction. It turns out Mr. Young owns most of the land Salton is being built on, along with Mr. Caldwell."

"Really." Del raised a brow.

"Adam seemed a bit surprised to learn he'd purchased the land for his house and clinic from the banker, not the town."

"Did you happen to ask about the school building?"

Lark slanted her a glance. "I was there to listen, not shut them up by reminding them that I was present. But you know the other night, when we were talking about a boardinghouse?"

Del and Lilac nodded.

"I have a feeling we need to start working on that while there is still land available. Once that train is running, I think land prices will rise accordingly. I think instead of paying off the homesteaded land, we use that money for a half acre or so in town, east on Main Street and on the north side of the tracks. The same as the water tower and train station."

"Who is going to build it?" Del asked.

"I don't know, but we should sit down this afternoon and write a letter to Anders to see if he wants to buy into our idea."

"Who will run it?" Lilac asked. "I mean, Del will be teaching school, Forsythia is busy being a doctor's assistant and working at the store, and Lark and I are the only two working full-time on our own big dream. You think Anders would sell the store and move out here?"

"And Jonah?"

"To run a boardinghouse?"

"No, to farm the land for us, and I'll take over the boarding-house." Lark shrugged. "The first step is a letter to Anders, and the second is talking with Mr. Young."

"You think Anders will go along with this?" Lilac asked.

"I have no idea. I asked Josephine to put half the garden there into zinnias for seeds. We'll have a good harvest of bachelor buttons and daisies here. I'm hoping the snapdragons will work well too."

"What about cosmos? Ma loved her cosmos."

"We planted all the seeds we have, so we shall see how it goes."

They climbed down from the wagon, and Lilac led the oxen off to the shed, parked the wagon next to it, then unyoked them and let them out to pasture in the one field that was fenced.

"Lark, did you hear Jesse talking about a herd of pronghorns just north of here?" Lilac asked.

"No, really?" Lark's face brightened. "You want to go hunting?"

"Today?"

Lark nodded. "At times like this, I wish we had another horse."

They headed inside, and Del began pulling out food for the noon meal.

"We can ride double till we find them and then sling the carcass up behind the saddle. Remember how Little Bear talked about hanging on to the stirrups to travel faster?"

"We could roast a haunch for the party."

"You two are crazy. Everything we have to do around here, and you want to take off hunting." Del continued slicing bread.

"I wish we had a smokehouse built," Lark said.

"Oh, sure, one more thing to build." Shaking her head, Del set to buttering the slices and spreading jam on them. She tried to squelch the tension building in her middle. Usually their time of fellowship after church left her uplifted, not disgruntled. "When shall I plan for supper?"

"We'll be back as soon as we can."

After they left, Del took a tablet and pencil outside and sat in the shade to write to Anders. She breathed in the fragrant summer air and closed her eyes. *Lord, forgive my anxious thoughts.* But someone needed to stay focused around here.

> *Dear Anders and Josephine,*
>
> *It's Sunday afternoon, and Lark and Lilac just headed out to hunt pronghorn. Lark mentioned again how she wishes we had another horse.*
>
> *Haying probably starts this week. We'll recruit everyone we can. Tell Jonah we could sure use some help out here.*
>
> *The big news is the railroad tracks are being laid through Salton and on west. They plan to dig the well this week for the water towers, so Salton will be the first water stop after Lancaster. Building a train station is high on the discussion list.*

She laid down her pencil and went in to feed the fire under the rabbit stew she had made. Lilac had snared a couple of rabbits and given one to Forsythia. A slight breeze tickled the short hairs at the nape of Del's neck, easing peace into her soul.

> *We have an idea—not that we don't have enough work as it is—to build and open a boardinghouse with a café*

that will be open to the public rather than just those paying for a room. There is such a need for housing both for those working here now and others that are coming. We thought that since the wagon trains are less frequent, we'd have fewer visitors, but the train tracks are bringing more change. I don't know if you are aware of the emerging salt mines, but they are not far from here.

Anyway, we are hoping you will share our interest in a boardinghouse and be willing to invest in building materials and the other expenses of opening such an enterprise. Leah's Garden is still our primary interest and dream, but like Lark keeps reminding us, cash flow is critical. My teaching is the only real money we have coming in, and Lark says her purse is thinning down.

I hope and pray that all is well for you back there. How is little Marcella doing? How we aunties wish we could see her. Looking forward to hearing from you soon. You know how Lark is once she gets a bee in her bonnet. Someone in this family needs to keep our feet on the ground, and it looks to be my job.

Love and prayers from the western part of the family.

> *Your sisters, Del, Lark, Lilac,*
> *and Forsythia with the little*
> *ones*

She raised her face to the calming breeze. The fragrance of rabbit stew drifted by, reminding her to stoke the stove again. Being all alone here felt strange. She missed Forsythia. It was only last month that her sister had gotten married. It used to be the two of them who managed things at home when Lark and Lilac went off gallivanting. Now it was only her.

Del folded and slid the letter into an envelope, waiting to

seal it in case the others wanted to add more. Picking up her knitting, she watched the sun begin its descent to the horizon. The breeze picked up, cooler now. It was time to make sure the chickens had all gone into their house, and she glanced out at the pasture to see Buttercup and Clover following their trail to the fence. Almost milking time.

She stared off toward the setting sun. Lark and Lilac had headed northwest. What was taking them so long? But they always forgot everything else once they headed off hunting. Never mind that they'd left her to do all the evening chores by herself. Fighting a prickle of resentment again, she let Buttercup into the barn and poured grain in front of her stanchion. Clover bawled from outside the door. The windmill creaked and squealed as it turned to face the evening breeze that had sprung up. Someone needed to climb up to apply grease to the gears.

With the last drop of milk in the bucket, Del stood and hooked the three-legged stool up on the post, then set the pail out of the way and let the cow out. Buttercup backed up and turned to walk out the back door. She always headed to the trough for a drink before ambling out to pasture with Clover right behind her.

Such a peaceful routine, especially during fine weather. It soothed Del's anxious heart a bit.

Carrying the bucket up to the well house, she poured the milk through a cloth to strain out any hair or dirt and then set the pans to let the cream rise to the top. They had enough cream now to make butter. A Monday job.

The sun had painted the layers of clouds in all shades of red and orange, and the yellow of the sun blazed near to white. Sunset, and no horse with two figures walking beside it. Del had better check on the stew and set the table. Her sisters would be hungry whenever they got back. And as usual, she'd have everything taken care of here.

Del squeezed her eyes shut. *Please, Lord, forgive me for being like this. I know we need the meat they're getting. I just . . . I keep thinking about the school—or lack of one, that is. I will trust you, Lord. I trust you.*

She stared up at the darkening blue above her. What if she had to teach at the church all year?

Lord, are you listening?

2

Why did weeds grow so much faster than flowers or vegetables?

Lark leaned on the handle of the hoe and used the back of her hand to wipe the drips from her forehead. July in Nebraska could be hot, but more than that, some days it was like breathing water. She leaned over to pull weeds from the row of carrots. The hoe could only get so close.

"Auntie Lark!"

She turned to see Robbie helping Sofie climb through the gate, and then the two of them charged down the garden row. Sofie squealed when she tripped and fell face-first into the just-hoed soil.

"Don' cry." Robbie sent Lark a pleading look and turned to help her up. "See, not hurt."

The little girl raised her arms to Lark, tears muddying the dirt on her face.

Lark winked at Robbie as she swooped Sofie up in her arms, brushing her off at the same time. What a pair these two made. "See, you can stop crying. You're dandy fine." She looked at

Robbie, who waited patiently. "Now, what brought you running out here?"

"Auntie Del said, 'Hurry up, dinner is ready.' So we hurried up."

"Good, you most surely did hurry up." Lark fought to keep the laughter inside so they wouldn't feel bad. It was a good thing Forsythia brought the children out most days. Sometimes, like today, she left them here and returned to assist her husband in the office. His practice was growing, thanks to an influx of people searching for land and a home of their own, many of whom had lost their desire to travel by wagon all the way to Oregon.

Everything was growing around here. If only Lark could manage to keep up with it.

She set Sofie on her feet, patted her on the back, and, after leaning her hoe against the fence, headed for the house.

Robbie slipped his hand into hers. "After dinner, can I help you pull weeds?"

"Me too." Sofie nodded emphatically.

"You need to take a nap," Robbie said. Definitely big brother to little sister.

Lark paused. "Hear that?"

"Meadowlark?"

She nodded and watched grins spread over the children's faces as they listened to the meadowlark's aria.

"Pretty." Sofie looked up at Lark. "You a bird?"

Lark swooped her up again. "No, Lark is short for Larkspur. That's a flower we will have blooming here later this summer."

"Oh." Sofie patted Lark's cheeks with her small hands. "Pretty."

Robbie pondered this. "And Mama is Forsythia, and she said that is a bush that blooms bright yellow after winter."

"That's right." How Lark enjoyed watching him puzzle things out.

"And Auntie Del?"

"Is short for Delphinium, a flower that also blooms in the summer."

"What color is your flower?"

"Blue, and Delphinium is also blue."

"And Auntie Lilac?"

"Lilac is a bush with purple blossoms that smell wonderful. We might have one bloom next year." She pointed to the other garden. "We have two growing over there and may transplant one closer to the house. They were too small to bloom this year."

They needed to plant more lilacs and forsythia around the vegetable garden too. She'd heard they could deter grasshoppers. The last thing they needed was another influx of the swarming vermin that had besieged the region last summer before the Nielsens arrived. There were so many things to worry over, or rather try not to worry over. *But, Lord, how do I not worry about tomorrow yet still be prepared for it?*

"Auntie Del said come eat." Sofie slid down to the ground.

Lark took Robbie's hand, and they trotted to the house.

"Wash your hands," Del called from the kitchen.

"Eat outside?" Robbie asked.

"On the bench. How did the hoeing go?" Del asked as Lark washed her hands at the basin.

"We hit a couple of rocks that we need to dig out. It got mighty hot out there. I think the oxen are as done in as I am." She lifted her face to the slight breeze, her sunbonnet hanging down her back. "Wading in the creek sounds like a good idea,"

"Me too, me too." Robbie and Sofie matched in words, then giggled at what they'd done.

Del set a plate of sandwiches on the bench. "Robbie, would you please say grace?"

They all bowed their heads.

"Dear Papa God, thank you for this food that Auntie Del made for us. Amen."

"Thank you, Robbie." Del raised an eyebrow at Lark, quickly blinking a couple of times in the same motion.

Lark sniffed and nodded. *Papa God. Lord, thank you for this child you have given us.* His trust was a lesson she needed. She looked at Lilac, who was cutting half a sandwich in half again for Sofie to hold, a smile tugging at the corners of her mouth.

The children each drank milk from tin cups while the women drank coffee.

Lark finished her sandwich and got up to bring the coffeepot for refills. "Our plowshare needs sharpening. We sure could use a blacksmith in town."

"It's a shame that one with the railroad moved on with the crew." Lilac took another bite of fried-egg sandwich. "You sure make good sandwiches, Del."

"Fresh baked bread makes anything taste special," Del said. "What do towns do to get someone like a blacksmith to move in?"

"Well, they post notices in newspapers, for one thing," Lark said. "But there has to be enough business for them."

Lilac leaned back against the wall of the house. "Remember how Mr. Holt used to shoe his own horses? Sometimes he fixed a wagon wheel or something. He always said that if a man wanted to ranch or farm, he needed to be able to fix his machinery and care for his livestock."

"You think this might be something to bring up at the town meeting?" Del asked. "Maybe someone knows how to sharpen a plowshare, at least."

"Sharpen it too many times more, and we won't have any plowshare left." Always something else needed in this new life. Here Lark had thought their first year of homesteading would be hardest, but they'd barely begun. Establishing the farm, getting

Leah's Garden going, helping build the town—it all made her feel out of breath at times, even when sitting still.

"Auntie Lilac, are we going to the creek?" Robbie asked.

Lark looked at the children. Sofie was fighting to stay awake, almost slumped against Robbie. "I think someone is ready for a nap."

Del smiled as she stood and scooped up the little one. "I'll put her down. Robbie, we'll go to the creek later."

"Then I can help weed in the garden?" He looked to Lark, who nodded. "And maybe go fishing in the creek too?" Now he looked to Lilac, who grinned and nodded back.

"I'll come weed too," Lilac said. "Good thing it rained yesterday so we don't have to haul water to the garden. Of course, that means the weeds sprouted and grew overnight."

Lark nodded. "As a child, I thought the rain showered weeds as well as water."

Robbie stared at her. "Does the rain do that?"

"No, the seeds are already in the ground, and the rain makes them sprout faster."

"So if you pull out the weeds before they go to seed," Lilac added, "we won't have so many weeds to fight."

He studied Lilac. "So weeds are bad?"

"They choke out the vegetables." Lark held out her hand. "Come on, let's go get them."

"Could we feed the weeds to Buttercup?"

Lark and Lilac exchanged wide-eyed looks. Lark grabbed her hoe. "Some weeds are not good for cows."

She waited for the next question, but Lilac took his hand and showed him the carrot tops.

"You have to pull out the weeds gently so the carrots stay in the ground. And if a carrot comes out, too, you dig a hole with your finger and stick it back in the ground." She made sure her actions were the same as her words.

She and Robbie each took a carrot row, and Lark moved on to the beans. Another month and they'd be picking beans. She looked off to the pasture, where dandelion blossoms dotted the field. Time to go pick greens again for supper. She reminded herself to look for wild onion and curly dock. And they could pull some cattails from that swampy area. In the spring, they'd enjoyed wild asparagus and the tender young leaves of stinging nettle—boiled to take out the sting, of course. And morel mushrooms. Her mouth watered at the memory. She hilled up the potatoes to make sure the tubers didn't get sunburned.

"Robbie, would you go get us some water to drink, please?" Lilac asked.

He bounded up with a big grin and ran toward the house, then brought back a jug of water. "When can we go fishing?"

"As soon as we finish weeding the beans. They go fast." Lilac set the jug back by the fence. "You want to go over to the old manure pile and find us some worms?"

"To eat?" His eyes danced with his giggle.

Lilac rolled her eyes and wagged her head, making him laugh even more. "There's a tin pail by the well house."

He took off for the house with the jug.

Lark wiped her forehead again. "He seems much older than five."

"I know. He can even read simple words. I think he could do all right in school, although Del says to wait until he's six. That's the usual age to start first grade. The other day he drew letters in the dirt with a stick and taught Sofie to recognize them too."

Lark shook her head. "Does Del know this?"

"Probably not, but I'll tell her. She's been lesson planning every chance she gets lately. She seems to feel extra pressure with all the new students coming in."

"She knows we depend on her salary to help us stay afloat.

If we can get a good wheat crop this year, that'll bring in some cash and help a good deal."

"As long as we get enough rain but not too much, and no storms ruin the harvest or grasshoppers or . . ."

"Don't remind me." Lark tipped back her hat, hoping for a breeze against her sweaty face. *Lord, farming sure is full of reasons to trust you.*

The next morning, coffee cup in hand, Lark studied the tall grasses rippling like waves in the breeze. Good thing they'd gotten the garden weeded yesterday. She fetched the whetstone out of the tool storage and set to sharpening the scythes.

Lilac, also cup in hand, joined her on the bench. "Del out milking?"

Lark nodded. "It was nice of her to start the coffee first." Looking to the east, she watched the sun peep its first bit of golden glory over the horizon. As if attached, the aria of the birds burst forth, announcing and welcoming the sun.

"Just think," Lark said, "when we have more trees around the house, we'll have more birds singing."

"Cutting hay today?" Lilac took a sip of coffee.

"As soon as the dew dries."

"Jesse said he'd be out early."

"Good. Three of us scything will get a lot done, especially if Del spells." Lark dumped the dregs from her coffee cup on the clumps of grass growing by the sod house. "Those fish were such a treat last night. You and Robbie need to go fishing more often."

"We saw a rattler pattern across the path."

"That's all we need. I'll cut the bread. Del said she was churning butter today, since she didn't get to it yesterday, and the soft cheese in the well house should be ready."

They went inside to make breakfast, and a few minutes later, Jesse stepped in the door. "Mornin'."

"Figures. Breakfast is ready, and you appear." Lark smiled.

"Perfect t-timin'."

"Thank you for coming."

"'D'rather work outside than in any day."

After a breakfast of soft cheese and bread, Lark filled a jug with water, and each of them picked up the sharpened scythes leaning against the house. After walking past the fenced-in gardens and pasture, she set the jug next to a fence post and settled her straw hat. "Let me get a couple of lengths in, and then you each do the same."

She swung the scythe, and the tall grass lay flat to dry. Three steps as she swung the scythe back, and the second swath lay, the pattern developing. Humming in her head, she continued to the far corner of the pasture fence, turned to the right, and continued. Her arms and shoulders were already complaining.

Looking back, she could see how the others were doing. Keeping the pace she'd set meant they would all be dragging before long. She took two more swathes, then something made her pause.

Sure enough, a nicely coiled rattler warned her away.

"Thank you, Lord." She raised her voice. "You two, stop. We have a guest."

Jesse joined her. "You want me to kill him?"

"With what?"

"The scythe."

"I'd rather let him go."

"And be here another time? Not a good idea."

"They help keep the rodents at bay." Holding her breath, Lark slid the tip of her scythe under the snake and flung it toward the gully.

"Anthony Armstead s-says they're good eatin'."

"I'd have to be mighty hungry." Lark felt a shudder charge from her toes to the top of her head. She took off her straw hat and fanned her face with it. "That was a bit close."

When they'd made the circuit of the two-acre field, they stopped for a drink from the jug and sat for a rest.

Jesse flopped back onto the ground, eyes closed under his straw hat. "Wake me in a m-minute or two."

"What use is that?" Lark swatted at him with her hat, then stretched her neck from side to side. "I read about a horse-drawn sickle bar mower. I want one."

"We could mow our fields first and then hire out to mow others." Lilac lay with the back of her hand shielding her eyes.

"Who has money to pay for mowing?" Lark asked.

"You watch. I think we should order one for next year. Save up our money."

"We'd need a team of horses too." Lark waved her hat to shoo the flies. "We could dream all day, but let's get back to it."

They'd made another round when Robbie met them at the post. "Come eat dinner."

"Where's Sofie?"

"With Auntie Del. I wanted to run, and she can't run too good."

"Let's bring the scythes. We need to sharpen them." Lark stared out over what they had done. And to think they had three more fields this size or larger to cut.

The week passed in a blur of haying and keeping up with the garden. Adam and Jesse spent one morning building a roof extension out from the side of the soddy to add extra shade, since their trees didn't help much yet. The sturdy beams holding up the roof almost gave the feel of having a front porch.

"We'll be glad of this for more than the party." Del nodded, scanning it with her hands on her hips. "We should eat out here often in the summer."

Saturday morning, the day of the party, Lark assigned Jesse and Lilac to rake the hay to turn it while she continued cutting. Del had given them strict orders to stop at dinner so they could finish getting ready for the evening. Meanwhile, she had been baking and cooking since before dawn, never mind that everyone would be bringing food.

"You're coming tonight, right?" Lark asked Jesse as they walked back to the house.

"Uncle Adam s-said so." Jesse ducked his head. "But I'm not much g-good at dancing."

Lark's heart pinched at the rare angst on Jesse's face. A hard life he'd had, passed around from relative to relative until Adam took him under his wing. His stutter had improved under Adam's gentle coaching but would probably never be entirely absent. *Lord, he's become like another brother, but how often do I stop to think what is going on in that quiet head? Or what future there might be for him?*

"Well, we Nielsens are all good teachers." She whacked him on the arm with her work glove. "So you'd better save me a dance, you hear?"

The return of Jesse's shy grin lightened her heart.

It lightened further still when Lark surveyed the gathering throng that evening, wagons arriving full of chattering children and parents who seemed nearly as excited.

"It's been too long since this town had a merrymaking to go to." Beatrice Caldwell pressed Lark's hand, her eyes bright. "Leave it to you girls to fill the gap."

Lilac tuned her fiddle by the wide patch of dirt they'd cleared for a dance floor, while Del oversaw the refreshments at a table under their young cottonwood tree. They had strung lanterns from the trees and between the house and barn. Forsythia followed a tottering Mikael with outstretched hands. The baby had taken his first steps a couple of days ago and now careened headlong between skirts and trousers, heedless of anything or anyone in his path.

"Mighty fine party, Miss Larkspur."

At the familiar drawl, Lark turned with a smile. "Isaac Mc-Tavish. Should have known you'd show up in town again the minute we had some music."

The drifter they'd first met on their wagon trip west tipped his worn hat. "I'd never miss a chance to hear the Nielsen sisters strike up a tune, that's the truth. But I've been back in town nigh on a week now. Came to sign on for buildin' the train station."

"And you didn't tell us?" Lark felt a pang of disappointment, though he had no obligation. After Isaac had helped finish their barn for winter and joined them for Christmas, she'd thought a real friendship had sprung up between them. Come spring, though, he'd taken off again, searching for work elsewhere.

He angled his bearded head. "I meant to, truly. Just been run near off my feet. That building master keeps us at hammer and saw sunup to sundown."

"Well, I'm glad you heard about the party and knew you'd be welcome. You got some refreshment?" She nodded at the cup in his hand.

"I did." He drained the lemonade and held out his hand as Lilac and Forsythia—now that Mikael perched safely in Adam's arms—struck up the first dance tune. Rev. Pritchard and a few other musicians had brought their instruments and joined in too. "Would you care to dance?"

"I'd love to." But she hesitated as she caught sight of Del heading toward her, thunder on her brow. "I'm so sorry, excuse me a moment." She caught her sister's arm and pulled her aside as fiddle and harmonica music twanged through the air. "What's wrong?"

"I just overhead Mr. Young talking with Mr. Caldwell and some new businessman in town." Del folded her arms across her best calico bodice. "They were talking about not building the schoolhouse this summer at all."

Lark frowned. "Without consulting you?"

Del huffed. "Well, they certainly didn't invite me to join the conversation. Though it was all I could do not to break in right then and there."

"Probably best you didn't." Lark rolled her lips together. Rarely had she seen her steady sister so upset.

"We had that whole Thanksgiving fundraiser, but nothing has happened. If educating our children isn't important, what is?"

"Well, the train coming through is rather urgent just now, but it won't last forever." Lark squeezed her sister's elbow. "Maybe you can talk to them after church tomorrow."

Del blew out a sigh and lowered her arms. "I suppose."

"Why don't you go join in the music? They're missing you on the guitar."

"I better check the refreshments." Del headed off.

Lark glanced around for Isaac, but he stood deep in conversation with Adam now. Ah well. Perhaps she'd better look for Jesse instead and claim that dance. Hopefully no other fuss would sneak in and spoil the evening.

By the time the musicians decided to call it a night, some of the wagons had already left.

Forsythia laid her fiddle back in its case and sighed. "This has been some party."

"That's for sure." Lark yawned. "Everyone seemed to have a good time."

"Even Del, although it wasn't looking too promising at one point."

"She told you about the school?"

Isaac stopped beside her. "Sorry, Miss Larkspur, we never did get that dance."

"Well, I'm sure we'll have more parties like this before the snow flies. You going to stay on around here?"

"Well, I might follow the railroad for a spell. But I'll be back, as long as there's work here to keep me busy."

"I know for a fact the schoolhouse needs to be rebuilt, and we're thinking on a boardinghouse. I'm sure there will be plenty of work."

"Good to know." He touched his forehead in a gentle salute and strode off toward town.

The clock had ticked past midnight by the time the sisters fell into their beds.

Lark laced her fingers behind her head on the pillow, thinking of tomorrow. "Sunday is supposed to be a day of rest, but like that old saying—make hay while the sun shines."

"How are we supposed to do both things at once?" Del asked from her bed.

"We need more hands for the scythes and someone else to keep turning the cut hay."

It was probably a good thing one couldn't cut hay at night. The other side of her mind slipped in with *But you could sharpen scythes by either moonlight or lamplight.*

Did everyone have a nagging voice inside their heads?

3

R J Easton sat straight up in bed.

The blazing artillery and rifle fire, the screaming— all now a dream. No, not a dream but a horrific nightmare. The morning breeze danced with the lace curtains, the dog's toenails clicked across the white pine floor, and stove lids clanked in the kitchen below his room. His room. He was home. Relief collapsed him back against the pillows. The war was no longer his life.

His eye itched. Bringing his fingers up to rub his eyes, he remembered. He only had one eye. Somehow—only God knew how—he'd come through the war with no visible scars after three years in the Army Corps of Engineers. He had entered the Union army as a second lieutenant due to his three years toward an engineering degree at college.

He made it safely through the war, only to lose his eye on his long-awaited journey home. RJ pressed his fingers against the throbbing scar, against the memory. The scream of the renegade who had jumped him that night at his campsite, the expletives he'd hurled at him for being a Yankee. The slice of the man's knife across his face, then the feel of that knife in RJ's own hand when he wrested it away and killed the man.

So much for his record of not taking any lives in the war.

His empty eye socket throbbed. The dog whined from the rug beside his bed. At least one creature cared that he was home. RJ dropped his hand over the side of the bed and stroked Barker's ears. The black hunting dog had not left his side since he dismounted at the hitching rail in front of the two-story brick house once filled with music and laughter. With the death of both his parents, his older sister and her husband had taken over the homeplace, but it no longer felt like home. But then, he was no longer the same man who had stridden confidently off to war.

With no eye and blood on his hands, would Francine even want to marry him anymore? They'd promised their hearts to each other four long years ago, before he joined up. Her letters had grown sparser as the months passed, but she had promised to wait for him. He needed to see her. Between his time in the hospital and his slow journey home, it had already been far too long. If Francine still wanted him, and if he could still build the dream house he'd planned for her, before war split their country and their lives in twain . . . well, then maybe he could find a reason for living again.

Barker yipped and put both front feet on the bed. He dug his nose under RJ's arm and, eyes pleading, whimpered.

The fragrance of brewing coffee called his name. "All right, fella, I'm coming." He rolled to his side, the dog dropped to the floor, and RJ stood, all in one smooth motion.

His room still looked the same, rocking him for an instant, as if time had stood still. His engineering books from college still sat on his desk.

One year left—such mockery. Who cared if he returned to college? For certain, he didn't. His service in the army qualified him for any position he'd apply for.

He heaved a sigh, the weight of the burden lessening enough for him to pull on the pants he'd hung on the bedpost and slam his feet into the boots waiting with military precision at the end of the bed. The habits of military life were now part of his being.

"RJ, breakfast is ready," Esmay, his sister, called up the stairs.

"Coming." He stopped at the dresser to brush his dark hair and pull it back with a thong. The face in the mirror, with its scar flashing like a beacon, was no longer the man he'd known. He snapped the black patch in place and, slapping his thigh to call Barker, made his way down the stairs.

RJ joined the family in the dining room, where Esmay, George, and their young daughter waited at the table. Jemmy stood nearby, the cook and general do-anything-needed freedwoman who had helped RJ's mother raise her children and maintain the home. She lived in an apartment over the carriage house along with her husband, Jehosephat, also freed. RJ was thankful the couple had decided to stay after his parents passed—at least that part of home hadn't changed.

"Good morning, RJ," George said as he folded the paper and laid it beside his plate. "I trust you slept well."

RJ nodded and pulled out the chair next to Emmaline. His niece grinned up at him, showing a gap where her front tooth used to be. He gently tugged on her pigtail and returned the smile.

At least he could still smile at children in spite of the horror on some small faces when they saw him.

Jemmy set platters of bacon, eggs, and fried potatoes on the table while Jehosephat poured the coffee. "Now, you eat up, RJ. Don't you go pickin' at yo' plate."

"Yes'm." He'd eat fast, then go find Francine. His urgency was increasing by the moment. How had he even waited this long? But after he arrived yesterday, it had been a blur of seeing his family and filling them in on his story. As much as he preferred not to relive it.

"How is your friend—you said Anders, correct?" George tried to start a conversation. "Isn't that who your letter was from? We wondered. It's waited here for you for weeks."

RJ nodded and patted the folded paper he'd stuffed in his chest pocket, having read it last night. "From Ohio." He exhaled. "He invited me to visit him."

"Really." Esmay laid down her fork. "How lovely. Are you going to?"

"I—I don't know." It was too much to think about just yet. "I need to see Francine first. I'm heading over as soon as I eat."

"Ah." Esmay glanced at her husband. "So soon?"

RJ stared at his sister. "It's been four years."

"Yes, but . . ." George tapped his finger on the folded newspaper. "Well, people can change in four years. Perhaps you should give it some time."

"Doesn't Uncle RJ know that Miss Francine got married?" Emmaline's pigtails swung from one side to the other.

"Emmaline," Esmay hissed.

Emmaline shrank down in her chair under her mother's glare.

RJ dropped his fork. A dull pounding began behind his eye. "What?"

"We wanted to break it to you gently," Esmay said.

RJ's vision darkened around the edges. He focused his good eye on his sister. "Tell me."

Esmay glanced from side to side. Did she not want to meet his gaze, or did she find him that repulsive? "I'm sorry, RJ, but you were gone so long. And I never did think Francine was right for you. She's always been flighty. I do think you're better off—"

"What *happened*?" He gripped his knees under the table to stop their shaking.

Esmay sighed. "She married that haberdasher on Third Street last spring. He opened a millinery for her to run next door, attached to his shop."

RJ lunged to his feet.

"Robert Joseph Easton, wait."

But RJ was already stumbling out of the dining room and down the hallway. He nearly collided with an end table—his peripheral vision was still learning to compensate—then slammed open the front door.

Blindly, he strode down the street, his feet pounding with the pain behind his eye sockets. He couldn't speak, couldn't think. But he had to see for himself.

Hardly knowing how he got there, RJ found himself standing on the corner of Third Street, under a beech tree heavy with summer foliage. He leaned his hand against the slender trunk a moment, catching his breath.

There, directly across from him—Miller's Haberdashery. He remembered Morton Miller vaguely, a stout, nervous man with a tight hold on his purse strings and balding early, though he couldn't be out of his thirties. Morton had climbed to business success young and gained a spot on the town council, then avoided the draft by paying some other soldier to go in his stead.

But it wasn't the haberdashery that held his focus like a moth to a candle. It was the millinery next door, the sign still new-paint bright.

Ladies Millinery, Hats and Notions.

Just what Francine had always dreamed of running. Just what he had promised to build for her someday. They'd already laid out the plans for it together by lamplight on his parents' dining room table, full of laughter and hope and young love. And after RJ had asked her to marry him, he'd begun laying other plans with the added expertise of his budding engineering degree. This time, for a house. A home for them, for their family.

But that was before. Before his parents died. Before he lost his eye. Before he learned that sometimes, love is no match for time and pain and distance and war.

A faint jingle across the street, and RJ's gaze shot to a young woman approaching the shop. Her fashionable hat and bustled gown gave her figure a foreign shape, but he knew that piquant face under the hat, those dark curls.

RJ stepped farther under the tree's shadow, his heart thudding painfully. He couldn't let her see him. Not now, probably not ever.

Keys in her gloved hand, Francine unlocked the millinery door and stepped inside. The door closed with a smart slap behind her.

RJ sucked in a breath, then turned and headed back the way he'd come, hands shoved in his pockets.

So. That was that.

Back down the familiar yet foreign streets, back up the stairs of his childhood home. He ignored Esmay's feeble attempts to engage him, Jemmy's understanding glance. In his room, he yanked the faded plans he'd drawn for his and Francine's house from his desk, crumpled them in his fists, and stuffed them into the bin.

I can't stay here. The thought poleaxed him, knocking him back to sit on the edge of the bed.

What do you mean, I can't stay here? he demanded of his mind. *This is home.*

No longer.

He scrubbed his scalp with shaking fingers. Looking up, he saw his dreams flutter out the window.

RJ drew Anders's letter from his chest pocket. He considered writing back, but he'd get there about the same time as the letter. Instead, he would send a telegram from the train station. And inquire about tickets while he was at it.

Anger raged through his veins. He had no fiancée, no one to

build a new life with. He had no home, not here, not now. He'd lost his eye. He'd lost his life.

He had to get out of here.

"But you just got here." Esmay shook her head, her tears gathering again.

It had been nearly a week now, a long week, but RJ ignored his sister's words this time. There was nothing for him here. He'd tried to make her see that, and he would not try again.

"That—that hussy," Esmay spat. "I wanted to slap her silly when she announced she was getting married. Just as if her decision had no impact on anyone else at all."

"Now, now." George tried pouring oil on the troubled waters of his wife's fury. "And when will you be returning?" He stared at RJ. "I can't hold that position I wrote you about forever, you know."

"I don't know. You better find someone else." RJ hugged his sister. "Thank you, Esmay. Captain and I will catch the westbound train this afternoon."

"Can't you stay?" Emmaline asked, a tear leaking from her hazel eyes. "Ma said . . ."

RJ swallowed and shook his head. How could one little girl have trapped his heart so quickly? "No, I can't."

Her cry near to strangled him. He hugged his niece, then heard Esmay comforting Emmaline as he strode toward the front door.

"You'll write?" Esmay asked as he slung his saddlebags onto Captain, the blood bay stallion who'd waited for him here at home. "I'll keep praying for you."

RJ nodded. How to say he was sorry? Sorry he was no longer the man he had been, sorry he couldn't stay, sorry he no longer believed in the God she would pray to.

He swung up onto Captain and reined the horse around. "Barker, you stay here."

The dog sank to his haunches.

RJ forced the words past the boulder in his throat. "Love you, Esmay. All of you."

Leaning slightly forward, he signaled Captain into an immediate canter. A sharp bark made him glance over his shoulder. Barker was tearing after them with Esmay waving him on. So much for the dog obeying orders, but then, why should RJ expect that? He hadn't the energy today to argue with man or beast.

The westbound train would leave at twelve forty. Jehosephat had already delivered RJ's trunk to the train station. Jemmy had made sure he had food in his saddlebags for the two-day train ride. A full canteen hung from one of the buckles on the saddle, as well as his rifle and scabbard, and a bedroll wrapped in his slicker was tied behind. He'd heard he could buy additional food at train stops if he needed, so he wasn't concerned.

At the station, he led Captain into a cattle car, Barker right on his heels.

"No, I'll stay with my horse," he told the conductor who checked his ticket. "I see we have a barrel of water, and there is hay, so we'll be good."

"But, sir . . ." The conductor stopped at the look RJ sent him. "As you wish. You can open this door from the inside if you desire."

Welcome darkness flooded over them as the conductor rolled the door closed. RJ tethered his horse and sank onto a bale of hay, leaning against the wooden side of the car. Captain nickered, and RJ reached out to stroke his inquiring muzzle.

"It's okay, boy. This is our space for now." Barker laid his head on RJ's knee, and he ruffled the dog's ears. "You disobedient rascal." Yet something in him was glad his dog was here.

The wheels rumbled beneath them. The car lurched as the train got underway, then soon settled into a rhythmic sway. RJ rested his head back and closed his eye, letting the steady rocking lull a certain peace into his bones.

"On our way, Captain, old boy." To what he didn't know. Nor did he care.

By the time the train rolled into Linksburg, Ohio, RJ was grimed head to toe with sweat and coal dust from days of hot, sooty air swirling through the cattle car. He knew he smelled worse than a wet dog, and trying to get a comb through his hair made him consider cutting it off. But at least Captain was groomed and hadn't complained, not once.

Wearing his uniform without insignias of any kind, since he was now a civilian, and a holster with his pistol and bullets belted under his jacket, he straightened. He would have shaved, but without hot water, he'd changed his mind. Maybe he'd wear a beard from now on.

He tried wiping his hands on his trousers before climbing out to look for Anders, but it was no use. Shaking his head, RJ clambered out of the car, then turned back to click his tongue at Captain.

"Be right back, old boy."

The horse nickered at him and shook his head. Though the car had been well supplied with hay and water, and RJ by Jemmy's generous rations, Captain was as ready to get out of the train as he was. Still, it had been better than having to talk to people.

"Where've you been, stranger?" A hand clapped his shoulder, and RJ wheeled around to see Anders's grinning face.

To his credit, his friend didn't give the barest flinch at the sight of RJ's eye patch, only slapped him on the back. "I'd hug you, but you're too dirty. What'd you do, sleep in the coal car?"

"The cattle car."

With Anders already here, RJ headed back for his horse. He unhitched Captain's bridle and carefully led him down the plank ramp to the ground.

"Didn't want to leave your mount alone, huh?" Anders held out his hand to Captain's inquiring muzzle and whistled low under his breath. "Don't blame you. He's a fine one."

RJ stroked his horse's broad cheek. "I hope it's all right I brought him along." Barker whined. "And the dog."

"Of course. We've got plenty of room in the stable." Anders eyed the bedroll, knapsack, canteen, and rifle slung over RJ's shoulder. "You look like you're joining the army again. That all you got?"

RJ nodded. His words seemed to have dried up, left behind in New York. With his heart. "Just this and a trunk," he managed to get out.

Anders's gaze grew keener—his friend always was perceptive. But thankfully, all he said was, "Come on home. Josephine can't wait to meet you."

Home. Something he might never know again.

But he had to go somewhere. So RJ followed Anders through the falling summer dusk.

His spirits lifted some as he sat in the circle of lamplight at the Nielsen family table, eating his first hot meal in days and watching the antics of little Marcella, Anders's and Josephine's five-month-old daughter. She sat kicking and squealing in her mother's arms, bringing laughter to her parents and even a reluctant smile to RJ's face.

Climie Wiesel, a youngish woman Anders had introduced as their friend who helped at the mercantile, sat quietly at a corner of the table. RJ wondered what her story was. An irregularity in her nose spoke of some past trauma, as did the shadows in her eyes. A tender longing touched her face as she watched the baby.

Jonah, Anders's brother, joined them also, though he apparently lived and worked on a ranch outside of town. Not yet out of his teens, Jonah livened the gathering with his laughter. Yet every so often he'd make a comment that made Anders shake his head. With his ready wit and feeble attempted mustache, the boy seemed to be aiming to be older than he was, yet RJ noted a fleeting insecurity that crossed Jonah's face whenever he thought no one was watching. This must be the troubled youngest-in-the-family Anders had worried about during the war. Prone to . . . gambling, was that it?

RJ pushed the thoughts away. He really wasn't up to dealing with anyone's problems but his own.

"I think I'll go out and check on Captain." He pushed back from the table. "All right if I bed down in the barn?"

Anders frowned. "The barn? We've plenty of room in here. Come sit by the fire awhile. I want to hear about your time in the army after we parted ways. And to tell you about this letter from my sisters and see if you'd be up for a trip out west. There's a lot of opportunity out there right now for a man good with his hands."

"I don't know if I am anymore." RJ hesitated. "And I don't think I'd be quality company for swapping war stories tonight."

Anders started to protest again, but Josephine laid her hand on his arm. "Let him go, Anders. He must be worn out. RJ, there's a cot made up for you in the sitting room if you change your mind."

RJ nodded, gratitude closing his throat. "Thank you, ma'am. Maybe tomorrow night."

He should say more but couldn't. Hoping his nods all around would fill in the gaps, he headed out into the welcome darkness, weariness weighting his limbs.

The murmur of voices and the clink of dishes followed him to the barn, as did Barker, tail wagging. RJ stumbled over a root in the unfamiliar terrain but regained his footing. Finding the barn latch, he shoved the beam up and slipped inside, then secured the door behind him.

The warm darkness and familiar scent of hay and horseflesh soothed the jagged edges of his heart, though his missing eye was burning again, a grinding agony that made him want to claw at it. The army surgeon had been able to give him no definitive answer as to why the pain existed or how long it might last.

Captain nickered from the stall Anders had provided, and RJ made his way over to his horse and ran his hand over his whiskery muzzle. The stallion whooshed warm breath against his face. RJ leaned his forehead against the horse's broad nose and closed his eye. He hated himself for walking out on Anders and his family like that. Anders was a good friend, the best, and they had opened their home to him.

But sitting at Anders's hearth and seeing his contentment with wife and child . . . The stab of all RJ had lost twisted anew, drawing fresh blood.

Francine, why wouldn't you wait for me? I waited for you.

Tears burned, stinging as they seeped into his scar, then bringing a strange relief. RJ untied his bedroll and lay in the straw near Captain's stall. Barker curled beside him, pushing his nose under RJ's arm.

He'd apologize to the Nielsens tomorrow. He didn't have it in him tonight.

4

Did she dare confront the men directly?

Trying to listen to the women's conversation around her, Del glanced over at the circle of menfolk across the churchyard.

"That was a delightful party last night," said Mrs. Caldwell.

Del turned back and put on a smile. "Thank you. Our first real party in our new home."

Mrs. Caldwell smiled and shook her head. "I'm amazed at all you sisters have accomplished in just one year."

"We've had a lot of help." Del glanced away again, this time toward the site of her former school, just within view from where she stood. She and some of her pupils had cleaned up the debris left by the tornado, but the schoolhouse itself had been erratically dropped in pieces, none of which were large enough for anything but firewood. The scattered pile looked lonely and forgotten, a bit like she felt herself lately. Though that was silly with a whole community around her, not to mention her family.

"Don't you think, Del?"

Her attention jerked back to the conversation. "Pardon me, I missed that."

"I asked if you had any idea yet how many new students you will have," Mrs. Weber said.

Del squinted to refocus her thoughts. "At least six, from beginners to . . ." She took a moment to ponder. "I think our eldest is fourteen."

"I heard Mr. O'Rourke saying his two older sons weren't going to waste any more of their time in school. He needs their help on the farm."

"I know. He was adamant." Del's mind leaped back to when she met the new family after church a few weeks ago. The mister was downright rude. She felt sorry for his wife, who was so grateful her children could go to school again. At least the older boys had had early years of school before they moved out west.

Another burst of laughter from the male circle caught her attention.

"Excuse me, please," she said to the women. "I need to ask about rebuilding the school."

Most of the other men were heading to their wagons, but Mr. Young and Mr. Caldwell were still talking as she stopped next to them.

"Pardon me, but may I ask you something?"

"Of course, Miss Nielsen. How can we be of service?" Mr. Young's smile didn't make it from his mouth to his eyes.

Del inhaled and smiled with her full face. *Lord, help me.* "I'm getting concerned about the schoolhouse. With all the new pupils moving to the area, we are in need of our building more than ever." Best not to let on that she'd overheard their discussion at the party. Men didn't like it when a woman knew too much.

The two men swapped glances, and then both nodded in unison, as if they had planned it.

"We've been meaning to speak to you about that." Mr. Young adjusted his coat lapels. "It looks like we're going to have to put the school off for the time being."

"Put it off?" Hearing the words so plain slapped Del hard.

Mr. Caldwell stepped in. "I know how dedicated you are to teaching our children, and I wish we could do both, but the train station has to come first. Hopefully we can begin work on the schoolhouse later in the fall."

"Provided no other more urgent projects come up," Mr. Young added.

Del's heart sank. "Can't you spare any men sooner? Surely the schoolhouse wouldn't take as long as the station. Though I think we should build for the future and make it large enough for two classrooms, at the rate we're growing."

Mr. Young pursed his lips. "You give your opinion mighty freely, Miss Nielsen."

"I am the town's sole teacher." Steel slid into her voice despite her efforts.

"And we value your opinion." Mr. Caldwell sent the banker a glance. "But you seemed to manage quite well in the church last term, didn't you?"

Del bit her tongue. Only she knew the burden it had been to set up and tear down her classroom each week, to work around prayer meetings and social gatherings. Rev. Pritchard was always gracious yet often underfoot, even though his circuit was divided between Salton and his other church in Antelope Creek, a neighboring town. To be unable to keep her own books and supplies at school but constantly toting them back and forth. Attendance had seemed more sporadic too. She had a nagging sense that as long as the school remained without a permanent place, some students would give less effort to their learning, and even be less likely to stay enrolled at all, especially the older ones. Yet she'd been truly grateful for the space, consoling herself with the promise of a brand-new schoolhouse all her own for the coming fall.

A promise that was now only a dream after all.

Mr. Young glanced at someone behind her. "Ah, just in time. Reverend Pritchard, you don't mind us using the church as a school building again this term, do you?"

"Us?" Del clamped her teeth together. *Interesting word choice.*

"Not in the least. I'm just grateful we can use God's house more." The pastor nodded to Del with his customary beam. "Do let me know if you need help setting up Monday mornings. I thought we might use some of the Thanksgiving benefit proceeds to order more school supplies and books for you. Perhaps even build bookshelves to fit under the windows."

But those proceeds had been meant for the new building. Still, with new students, she should be grateful for new books.

Del forced a smile and a nod. "Thank you, I appreciate all your efforts. I see my sisters are waiting for me. We will make do—for now. Good day, gentlemen."

She turned and strode to their wagon. Though as hot as her head was pounding, walking might help more than riding.

"You go on." She motioned to Lark. "I think I'd do more good walking today."

Lark gave a gentle head shake. "Come on, get in and tell us about it. You can't let this get under your skin."

Easy to say, hard to do. Del settled next to Lark, with Lilac on her other side. Usually they would have Robbie and Sofie along, but today Forsythia said she wanted them to remain at home.

"I gather it didn't go well." Lark could always tell.

"You might say that." Del rubbed her forehead, fighting a sudden urge to cry. "I'm stuck with the church, at least for now."

"When are you thinking of starting school?" Lilac asked. "You know we'll all help set up."

Del blew out a sigh. "Usually mid-August, and I think we will stay with that. Someone suggested we wait until September when it is cooler. Harvest won't affect too many of the children this time."

"Whoever thought you'd be needed as a schoolteacher like this? I mean, I figured hopefully in a couple of years. You were wise in going ahead and getting your certificate when you did." Lilac squeezed her hand.

Del had done it because their family needed income. Little had she known how much she'd love teaching. Yet for all the townsfolk claimed to value education, they had little notion what it truly demanded of her.

"After dinner, let's write another letter home and let Anders know what's going on," Lilac suggested. "It might help him decide if he's coming out for a visit."

"Fine idea. Have you noticed more grasshoppers lately?" Lark turned to her sisters.

"That's mostly what the chickens are eating. Those two young roosters are going to taste mighty fine all fried up in a pan."

"True, but not today. We have leftovers from last night."

Del looked up and smiled as they drove past their *Leah's Garden* sign, her spirits lifting at the sight as always. "I hope Mama likes our sign."

"Of course she likes it." Lilac grinned at Del. "I dream of her nodding the way she did and saying how proud she is of us and then shaking her head and adding, 'But we must not get puffed up now. After all, everything we have is a gift from our heavenly Father.'" She stepped down out of the wagon and walked around it to stroke their mare's nose. "I'll unhitch her and leave her at the barn for a bit. Riding over to the creek to go fishing again sounds like a good way to spend the afternoon after we write the letter."

They ate a cold dinner so as not to have to start up the stove and sat around the table in the roof shade to pitch ideas to Lilac, who was doing the writing.

"Remind him to bring more starts of forsythia when he comes." Del leaned her chin on her hand. "And to let us know if he does want to invest in the boardinghouse."

"When we finish the letter, I'm taking Starbright and going fishing." Lilac sketched a forsythia branch in the margin. "Didn't we also talk about putting up a tent to cook and serve meals to the workers?"

"We did?"

"Didn't someone mention that?"

The sisters looked at one another and shook their heads.

"Hmm, I thought for sure I heard meals," Lilac said.

"That amazing creative mind of yours just took flight." Lark nodded. "But that is a real possibility."

Always another project. The pressure in Del's chest rose again. "Oh, come on, Lark. Pretty soon you'll think we should open up the church to take care of the transients from the railroad. Or shall it be tents for them too?"

"Del . . . what's come over you?" Lark stared at her. Lilac kept her head low and doodled a pair of fists.

"Well, maybe I could teach school in a tent or—" Del slapped her hands on the table. "In case you haven't noticed, we need the money I bring in. But no one seems to care." She started to stand up, but Lark grabbed her arm and forced her back into her seat.

"I don't know what's really bothering you, Delphinium Joy Nielsen, but we need to talk about it." Lark's voice was soft. "Like Mama always said, bring these things to the Lord."

Del tipped her head back, tears streaming down her cheeks. "I don't know." She shook her head. "I just feel like I'm standing at the bottom of a big hole, and nobody is listening to me." *And, Lord, this is not like me. What is going on?*

Lilac laid her hand on Del's tanned arm. "Maybe you're the one who needs to go fishing."

She wagged her head slowly from side to side and heaved a sigh. "Let's just finish this letter so we can get it in tomorrow's mail. When I figure this out, you'll be the first to know." She sighed again. "I sure wish Mama was here." She rolled her lips together and tried blinking the tears back.

Lilac drew teardrops on the side of the letter, but the splotch that hit the paper was one of her own.

"Ask if they've heard anything about the gambler or that reprobate deacon," Lark suggested. "I keep thinking we need to get Climie out of that town."

Del mopped her eyes and blew her nose. "You think Anders might actually move out here one day?"

Lark shook her head. "That won't happen. They'll never leave Linksburg."

Lilac tipped her head. "You know another thing Mama said, 'Never say never. But watch out if God says never, because that's real for sure.'" She shrugged. "Let's get this finished."

We are so hoping you will decide to visit. We wish you could all come, but then who would mind the store? Forsythia helps out at the general store here once in a while, but Dr. Brownsville is getting busier, and she helps him too. Sofie and Robbie are out here often. Robbie and Buttercup are best friends.

Lilac read aloud what she'd written. "Anything else?"

They are seeking more laborers, so if you know people who are dreaming of heading west, Salton and Lancaster (the town about twenty miles southeast of us) are both growing.

We love you. If you have any drawing or painting materials around the house, I would appreciate you bringing those too if you come.

Love from all of us to all of you.

Lilac, Lark, and Del

Lilac folded the letter, stuck it into one of the envelopes she had made during the winter, and addressed it. "Whoever goes to town first needs to mail this."

Del watched her younger sister mount Starbright and, with a bucket of worms and fishing pole in hand, jog off to the creek. Maybe she should have gone along.

"I'm getting a glass of buttermilk from the well house. You want some?" Lark asked.

Del nodded and drew a long breath. "Bring the jug. I think I'll bake some buttermilk biscuits."

"Let's go check on the plants before you begin baking. I'll fill the water barrel."

"Remember to add a cow pie to the barrel. They can all use fertilizer too."

Their mother had sworn by using manure tea for her plants and was absolutely convinced that after fish water, manure tea was best. Horse manure worked well too.

Del put on her straw hat, and after draining their cups, the two sisters pulled the wagon out to the flower garden. They took turns pulling the wagon and dipping water for each plant. The cuttings of forsythia, lilacs, bridal wreath, and snowball bushes were well leafed out. The fruit saplings had sprouted branches, as had the sugar maple and other shade trees.

As soon as perspiration ran down their faces, the flies attacked them, as if one had found them and invited friends.

They emptied the last of the barrel and hauled it back to its place by the well house. The creaking song of the windmill reminded them that it needed grease. As the sun sank toward the horizon, the evening breeze sprang up, driving away the flies and blessedly cooling the air in time for supper.

Another day gone.

Morning was only a thin line on the horizon when the sisters left the comfort of their beds to start the day. The dew-laden grass dampened their skirts on the path to the outhouse. They each loaded their arms with split wood to dump in the woodbox by the stove.

"I'd much rather wear my britches than this skirt," Lark grumbled as she dressed. "It shouldn't matter what everyone else thinks. Skirts do not add ease to scything hay."

"Should we yoke up the oxen and start the stack by the barn?" Lilac asked.

"This afternoon, make sure those turned rows are real dry."

They'd just sat down for breakfast when they heard Jesse's whistling.

"Perfect timing," Lark greeted him as he came around the corner of the house.

"Good m-morning, the l-little ones will be out later. Forsythia said she'd b-bring them and get away from all the hammering." He sat down on the stump seat at the end of the table and smiled up at Del as she set a plate of pancakes before him. "Thank you."

"I chopped some ham and mixed it in the batter. That's what the lumps are."

"Good idea." He spread butter and poured syrup.

"Let's have grace." Del paused in her hustling.

"I will." Lilac bowed her head. "Thank you, Lord God, for this new day, for our home and life here, for Jesse coming to help us, for this food, for Del, who is such a fine cook, and for your loving care and protection. Amen."

"How long until they'll have the upstairs done, do you think?" Lark asked Jesse around bites.

"Should b-be this week, Adam said. Then we have to plaster the walls. But I think they'll l-leave that for now. Good winter project." Talkative this morning, he forked a couple more pancakes from the platter.

"I'll fry more if anyone wants." Del ate the last of hers. "I made plenty of batter so we can have some cold for break time."

"If Robbie doesn't eat them all." Lilac grinned and wiggled her eyebrows. Robbie's love of pancakes was nearly legendary.

Del and the children brought cold water and pancakes rolled with butter and sugar out to those in the field midmorning, after Forsythia and her brood arrived.

"Auntie Lark, we gots pancakes," Robbie hollered as he dodged around the turned hay and met them where they laid down the scythes and mopped their foreheads.

"Where's your ma?" Lark asked.

Sofie pointed back to the sod house. "With Mikael. He's crying."

Lilac passed the water jug to Jesse. "Why's he crying?"

Robbie and Sofie looked at each other and shrugged, as if they were marionettes on strings pulled by one master.

Robbie cocked his head. "He cries lots."

Del handed the bag of pancakes around. "You better eat quick before the pancake man eats them all." She grinned at Robbie. "He helped me roll them."

"Me too," added Sofie.

Robbie pulled at Del's skirt.

"What?" She frowned at him, then looked where he was pointing. Her eyes widened. "Uh, Lark, do you see what Robbie sees?"

Lark straightened and stilled. Del reached for Robbie's hand and clung to it.

A column of dark cloud shadowed the sky to the north, casting its shade over the sun and approaching rapidly.

"What is it? Another tornado?" Del's heart thudded painfully.

Jesse pushed back his hat and stared, dread on his gentle face. "Don't think so. I think that's g-grasshoppers."

5

"So what do you think? Up for getting back on that train and heading to Nebraska?"

RJ hesitated at his friends' breakfast table, sipping the coffee Josephine had poured him. He glanced at Anders, sitting there expectantly and jiggling little Marcella on his knee.

"Maybe. I don't know. The Union Pacific has already built that far?"

"Well, it starts in Omaha, which is already close, and then they're building west. I hear they're starting a branch southward too. Should at least get us close enough to reach Salton someway."

Salton. RJ tasted the unfamiliar name. Unknown town, unknown people. Sounded good to him. "How soon would we leave?"

Anders grinned. "As soon as I can get someone to help the ladies take care of the store. Josephine thinks her brother and cousin will pitch in. I want to get home well before harvest. Business always picks up around then."

"You said there might be construction work?" RJ dug into his pancakes and bacon, his appetite suddenly sharpened.

"Del—that's my second-oldest sister, Delphinium—wrote that the railroad is coming through, and they're building a train station and water towers. And my sisters have this boarding-house idea I told you about. That's the main reason for my going. They'll need lots of workers for that, and there's bound to be more construction needed if the town is booming like they say."

"You think I can"—RJ forced the words out—"still do good work with my . . ."

Anders nodded vigorously. "Sure you can. I had an uncle, a carpenter, who lost an eye in a building accident. His other eye compensated, and he was as good a craftsman as ever. Maybe better."

RJ nodded, relief tightening his throat. It was true that he already barely noticed the limitation to his vision anymore—only if he really needed peripheral on his bad side. But he hadn't tried crafting anything yet.

"Well, I'd better head to the store while you men plan your trip." Josephine planted a kiss on Anders's head and scooped Marcella from his lap. Anders had said they kept a large basket behind the counter for the baby to play in while Josephine worked.

"I'll be along soon, love." Anders pressed her hand. "I just want to walk over to the station on my way and check out the train schedules." He glanced at RJ. "Come along?"

The sun beat on RJ's shoulders as they strolled the dusty street of the town, the late July heat already rising, though it was still early. Horses clopped along the street, and jangling music already sounded through the half doors of the saloon.

Anders frowned as they passed the establishment. "I sure hope Jonah's steering clear of that place these days."

They headed to the edge of town where the train station stood, and Anders checked the schedules. "We could leave the day after tomorrow or wait until next week. What do you say?"

RJ shrugged. "Whatever you do." He'd just as soon keep going, going, going, but it wasn't his place to decide here.

"Might be best to wait." Anders rubbed his chin. "My sisters want me to bring all manner of seeds and starts for their garden business, and it'll take time to pack it all up right. And to get the store ready for others to handle for a while."

"You're not worried about leaving Josephine and the baby?"

"Her folks live close by, and they'll help out. As will Climie. Someday we'll all go visit." The light of adventure sparked in Anders's eyes.

"Ever wish you'd gone out west with them to begin with?"

Anders gave the schedule one last scan and turned to go. "Never really considered it. Josephine was here—we weren't married yet—as was the store my father left me to run. I've always thought of myself as a responsible family man. But thinking of the great railroad spanning the continent . . . well, it does fire a man's imagination." He stepped back out onto the street. "Right now, though, we'd better grease our heels for the store, or my wife will fire something else. It's near time for the morning mail, and we always get a mad rush about then."

Sure enough, Josephine looked up from behind a crowd of customers at the mercantile counter when they arrived, her face strained.

"Sorry we didn't get here sooner." Anders squeezed his way behind the counter to join her, tying on his apron as he spoke.

"Anything I can do?" RJ skirted to the side of the counter where dry goods were stacked.

"Climie's sorting the mail in the back room." Josephine raised her voice above the din of customers. "If you could bring out what she's finished, that would help."

Grateful to escape the crowd, RJ ducked into the back storage area, its walls filled with shelves of canned goods and boxes of hardware, and its floor lined with barrels and buckets. Farm implements leaned in corners.

Climie stood with her back to him, the mostly empty mail sack on a small wooden table before her.

"Uh, Josephine asked me to come get some more mail," RJ said.

The slender woman stood motionless.

RJ cleared his throat and stepped closer. "Is this it?" He reached for the three stacks that seemed sorted on the table before her.

Climie gasped and jumped back from him. She clutched an open letter to her calico bodice, her gaze darting from him to the corners of the storeroom like a spooked horse.

"Sorry." RJ stepped back, raising his hands. "Thought you heard me come in."

"I didn't—that is—I'm sorry. It's my f-fault." She stumbled to a barrel and half-collapsed onto it. Her stooped shoulders folded inward, her chest heaving. "I—I—could you get Anders or J-Josephine, please?"

RJ bolted out of the room and behind the counter. "Hey, could one of you come back here? Climie's upset about something."

Anders and his wife exchanged glances. Josephine handed one more stack of mail to a customer, then followed RJ, glancing at Marcella's basket as she passed to be sure the baby was asleep.

"What's wrong, dear one?" Josephine knelt before Climie in the back room, clasping the other woman's trembling hands. Climie was shaking so hard that the barrel wobbled. Tears dripped unheeded off her chin.

"RJ, would you bring a cup of coffee from the front, please? We keep a pot on the stove in the corner for customers."

RJ hurried to obey. Dread tightened his gut as he poured the coffee into a cup he found nearby. Only once had he seen a living creature this spooked, when he'd come upon a horse during his days in the Corps of Engineers that had been habitually abused by an army sergeant. He'd been able to report the man and get the horse removed, but he'd never forget how the mare flinched and trembled at every movement around her.

Whatever Climie's story was, it wasn't good.

Josephine still knelt before her friend when RJ returned, gently rubbing her forearms, murmuring a soothing word now and then. She took the cup from RJ and held it for Climie to sip. The young woman did, her teeth clattering against the cup, then finally drew a longer, less gasping breath.

"Now." Josephine's voice came gentle but firm. "Tell us."

Climie shuddered anew, then drew the crumpled letter from the folds of her skirt. She held it out to Josephine. "It's—it's—f-from *him*."

Josephine took the letter as if handling a rattlesnake. She smoothed out the wrinkles and scanned the scrawled message within. For a moment, she knelt motionless, and then she pushed to her feet. When she turned toward him, RJ saw a hardness he'd never imagined on the face of his friend's gentle wife.

"RJ, go get Anders. Climie's going to need to go with you out west."

"So he beat her?" RJ thrust his pitchfork under the dirty straw in the stall Captain had been using.

From a neighboring stall, Anders huffed a humorless laugh. "Beat her, kicked her, nearly killed her the last time. Did kill their unborn child. She lost the baby the next day. Then he hightailed it out of town and hasn't been heard from since—until today."

"What did the letter say, exactly?"

"Just that he's on his way home—coming for her. To collect

his rightful possession, as he put it." Anders jammed his fork into the muck as if the sender of that letter lay beneath the straw.

"And he was a leader in your church?" RJ might have nearly lost his own faith, but the juxtaposition still clashed.

"Deacon Wiesel. A devout guide to those seeking humble Christian living, if you listened to him tell it." Anders finished mucking out the stall and rolled the wheelbarrow near for RJ to add his pile. "Though *his* living stank worse than this horse dung does."

"Why didn't anyone do anything? The sheriff?"

"Legally, he couldn't—wife beating isn't a crime, hard as it is to believe." Anders set down the wheelbarrow so hard that some manure bounced out. "Some of us in the church tried to get rid of him, but I often think there must have been something else we could have done. His shenanigans are part of the reason my sisters left when they did. He blamed Larkspur for stirring up Climie to rebel against him and threatened her. Even showed up at the house in the wee hours once and routed them all out of bed."

RJ forked the muck into the wheelbarrow, anger simmering low in his gut. One thing he couldn't abide was cruelty to the innocent, be they person or animal. "I can't imagine Climie's got a rebellious bone in her body."

"You'd be right on that. It's by God's mercy she still *has* any bones in her body."

"It seems like by your mercy and Josephine's." The retort came out sharper than RJ intended.

Anders cast him a quick glance.

"Just sayin'." RJ jabbed the pitchfork into a nearby heap of fresh straw and began spreading it in the cleaned stall. "It appears God turned a blind eye to her suffering for a long time is all. Until you stepped in." God turned a blind eye to plenty of suffering from where he stood.

Anders was silent a moment. "You saw terrible things in

the war, I reckon. I know I did. Especially once I was taken prisoner."

RJ flinched. He'd nearly forgotten his friend's time in a Confederate prison camp. The horror stories he'd heard about those places made his skin crawl. Anders still limped occasionally from that terrible time. RJ had never heard the full reason why.

"But you still trust Him." The words tore from his throat, part challenge, part plea. "Why?"

Anders leaned one hand against a barn post. "I suppose, like Simon Peter said when he realized following Jesus wouldn't be easy, 'Lord, to whom shall we go? Thou hast the words of eternal life.'"

Silence hung in the barn for a moment. Then Anders lifted the wheelbarrow handles. "We better finish up. Josephine will have supper on the table. We've got a lot to do, now that we're leaving sooner than we thought."

After a quick supper of ham, baked beans, and fresh garden vegetables, RJ joined the others outside in the garden. The summer evening twilight cooled around them, and Marcella kicked sleepily in her basket, gazing up at the pearly sky. Climie sat near, sorting seeds or something in her lap.

"What can I do?" RJ blinked back the pain trying to beat behind his eye sockets again.

Anders shoved a wooden bucket filled with loose loam toward him. "Help me get these cuttings rooted. We're taking starts of raspberries, strawberries, roses, and also seedlings of sugar maple and oak."

"What for?"

"Leah's Garden, my sisters' business. They asked me to bring as much as I could. They'll plant some now, nurture others over the winter, and then plant and sell more in the spring."

"Don't forget the daylilies and irises. And the forsythia,"

Josephine put in. Wearing work gloves, she handed RJ a raspberry cutting.

Anders had said something about this, but RJ hadn't realized the quantity intended. He loosened the soil in the bucket and accepted the bare stems and fragile root balls, settling them carefully inside. "How are you going to get all this on the train?"

"Figured maybe Captain could share his cattle car." Anders cocked a brow. "Or will you be keeping him company again?"

"Yes." RJ's sharp tone wiped the grin from his friend's face. Softening his voice, RJ added, "But there should still be enough room." He reached for another bucket of soil, but a sharp stab made him bend over and groan, clutching at his lost eye.

"You all right?"

The concern in Anders's voice brought RJ upright again, smarting with embarrassment. He dragged his hand from the black patch, willing the pounding back. At least it wasn't as blinding anymore. "Sorry. My . . . scar aches at times." More like burned like fire, but he wouldn't say that. "I'll be all right."

"That doesn't seem all right." Josephine frowned. "Anders, you should take him to see Dr. Bishop before you leave."

RJ shook his head. "That's really not necessary."

But Anders was nodding, his face set in a resolve RJ was learning to recognize. "She's right. I'm not taking you to the frontier, not with pain like that. Not until you are at least checked by a physician. No doctor, no trip west."

RJ met his friend's gaze for a moment, then sighed and reached again for the bucket. "Fine."

The next day, RJ sat on the examining table in the office of Dr. Bishop, a fine-featured man with a neatly trimmed white beard and kind eyes behind his spectacles. Despite the doctor's considerate manner, RJ had to breathe deeply through his nose to keep himself in his seat as the man examined his exposed scar.

"I see the entire eye was excised, though preserving most surrounding tissue. And signs of a knife wound, yes?"

"Yes." RJ spoke without moving his head.

"Well, I see no evidence of infection." Dr. Bishop stepped back and adjusted his spectacles. "But war-wound pain can't always be explained. It could be some nerve was damaged or some small foreign matter remained behind the stitching. It may improve over time."

"That's what the army surgeon said." RJ replaced his black patch, the tension in his chest easing as soon as it was in place. "Guess there was no reason for me to come here, then." He shot a look at Anders, who sat on a stool in the corner of the room.

"Not necessarily." Dr. Bishop held up a hand, searching through a wooden cabinet of various bottles, liquids, and powders. "We may not be able to determine the source of the pain, but that doesn't mean we can do nothing about it." He held out a small glass bottle stopped with a cork. "I can prescribe you these opium pills to take when the pain gets severe. They are safe and effective."

Dubious, RJ took the bottle. "I'm really not sure I need this."

"Just take it," Anders put in. "Better to have them and not use them than to need them and not have them."

He had a point there. "All right."

Early the next morning, Josephine's father drove them to the train station in his buckboard. Josephine and Marcella perched on the wagon seat beside the older man, with Anders and Climie in the back. RJ rode Captain alongside, while Jonah drove another wagon just for all the seedlings and cuttings. RJ inwardly questioned the wisdom of transporting so many plants in this heat, but Nielsen determination seemed just about strong enough to carry them through. Or at least strong enough not to argue with.

As the engine belched steam and smoke like an impatient bull, RJ helped Anders and Jonah load the wooden boxes they had built to hold the tree seedlings, along with buckets and planters holding the smaller starts. Mr. Holt, the neighbor whose ranch Jonah worked on, had also sent along a young cattle dog for the sisters' homestead, a puppy of about four or five months, who leaped and licked at everyone despite Climie's efforts to contain him. He and Barker circled each other, tails flapping.

"He'll keep your journey lively." Josephine nodded at the dog, her own hands full of an excited Marcella, who seemed determined to propel herself out of her mother's arms toward the puppy.

"I hope we don't regret taking him along." Anders hoisted the mass of fur and wagging tail and jerked his head back from an enthusiastic tongue bath. "We'll try him with us in the passenger car but may have to relegate him to be with you, RJ."

RJ shrugged. So much for quiet alone time, but nothing about the past weeks was following his expectations anyway. At least the throbbing behind his eye sockets had dulled after he acquiesced to one of the opium pills in order to sleep some hours before dawn. He didn't like the vague fuzz that blurred the edges of his brain, but some trade-off was to be expected. And relief was not to be taken lightly. Perhaps Anders had been right to insist on a visit to the physician.

Jonah joined them. "All right, we've watered everything well and put two barrels of water in the car. That should tide you over till Omaha."

Anders shook hands with his father-in-law, then embraced Jonah and his wife and child. Josephine's smile looked wobbly, though she put on a brave face.

How long would they be gone? RJ had no notion. Nor did he particularly care at the moment, at least for himself.

Climie stood back, her face shadowed yet resolved, holding tightly to the puppy's rope. RJ wondered if she was braver than he, fleeing an evil man who shattered bones rather than merely a fiancée who shattered dreams. But he hadn't the mental energy to ponder it.

At a whistle from the train and a hollered "All aboard," RJ gave nods and thanks all round, then climbed in with Captain, welcoming the darkness when the door slid shut. The pain was beginning to lance again, the opium's fuzz wearing off. He was determined not to take more, though, not during the trip. The thought of slipping into a habit sounded warning bells in his mind that he only vaguely understood but heeded.

6

L ark had never seen anything like it. A horrid, glinting cloud, dark gray in the middle and flickering red around the edges. Like a tornado, only alive. And coming fast.

"Run," she yelled, grabbing Sofie.

Del snatched up Robbie, and they dashed for the soddy, Jesse on their heels. They could hear the sound of the grasshoppers now, a million wings beating the air behind them like an unholy host.

Forsythia and Lilac met them at the door. "Is it grasshoppers? What do we do?"

Lark set Sofie down inside and pressed her fingers to her temples. "I-I don't know." She, Lark, who always knew what to do. But her mind was spinning with the roar of the devastating cloud outside until she couldn't hear herself think.

"We've got to protect the garden," Lilac said. "I've heard smudge pots can help ward them off."

"Good." Del took charge. "Lark, let's get some milk pails, feed bins, anything metal we can find. Jesse, can you kindle fires in them?"

He nodded and dashed outside. Lark followed Del and Lilac

on numb feet. Forsythia stayed inside with the little ones, closing the door and windows. There was no sense in trying to make it back to town.

All around them the grasshoppers were falling, hitting their sunbonnets, their shoulders, their hands. Already descending on any living plant.

The smattering blows roused Lark to her senses. Shielding her face from the harsh-winged insects, she dashed for the barn, joining her sisters to dump feed from metal pails and scooping manure and dirty straw inside, then back out to the garden. His hands surprisingly steady, Jesse kindled fires in each one, the damp fuel sending up smoke like little sentinels around the garden's edge, rising like their prayers around the precious vegetables, Mama's flowers, the seedling trees.

Yet they could already hear the sound of the grasshoppers munching, eating, devouring. Lark had heard of it but hoped never to hear it.

"Lark, the wheat!" Lilac's cry turned them all. Part of the swarm moved toward the green-gold field, their precious cash crop for winter.

No. Lord, please, no. Lark ran for the field, flapping at the grasshoppers with her skirts, yelling herself hoarse as if she could scare them off like a flock of crows.

"Lark." Del caught her arm, panting. "It's no use. There're too many."

"Fire." Lark whirled on her sister. "We need to light more fires, around the grain fields."

"We used all the buckets on the garden."

"Then we'll just make piles of manure and straw all around, set them alight." Lark charged toward the barn, heedless of her sister calling her back.

The grasshoppers hopped haphazardly through the barn, giving the chickens a feast as they scurried one way and then the other, gobbling the beasts as best they could. Lark snatched the wheelbarrow and pitched manure into it.

"Lark, we can't." Del appeared at her shoulder and grabbed the pitchfork handle.

"Yes, we can." Lark yanked it back.

"The fields are too dry. We could start a prairie fire."

Lilac shut the barn door behind her. "Jesse says we've done all we can do."

Del grasped the pitchfork again, surprisingly strong. Sweat slicked Lark's hands, and the handle slipped from her grasp. Balling her fists, she fell to her knees in the dirty straw.

"God, please." She pounded her fists on her knees. "Not our harvest. *Please.*"

Her sisters sank down beside her. Silence hung, but for the awful whirring roar outside.

Then slowly, almost imperceptibly, it lessened, overridden by the rising wind that often came toward evening. Lark lifted her head.

Lilac jumped to her feet and pushed the barn door open. "I think they're leaving." Relief wafted into her voice as the wind lifted her dark curls, her sunbonnet hanging forgotten down her back. "Jesse's coming."

He appeared in the barn doorway and wiped his brow with his sleeve. "Wind is ch-chasing them off, I think. Th-they got part of the garden, but I think we s-saved some."

Lark pushed to her feet and headed for the door, legs wooden. She braced herself against the doorframe for a moment, then headed out, flanked by her sisters, to survey the land. Forsythia stepped out of the soddy, her children huddled about her, a few stray grasshoppers jumping away from their feet, skittish now that their horde had passed.

Lark scanned the land, their homestead tilled with blood, sweat, and tears. Those same tears rose to clog her throat.

Part of the wheat field still stood, though it was ragged about the edges. But a cry tore from Lilac, and Del reached to draw her close.

Their garden—Leah's Garden—was spotted with green, perhaps protected by the smoke, but much of it was stripped down to the ground.

They spent most of the next two days trying to assess damage and salvage as much as they could. Neighbors and friends stopped by—the Caldwells, Armsteads, Webers, Youngs—to bring news and see how the Nielsen sisters were faring. The grasshopper cloud had touched down with the scattered havoc of a cyclone, with some families' crops devastated and others untouched.

"You ladies should be grateful," Mr. Young observed from his gig. "You only got the tail end of it before that wind blew them out." Of course, his farm had been spared entirely.

Lark was kneeling in the garden bed, sorting through damaged cabbages to see which ones could be saved, when Del found her.

"I guess they didn't have time to eat through all these, since they're so dense." Del turned a ragged green head. "How much do you think we can replant?"

"Beans grow fast, so we can get another crop of those for sure." Lark blew out a breath. "Same with all the greens, and the root vegetables were mostly spared. It's the tomatoes, cucumbers, and melons that need the months of warm growing season, and I don't think there's time for those. And the flowers . . ."

Both sisters looked toward the decimated flower beds, the saplings stripped of their leaves as if fall had come early.

Del reached out to squeeze Lark's hand. "At least Anders will bring more."

"Yes." But they were still set back most of a year in building their business, their dream. Neither of them needed to say that out loud.

"I've been thinking." Del withdrew her hand and began piling the usable cabbages into her apron. "I should ask the town for a raise."

Lark raised a brow. "A higher salary? You think you could get it?"

"I remember hearing about teacher pay rates back when I took my certificate exam. Salton was definitely on the low end in what they offered. I said nothing—after all, I was inexperienced then."

"But you're not now." Lark narrowed her eyes. "You think it's worth asking?"

"Well, they're not giving me my schoolhouse." Del rose, her apron sagging with cabbage weight. "And I'll be teaching far more students this year than last. So I aim to try. The worst they can say is no." She smiled, lifting her chin.

Lark felt a slow smile respond on her own face. "That's my sister."

She watched Del head back into the house, then scanned the garden around her, the stripped flowers and withering vines. Her heart sank again.

They sure could use a raise for Del. Otherwise, their dream of a boardinghouse—not to mention enough food for the winter— might shrivel as fast as their beloved garden.

For RJ, the days by train passed in a blur of rocking motion and sooty breezes, of keeping Captain calm and the dogs entertained—for Scamp, as the puppy was soon christened, indeed found himself banished to the cattle car by the second day. RJ welcomed the distraction, as it turned out—too many hours sitting gave one too much time to think, and Captain only had so much advice to give. He was even grateful for the need to get out of the car at stops to allow Barker and the pup to relieve themselves, holding the rope while Scamp chased his tail in circles.

After a couple of days, they reached Omaha, where they would take the new Union Pacific line. Having a longer water break than usual, RJ and Anders headed into town to buy a newspaper.

"You boys heading west?" the friendly owner of the general store asked.

"Just for a visit." Anders handed over a coin and accepted the paper the man handed back. "My sisters homestead somewhere near Lancaster."

The man gave a low whistle. "Lancaster. I hear tell they got hit by grasshoppers down that way this week."

"Really." Anders stared. "That's bad."

"Yep, folks had hoped last summer was the last they'd see of the varmints. You know, they're thinking to make Lancaster the capital, once we get statehood next year."

Anders cocked his head. "I didn't know the town was big enough."

"It ain't, not right now. Makes little sense to me, nor most folks around here. But you know them politicians. They got their own ideas, and it makes no nevermind what the common people think. They've got some notion of laying it out as a paper town, building it from the ground up. There's even talk of changing the name from Lancaster to Lincoln."

"In honor of our late president." Anders nodded slowly.

A man stepped up to the counter and scoffed. "Just another political move."

The owner moved to ring up the customer's order. "It makes little difference to me. I got business enough of my own to worry over. But some folks are awful fired up about it and think the capital should stay here in Omaha."

"And so it should," put in the other man, a burly fellow buying bridles and tack. "There's nothin' down there but salt marshes anyhow. Like that paper there will tell ya"—he jabbed a finger at Anders's purchase—"they got no river, no railroad, no steam wagon, nothin'. We've been leading the territory this long. The seat of government should stay right here where it belongs."

The general store owner sent the customer on his way, then quirked an amused brow at Anders and RJ. "As I said, it's a mighty sore subject around here. You boys have a good trip, now."

They stepped back into the sunshine, Anders unfolding the newspaper as they walked. He scanned the front page and chuckled. "That man wasn't joking. There's an article right here on the state capital debate. 'Nobody will ever go to Lincoln who does not go to the legislature, the lunatic asylum, the penitentiary, or some other state institution.' Sore subject indeed. It'd be mighty interesting if the capital did end up down near Salton, though. I wonder what change it would bring to the area." Anders read further. "And here's something on the grasshoppers. It sounds like they hit sporadically. I sure hope they spared my sisters' place. That could set them back terribly." He shook his head, then folded the paper and nudged RJ. "If they do build Lancaster up as a paper town, they'll be needing a lot of construction men. Maybe you should consider sticking around this territory. Or state, as it soon will be."

"I'll think on it." RJ squinted in the sunshine, ready to return to the soothing dimness of the cattle car.

Their train rumbled on over the newly laid rails west, then took the beginnings of the southward branch toward Lancaster. By the time the engine pulled up at the Salton water stop, the pain had begun again, sending flashes of agony into RJ's skull till he nearly acquiesced to the opium once more. He might have if the conductor hadn't hollered out their stop.

They stepped onto the roughhewn train platform, the summer sun still well above the horizon, though it was early evening. Construction of the station looked well begun. Anders's oldest sister, Larkspur, met them with a wagon. She was tall and strong for a woman, wearing a man's hat despite her calico dress.

"Welcome." She climbed down, her face weary but beaming, and embraced Anders. "You're a sight for sore eyes, big brother."

"As are you." Anders hugged her hard, lifting her boots off the ground despite her height, then released her. "I've brought a couple of guests. I don't know if you got our telegram."

"We did." Lark stepped back and turned. "Climie." She wrapped the frail young woman in her arms. "I'm so glad you came."

Climie clung to her, her thank-you barely audible.

"And you must be RJ." Releasing Climie, Larkspur extended her hand. "Welcome. We'll have to squeeze you all in at Adam and Forsythia's house. They're the only ones with extra room, but they don't mind."

RJ shook her hand. "Pleased to meet you, Miss Nielsen."

"Lark, please. Everyone calls me that." She blew out a breath. "You'll find us reeling a bit just now, I'm afraid. But we're so glad you're all here."

Anders's eyes darkened. "What happened?"

"Grasshoppers. They hit our wheat. Not as badly as some other families, but we took some damage. The worst was the garden." She blinked hard, her jaw tightening. Even RJ, despite his pain, could see her fight against the tears. "They destroyed most of what we'd planted from Mama's seeds this year. Smoke from pails we lit did manage to save some of our food for the winter, at least."

"Oh, Lark." Anders rubbed a hand over his face. "Can you replant?"

"Some. Thank heaven for what you've brought with you."

She gestured to the boxcar. "Speaking of which, we'd better get it all unloaded."

By the time all the boxes and buckets of young plants were lugged up to the wagon, some of the seedlings a little worse for wear, the flashes of pain had become a steady throb. RJ refused a seat in the wagon and rode Captain the short distance to the Brownsvilles', but the jostle of his horse was little better, gentle though Captain's gait was. RJ gritted his teeth and bore it. Clearly, he wasn't the only one suffering around here.

But by the time they reached the doctor's house, all he could think about was a spot to lie down—a bed, a floor, even cool dirt would do. He dismounted and helped Anders stable and care for the horses, then followed his friend up to the house. They'd left the dogs in the stable for now and would unload the wagon later. At least the evening air was cooling now.

The door opened, spilling light and people exclaiming, laughing, embracing.

RJ had a moment's thought of fleeing back to the barn. But he was carried on a wave of welcome into the two-story frame house, where Anders's laugh filled the entry and his bright-eyed sisters seemed everywhere at once.

Anders grabbed RJ by the shoulders and introduced him to the lineup. "You've met Larkspur. This is Forsythia and her husband, Adam."

"We hope you'll be comfortable here, RJ." Forsythia jiggled a toddler on her hip, her gentle face wreathed in welcome.

RJ shook their hands and barely got a word out before Anders marched him on.

"And this is Lilac, the baby—well, except for Jonah back home."

Lilac had dark pinned-up braids and an impish smile. "Glad you're here, RJ."

"And last but not least, fresh out of the kitchen by the look of things, my sister Del." Anders propelled him toward a young woman holding a tray of baked goods.

"Welcome, RJ." She smiled, and he vaguely noticed her eyes were a striking deep gray-blue. "Would you like a raspberry fritter? You all must be famished."

RJ eyed the hot pastries, but amid the blinding pain, the smell just turned his stomach. "No. No, thanks." His words came out clipped.

Her face fell slightly, but Del lifted her chin and offered the tray to Anders.

His friend took one, casting RJ a frown.

Remorse twisted RJ's middle as the family chatter rose again. Yet another thing he should apologize for, but he couldn't, not right now. He just needed a place to lie down.

A fine start for his visit to the Nielsen family. And here they were dealing with a crisis of their own.

Maybe he never should have left New York.

7

*W*hat a churlish young man.

Del pushed away the uncharitable thought and tried to focus on the joy of Anders being here, a blessed ray of sunshine in the devastation of the week. But RJ Easton glowering across the table from her didn't help her mood.

"Forsythia, your cooking has gotten nearly as good as Ma's." Anders took another bite of roasted young chicken and new potatoes, rolling his eyes in pleasure. "Or maybe anything would taste good after cold train fare for days." He ducked away as she swatted at him.

"Now we know Anders is really here. He's teasing again." Lilac's eyes danced. "I'm just glad the grasshoppers left the potatoes alone."

Lark dabbed her mouth with her napkin. "What do you think about the boardinghouse idea?"

"Do you still want to pursue that?" Anders accepted a roll from the basket Del passed with a nod of thanks. "I thought the grasshoppers might have changed your mind."

Del had thought so, too, but Lark seemed more set on the idea than ever. Sometimes the desperate determination she sensed in her sister these days worried her.

"The need is still there, with the railroad bringing more workmen all the time. And the uncertainties of farming are all the more reason for us to have another source of income."

"Where were you thinking to build?"

"I've been casing the town for available land and found a couple of possible lots I'd like to show you. With the railroad coming through, land value is going to skyrocket, so we'd best buy soon. Only recently did I learn that most of the town is owned by Mr. Young, our banker."

"And what sort of man is he?"

Lark furrowed her brow. "Fair, as far as I can tell. A bit shrewd, and cares more about the bottom line than anything. But the part of our land we bought outright we bought from him, and he seemed to treat us well."

Lilac began to clear the plates. "Didn't you say Mr. Caldwell owns some of the land around here also?"

"Yes, he has the more undeveloped portions outside of town, I think."

"Ah, Henry. I can't wait to see him again. You'll like him, RJ. He was one of my army officers in the war. It's thanks to him my sisters even settled in this region, actually." Anders clapped RJ on the shoulder. "What would you think of taking on this boardinghouse project, my friend?" Anders glanced around the table. "I'm not sure I told you, but RJ is an engineer by training."

"Really." Lark leaned forward. "So you know about drafting building plans and such?"

RJ flinched and shifted in his chair. "I didn't finish my degree. But yes, somewhat."

"You know more than any of us, that's certain. We'd love your help, if you'd be willing."

The young man leaned back, his face a mask even without the black patch covering one eye. "I'll think on it."

"I may also need help getting the school rebuilding project going," Del said. Perhaps this was a way to build a bridge. "I don't know if Anders told you, but our school building was destroyed in a tornado last fall, and with the train coming through, the town hasn't yet managed to rebuild it. Have you ever laid plans for a smaller building like that?"

RJ fixed his one eye coldly on her. "I said I'll think on it." He pushed back his chair. "If you'll excuse me, folks, I'm afraid I need to turn in. All right if I bed down in the barn?"

After an awkward silence, Forsythia stood. "Of course. You must be weary from your journey. But we have a bed made up for you upstairs, RJ. You'll share a room with Anders. Adam, would you show RJ where?"

Adam nodded and pushed back his chair also.

"I'm going to tuck this little one into bed too." Forsythia lifted a drowsy Mikael from his high chair. "And then perhaps everyone will be ready for dessert? You sure you don't want some before you head up, RJ?"

"No, thank you." He hesitated. "Thanks for the good supper, though. 'Night, folks." He nodded to everyone, then followed Adam up the stairs.

"Quite a man of few words, your friend," Lilac observed, taking Anders's empty plate.

Their brother shifted in his seat. "He's had a hard time since the war."

Hasn't everyone? Del headed to the kitchen to help Lilac with the dishes, scolding herself again for her uncharitable thoughts. After all, the man had obviously been wounded. Though hadn't Anders said he was in the Army Corps of Engineers? Well, they weren't fully shielded from the horrors of war, clearly.

But everyone suffered. RJ had lost an eye, and Anders had

been imprisoned. They'd lost their parents, and now much of their best remnant of their mother in the garden, at least for this year. Del's fiancé had lost his life.

That thought made her pause in scrubbing stuck bits of potato from a plate. She hadn't thought of Everett Hastings in months, and not frequently for a couple of years. But suddenly, unbidden, the memories came flooding back. Summer evening walks together down their quiet lane in Ohio. Long talks on her parents' front porch, Ma or Pa always not far off, smiling their blessing. She had been the first of the Nielsen girls to be courted, the first to be engaged, that Christmas she'd been eighteen. Since Everett was the only son of a widowed mother and a farmer, they'd hoped faithfully growing crops and donating them for the war effort would be his only needed contribution.

Then came the draft, only a few months after their betrothal. And he'd had to go. Del had put on a brave front, but almost before she realized he had left, he was dead, struck down by a minié ball at the Battle of Chancellorsville. Her parents had passed within the next year, succumbing to a fever, and then the six siblings were on their own.

Del dashed the back of her soapy hand against her eyes. Why, after all this time? It must be all the emotion of this past week. Her loss was by no means a solitary one, she knew that. Forsythia had lost a sweetheart in the war too. So had probably half the young women in the country.

Well, no one had ever claimed life was fair. Generally, Del didn't let herself succumb to sentiment over it. She had known love, and that was more than many women would get in this lifetime, with hundreds of thousands of the nation's young men buried on battlefields. She had her school—not just a source of personal purpose now but real survival for her family.

"You sure are quiet tonight." Lilac picked up a dish towel to dry. "Is it the grasshoppers? Or just brooding over your school-house?"

"I'm not sure why everyone thinks it's of such little impor-tance," Del snapped, dunking another plate in the rinse water. "I'm merely educating the next generation of a soon-to-be state."

"I didn't mean it wasn't important." Lilac sounded taken aback. "Just asking a question."

Del sighed and swallowed back the lump aching in her throat. "I'm sorry. I'm awfully on edge tonight, I'm afraid."

"Aren't we all? I'm just glad Anders is here. He makes every-thing seem better." Lilac dried in silence for a moment. "Why don't you talk to Reverend Pritchard about the school? He'd be on your side, surely. He helped organize the Thanksgiving benefit and all."

"On Sunday, he seemed right in agreement with all the other men. But I could try approaching him about increasing my salary, I suppose. Maybe his opinion there would carry some weight with the others."

Forsythia entered, Robbie and Sofie trailing at her heels.

"Pie, Mama Sythia, Sofie want pie!" The little girl danced on her toes to see the flaky slices of peach pie Larkspur was slicing. It was a mercy most of the peaches had been picked before the swarming locusts, or there would be few pies in Salton at all. It would still be slim pickings from now on.

"What do you say, little one?" Forsythia rested her hand on her daughter's blond head.

"Pie, *please*?"

"Very well, you may have some." Forsythia scooped her up and kissed her cheek. "But let's take some out to Uncle Anders first."

Something pinched in Del's heart, watching them. Not jeal-ousy, surely. Forsythia had had her own losses, true enough. But here she was, happily married at twenty-one, with three ready-made children as well.

It was best not to dwell on such thoughts. There were far more important things to worry about than buried dreams or even an absent schoolhouse. Time to quit bellyaching and make the best of it all.

The next morning, Del rose even earlier than the Nielsen sisters usually did. She crept out to the darkened main room of their soddy and lit the lamp on the table, then dug out her set of McGuffey Readers from the trunk. Locust plagues and uncertain school location notwithstanding, at least she could lay out a solid plan of course study for the year. Her students deserved that much. Her heart ached to think of the families whose crops had been hit far harder by the grasshoppers than the Nielsens' had. For those without any other stable income, how would they survive?

Del leafed through the readers and began making notes in a slim journal within the circle of lamplight. Recitation, reading, penmanship, and arithmetic—these were the core subjects required, but she wanted to incorporate more history and science this year. Their parents had always made sure the Nielsen children—boys and girls—were well educated in all respects. Lark could still teach a lesson on botany, even if the samples available from Leah's Garden would be much sparser than she'd hoped. And music—she definitely needed to have more music this year. Perhaps even a special program at the end of the year, with recitations and singing. A spark of excitement kindled in her middle.

"Goodness, you're up early." Lark yawned and laid a hand on Del's shoulder. "Planning for the school year still?"

"The term begins in just over a week. And I know we've got all the plants Anders brought to get into the ground today." Del glanced up at the window. Black had turned to gray, signaling dawn. She closed her notebook and stacked the readers. "I'll get breakfast started."

Lilac wandered in from the bedroom also, still buttoning her work dress, then she tied on her chore apron and tugged on her boots. "I'll milk."

"I'm coming too." Lark snagged the milk pails and headed out the door after their little sister.

Del stoked the fire in the stove and lifted the crock of sourdough starter from the warming oven above. Scooping some out into a bowl, she added flour, salt, lard, and a little soda and mixed biscuits. She slid the tray into the now-hot oven, then started a pot of porridge on the back of the stove. Leaving it to simmer, she fetched the empty egg basket and headed outside to fetch eggs from the well house.

The twitter of early morning birdsong and sunrise clouds pinking in the water-blue sky lifted her spirits, and Del breathed deeply of the blessedly cool air. The heat would rear its oppressive head soon enough. Hopefully, they could get a start in the garden before then.

She stopped short next to the chicken coop. "Oh no."

Lark came around the corner of the barn, milk pails brimming. "'Oh no,' what?"

"You didn't see? Something got at the chickens." Del stepped inside, shutting the gate behind her. The hens fluttered about at her feet, clucking in distress. Feathers lay strewn about, some of them bloody. One bird lay dead, bite marks on her neck, and she counted at least two birds missing.

"Coyote." Lark set down the milk pails and joined Del inside the enclosure.

"How can you tell?" Del scooped up one of the birds and stroked her feathers, murmuring comfort. The hen was still trembling.

"See the place in the chicken wire that's chewed with a hole dug beneath? Coyote are the main ones who do that, as far as I know. And they leave more of a mess. Foxes or bobcats will just take the birds back to their den."

Del shuddered. "I thought this coop was secure."

"Best as we knew to make it. These are the first birds we've lost, but now that critter may be back." Lark blew out a breath. "I'll have to ask Jesse if he has any more ideas. Maybe we could add sheet tin to the bottom of the coop walls and dig it into the dirt so they can't dig under the fence."

"That's a thought." Del swallowed. "Well, we'd best clean up this mess. Then maybe the rest of the flock can start to calm down. Poor things."

"What in the world?" Lilac halted by the coop too. "A fox?"

"Coyote, Lark thinks."

"First the grasshoppers, now this. It never rains but it pours. I'll get the shovel." Lilac headed back to the barn.

The chicken squirmed and kicked in Del's arms, so she set the bird down with another murmur. There likely wouldn't be many eggs today, if any. Del swallowed. Well, she'd lost her appetite anyway.

Lilac returned with the shovel, and together they cleaned up the bloody feathers and buried the dead bird. With the chickens comforted by an extra scattering of feed, the sisters headed back to the soddy to wash up.

"You never know what a day may bring forth, as Ma would say. We sure have been putting that to the test lately." Lark dried her hands. "Any breakfast, Del?"

"Oh, the biscuits." Del dashed for the oven and snatched a dish towel to pull out the tray. Well-browned but not quite burned. "I'm afraid they'll have to do. I was going to get eggs from the well house, but maybe we should save them, since the hens probably won't lay much today."

"Just fry up some bacon," Lilac suggested.

"Good idea." Del hefted the cast-iron skillet onto the stove, then checked the pot simmering on the back. "There's porridge too. That didn't burn."

"See, we'll eat fit for a king."

Del's appetite returned enough to eat a tolerable breakfast, and then she and her sisters tied on their sunbonnets to head outside.

"Is Forsythia coming out today?" Del asked.

"She said she'd bring the little ones and help us in the garden," Lilac said. "Jesse and Climie too, I hope."

"Good. We can use the help."

Still, Del's chest tightened at the thought of facing their devastated garden. *Lord, give us strength.*

Lark thought she was prepared, but the sight of the garden twisted a knot in her stomach again. How could such small creatures cause such destruction?

Lilac and Del plunged right in, bless them, pulling up the stringy dead remnants of bean and cucumber plants, and, more painfully, Mama's flowers. The forsythia and lilac bushes had fared better but hadn't deterred the grasshoppers enough to protect the rest of the garden.

The root vegetables seemed mostly to have survived, though the carrot and beet tops were shorn. Lark frowned and pulled up an onion.

"Look at this." She held it out to her sisters. The onion was eaten through from the inside, the outer shell of the bulb still intact.

Lilac sat back on her heels. "Those sneaky little monsters. I guess the onions stick up just enough from the earth for them to get at."

At a wagon rattle and call behind them, Lark turned to the

welcome sight of Forsythia arriving. Jesse drove beside her, with Climie and the children in the back. They climbed down and headed over.

"Reinforcements are here." Forsythia smiled beneath her sunbonnet, Mikael on her hip. "Anders sends his apologies. He's helping Adam with a difficult case today. Where would you like us to start?"

Lark stood, stretching her already aching back. "Maybe the children can help pile the dead plants we've pulled, and you can help us sort through which ones can survive and which won't. Jesse, if you could start tilling up the soil as we clear it for replanting, that would help."

"Where are the plants Anders brought?" Forsythia asked. "Thank heaven for those."

"In the barn. I'm hoping we can get them in the ground by the end of the day, and then they'll have the coolness overnight to adjust before the heat sets in again."

"Good thinking."

"Here." Climie reached to take Mikael from Forsythia's arms, her gentle face resolute and kind. "I'll watch the children, and you go on. Where do you want the dead plants piled, Lark?"

Lark smiled at the rising strength in their friend's voice. Give her someone else's troubles to focus on, and she came alive— that was Climie. "The edge of the garden is fine. Jesse can haul them to the pile to compost for next year. Throw anything that is left of the corn in for the cows."

By next year, those dead plants would help bring life to a new garden. There lay a comforting thought.

With many hands, by noontime the garden was mostly cleared, both the kitchen section and Leah's Garden, the decimated flowers and vegetables joining the pulled weeds in a decomposing pile outside the garden fence. Lark rolled her aching shoulders and surveyed the lumpy brown expanse, so full of green and life only a week ago, though surviving plants still struggled bravely wherever they grew. Yet the bare earth held hope, too, for new seeds and the starts Anders had brought. *Lord, we little knew how much we'd need him to do that, but you did.*

"I'll go rustle some dinner together." Del pulled off her gloves and sneezed. "Got some dirt in my nose."

"We could all use a break." Lark glanced up at the sun.

They trailed toward the soddy, Mikael insisting on walking on his own two feet, clinging to Climie's finger. Lark followed Climie, seeing her look down at the little boy with a loving ache on her face. *Lord, she's wanted babies of her own for so long and had them literally kicked out of her by that monster.* Lark swallowed back a sudden hot rage. *She's safe here with us, but it's a good thing you have a plan for her future.*

Since they'd left the makeshift table for the party set up outside, Del and Lilac spread the cold dinner there—bread, ham and cheese, and a jar of canned peaches.

Lark quirked a brow as she sat down. "I thought we were out of fruit?"

"We are, but Forsythia brought this, and I thought this day deserved a treat."

Lark tipped her head in acquiescence.

The young cottonwood provided only meager shade, especially this time of day, but they welcomed every fluttering leaf, along with the faint breeze that cooled their sweaty faces. They joined hands around the table, Jesse and Climie holding Robbie's between them.

"Would you pray for us, Robbie?" Lark smiled at her nephew. She could use some childlike faith about now.

Robbie nodded and squeezed his eyes tight, scrunching his whole face.

Biting back smiles, the adults all closed their own eyes.

"Papa God, thank you for the day. Thank you for the food. Thank you Uncle Anders brought new plants 'cause the old ones got eaten. Please help the grasshoppers go eat their own food and not take anybody else's anymore. Thank you for taking care of us. Amen."

"Amen." Lark felt something release inside her. She couldn't have said it as well.

"We made even more progress than I thought we would this morning." Forsythia broke Mikael's bread and cheese into tiny bits for him to palm. "What do you want to do this afternoon, Lark?"

"Let's rest a bit and then replant what we can in seeds—beans and greens, and I want to plant more carrots and beets and turnips since they can grow into the fall and give us more food for the winter. I wish we could replant the onions, too, now that I know the grasshoppers got to them, but it's too late to grow more from seed."

"I have some onion sets a neighbor gave us," Forsythia put in. "I'll share some with you."

"That would be wonderful, thanks."

Lilac passed the plate of ham. "So seeds this afternoon, seedlings and starts when it gets toward evening."

"That sounds good." Del stood and lifted the water pitcher. "Anyone need a refill?"

Jesse held out his tin cup. "Lark, d-did you still w-want to plant winter wheat too?"

"I do, but that won't be for another month or two. In my understanding, it germinates but then doesn't really grow until spring, so it will help make up our loss, but not for this year."

"So what kept Anders and Adam back today?" Lilac asked.

"A man with a broken leg. It sounded like a hunting accident." Forsythia shook her head. "It's a young family, just a wife and young children, so there was no one to help hold him down. That's why Anders went to help."

Lark winced. Not a pleasant job, but Adam would be grateful for their brother's strong arms.

"What about RJ?"

Lark glanced at Del, surprised by her sister's question. As was Del, by the look on her face.

"He went to give input on the train station today and maybe help out a bit," Forsythia said.

"I'd like to ask him again about helping with the boarding-house too," Lark said. "See if he's given it some thought."

"Are you still going into town with Anders to look at possible lots tomorrow?"

"Planning on it. As long as we can get everything planted today." Lark rubbed a sore spot on her shoulder.

"Who will run the boardinghouse?"

Lark glanced over at Climie's quiet question.

"That's something we still have to sort out. We'll all be involved, of course, but we may need to hire someone to run it eventually. Between the farm, Leah's Garden, Del's teaching . . . well, my sisters tell me that, despite all appearances, there is some limit to what the Nielsens can do." She made a wry face, making Robbie and Sofie giggle.

They spent the afternoon planting seeds, then, as the sunlight slanted toward evening, hauled from the barn the wooden buckets and tubs Anders had brought. The bravely waving leaves and seedlings lifted hope to Lark's heart, and she passed a gentle hand over a young raspberry start. *Lord, please protect these precious gifts.*

The sun slipped toward the horizon as Jesse settled the last sugar maple seedling by the house, Climie holding it steady as he poured water around it to settle the soil. Forsythia was already loading three tired children into the wagon, Sofie nearly falling asleep on her feet.

"Thank you both so much for all your help." Lark clasped

Climie's shoulders from behind as Jesse straightened and brushed the dirt from his hands. "We could never deserve friends like you, but we're grateful."

Climie turned toward her, a pucker between her brows. "I have something to ask you."

Lark lowered her arms, her pulse quickening. "Of course, dear one." Something about her weasel of a husband?

But Climie's gray eyes were thoughtful, not afraid. "I was thinking of what you said about the boardinghouse. It looks as though I'll be staying on in these parts, for the time being, at least. Forsythia and Adam are so kind, but I don't want to be a burden. I wondered . . . do you think you might train me to run it?"

Lark blinked, then felt a smile warm its way up from her middle. *Lord, this day has certainly been full of surprises.*

But could Climie truly shoulder such a job?

8

So where are these lots you've found?" Anders asked.

Lark led her family down the dusty street with a spring in her step. "One is right near the train station. That's the one I like best. The other is a little farther away, some unused land not far from the church."

"By the train station sounds good."

"Come on, girls, keep up. We don't want to keep Mr. Young waiting." As the banker owned the land, he'd agreed to meet them to look at the lots.

Forsythia, Lilac, and Del hurried to catch up.

"I'm so grateful Climie kept the children so I could come," Forsythia said. "This is exciting." She squeezed Lark's arm.

"Have you any idea what Mr. Young might charge?" Del pulled her sunbonnet farther over her face, as the August heat was fierce today.

"I have some idea of land prices around here, but they are going up. Hopefully he'll be reasonable." Lark glanced at Anders. "You and Josephine are willing to invest in this?"

He gave a firm nod. "We agreed we would be, as long as the

plan seemed sound. And if we can get a decent price for the land."

"She knows you'll get a percentage of the profits?"

"She does. We agreed it seemed a worthwhile project."

"There's Mr. Young," Lilac put in.

The portly banker stood in front of the unfinished train station. He nodded as the Nielsens approached and shook hands with Anders. "So you are the brother to this bunch of strong-minded women."

"Well, the older brother, at least. Our youngest is back in Ohio."

"Fine, fine." Hiram Young rubbed his hands. "Well, shall we take a look at the lot? I must say, I wish I'd come up with this plan before you did, Miss Nielsen. It should be a real moneymaker."

"It seemed like a growing need." Lark smiled but kept her caution up.

"Indeed. Well, as you can see, this location would be ideal." The banker led them over to the expanse of bare prairie just beyond the station. "Close to the water towers, so we know there's water, and you could dig a good well of your own. And obviously convenient for attracting customers, as you can catch people right off the train."

Lark exchanged a glance with Anders. "Yes, that's why I thought of it. I'm surprised no one has snatched this land up yet."

"Oh, I've had other inquiries already. But you spoke to me first, so I've been saving it for you." The banker cocked a brow. "Although I will need an answer today."

Today. Well, that put the pressure on.

"What price were you thinking?" she asked.

"Oh, let's not haggle over money just yet. Take your time, walk over the lot a bit."

Lark strode the boundary of the lot, her siblings trailing behind. The prairie grass, drying in the summer heat, swished against her skirt. It was a big enough lot to build a boarding-house and a stable too, which they would need for customers' horses. Especially in winter.

Del joined her. "No trees yet."

"No, but we can plant some. Just like we did on our land."

"But the previous owner had planted that other cottonwood sapling already. That gave us a head start."

"True. But I don't think that alone is a reason not to buy this lot."

"Just bringing it up." Del's tone bit sharper than usual.

Lark eyed her sister. "You all right?"

"Sorry. Just wondering if I should talk to Mr. Young about the salary issue today." Del glanced back at the men chatting behind them and bit her lip. "He's the one with more control, after all, not Reverend Pritchard. But I'm not sure how to bring it up."

Anders approached. "There are lots of advantages to this property. I like the water source, and its location by the train station can't be beat. I'm thinking we should snatch it up."

"Shouldn't we at least look at the other property first?" Del put in.

Lark nodded. "Definitely. I agree, Anders, I like this one. But we don't want to be hasty either."

"Certainly not," Mr. Young said. "But once you see the other lot, I think the virtues of this one will stand out clearer than ever."

They headed back toward the center of town, then down the main street all the way toward the church. Lark and Mr. Young led the way, followed by Lilac and Anders. Lark glanced back to see Forsythia linking arms with Del, chatting quietly with her as they walked. Trust Forsythia to seek out whoever needed comfort, even if she didn't know the reason.

"Here it is," Mr. Young said a little while later, slightly out of breath, his face flushed. "As you can see, it's quite a walk from the station."

"But not that far." Del loosed her arm from Forsythia's and stepped forward, her face brightening. "And, Lark, look at those trees—the grove behind the church extends onto this land also. They'd provide wonderful shade for the boardinghouse."

"They would at that." Lark nibbled her lip. She'd dreamed of weary travelers being able to see their sign as soon as they stepped off the train, though. *Nielsen House*, perhaps? "Do you know if there is water available for this land, Mr. Young?"

The banker took off his hat and wiped his forehead. "Not right on the lot, as far as I know. The church shares a well with the nearby businesses, so you'd have to negotiate there."

"Yes, that's where we draw water when we're holding school in the church." Del nodded. "It's good and deep."

Lark slanted a glance at her. "You like this property."

"It just seems . . ." Del shrugged. "Friendlier."

"Friendlier, when it's so far from the station? It seems less of a welcome to me," Lark said.

"I see Del's point, though," Lilac put in. "The trees and being near the church—it has more of a stable, homey feel. And not having to dig a well is a saved expense."

Anders shook his head. "I agree with Lark and Mr. Young. Location is always most important with real estate."

"Well, it's not like we'd be competing for customers," Del pointed out. "There are no other boardinghouses in town."

"No guarantee there won't be soon," Mr. Young said. "The way the railroad keeps bringing folks out, this area'll be booming before you know it. Hotels springing up every which way, I wouldn't be surprised."

"Won't most of them continue on farther west once the railroad does, though?" Anders frowned. "It's not like there's any huge draw right here in Salton."

"Sure there is. There're the salt deposits—no one's succeeded much at developing that into a business yet, but some lucky fella will. And if they do move the capital to Lancaster, we're bound to get more traffic and business, being so close by."

"That's true." Anders nodded. "We heard talk of that in Omaha. They said they're thinking of changing the name to Lincoln."

"That's right," Mr. Young confirmed. "All that to say, you're smart to buy up land early and capitalize on your profits. And to do that, I'd say choose the lot by the train station."

"It's all about business for you, isn't it?" Del said tartly.

Hiram Young shifted his jaw. "What should it be, young lady?"

She said nothing but pressed her lips into a line.

Oh dear. *Del, keep your knickers out of a knot long enough for us to settle the deal.* "Perhaps you could tell us what you'd be charging for the land, Mr. Young," Lark said. "That may help in our decision."

"As you know, prices are rising fast, but seeing as I know you folks, I'll give you a good deal, even for that plot by the station." He named a price that made Lark swallow.

"That much? Just for the bare land?"

"Land is gold out here, Miss Nielsen. You know that. And that piece is prime real estate. Someone else will snatch it up tomorrow if you don't buy it today."

Lark glanced at Anders.

Her brother shook his head. "What about for this piece by the church?"

The banker hesitated. "Well, this piece won't be as much in demand. I'd charge only half what I would for the other. But I still say by the station is your better investment by far."

"Well, our resources are limited, Mr. Young. Especially now." Lark's heart sank, but at least the choice was clear. "You know we were hit hard by the grasshoppers."

"Many were." Mr. Young's gaze didn't flinch.

"And we still have to pay for the building of the boardinghouse itself. That will cost a pretty penny. Not to mention stables and an outhouse." She exchanged glances once more with the others. They all nodded. *Well, Lord, we asked you to make it clear.* "We'll take this lot, then."

Hiram Young frowned. "If you're sure."

They settled the deal and that they would pay the next day at the bank. The sisters needed to collect their money from home, and Anders had brought some cash with him.

"Good doing business with you folks, as always." Mr. Young tipped his hat, seeming only slightly miffed they hadn't taken the pricier property. "See you tomorrow."

"Excuse me, Mr. Young." Del stepped forward, her shoulders straight. "I wondered if I could speak to you about something."

He sighed. "If it's about that schoolhouse again, I thought we'd made the situation clear."

"It's not. At least, not exactly." Del twisted her fingers together, a gesture Lark knew well. "It's about my salary."

Mr. Young shifted his jaw. "What about it?"

"Salton pays the lowest end of the going rate for teachers in Nebraska, only twenty-four dollars a year." She lifted her chin, seeming undaunted by the refusal dawning on the banker's ruddy face. "I didn't complain last year, as I lacked experience. But I don't now, and with how our school is growing, I would like to request a raise. To thirty dollars."

Mr. Young coughed and lifted his brows. Lark bit back a smile. Her sister didn't pull punches when she got something into her head.

"Well now, I don't have the authority to do that. That'll be the decision of the school board."

"But you're the head of the school board. And one of the founders of the town, isn't that right?" Del tipped her head with a sudden beguiling smile. "I'm sure they'll follow your lead, so I wanted to speak with you first."

Lark had to turn away to hide a full grin. *Stooping to flattery, Delphinium Nielsen?*

"Well now." Mr. Young took off his hat and scratched his balding head. "I suppose I appreciate that."

"Would you be willing to speak to the board on my behalf?" Del's voice could melt a plowshare now.

"Well. I guess I could do that."

"Thank you so much, Mr. Young." Del stepped back with a gracious dip of her head. "We won't keep you any longer."

They all watched the banker amble away down the street, glancing back at the group of Nielsens once as if wondering what had just happened.

Once he was out of earshot, Anders bent over, slapping his knee. "Leave it to my sisters. Del, I didn't know you had it in you."

"Had what?" Del gave him an arch smile, then sighed, her shoulders sagging. "I thought it was worth a try, at least, catching flies with honey rather than vinegar, or whatever it is Ma used to say."

"Well, you certainly set him off-kilter a bit. Who knows if it will have any effect, though." Lark scanned the windswept bit of prairie they'd just bought. "So, here's our property. You're right that those trees provide some good shade, not to mention shielding from the wind."

"And it's convenient for Del, with teaching right next door," Forsythia added.

"Sure that's not why you argued for it?" Lark waggled her eyebrows at her sister.

"No. I mean, it *will* be handy, but I just liked it better. And we didn't have much choice."

"No, we didn't." Lark sighed and scanned the land once more before they headed back to the wagon. *Lord, I sure hope we haven't made a mistake, taking on this project right now.*

"Have you thought of all the help you'll need to hire?" Anders propped his boot on the edge of the wagon as they drove home. "Not just building, but cooking for your boarders, cleaning, laundry. Keeping up the stables."

Lilac spoke up from the back of the wagon. "I heard the town leaders are planning to advertise back east for more workers for the construction in town. Maybe we could include an ad for the boardinghouse."

"Maybe." Lark's head spun with it all. "Actually, Climie spoke to me last night, asking if she might run the boardinghouse."

"Really?" Forsythia cocked her head. "Do you think she'll stay here?"

Lilac narrowed her eyes. "I don't think she'll want to head back to Ohio anytime soon, not with the deacon threatening to come back."

A frisson of anger tensed Lark's spine at the thought of that man. "I can't believe his nerve." Or maybe she could, but she sure prayed they'd seen the last of Deacon Wiesel. He chased every charitable thought and feeling right out of her every time she heard his name.

"I'll talk to her," Forsythia said. "Del, you probably won't have much time to give to the boardinghouse, not with teaching."

"I'll do what I can." Del rubbed her arms as if the air weren't still heavy with heat and humidity. "I just hope I haven't jeopardized my job, talking to Mr. Young like that."

"Well, who else do they have to teach school?" Lark halted the horses at the Brownsville house. "Thanks for coming along, Sythia."

"Of course. Want to come in for a bit?" Forsythia climbed down, assisted by Anders.

Lark glanced at her sisters.

Del shook her head. "I've got too much planning to do."

"Soon then," Lark said to Forsythia. "Actually, I want to have you all out for supper, maybe Sunday night? We haven't had a family meal at the farm since Anders arrived."

"Sounds good. I'll speak to Adam."

"RJ, Climie, and Jesse too."

"Of course. 'Night."

They drove home as the sun slanted golden over the prairie, then hurried to milk the bellowing cow and feed the animals.

"We should have music Sunday night. It's been too long since we had a sing-along. We ended up just dancing and visiting at the party." Lilac slapped at a mosquito as they headed into the soddy under falling twilight. "Want to invite anyone else?"

"Like who?"

"Maybe the Caldwells, Reverend Pritchard. He loves our music."

Lark strained the milk. "Good idea. Isaac McTavish too, if he's still in town." Or had the drifter already moved on with the railroad? She hadn't noticed him anywhere in town today.

"It sounds like a good way to cheer everyone up." Lilac sat on a chair to pull off her boots, then jerked back as Scamp hurled himself onto her lap. "Whoa, little fella."

"I wonder if RJ Easton *can* cheer up." Del pulled out provisions for a cold supper. "He's the most sullen young man I've ever seen."

"You know Ma would have welcomed him in all the more for that," Lark said. "He seems like a lonely and hurting young man. And he might be just the one to build our boardinghouse."

"I suppose."

A yawn caught Lark by surprise. "I guess it's been a long day."

"A long day but a good one. We now have land for our boardinghouse." Lilac ruffled Scamp's ears.

"So we do. I wonder what we should call it. It'd be nice to honor Pa somehow in the title, like we do Ma in our garden business. I thought perhaps Nielsen House."

"I like that." Del sat down in the rocking chair and picked up her knitting, which she could do anytime, day or night, not needing to look. "Or Nielsen Hotel?"

"That sounds a bit pretentious." Lilac wrinkled her nose. "But I like using our name like that. That way even if all of us get married, we'll still have Pa's name there."

Even if all of us get married. No doubt Lilac would, and Forsythia already was. Lark knew Del was set on not marrying, and Lark often doubted she would herself. There was always too much to do, too much leading and caring for this family, to think of starting another one of her own. Most of the time.

But she just smiled at their youngest sister for now. "I like it too."

Scamp snoozed at Lilac's feet while she read them a chapter from Matthew, a habit Ma had started and that the sisters were trying to reinstate. Then Lark got up, wound Pa's clock, and secured the door.

"Best to bed, girls. Morning comes early."

Yet when she lay beneath the sheet, listening to her sisters' soft breathing, Lark's mind wouldn't unwind. Tomorrow, taking the money to pay Hiram Young—had he given them a fair price? Had they made the right decision in taking the land farther from the station—would it make little difference in such a small town? At least it was small for now. Who knew what the future held. *God does, and leave it there,* Ma would say.

Lark turned over. But now to find a way to build the boardinghouse, all while trying to recover from the grasshoppers. If only RJ would take the project on, as she'd no inkling of how to design a building. Or to get the workers needed.

She squeezed her eyes tightly. *Forgive me, Lord. You've guided us this far, surely you'll get us the rest of the way.*

Sometimes casting all her cares upon Him sure was a hard command to keep.

9

If only she felt ready to start.

Del stood at the front of the church, the altar behind her, and stared around the room, searching for anything that was missing. Benches for sitting, narrow tables in front to form the desks. Four students to a bench, a sure cause for devilment. At least she knew her students from last spring, so she had a head start over last year, when she took over the schoolroom mid-fall. The woman who'd been Salton's first teacher had to leave rather abruptly, so Del had been able to get a last-minute meeting with the county superintendent. After passing the exam for her certificate with flying colors, she had stepped right into the job—and loved it.

So far she had eighteen pupils registered, but she wasn't sure she had contacted everyone. It promised to be a blistering August day, so she'd already opened the windows to get some ventilation moving the heavy humid air out or up or somewhere.

She still hadn't heard a word about increasing her salary. Well, she had tried.

Since all their materials had blown away with the schoolhouse in the tornado, they had fewer textbooks, chalkboards, slates, paper, and pencils to start with, along with a total lack of library books. Their current supplies failed to fill the shelves under the window that Rev. Pritchard was so proud of. Mr. Caldwell had asked her to make a list of all the things they needed, the most important at the top.

Even her desk consisted solely of a chair with a narrow table in front of it, like those for the students. There wasn't one drawer in the place.

Lord, I know you know all about this, and I try not to complain, but surely our schoolhouse should be of more import than the completion of the train station. Or at least we should have enough supplies. I know, I know, in everything give thanks. When *thanks for nothing* snuck through her mind, she clapped her hands over her face. *Forgive me, Lord, for being so very ungrateful. Help me, please help me.*

At the sound of a door opening behind her, she dropped her hands and pasted at least a portion of a smile on her face.

"Good morning, Miss Nielsen. What a wonderful day to start school." Rev. Pritchard stopped beside her and looked around the room. "We're missing a stand and a bucket and dipper for the water."

Her shoulders slumped. "You're right. We are."

"I'll run over to the store and get a bucket, and we can set it on a stool there in the vestibule."

"You could wait until after school starts. The children will be coming any minute."

He smiled and nodded. "All right. I'll give the blessing, we can salute the flag, and then what song are you planning to sing this morning? You can play the piano, correct?"

"A little. Enough to find the opening chord. I should have asked Forsythia to come play the song for today." Another strike of *should* against her.

She could hear the children chattering outside as they waited to be called in. The desire for a school bell—they'd never found the one sucked off by the tornado—chewed on her. She didn't even have a handbell to ring. Perhaps they could rig an iron triangle with a hanging bar like the one Jesse had made for the soddy.

Rev. Pritchard pulled a round watch from his pocket. "It's time."

She stepped out onto the front steps, ready to call for the children to line up. Mr. Caldwell stood off to the side of the group and held up an arm to catch her attention.

"Sorry I didn't get here sooner, but my wife found this bell and wants you to have it for the school." He handed her a brass bell with a black handle.

"Why, thank you." *Lord, you did it again. I hardly even asked, just mentioned it in my musings.* She hated to admit to complaining.

She took the bell and, now smiling, rang it, the cheerful notes catching the children's attention. Those from the year before ran to get in line, one of the older girls guiding the new children into their places. The line started with the youngest leading to the oldest, with all of them looking at Del.

"Very good. Now we will walk in and sit down according to grades. If you are not sure where you should sit, we'll attend to that after our opening. Put your dinner pails on the benches in the entryway. Elsie, will you please help seat the first graders?"

"Yes, Miss Nielsen." Elsie, a girl tall for her age, with one dark braid hanging down her back, smiled at her three charges.

The other children filled up the rows of benches with a minimum of scuffling, and when the experienced ones remained standing, those who'd sat down quickly jumped up again.

"Reverend Pritchard, if you will please give our opening prayer?"

He nodded and stepped forward. When everything was

quiet, he bowed his head. "Heavenly Father, thank you for this day that begins a new year of school. We ask you to bless each pupil here. Help these your children to learn to read, to write, to do arithmetic, and best of all, to learn of your Word. Help us all to grow daily in grace and to be grateful. Bless Miss Nielsen as she teaches and helps these children grow. In the name of your precious son, Jesus, Amen."

"Thank you, Reverend. Would you like to lead us in the Pledge of Allegiance also?"

He turned to look at the flag in the corner of the room and laid his hand over his heart. All the children copied his actions, Elsie guiding the little ones. "I pledge allegiance to the flag of the United States of America. . . ."

Afterward, Del made her way through a fumbling rendition of "Home, Sweet Home" on the piano, but the children's enthusiastic singing covered her mistakes. Give her a guitar or a fiddle any day.

"You may all be seated." Del rose to stand before them. "For those of you who are new, my name is Miss Nielsen, and I will be your teacher this year. My three sisters and I moved here a little over a year ago. I began teaching in the Salton school last fall, and I'm glad to be back here again. Now, I would like you each to stand at your desk and tell us your name and how old you are. Let's start with Elsie."

"I am Elsie Weber. I am in the seventh grade, and my family moved here two years ago."

The boy next to her stood. "My name is Curtis Jeffers, and I'm eleven years old and in the sixth grade."

Next to him, a boy sat staring at the floor.

Curtis prodded him. "Your turn."

The boy with one shoulder strap holding his overalls in place shook his head.

Del waited. He was new, so she had no idea what his name

was. "You are next. Stand and tell us your name." She spoke firmly but still in a friendly tone. Why hadn't his parents brought him in to be registered?

"Come on," Curtis whispered.

The boy shook his head and stared at the floor.

Del debated, then smiled at the girl at the end of the row. "Betsy, you go ahead, please."

Wearing her blond hair in two braids with red ribbons, the girl announced, "I am Betsy Jorgensen. I am in the fifth grade, and I like to read. My grandpa owns the general store."

"Thank you."

They continued back and forth on the rows. Another unknown child, a girl this time, took her turn.

"My name is Bethany Kinsley, and he is my brother, John." She pointed to the boy who would not stand. "I am nine years old, and he is ten."

"Thank you, Bethany. How long have you lived here?"

"Four months. My ma said we was to come to school here."

"Have you ever been to school before?"

"No, but Ma taught us to read and do sums. I can write some and so can John, but he don't talk much."

"Thank you, Bethany."

They continued around the room, with an older child sometimes introducing a younger one, until all eighteen students had taken their turns. Who were they missing? She trailed down the list with her pencil. Two registered children were absent. Should she call on them after school?

Del nodded and smiled at her charges. "Well done. Those of you who were in school last year know what grades you are in, but for our new students, I have questions and special exercises. So those of you third grade and up will spend the next hour writing about something special you saw or did since school finished last spring. Second graders will read a story aloud from the textbook Elsie will give you. If you have any questions, raise your hand."

She called the youngest children to the front. "Abel, Josie, and Clarabelle." She motioned for them to join her in the front corner, where she sat on a stool and seated them on the floor. While none of them had been to school before, Clarabelle knew her alphabet and her numbers, but the other two needed to start from the very beginning.

"Miss Nielsen." Josie fidgeted and raised her hand.

At the look of distress on her face, Del leaned forward. "What is it?"

"I have to go bad."

"Do you know where the outhouse is?"

"No."

"Elsie, can you help?"

Elsie took the little girl's hand and took her out through the side door.

Del sent the other two back to their seats in the front row and then called John and Bethany to join her. As they sat down, she looked up to see Elsie beckoning her.

"She didn't make it in time, and she's wet into her socks," Elsie whispered.

"Poor little one. She's still in the outhouse?"

Elsie nodded.

"Take her over to Dr. Brownsville's house and ask my sister Mrs. Brownsville to help you. Tell her I sent you."

"Okay."

Del returned to the two students waiting on the floor for her. "I'm glad you are here for school. John, what is your full name?"

He stared down at his hands and shook his head.

"His name is John Jacob Kinsley, and I am Bethany Ann Kinsley." She leaned forward and whispered, "John don't like to talk to anybody, 'specially strangers."

Del kept her frown at bay. "Thank you." How should she handle this? *Lord above, help.* She leaned closer to John. "Can you hear me?" The boy nodded and sneaked a glance at her.

"Good. I'm going to show you some things, and you need to answer me." She held up a page of letters and pointed to the *K*. "What is this letter?"

No answer.

"Point to the *K*."

He did.

"The *R*."

She did the same thing with numbers. He knew them all. Bethany did too.

Del opened the textbook beside her and handed the open book to Bethany. "Read me the first page."

Bethany read it without hesitation. "We learned to read from Ma's Bible. We memorized verses too."

That's surely more difficult than the McGuffey Readers, Del thought. *But how do I get him to talk?* She looked at John. "Can you talk?"

A look of terror whipped across his face before he set to studying his hands again. Del looked to Bethany, who shrugged.

"All right. You will both start in the fourth grade, and we'll see how that goes. You may go back to your seats." *And, John, you are going to learn to talk with me.*

She excused the children for recess and met Elsie bringing Josie back with a big smile on her skinny little face.

"All is well?"

Elsie nodded, then bent to tell Josie to go play with the others. "Mrs. Brownsville gave Josie a pair of drawers and socks and told her she could keep them. She said she'd rinse Josie's out and bring them over before school is out."

"Thank you, Elsie." *Thank the Lord for Forsythia.*

"Someday I'm going to be a teacher like you."

"You will make a good teacher. Now, you go play and enjoy your recess."

Del sat down at her desk and looked through her notes from talking with parents. The two missing students were Timothy and Iris O'Rourke from one of the homesteads. Their resistant father said the two older boys were needed on the farm and would not be attending school anymore. While she hated to accept that, the law said children had to attend only up to age twelve. But why were the two younger children not in school today? After school, she would ride Starbright out to their homestead and find out, as much as she disliked confrontation. But perhaps Mr. O'Rourke would be out in the fields, and she could visit with his wife.

By dinnertime, all the testing was finished and the stack of papers on her desk attested to her pupils following instructions to write about their break. She planned to read them aloud after noon recess.

"You may all fetch your dinner pails and sit back down to eat before you go outside for recess. Walk, don't run in school, and if you need to use the outhouse, after you eat is the time."

"Miss Nielsen?"

She looked up to find one of the boys in front of her. "Yes, Curtis, what is it?"

He leaned closer to whisper. "John and Bethany don't have no dinner pails."

Del looked up and, sure enough, the two children were sitting silently. "Thank you." She wrapped up her sandwich and two cookies and took them to the children. "Here, I have plenty. Tomorrow you will know to bring food for dinner."

"Thank you, Miss Nielsen."

She watched them eat as if . . . *I wonder if they had breakfast before they came.* While she drank her coffee—cold now but still welcome—she flipped through the tablet pages, interested in seeing what the students had written with so little instruction. Several made her smile. Not all of them had names on them, as some had obviously forgotten, and what could she say, since she'd forgotten to remind them?

She rang the bell to call them in from recess and waited until those lined up at the water pail found their seats. "When I hold up a paper, you recognize which is yours and come up here to read it. Everyone understand?"

At the first one she held up, Betsy Jorgensen raised her hand.

"Please come up here and read."

"'My name is Betsy Jorgensen, and I live on a farm. Our cow had a calf, and my pa said I could name the calf. Since it is a heifer, I named her Daisy. We once had a cow named Daisy, but she died. She was a good cow, so now we have Daisy again.'"

"Thank you, Betsy. You did well." Del held up another paper, this one without a name. No one moved. "Thomas, isn't this your paper?"

The boy nodded.

"Please come up and read it."

He dragged himself off his bench as if he were stuck to it with dried paste. He took the paper and, without looking at anyone or anything, read it. "'Pa and me went fishing. I caught three fish. He din't catch none.'" He nearly ran back to his seat, the paper clutched so tightly in his hand that it ripped in one place.

Someone snickered. Del glared at where she thought it came from.

Once they'd all read their papers, she sent them out for recess again. She'd considered skipping this recess, but it was important to set the schedule for the year. When she rang them back in, Del was more ready for the day to be over than the children.

"Will you read to us like you did last year?" asked Elsie.

"Yes, if everyone has done their work for the day. Since this is our first day of school, I thought we would start out right. Our first book for this year is *Robinson Crusoe,* written by Daniel Defoe. This was one of my father's books, and my brother brought it here on the train just so I could read it to all of you." She sat down in her chair and opened to the first page. "'Never any young adventurer's misfortune, I believe, began sooner or continued longer than mine.'"

At the end of the chapter, she closed the book and smiled at her students. "Remember to bring your dinner pails, and I will see you in the morning. You are now dismissed for the day."

When the room was empty, she blew out a long breath. Then she straightened her desk and closed all the windows in case it rained during the night.

"So how was your day?" Forsythia asked as she walked in the classroom door. "I brought back Josie's things."

"It went well, and thank you. I have two new students who did not register. They didn't bring dinner pails, and when I gave them my sandwich and cookies, they ate like they'd not had breakfast either. I think I'll go home and get Starbright and . . ."

"Do you know where they live?"

"Not really, but north of town. I thought I'd ask at the store. That's usually the first place people go."

"How about if I fix something tomorrow, in case they don't bring their dinner, and you go home with them after school to meet their folks?"

Del nodded. "I'd appreciate that. Their mother has taught them to read and write and do sums. Are Robbie and Sofie with Climie or out at the farm?"

"The farm. I'm taking the buggy out to get them and can give you a ride home."

"Thank you." Del blew out a breath. "The two younger children of the O'Rourkes didn't come either. If they're not here tomorrow, I'll need to call on them too."

"Maybe you shouldn't be alone for driving out to call on these families. It's not like we know them well—or at all, really."

Del stared at her younger sister.

Forsythia shrugged. "I think you need a man along, just in case."

10

RJ stared at the bottle of pills on the dresser. To take or not to take?

He hadn't succumbed to the opium again since arriving in Salton, but they were about to leave for dinner with the Nielsen sisters, and the pain in his scar was acting up something fierce—burning, shooting knives until he wondered if there were some sort of infection in there despite the Linksburg doctor's words.

"Hey, RJ! You comin'?" Anders hollered up the stairs.

RJ grabbed the bottle and tapped a pill into his hand. "Just a moment." He filled a glass from the water pitcher on the washstand and downed the pill with a quick swig.

He sat on the bed and blew out a breath. He didn't like taking the medicine, but if he wanted to have any chance at redeeming himself with Anders's family after his surliness the night they arrived, then he needed to be in less pain. That was the simple fact.

RJ leaned his forehead in his hand, willing the throbbing to subside. Evening sunlight streamed through the window, and a blessed breeze eased the day's heat. This room was barely finished, along with the rest of the upstairs bedrooms, and it still smelled of sawdust and fresh wood. But it had a homey feel, with quilts spread over the two cots and curtains at the windows. Forsythia's doing, he knew. He shut out any thoughts of how, by this point, he might have had a good start on his and Francine's house if things had been different. If he hadn't been laid up in the army hospital all those months. If she hadn't found someone else.

A gentle fuzz crept over the ragged edges of his brain, dulling the pain. RJ drew a long breath and pushed himself to his feet. He couldn't keep the others waiting any longer, however he might dread a social gathering.

RJ rode Captain alongside the Brownsvilles' wagon to the Nielsens' homestead. There wasn't room in the wagon anyway, and his horse needed the exercise. Barker loped along at his heels, tongue lolling out in delight. His dog would be glad to see young Scamp again. They'd bonded during the long train ride. The familiar feel of the saddle beneath him and Captain's gentle gait soothed peace into RJ's heart as they crossed the expanse of prairie. A flock of birds swooped and dove over the waving grasses, snatching an evening meal of insects.

Dr. Brownsville turned the wagon down a narrow lane, passing by a wooden sign hung between two posts.

"See, that's my sisters' business." Anders pointed. "Leah's Garden, named for our ma. It took a hit this year, but they'll weather the storm, I've no doubt of that."

The roughness of the soddy struck RJ as they pulled up beside the barn, which was also made of dry, stacked sod. He dismounted and scanned the farm. He knew most Nebraska homesteads had sod buildings due to cost and practicality, but seeing one . . . it was a bit of a shock to his engineer's eye.

"Welcome." Lark stepped out from the soddy, arms outstretched. Del and Lilac followed, the puppy darting between their skirts to nose and circle around Barker.

"Scamp will be glad to have a playmate." Del stood back a bit, arms folded across her apron, but she smiled at the group. "Good to see you, Climie, RJ." She met his gaze with apparent effort. No doubt thanks to his rudeness when they first met.

Guilt smote RJ, and he dipped his head politely. "And you, Miss Nielsen. Thank you for having us."

With a slight arch of her brow, Del bent to hug Sofie as the little girl threw her arms around her aunt's skirts. "We thought we'd eat at the table we set up outside. More room."

"Good idea." Forsythia set Mikael down to toddle toward the puppy. "Easier to watch the children as they play too."

"Exactly." Lilac grabbed Sofie's and Robbie's hands. "Come, you two, help me finish setting the table."

The rumble of another wagon announced Attorney Caldwell and his wife, whom RJ had met at church this morning. An unfamiliar man in a shabby army hat jumped down from the back of their wagon.

Another returned soldier. Well, few young men weren't these days. Hopefully this stranger wouldn't be eager to swap war stories. RJ glanced around for an excuse to avoid the man, but he was already approaching, his smile warm behind his scruffy beard.

"Howdy." The man extended his hand. "I'm Isaac McTavish."

"RJ Easton." But RJ stiffened at the Southern accent. Was this man a former Confederate, like the renegade who had jumped him? The man's hat was so faded that he couldn't be sure of its color. He well knew that not all who had fought for the South were tarred with the same brush, but . . .

Isaac nodded at RJ's own worn army jacket. "What unit were ya with?"

"Army Corps of Engineers." RJ shifted his shoulders. He should have just worn shirtsleeves tonight. It was warm enough.

"I was with the 7th West Virginia Volunteer Infantry."

RJ's tension eased a bit. *West* Virginia. That state had only formed through their choice to join the Union three years ago. "I guess you saw a good bit of action, then."

"I did." Isaac's friendly eyes sobered. "Chancellorsville, Gettysburg. Plenty I'd like to forget. But that's the truth for all of us, sure enough." He clapped RJ on the shoulder, a familiar gesture he somehow didn't resent. "And here we all are in this new territory, makin' a life for ourselves one way or t'other. What brings you out to these parts?"

"Anders Nielsen. We met during the war." RJ nodded at his friend, who was talking with Henry Caldwell and Jesse. Climie and Forsythia helped set food out on the plank table under the shade roof that extended off the soddy, the children and dogs scampering around.

"Ah yes. The brother to this fine group of women." Isaac tipped his cap back with a finger. "They've welcomed me like kin whenever I've imposed my sorry hide. This is the only place I've felt that since the war, and that's the truth."

A sudden clanging rent the air as Robbie rang an iron triangle with all his might, his face scrunched in the effort of his task. Chuckling, the group gathered around the table near the soddy.

"Anders, would you say the blessing?" Lark sat at the head of the table and extended her hands.

RJ found himself holding Jesse's hand on one side and Isaac McTavish's on the other. He bowed his head, more from habit and respect for the family than anything else.

"Father, we thank you for bringing all of us together this evening, for the food you have provided for us from this good land, and for family and friends who have become family. Bless this food and our fellowship this night, we pray. In the name of your Son, Amen."

Amens murmured around the table, RJ joining before he thought about it.

"So, Hiram told me you purchased land from him for a boardinghouse." Henry Caldwell dug into the tender fried chicken and new potatoes. "He treat you right?" His eyes twinkled.

Lark chuckled. "He was disappointed we didn't go for the higher-priced lot by the train station, but yes, well enough, I think. I liked the other location, but the cost was just too high."

The attorney nodded. "Well, it's not like the church is too far of a trek. I'm glad you're doing this. People will be more likely to stop and settle here rather than just pass through if they've got a decent place to stay."

"A commodity rare and precious on this frontier." Isaac wiped his mouth. "I could tell y'all stories of so-called lodgings that would raise the hair on your heads."

"Really?" Robbie put his hand wonderingly to his curls. "Like what?"

The adults chuckled.

"Well, the food for one thing." Isaac winked at Robbie. "No fine fare like this here your aunts spread out for us, no sir. Most places I've stopped, you're lucky to get some side meat swimming in grease alongside pickled cabbage and hard biscuits, with coffee so black you could stand a spoon in it, and no milk or sugar to relieve it neither."

"Yuck." Robbie made a face.

Henry Caldwell chuckled. "When I was first on my way out to this territory, before I brought Beatrice to join me, I stayed in a hotel run in a big tent. There was one side for men and one for women, with just boxes stacked in between."

"I've come upon some of those tent establishments too. Down in Kansas, two enterprisin' ladies started a boardinghouse right out in the open air. They just laid rough boards across logs for a table." Isaac nodded to the Nielsen women. "A mite like this, and the meal was better than most too."

"Leave it to a woman," Lark said archly.

"Rightly so." Isaac tipped his head gallantly. "Then once, when I'd been ridden hard and put up wet, I happened upon a hotel in an actual building. Never again. Everyone crowded upstairs in one unfinished room, and whee-oo, you could sure tell many of those fellas hadn't bathed in a coon's age. Not enough blankets neither. Some men came in late and took the blankets off others, and it turned into a regular row."

"Goodness." Del shuddered and passed the biscuits.

"From then on, I just slept in the open air, as long as the weather obliged." Isaac raised his fork toward the leafy canopy overhead. "One place I heard of, though, had a system that was right resourceful. One room for married folks only, and one giant bed. Any notion how they managed it?"

Everyone shook their heads. Robbie bounced in his seat. "How?"

"Well, they'd have one lady go in first, then her husband next to her. Another husband next to him, his wife beside him, then tuck in the next woman and so on. Accommodated several families that way."

Disbelieving laughter rose around the table. "Well, I never." Forsythia shook her head.

"Creative, I suppose." Still chuckling, the doctor reached for another biscuit. "Though I prefer closed doors when I bed down with my wife."

"Adam!" Forsythia slapped his hand, cheeks scarlet.

"So, RJ." Anders raised his eyebrows across the table at him. "Does this give you any inspiration? There's certainly a lot of building needed out in this country."

"I did want to ask you, RJ." Lark laid down her knife. "Have you given any thought to heading up our boardinghouse project?"

RJ swallowed, all eyes suddenly on him. And here he'd actually been enjoying the conversation. "Not a lot, I'm afraid." He should have, and mentally he kicked himself. "Could you tell me a bit more about it?"

Lark exchanged a glance with Anders. "Well, I'm not sure how much more there is to tell. We have the piece of land now and want to build a boardinghouse on it. As economically as possible, of course, but we want it to be a quality establishment."

"So enough blankets to go around," Isaac put in.

"And beds too, I take it." RJ added drily.

He hadn't exactly meant a joke, but the gathering chuckled, still merry from Isaac's stories. The friendly sound heartened him. He'd hardly known he still had the ability to provoke a laugh in anyone. Even Del looked up with a sudden smile, the deep gray-blue of her eyes catching him by surprise. Had they always been such a startling color?

RJ refocused. "You'll want a good half-dozen rooms for boarding, then. Possibly more. Two stories?"

"Certainly. Though the upstairs can just be one long open room to start. Downstairs we'll need an office, a good kitchen, and a large dining room. I've even heard of some boardinghouse dining rooms being used for civic gatherings, speeches, town assemblies, and such. President Lincoln spoke in one out west before he was elected."

"We've usually used the church for such things." Attorney Caldwell cocked his head. "But it could be good to have another space as well."

"Especially since the church is already doubling as the school," Del put in. "Won't we want a washroom also?"

"Off the dining room, maybe." Lilac popped a bite of beans into Sofie's mouth, earning an appreciative pat on the arm.

"And we'll need an outhouse built outside," Climie added.

RJ glanced at her, glad to see more brightness and less terror in her eyes these days.

"You're right, we will. Along with the stable." Lark blew out a breath. "I'm excited about this, but sometimes I hope we aren't taking on too much."

The conversation swirled while RJ ran numbers and plans through his head, sketches forming in the back of his mind. He'd never planned and built such a large project as this, but as the building took shape in his mind's eye, suddenly he knew he could. He could see the broad front porch, the tastefully appointed upstairs windows. And for the first time since the renegade's knife, a frisson of excitement made his fingers itch for a pencil to start sketching.

"I'll do it," he blurted.

Everyone at the table turned.

RJ's neck heated. He hadn't realized he was interrupting. Now he hadn't even a clue who had been speaking. "I'm sorry, I didn't—"

"Wonderful." Lark beamed and clasped her hands. "Now our dream can really begin to take shape."

Anders reached around the corner of the table to clap RJ on the back as the chatter resumed. "I knew you'd come through."

RJ blew out a breath and dug into his neglected meal. Well, he'd said it. Now it only remained to see if he could make good on his word.

The next afternoon, he was beginning to doubt it. Lacking a desk upstairs, he sat at the Brownsvilles' kitchen table, trying to draw on paper the plans he'd seen so clearly in his mind's eye last night. Robbie and Sofie dashed through the downstairs rooms in a riotous game of tag, while Mikael wailed upstairs as Forsythia tried to settle him for a nap. She'd said something about teething.

RJ pressed the heel of his hand against his good eye and gritted his own teeth against the stabbing pain in the other.

Last night had been so . . . good, almost. Mostly free of pain, and amid the laughter and conversation of the Nielsen family and their friends, he'd felt nearer to a whole man than he had since the war. Especially when they gathered for music under the stars at the end of the evening, the Nielsen sisters plying fiddle, guitar, and harmonica with surprising skill. Voices blended in hymns he'd nearly forgotten the words of, but they came back to him, songs of his boyhood gentle and healing on his tongue.

RJ groaned softly and lifted his head as his scar throbbed afresh. The opium bottle upstairs beckoned, but he resisted. He'd already succumbed again last night in order to sleep, and he didn't like how the frequency of the pills was increasing. Today he would stick it out, come what may.

He bent back over the paper, forcing himself to concentrate. He had the downstairs mostly laid out and a rough sketch of the front of the building. He still needed to figure how many rooms to divide the upstairs into and if he should include an extra washroom.

A ringing shriek sent a flash of blinding pain through his skull. Robbie crashed into RJ's chair in pursuit of Sofie, knocking RJ's elbow into the edge of the table and sending a dark slash from his pencil across the fresh drawing.

"Would you kids *watch* what you're doing?" He flung his chair back and jumped to his feet, holding his elbow. "And must you scream all the time!"

Robbie and Sofie stood together in sudden solidarity, small running feet now still, and stared up at RJ. Sofie's tiny chin wobbled, and Robbie put a protective arm around her shoulders.

"Sorry, Mr. RJ." Robbie rubbed one bare foot atop the other. "I din't mean to bump into you."

"Everything all right in here?" Adam stepped in from his office off the sitting room, brows raised. "Robbie, Sofie, have you been bothering our guest?"

"It's fine." RJ rubbed his forehead where the eye-patch band irritated. As did everything today, it seemed. "I just need to find a better place to work. Sorry I was sharp with you, Robbie, Sofie."

His chest pinched at their sober faces, making him miss little Emmaline back home. He never used to be short with children.

Adam nudged the little ones toward the door. "Why don't you two go play outside for a bit? Keep her in the yard near the porch, Robbie."

RJ leaned his hands on the kitchen table to survey the damage to his plans. The dark pencil slash streaked right across the detailing of the downstairs layout. He might as well start completely over. He grabbed the paper, crumpling it into a ball. What a waste. Just like his life.

"RJ?" Adam said. "Might I speak with you in my office, please?"

Dread settled hard in RJ's gut. Well, it hadn't taken him long to wear out his welcome. He stuffed the ruined plans in his pocket and turned, avoiding Adam's gaze. "Of course."

He followed Adam through the sitting room and into the doctor's home office. Neat shelves of medical books lined the walls, while a clean examining table filled the corner by a medicine cabinet. Adam shut the door, then glanced out the window at the children playing before sitting down in the chair behind his desk.

"I don't know where they get their energy. Forsythia and I often wish they would share a bit with us." Adam chuckled drily. "But I'm truly sorry they caused damage to your work. Was it the plans for the boardinghouse?"

"It's I who should apologize." RJ clenched his hands on his thighs. "You have opened your home to me. I know I must seem ungrateful—"

Adam held up his hand. "I didn't call you in here for a reprimand. I want to ask about your eye."

RJ stared at him for a moment, tongue-tied.

Adam leaned forward, clasping his hands on the desk. "How long ago did it happen? Was it a minié ball?"

"Six months." RJ swallowed. "And no, it wasn't in battle. It was a bushwhacker on my way home to New York State. A Confederate renegade with a knife, thirsty for Yankee blood." The gruesome memory encroached, and he shoved it away.

"I see. I thought most of them were in the Missouri-Kansas area."

"Not all."

"Did you see a surgeon?"

"Yes, and spent time in an army hospital." RJ drew a long breath. "He removed the remainder of the damaged eye and stitched me up."

"But you have pain." Adam's brown eyes were keen. It wasn't a question.

RJ shrugged. "Sometimes." He shifted his jaw against the stabbing that belied his words. "Anders made me see his doctor in Linksburg before we left, and he gave me some opium pills for when it gets bad." Which seemed more and more to be all the time.

"I wondered."

RJ cocked his head. "Why?"

Adam shrugged and frowned. "The way your moods seem to go up and down. I've seen it with patients on opium before. The drug is still new in many ways, at least in its present form. Many see it as a miracle, and so it is in acute situations. The invention of the hypodermic needle and the distillation of morphine have relieved untold suffering during and after the war. But a few of us physicians, myself included, see some evidence that it may be addictive. Which could make it as damaging as the pain it purports to cure."

RJ sat back, his heart sinking. "I've been tempted to take it more and more."

"Which is only natural when you are in pain. But regardless, the opium will only mask the symptoms." Adam tapped his fingers on his bearded chin. "Let me look into this."

"Look into what, sir?" RJ appreciated the doctor's concern, but what was done was done.

"What could be causing your pain. Any alternative remedies that might help."

"With respect, nothing's going to bring back my eye."

"No." Adam met RJ's gaze, and the compassion in the doctor's eyes made RJ swallow. "But that doesn't mean there's no chance of healing." He stood and stepped forward to lay a hand on RJ's shoulder. "Let me pray about this and check with some colleagues. You're not in this alone, RJ. I believe God has brought you out here for a reason."

Did that reason include exploding his life to bits? RJ held his tongue and thanked the doctor.

But as he strode up the stairs to fetch more paper, as much as he tried to quench it, something deep in RJ's chest wanted to hope.

11

W hen do you think you'll be leaving?"
Anders turned to Lark. "I hate to leave here because so much is going on, but I need to get home
too. I can't let Josephine carry everything too long, with the
baby and all. So I was thinking, let's get the plans ready for the
boardinghouse and get it staked out before I go. We need to
work with Mr. Young."

"For what?" She brought the coffeepot and filled their cups.

"I don't have cash to pay for building supplies, and I don't
think you do either." He cocked an eyebrow.

"No, of course not, but I don't really want to be beholden to
the bank either. You hungry?"

Anders glanced out the one sunlit window. "Where's Lilac?"

"Right here." Lilac popped in the soddy door, face and hands
still damp from washing up outside.

"I thought I might have to come get you," Lark said as she set
their bowls of rabbit noodle soup in front of them.

"I was picking the flower seeds that are dry enough. It's amazing how the marigolds and zinnias sprang back and keep blooming." Lilac poured herself a glass of buttermilk.

"Well, bugs never like marigolds. I know you were hoping to have seeds to sell next year, but it seems to me you would have needed another planting using all of this year's seeds to have enough. Even without the grasshoppers." Anders rubbed his chin with a forefinger.

"We figured that out." Lilac buttered her bread. "Sit down, Lark, so we can have grace."

"Yes, ma'am." Lark ducked her head as if saluting. Ah, how wonderful to have at least the three of them together. "You ever think of moving out here, Anders?" she asked after he said grace.

"Yes, and surprisingly, now that I've been out here, even more so. But that store is earning us a good living and making enough that I can invest in your boardinghouse."

"*Our* boardinghouse."

"All thanks to the store." He tipped his head and shrugged. "And Josephine really doesn't want to leave her family."

"Bring them out too. There's plenty more land to homestead, or perhaps they could start another kind of business in Salton. You know any blacksmiths? Let's see, what other businesses had we figured out?" She looked to Lilac, who thought a moment.

"The blacksmith, a livery stable. Something with salt mining machinery might be useful in a few years, and any kind of farming."

"Yes, I'd give anything to buy a mower next year, but I'm not sure if oxen move fast enough to keep that blade at top speed," Lark said.

"We thought of buying a mower and then mowing for others," Lilac said. "You could do it so quickly. And then the rake. It'd be best if we had a team of horses."

"All that and build the seed business too?" Anders shook his head. "You two never give up dreaming, do you? It looks to me like you have more to do than you can handle already."

"So ship Jonah out here to help us. We'd just have to keep him away from the liquor tent I hear has gone up for the railroad workers." Lark shook her head in turn.

"I bring you Climie, and now you want Jonah too? Who's going to help me in the store?"

The sisters shrugged and smiled at each other. "I guess you better grow your children up fast," Lark said.

Lilac got up to get more soup. "By the way, I'd like to find a good stud and get Starbright bred."

"What about Captain, RJ's horse?"

"He hasn't been gelded?"

Anders shook his head. "Want me to mention it?"

"If you want. No—yes, that might be best. Ma would have a conniption if she knew her daughters were talking of such unmentionable things. Mr. Holt might be confounded too."

Anders shifted in his seat. "Well, I can tell you this discussion isn't the most comfortable I've ever had."

Lark rolled her lips together and nodded on the sly to her sister.

"Anders, Anders, this is Nebraska," Lilac said. "We are four sisters—well, three now—with no man in our house to do these kinds of things. Should we simper and be embarrassed and—"

"And never get anything accomplished?" Lark finished. "I had to find a bull for Buttercup. What was I supposed to do, don my Clark clothes in order to talk to a bull-owning farmer?"

Anders wagged his head. "I will be careful not to mention this conversation to Josephine." He finished the soup in the bottom of his bowl. "It seems to me this is another change to blame on the war."

"I think you're right. With no men around, women were forced to step into situations they would not have needed to before." Lark shook her head. "And we're too level-headed, thanks to our parents, to curl up and simper ourselves to death." She gathered the bowls. "Coffee anyone?" Sitting back down, she continued. "Let's go back to dealing with Mr. Young. What kind of process are we looking at?"

"Well, there are several ways," Anders said. "We set up an account with the bank so we can draw on the funds as needed. This is business for a business. So when we order construction materials, we will have money to pay the bills as they come in."

Lark nodded. "So we need to set up books for this from the beginning. Similar to the ones you have for the store."

"Yes. You will have no problems with that. I'm surprised you've not already done so. Do you still have money left from your association with the gambling man?"

"Not much. A couple hundred."

"Did you put it in the bank?"

"I put some in the bank and kept some cash for buying things we've needed, usually food for us and the animals."

"Do you have an account at the merc?"

"When I need it. We trade as much as we can."

"Does Hiram know of your skills with numbers?"

She shook her head. "He thinks of us as simple women in need of a man's protection. But he doesn't mind taking our money, like for the property for the boardinghouse. I'm sure he figures all this is thanks to you."

Anders rolled his eyes heavenward. "Lord help the man."

"I've not set him straight. It seems to me there is strength in misconceptions at times. Like a feint in military strategy." Lark tipped her head back, remembering. "I can hear Pa saying, 'Strategy, Lark. Think this through,' when we were playing chess." The memory grabbed at her throat and set her to blinking back tears. "Sometimes I miss them so much I want to go howl at the moon. It makes me wish I had sat at his feet more. He was so wise."

"They both were," Lilac said softly, as if dreaming back along with Lark.

Anders flattened his hands on the table and stood. "Get your hat and whatever you need, and let's go to town and get things rolling. Lilac, you coming too?"

Lilac shook her head. "I'll stay here and harvest more seeds. The cream is ready for churning, so we'll have fresh butter for supper."

"Thank you." Lark snagged her hat off one of the pegs driven into the sod wall and picked up her reticule. Outside she whistled for Starbright, who picked up her head and, at the second whistle, broke into a lope up to the gate where Anders waited.

"She gets a reward when she comes like that." Lark dug in her pocket for a small carrot and palmed it for the mare, who chewed and swallowed while Lark took hold of her halter. Anders pulled back the bars so Starbright could walk through.

Lark slid the snaffle bit in her mouth and the headstall over her ears. "Good girl, let's get you harnessed."

"Where do you keep the harness?"

"On the inside wall of the barn to the right of the door." She led the horse over to the wagon and backed her into the traces. Anders slung the harness over her back, and while Lark buckled in one side, he did the other, and then they both stepped up into the wagon.

"Is she still mostly Lilac's horse?"

"Lilac has done most of the training and care, but as you saw, she responds to all of us. We wrote you about the day the Indians stopped the wagon train. When they indicated they'd take Starbright, Lilac turned white as a sheet. I figured better the horse than the girl, but they settled on an ox from the Durhams' wagon. That was Robbie's family. Both his parents were gone by that time."

Anders shook his head. "It's easy to forget all that little boy has been through. But then the Indians left you alone?"

"Mm-hmm. The guide for our wagon train told us the government was not honoring their agreement with them to provide food, so in order to hunt they had to leave the reservation." The memory still weighted her heart. How were Little Bear and his family faring now?

"I heard rumors of that. I'm grateful the reservations are farther north so they shouldn't create a problem for you."

She looked at her brother, who'd taken over the reins. "Your friend RJ, has he always been so surly?"

Anders shook his head. "It's his eye socket. The pain is often excruciating. The doctor at home gave him some opium, but he had no idea what was causing it. I've seen RJ almost pass out from the pain. Adam is looking into it to see if he can find a solution. It's good to have a doctor in the family."

When Starbright trotted into town, they stopped at the bank. "Not too imposing, is it?" Anders commented.

"It serves its purpose." She waited for Anders to assist her out of the wagon. He held the door for her too, and she nodded and smiled at Mr. Young, who stood up from his desk.

"Why, Miss Nielsen and Anders, to what do I owe the honor of this visit?" The two men shook hands, and Mr. Young motioned for them to join him at his desk.

"We plan to get the boardinghouse started before I leave," Anders began.

"I was hoping you would decide to remain here in Salton."

"No, I need to get back to our family store in Linksburg, but now that we can travel here by train, we plan to take advantage of that. I'm inquiring if you are set up to work with construction financing?"

"I am open to any needs as we grow Salton into the thriving town of our future. What do you have in mind?"

"Since the boardinghouse is much needed here, we plan to have it open as soon as possible. Construction costs will be higher due to the need for more workers to expedite the opening."

"And you will need funds to make this happen." Mr. Young nodded as he spoke. "Because Miss Nielsen already has an account here, we will draft an agreement of the funds you will borrow and the timeline for repayment."

"Understanding, of course, that repayment will not begin until the boardinghouse is open and bringing in cash above operating expenses," Lark said.

Mr. Young tilted his head. "Within reason, of course."

"And you could have that ready when?" Lark glanced over to catch a nod from her brother.

"The day after tomorrow?"

"Fine. Thank you." Lark started to rise, so Anders did the same.

Anders extended his hand. "Good day to you."

"I hope this is the first of many agreements," Hiram Young said. He smiled and nodded to Lark. "Miss Nielsen."

The two of them walked back out to the hitching post, where Starbright stood with one back foot cocked, tail swishing at the flies.

Lark blew out a breath. "I'm surprised at how smoothly that went."

"Why? You've worked with him before. I mean, you bought that property and gave him cash, which might not have been the best plan, but . . ."

"We should have paid half down and asked him to carry the rest?"

"Possibly. I mean, you purchased that section with the house and windmill, and you have increased the value of the land with the addition to the house and building the barn, plus fencing, and you're homesteading the next section. You've accomplished a great deal."

"All because I outplayed a gambler."

"And had been saving money. And made drastic decisions but carried them out for the best."

"You think RJ will have some of the plans drawn up?"

"I know he was working on them this morning. We'll see how far he has come."

When they reached Forsythia and Adam's house, RJ came down the stairs, rolled paper in his hands, after Robbie ran up the stairs to tell him he had company. "I was hoping you would come so we could talk about some of this." RJ held up the roll.

"Use the table. I'll put the coffee on." Forsythia headed for the kitchen. "Robbie, please bring in some wood."

"Me too," announced Sofie and followed him out the door.

Lark arched an eyebrow at her sister.

"He wanted to do it, and I figured he could carry some, so now he fills the woodbox."

A thud and a screeched "Maaa!" came through the back door.

"Now what?" Forsythia headed for the door, Lark on her heels. "Oh, Sofie."

"She dropped that on her bare foot." Robbie patted his sister's shoulder. "Shh. See, no blood."

Forsythia scooped up the little girl and set her on the porch rail to check out the foot. "No blood, no slivers. You'll be fine." Sofie raised her arms, and Forsythia scooped her up. "See, it's all better now."

Robbie carried his armload inside and dumped it in the box. Lark stacked split wood on her arm and did the same. Sofie scrambled to get down, picked up two pieces of wood, and limped after them.

Lark went back to the table, where RJ was laying out his drawings.

"I've drawn this building to be done in several stages so we can open part of it more quickly. Two stories, like you said. We can rough in the first section of the building, which has the kitchen and eating area on the first floor, and you can rent out the upper floor for men, and a separate room for women. They will have a place to lay a pallet or bedroll. It will be out of the weather, and they will eat downstairs. Better than a tent or a wagon bed. Many places started this way in the early days."

Lark nodded and chewed on her lower lip. "You're right, we could open much faster this way."

"Are you planning on a cellar?"

"Yes." She looked to Anders, who was nodding slowly. "Then separate rooms could be added later. And a second wing, someday. Forty by fifty each?"

"For the first, anyway."

"We could go over and lay it out so they could start digging the cellar right away."

He nodded. "As soon as you have someone to dig."

Lark stared at the drawings on the table. They were really going ahead with this wild idea. She rose to check on Forsythia in the kitchen.

"Coffee's ready," Forsythia said. "Let's take it out on the back porch where it's cooler."

"Where's Climie?" Lark asked.

"Helping at the store. Adam is out on a call, a baby being born. The mother was in here last week, and there might be difficulties, so he asked them to come for him. He left early this morning."

"Oh my."

"I've been praying off and on all day."

"First baby?"

Forsythia shook her head and walked out of the kitchen. "Would you gentlemen like to enjoy coffee out on the porch?"

"We're going over to stake out the house, but we can do that too." Anders studied his sister and dropped his voice. "Something wrong?"

"Adam left early this morning to assist with a baby being born."

"I see." He closed his eyes briefly, then took the coffeepot from her. "RJ, coffee's ready." He paused. "Sythia, you have any idea where the cord might be from when they laid out this house?"

"All the tools and things are down in the cellar. I'll go look."

Outside, Lark poured the coffee, enjoying the slight breeze that kissed her cheeks. Shouts and children's laughter announced that school was out. Had Del said she might be going calling? And they had Starbright here.

"I'll be right back." She hustled out the door and over to the church, where she found her sister tidying up the schoolroom. "Del, are you planning on visiting a family this afternoon?"

"I don't think so." She shut the last window. "I'll try tomorrow, since it looks like it might rain tonight."

"That it does. Anders and RJ are going over to stake out the boardinghouse so we can get started digging the cellar."

"We?"

Lark grinned. "You think they'll let me dig?"

"Probably not. It's some different from spading the garden."

The two sisters shrugged and closed the door behind them. Dark clouds hovered to the west. Thunder rolled and crashed, lightning stabbing the sky just as they reached home. Lark stabled Starbright and hurried back to the soddy after her sisters. Throwing a towel over her dripping hair, she leaned at the window to breathe deep the fragrance of life-giving rain.

Such a gift for our replanted seeds and the new transplants, yet after the hay is safe. Thank you, Lord.

The next week, with the cellar a couple of feet deep, the family gathered at the station to see Anders off.

"Greet Josephine for us and tell Marcella about her aunties out west," Lark said.

"And her cousins," Forsythia added.

Anders hugged his sisters and the little ones. "How I wish we were not so far apart. I would never suggest you move back, but we will build Leah's Garden and the Nielsen Boardinghouse. We will." He mounted the steps the conductor had placed at the open door to the train and turned to wave again.

"Go with God, brother," Lark muttered. "Lord, please keep him safe."

"And us." Forsythia put her arm around Lark. "Only God knows what lies ahead."

12

Was teaching this exhausting last year?
Del waved to the last of her students as they ran off down the street, small feet kicking up clouds of dust, pigtails and dinner pails bouncing. She stepped back inside the church and began to erase the makeshift blackboard Jesse had finished for her last night. It was just a few boards nailed together and painted black, but along with a package of chalk from the general store and a rag, it certainly made teaching a bit easier. The only trouble was finding a secure place to put it, since it couldn't be fixed to the wall like in the schoolhouse. So far she'd made do with propping it on her desk and holding it still with one hand while she wrote with the other, but that wasn't ideal.

After a knock, the door opened, and Rev. Pritchard poked his head into the room. "How did it go today?"

Del placed the erased board on the floor and leaned it against her desk for tomorrow. "Overall, a bit smoother than last week, I think. No accidents in the outhouse, and students are settling into their assigned groups, as I've mostly figured out what readers they're in. The new ones are making friends, which also means more trouble. I had to separate two boys today and stand another in the corner for talking."

Rev. Pritchard chuckled. "Always the boys, isn't it?"

"No, sometimes girls can be the worst chatterboxes. But not today." Del sank into her chair. On the other hand, John Kinsley still hadn't said a word. And now she needed to deal with the O'Rourkes, since their children still hadn't shown up. Dread tightened her gut.

"Well, you seem to be managing beautifully." Rev. Pritchard rubbed his hands together. "I wanted to let you know that the school board met, and they voted to raise your salary. Twenty-seven dollars a year."

Del sat back in her chair. Not as high as she'd hoped, but every little bit helped. "Thank you."

"I was in favor of the whole thirty, but majority rules, you know." He sighed but gave her a wink. "Anything you need before tomorrow?"

"I don't think so." She made a few notes on her lesson plan, then looked up as the young minister headed for the door. Forsythia's words sprang back into her mind. She rose from her desk. "Actually, would you by chance have time to help me make a visit?"

"Do you know the O'Rourke family?" Del asked half an hour later as she rode beside the preacher in his two-wheeled gig across the prairie.

"Not well." Rev. Pritchard shoved back his hair, which seemed always to be falling forward. "They've come to service regularly since they moved here a few months ago, but they always leave right after."

"Yes, I had to practically accost them one day at the store in order to speak to them at all. Mrs. O'Rourke seemed eager for her younger ones to go to school, and they are registered. But now we're a week in, and they haven't shown."

"They have four children, don't they?"

"Mr. O'Rourke has already made it clear that the older boys won't be attending. I just hope he hasn't changed his mind about Timothy and Iris too." Del ran her proposed speech through her mind. Dealing with difficult parents certainly was a part of the job she'd be happy to skip—as would any teacher, no doubt.

Rev. Pritchard turned down a faint dirt track toward a soddy with smoke wisping from the chimney. Cultivated fields spread on either side, and Del could see several figures out working in them, though she could see clear damage from the grasshoppers. The older boys? Their father? She hoped they wouldn't have to call him in from the fields. That doubtless would do little to improve his temper.

"They came out to the area because Mr. O'Rourke was working on the railroad, didn't they?" she asked.

"I believe so. But once they reached Salton, they decided to homestead instead. More stable for a family."

Rev. Pritchard stopped the gig and helped Del down. She drew a breath to calm the twisting in her stomach, but it didn't quite work.

A slender woman with faded red hair pulled into a neat bun came to the door of the soddy. "Afternoon to ye, Reverend. And Miss Nielsen too."

"Good afternoon, Mrs. O'Rourke." Del stepped closer. "I wondered if we might speak with you and your husband. If this isn't an inconvenient time."

The woman hesitated and glanced toward the fields. "He's still out there workin', I'm afraid. But he and the boys should be stoppin' for supper soon. Won't ye come in and sit down?"

"We don't want to trouble you." Del glanced at the young minister. Had they been wrong to come unannounced? It was so hard to know about these things.

"No trouble 'tall." Mrs. O'Rourke stepped back and tipped her head. A little girl with red braids peeked around her skirts.

"You must be Iris." Del smiled as she stepped into the shadows of the soddy. It was similar in size to their own without the addition, but darker, having only one window. There was little furniture, merely a rude bedstead, a roughhewn table, and a few chairs. Wooden boxes and barrels apparently held the rest of the family's possessions. But the dirt floor was swept clean, and the open fire was well tended with a pot of stew simmering above.

"Would you like a bit o' coffee?"

Del started to shake her head, then wondered if that would be impolite. "Thank you, that would be nice."

"Iris, get me the cups please, darlin.'"

Del accepted the cup with a smile, as did Rev. Pritchard. "I was sorry not to see Iris in school this last week. And Timothy too. That's why we're here, actually."

"Oh, I see." Mrs. O'Rourke twisted her hands in her apron and glanced out the open door. "Aye, well—that's somethin' you'll need to be speakin' to my husband about."

As she'd feared. Del smiled and sipped her coffee. "We'll wait, then."

She sat in the chair the mother indicated. Silence hung, and Del focused on the little girl rubbing her bare toes on the soddy floor. "So, Iris, how old are you?"

Iris glanced at her mother, then met Del's gaze with shy blue eyes. "Eight, miss."

"And have you been to school before?"

She nodded. "Back home, in New York City. I learnt my letters and cipherin.'"

Then Nebraska wasn't "home" yet. Perhaps it might become so if the children were allowed a chance to make friends. "So you lived in New York City. This must be quite a change for you all, then."

Mrs. O'Rourke laughed softly. "Sure, ye might say so. My husband worked at the docks or wherever they would take him, and me as a washerwoman for rich folks. But I'm well content to have traded our crowded tenement for a soddy, and that's the truth. Even if the open spaces here make me long for a friendly face, 'tis better still."

"At least one can breathe free." Del studied the woman's face in the shadows. What stories did this family have to tell?

"How long since you came over from Ireland?" Rev. Pritchard asked.

"Near on nine years now. We came just before Iris here was born. 'Twas hard, havin' a wee babe in the tenements, but she's our American-born child." Mrs. O'Rourke touched her daughter's uplifted face.

A stamping of boots and rumble of male voices approached the door.

Mrs. O'Rourke turned with a slight intake of breath. "That'll be Mr. O'Rourke now."

Del stood, her middle tensing.

Mrs. O'Rourke stepped just outside the soddy. "Liam, the schoolmarm is here to see ye. And the preacher too."

Muffled muttering, then splashing as the mister and the boys washed up in the basin outside—just as the Nielsens had at their home. A moment later, the soddy darkened almost completely as Mr. O'Rourke's powerful form filled the open doorway.

"Reverend." He stepped inside, allowing slants of light again. "Miss Nielsen. What can I do for ye?"

"Good afternoon, Mr. O'Rourke." Del might as well get right to the point. "I'm here about Timothy and Iris. They haven't shown up for school this past week."

"Aye, well, they're needed here on the farm."

"And yet you registered them for this term." Del kept her voice gentle but firm.

"Doesn't a man have the right to change his mind?" Mr. O'Rourke ran a massive hand over his reddish beard. "Or some say over his own children?"

"Of course, sir. I merely wanted to see if we could find out what happened, if there were anything we could do to help. The education of our young people is a central priority for this soon-to-be state."

"My sons and daughter can read and write a fair hand and do enough figurin' to get by. Buildin' up the farm is what counts just now for our family. Even for this soon-to-be state, as you say. A homestead isn't held down by fancy letters, is it now? And since that plague o' locusts, we need every hand we can to replant what little we can."

Rev. Pritchard stepped forward, hands lifted. "But suppose some of your children want more than farming in the future. Would you deny them that chance? When you've come so far and sacrificed so much for them to have a life in this new land?"

"Listen here now, Reverend." Mr. O'Rourke held up his hand, voice quiet but deadly. "Don't ye go tellin' me how far I've come or what I've given up. Ye don't know nothin' about it. Book learnin' might be all right for a fancy preacher man, but it didn't make a bit o' difference for some of my friends who came over from Ireland with us. Didn't matter a titch that some of them were scholars, teachers, or even priests back home. No, all people saw in that city was that we were Irish. And 'No Irish need apply.' We had to take work where we could get it, down at the docks or buildin' the sewers. And no amount of book learnin' kept my friends from breakin' their backs in the filth like the rest of us."

"Liam—"

Mr. O'Rourke quelled his wife's timid remonstrance with a glance. "'Twasn't till I got work on the railroad and could bring my family out here, and had the chance to homestead, that I've been free for the first time in me life. Not back home, and not here in your supposed land of the free. Only when I can work with me own two hands on what will be me own land. And that's the only chance I can be sure of for me boys as well, grasshoppers or no grasshoppers. So, fine, Iris can go if her ma can spare her. But my boys need no more schoolin', and that's final."

"I'm truly sorry for the ill-treatment you have endured." Rev. Pritchard pressed forward, undaunted if slightly flustered. "But shouldn't your sons have the chance for a different path if they should so choose? The beauty of America is that anyone can climb high from low, anyone can be anything, if they put in the effort—"

Mr. O'Rourke erupted into chortles of laughter.

Rev. Pritchard stopped, looking nonplussed.

"Anyone?" The Irishman looked around the room, making a sweep with his arm. "Did ye all hear that? He actually said *anyone*." The laughter halted, and Mr. O'Rourke stepped closer to the pastor, towering over him. "D'ye really believe that, Reverend? That anyone can get ahead if they merely try? Tell that to my kinsmen still toiling away in the sludge. Tell that to your supposed freedmen now crowding the cities of the North, competing with the Irish for the jobs no one else wants to do, that no one wants to pay proper wages for. Go tell them, with your spectacles and your books someone else probably paid for you to learn from. Then come and talk to me about 'anyone.'"

Rev. Pritchard swallowed and pushed his spectacles up his nose.

"Mr. O'Rourke," Del began. Then she stopped. She really wasn't sure what else to say. *Lord, we could use your help here.* "We mean no disrespect, Mr. O'Rourke. Of course it is your right to choose whether to send your children to school. We merely want to ensure that you know they are welcome, and if there is anything we can do to help smooth the way, we wish to do so." She hesitated, then continued. "You speak truly that not all are free in this land, whatever we purport it to be. But at my school, all will truly be welcome. You may count on that."

"Da?" A small voice came from the doorway.

Mr. O'Rourke stepped back from the preacher. They all turned toward the door.

A slight lad stood silhouetted in the evening sunlight. When he stepped inside, where Mrs. O'Rourke had lit a kerosene lamp, Del could see his hair was dark, nearly black, in contrast to the red of his mother and sister. His eyes, though, shone the same bright blue, and his work shirt and trousers were worn and smudged. He looked about twelve or thirteen, though she sensed him small for his age.

Del stepped toward him. "Are you Timothy?"

"Yes, miss." He lifted his chin and looked at his father. "Da, I want to go to school."

Mr. O'Rourke sighed and rubbed his hand over his face. "We've talked about this, Tim. It's no good for you, ye must come to terms with that. And ye're needed here on the farm. We need all hands if we're to make it through the winter now—'tis a whole new world of farmin' compared to Ireland."

"I'll still help, Da, I promise." Timothy stepped closer, though he had to crane his neck to see his father's face. "I'll get up extra early to work before school, and then I'll hurry home after."

"Why do you want to go to school, Timothy?" Del took another step closer, her heart tugging toward the boy.

Timothy met her gaze directly. "I want to learn, miss."

His words hung a moment in the soddy, potent.

"You can learn here, son." Mr. O'Rourke's voice came rough. "Haven't I taught ye all ye need to know for life so far?"

"But I want more, Da. What we learned back at school in New York—'twas like I only got a tiny taste of a Christmas feast." He hesitated, seeming to search for a better argument. "And

William and Patrick say they'll work twice as hard as me if I'm gone. They do anyhow, bein' so much bigger'n me."

A half-suppressed chuckle ran around the room, faintly easing the tension.

"We do let the children off for harvest." Del lifted her gaze to Mr. O'Rourke again. "And if you had a special need for Timothy's help, that is always at your discretion."

Mr. O'Rourke let out a long sigh and scrubbed one hand through his hair, glancing at his wife. "It would seem I'm outnumbered, as usual." He bent forward, leaning his hands on his knees to look into his son's eyes. "It would just be for this term. Ye understand that."

Timothy seemed about to protest, then nodded. "If you say so, Da."

"I do. After that . . . we'll see." He straightened and aimed a general glare at Del and Rev. Pritchard. "But I don't aim to be cornered into anythin' else, mind."

"Of course, sir. Thank you so much." Del handed her coffee cup to Mrs. O'Rourke. "We won't intrude further on your evening. Timothy, Iris, I look forward to seeing you in class tomorrow?" She raised a brow at their mother, who nodded.

"Thank you," Mrs. O'Rourke mouthed, running her hand over her daughter's braids.

"Remember to bring dinner pails for the noon meal." Del smiled at the family, then led the minister out the door of the soddy.

"How did you learn to do that?" Rev. Pritchard asked as they drove back toward town, dusk falling over the prairie.

"Do what?" Del slapped at an impertinent mosquito trying to buzz down her collar.

"Handle an obstreperous parent like that."

"I didn't do much, really. Mostly listened. That's all most

people really want." She hadn't realized it until now, but much as she dreaded difficult encounters with parents, once she was in them, she often felt a sort of peace, even a divine guidance over the meeting. Like the Spirit was telling her when to speak and when to be silent. The thought lifted her heart. Perhaps teaching really was her calling after all, despite the discouragements lately. "I think Timothy was the one who made the difference."

"He did at that." The pastor huffed a laugh. "I nearly blew the whole thing up."

Del sat silently a moment, listening to the rattle of the gig and the jingle of the harness. Around them in the prairie grass, crickets struck up their summer evening chorus. "We often don't think about what life might look like through someone else's eyes. Someone whose experience has been different from ours."

"Yes." Rev. Pritchard flicked the reins and sat back. "I'm afraid too often I am quicker to speak than to listen, in contrast to Scripture's command."

"That's true of most of us." Del sighed and folded her hands in her lap, weariness sinking over her. "But I'm so thankful they've agreed to let Timothy and Iris come to school."

"At least for now."

"Yes. At least for now." Lord willing, she could make school valuable enough that Mr. O'Rourke wouldn't think of pulling Timothy out again.

Rev. Pritchard insisted on driving her all the way home, though Del told him simply taking her back to the church was fine, since nightfall was a good two hours off still. But she couldn't refuse the gracious offer, tired as she was. And she still had lessons to finish planning for tomorrow, not to mention a stack of new papers to grade.

"Thank you again for accompanying me." She accepted the preacher's steadying hand as she climbed down from the gig.

"Of course. Please feel free to call on me at any time, Miss

Nielsen." He held on to her hand just an instant longer than necessary, looking into her eyes.

Del pulled away her hand as if she'd touched a hot stove lid and hurried toward the house with only the briefest of good-nights.

Oh dear and botheration. Had she seen in the young minister's eyes what she thought she just saw?

13

Thank God that train station is finished, Lark thought as Forsythia passed on the news.

"And they set the date for the city celebration, two weeks from this Saturday. Mr. Young wanted to wait until October, but other heads prevailed. The station will be a great place to have a celebration before any benches or wooden seats get set permanently."

"So he thinks they can be ready?" Lilac asked.

"It looks to me like he's been planning this awhile. Mr. Young said he has invited General John Thayer from Omaha—he's on the state constitutional convention, hoping to be a senator—to come in and speak to us right from the back of the train. Young's all excited, says this will be a real feather in the cap of Salton and get us known on the map as a progressive town that is looking forward to Nebraska statehood."

Lilac and Lark swapped looks. "How much do we care about Nebraska statehood and moving the capital to Lancaster?" Lark asked.

Lilac shrugged. "What difference will it make for us?"

Sythia shook her head at both of them. "You're part of this town."

Lilac glanced at Del. "Now perhaps they will finally start the school building."

"That was my first thought but the celebration . . ." Del heaved a sigh. "Not that women should be consulted—after all, we're only the ones who will prepare the food and serve it. And in our case, provide the music."

Forsythia shook her head. "We should get some of those laborers to help on the boardinghouse now that the cellar is dug. The lumber is due for delivery next week, and the sooner they get going—"

At Del's look, Lark held up both hands, palm out. "Del, we all agreed that the sooner we got the boardinghouse going, the better. Two of the men who dug the cellar were working on the train station. Anders arranged for them to do this."

"I didn't realize the boardinghouse would come at the expense of the schoolhouse." Del stared at her. "I-I thought . . ."

Lark rolled her lips together, hating the feeling of being a traitor. Del had been working dawn to dusk both teaching and helping on the farm. Lark wished she could spare her sister more, but there just weren't enough hours in the day. Or enough workers to go around. And Del *did* have the church. Tension tightened her shoulders.

Del blew out a sigh. "So is RJ in charge of building our boardinghouse or are you?"

Lark shook her head. "Not me. But I am learning a great deal and keeping all the books and financial matters. Mr. Young is not very comfortable with that, but our wise brother Anders insisted it be so."

"Oh, I almost forgot. We got a letter from Anders today. He must have been writing it on the way home." Forsythia pulled the envelope out of her reticule.

Del fetched a pitcher of buttermilk she had brought in from the well house and poured them each a glass, and together they sat at the outside table.

Dear Sisters,
  Thank you for making me feel at home in Salton. For-sythia, I appreciated time with your family, and thank you for including a place for RJ. Lark, Del, and Lilac, I am amazed at all you have managed to accomplish in one year at Leah's Garden. Driving past that sign made me think of our mother and her love of gardening. You are all building such a legacy in her name.

Something eased in Lark's chest as she listened. It had been good to have Anders here, to not feel the whole responsibility for their family on her shoulders, even for a little while.

Forsythia finished the letter, folded it again, and put it back in the envelope. "I started missing him the moment the train headed east on that track. I sometimes dream about them all moving out here, and yes, I am aware that is a farfetched dream. But then, I never dreamed of any of us moving west."

"I'm sure Abraham's wife, Sarah, never dreamed of packing everything up and moving either. And she had no idea where they were going, only that her husband said that God told him to do this, and He would show them the way," Del pointed out.

Forsythia shuddered. "Not sure I could do that."

"Well, we sort of did." Lark shrugged. "And here we are. Land-owners, homesteaders, and now businesswomen with Leah's Garden and the boardinghouse. It goes to show women can do far more than most men believe."

"Speaking of men believing, I believe I better get home," For-sythia said. "No telling what has taken place since I left. Adam was called out on another birthing early this morning, so he was taking a bit of a lie-down. Climie has the children, who were sleeping when I left."

"Thank you for the ride home." Del hugged her sister. "I'm so grateful for the box of supplies Reverend Pritchard and Mr. Caldwell ordered for the school. We now have enough slates for everyone and textbooks for the older pupils too." Her eyes sparkled. "And Jesse is making me a proper desk. That young man is such a fine woodworker."

Lark nodded. "That he is." *And right now we have a glimpse of our Del who used to be. Please, Lord, let us see more of this one.*

The day of the celebration, butterflies jumped around in Del's stomach as she scanned the gathering crowd for her students. The children were to provide the music. Did she have time to practice with them once more? Some of the little ones were still unsteady with the words.

Rustles of excitement swelled the crowd like she'd never seen in Salton before. The day before the celebration, a sign had been strung above the street at both edges of town, proclaiming, *Celebrate Salton, Best Little Stop on the Rails West*, which had given the Nielsen sisters a good laugh. Flanked by American flags, another sign hung on the station, *Welcome to Salton*, for those coming in on the train.

Lark and Lilac had gone out hunting, and the two antelope they'd bagged were being turned on a spit over a long bed of coals. Tables were set up in the station for all the food people were bringing.

"What are we waiting for?" someone muttered.

"The train to come in."

The musicians set up chairs in the shade of the station, the platform being for dancing. The men had moved the piano out of the church and brought it to the station. Mrs. Caldwell sat down on the bench and lifted the cover off the keys.

Del gathered her students, who had been memorizing "Battle Hymn of the Republic," a new song that came out of the war. "Let's practice one more time." She slid the guitar strap over her head and tested the tuning, then nodded to Mrs. Caldwell, who played a couple of opening bars, and Del strummed and led the singing.

"'Mine eyes have seen the glory of the coming of the Lord; He is trampling out the vintage where the grapes of wrath are stored . . .'" Silence crept over the gathered folks. "'He hath loosed the fateful lightning of His terrible swift sword; His truth is marching on.'"

When they reached the chorus, other folks joined in, and everyone applauded as the children finished.

"Thank you," Del said. "We believe this will be a very popular song, and we are proud to share it with you. Mrs. Caldwell, would you please play it again, and I will shout out the words. The children and anyone who knows it can sing along."

When the song was over, someone was heard to say, "If that don't get your feet to tappin', what will?" Chuckles flitted over the gathering.

Mr. Young paced the platform, watching for the train that was supposed to have arrived by now, checking his watch and shaking his head.

Del and Mrs. Caldwell shrugged at each other. Forsythia lifted the fiddle to her shoulder. "How about 'America'? Everyone, let's all sing along."

The other musicians joined in, and they sailed right into "'My country, 'tis of thee . . .'"

Mr. Young came out of the station and waited until the song finished. "The telegram said they left right on time and should have been here by now. Something must have happened on the way." He mopped his forehead with a handkerchief and settled his hat back on.

Mr. Caldwell looked to Rev. Pritchard, who shrugged. Caldwell raised his voice. "Something has forestalled the train, but we don't need a fancy politician to bless our new train station. We can do this just fine."

Rev. Pritchard nodded in agreement and raised his hands. "Let us pray." He waited for folks to settle. "Lord God, heavenly Father, Jesus, and the Holy Spirit, we stand before the work of our hands. We come before you, asking that you will bless this train station and all the folks who have worked on it and for it. That this station will be welcoming to strangers, as is this town. That the trains that run on this track will help bring growth and prosperity to our town. Father, we thank you for all your provisions, the singing, music, food, and time to be together and become better friends. Bless everyone here and help us go forth in joy. In Jesus' precious name, Amen."

He nodded to Del, who led the students—and the gathering—in one more rousing chorus.

"Now, that was better'n a parade," Mr. Jorgensen said to Mr. Young, who clapped him on the back.

"That indeed was our parade. I sure wish I knew what happened to that train."

Despite the angst on Mr. Young's florid face, the rest of Salton's population, their ranks swelled by railroad and construction workers, flowed toward the tables laden with food. People sat wherever they could find room, their plates loaded with roasted antelope, corn on the cob, various pastries, pickles, and pie. Families spread quilts in the shade, and youngsters perched on the edge of the platform, feet dangling.

After making sure all her students had rejoined their families, Del joined hers last, plate in hand. With the performance behind her, her stomach rumbled in anticipation.

Lark met her with furrowed brow, though she and Lilac scooted to make space for her on the quilt.

Del bowed her head for a silent grace, then bit into her corn on the cob, butter dribbling down her chin. "Something wrong?"

"I just hate seeing that liquor tent." Lark jutted her chin at the dingy tent on the other side of the railroad tracks. "Isn't there anything we can do about it?"

Del glanced over her shoulder. Sure enough, a number of the construction workers and other single men had drifted that direction. Some lingered outside the tent, cups or bottles in hand. A burst of raucous laughter carried across the tracks.

"Like what? They've kept it outside the town limits." Lilac sopped up savory meat juices from her plate with a sourdough biscuit.

"I don't know, but something. I hear they have gambling too. I'm sure we're not the only women in town who don't want that kind of influence around."

"So let's gather the women." Del dabbed her mouth with one of the napkins she'd tucked in their picnic basket.

"What do you mean?"

Del shrugged. "Talk to them, hold a meeting. The men might think they run things around here, but each one I know has a wife with a lot of influence over him." Her conviction grew as she spoke. Why hadn't she thought of this before? "Actually, I should be talking to them about the school. Surely they care about their children's education." She thought of Mrs. O'Rourke. Would she come to such a meeting?

"You're rather brilliant, you know that?" Lark shook her head and popped one more bite of antelope in her mouth, then laid down her fork and rose. "I'm going to talk to Mrs. Caldwell right now."

Lilac and Del exchanged glances and grins.

"Now you've done it." Lilac pushed back her sunbonnet to let in the cooling evening breeze. "You've started Lark on another crusade. Do you think she's especially touchy about gambling because of what happened with Jonah and that lowdown snake Ringwald?"

"Likely. I mean, that's the whole reason we all ended up here."

"I think God had something to do with it too."

"You're pretty wise for a baby sister." Del reached to squeeze her hand. Lilac was growing up, her dark curls pinned up lady-like today, her girlish features turning into those of a woman as she gazed across the gathering, a pensive look in her eyes.

"It looks like Reverend Pritchard is gathering the musicians for the dancing." Lilac stood and shook out her skirts. "You coming?"

"Of course." Del pushed to her feet. "Good thing I'll be on guitar. I'm too full to dance for a while."

"We'll have to take turns on the music so we can all dance."

"Gather 'round, folks." Rev. Pritchard cupped his hands to his mouth to be heard across the gathering. "Grab your partners! We'll start off with the grand march."

Laughter sprinkled the falling dusk. Men pulled their wives to their feet, and single men hung around awkwardly, looking for an available partner among the shy or simpering young girls. Del frowned at the sight of several men sauntering over from the liquor tent, none too steady on their legs. Parents had better keep a close eye on their daughters tonight.

She and Lilac joined a couple of other musicians to sound the lively marching notes of the opening polonaise. She saw Forsythia leading off with Adam, Robbie and Sofie following close behind and winning many a grin. Climie bounced Mikael on the sidelines, a smile brightening her face. There were Mr. and Mrs. Caldwell, and even Hiram Young with his wife, who apparently had convinced him to forget the missing train for at least one dance. Many of her pupils' parents followed, and even her pupils, including Elsie Weber led by a red-faced Thomas Dwyer. Del chuckled, her heart lifting as she strummed. And there went Lark, promenading alongside Isaac McTavish, of all things.

The grand march finished with a flourish, and everyone clapped. Rev. Pritchard had just lifted his hand to announce the next dance when a man hurried up to the banker, and then Mr. Young strode to the front of the platform and whispered something to the minister.

"Mr. Young has an announcement for us, everyone." Rev. Pritchard nodded to the banker.

"We've just received a telegram from Omaha." Mr. Young lifted the paper as if it contained crucial news of the war, had it still been going on. "General Thayer is safe, but the train had to back up due to some danger on the tracks. We'll learn more details later."

The crowd murmured and rustled.

Mr. Young stood there a moment, telegram still raised, then lowered his hand. "That's all I know."

"Then let's get back to dancing," someone hollered from the back. Laughter rumbled through the gathering, along with cheers of agreement.

Slightly crestfallen, the banker stepped aside.

"Thank you, Mr. Young." Rev. Pritchard took charge again. He wiped his spectacles, then beamed out over the gathering. "Now that we know the missing train is safe, let's celebrate with the Virginia reel."

Whoops and applause. Couples separated, and new ones formed.

Del was just strumming the first chords of the reel when Rev. Pritchard appeared at her side.

"May I have this dance, Miss Nielsen?" The young minister's eyes were bright and eager.

"I—" Del glanced at the other musicians. "I'm needed to play."

"Go on." Lark appeared at her other side and reached for the guitar. "I danced the last one."

Del hesitated, holding onto the strap. But how could she say no without being rude? "Very well. But just this one." She lifted the strap over her head and handed the guitar to Lark, who slipped it on and joined in without missing a beat.

As the preacher led her away, Del caught a glimpse of Lilac's face that nearly stopped her cold. What—*Oh dear.*

She fought to focus as they lined up for the reel, clapping automatically as the head couple began sashaying up and down. At least this dance didn't require much close contact with one's partner. Did Lilac think . . . ? Del glanced back at her little sister, fiddling away, her face now in shadow. Did Lilac carry a torch for the preacher? And what kind of sister was Del not to have noticed before?

One who has been too wrapped up in your own problems, that's who. Guilt smote Del's chest as she circled a right-arm swing with one of the railroad workers.

The dance passed in a blur until she and Rev. Pritchard reached the head of the line and joined hands to sashay down and up.

"Enjoying the celebration?" he asked, slightly breathless.

"I am."

"So am I." He sent her another beam as they separated to begin swinging opposite partners up and down the line.

Oh, Lord, please show me how to let him down gently. He's a fine man, but . . . They met at the bottom and lifted their hands to form a bridge, other couples lining up to file beneath their arms.

Finally, the dance ended with a few exuberant chords and a burst of applause.

"Thank you." Del joined in the clapping and dipped her head at Rev. Pritchard. "Now I'd best go back to play for the next one."

"Can't I get you a cup of punch?" His face so resembled an eager little boy's that Del bit her lip not to smile.

"Thank you, but—"

"May I have the next dance, Miss Nielsen?"

Del turned at the voice, lower than Rev. Pritchard's. RJ Easton—the last man she would have expected to rescue her.

"Well . . ." Perhaps the musicians could do without her for another round. And the minister couldn't follow her this way. She accepted RJ's outstretched hand. "I suppose I could dance one more."

RJ quirked the brow above his good eye as he led her back out toward the center of the platform. "Don't let me put you out of your way, now."

Her cheeks heated. She and this taciturn young man might have clashed at times, but she truly hadn't meant to be rude. "Forgive me, I was a bit distracted back there. Thank you for the offer."

The musicians struck up again, this time a slower waltz, a needed breather after the lively reel.

"You may wish I'd take it back." RJ pulled her into the waltzing stance. "Engineering doesn't fit one to be the best of dancers."

Yet he led her surely, his other hand guiding gently on the small of her back, turning them deftly among the other couples.

The tension in Del's middle eased, and she relaxed into the steps and the music. She'd always loved waltzing, ever since Pa taught her as a little girl. "You seem to be doing just fine."

Around them other couples twirled, including Jesse guiding a beaming Climie—now that was a sweet sight. Lark had been giving him lessons as promised, and they must have paid off.

Del searched for something innocuous to say. "So you've started our boardinghouse."

He cocked his head. "It would seem so."

"We're grateful for your expertise. Have you supervised many buildings before?"

"Not many yet." A frown creased his forehead beneath the strap of his eye patch.

Oh dear, had she turned him cross again? Del focused on the steps.

"How did you come to teach school?" RJ twirled her away from a collision with Mr. and Mrs. Young.

Del glanced up at him. The frown had passed, miraculously. "The town needed a teacher, and we needed income. I'd always considered teaching, so I took the certificate exam and was teaching almost before I knew it had happened."

"But you like it?" He met her gaze, apparently really listening.

"I do." She glanced over at a group of her students circling on the edge of the dance floor, a smile warming her middle. "I love it, actually."

"Then they are blessed to have you for a teacher."

She looked up at him again, surprised at the sincerity in his voice. "What about you? Do you love engineering, building things? Or is it just a job?"

"I used to." His gaze faltered. "I . . . I was . . ."

The music ended. Snapping as if from a reverie, RJ dropped her hand and gave a curt bow, his jaw tight. "Thank you for the dance." He spun on his heel and disappeared into the crowd.

Well, so much for thinking RJ was growing past his surliness. Del's stomach sank. She'd merely been trying to make conversation.

Feeling alone amid the swirl of laughter and chatter, she made her way back to the musicians and touched Lilac's shoulder. "I can fiddle for a while. Why don't you go dance?"

"I'm fine." Lilac angled away from Del's touch, bending her head toward her bow.

Del dropped her hand to her side. She'd made a mess of this too.

"Here, you can have the guitar awhile if you're ready for a breather." Lark lifted the strap off her shoulders. "You were quite the belle of the ball out there." Her eyes twinkled.

"Hush." Del tipped her head toward Lilac. Had Lark noticed anything?

A sudden crash jerked all their attention to a commotion inside the newly finished station. There was shouting, then a string of words Del felt sure would burn their ears were they close enough to hear. She and Lark hurried toward the ruckus, following Rev. Pritchard and Mr. Caldwell.

Several men, unfamiliar workers, emerged from the station's open doorway hauling a man between them who spouted slurred nonsense.

"'Fraid someone's purty china won't be eaten off no more," one of the men hauling him volunteered—though he seemed only slightly less inebriated. "Mac here done smashed it to smithereens."

Several women exclaimed in dismay and hurried inside to examine the tables. The workmen exploded in guffaws, bending over and slapping their knees while the culprit between them slipped down to sprawl on the rough boards of the platform.

Tight-lipped, Rev. Pritchard hurried after the women.

"Get that man off the premises." Del had never heard Mr. Caldwell sound so stern, a hint of what he might be like in the courtroom. "And don't any of you show your faces again here tonight."

Sobered in mood if not in fact, the men managed to pull their comrade to his feet and stumble their way off the platform. The gathering stood subdued under the emerging stars. The faint wheeze of the concertina when Anthony Armstead shifted his feet was all that remained of the gaiety.

Del and Lark exchanged glances. So much for a happy ending to Salton's first celebration.

14

The heat was stifling.

RJ pulled off his wool army hat to wipe the sweat from his forehead with his sleeve, then settled the hat back in place and scanned the building site of the boarding-house. He needed to get himself a straw hat for working. The sweat seeped under his eye patch, causing the wet cloth to rub against the flesh and further irritate his scar.

Clive Johnson, one of his workmen, approached, a wad of tobacco bulging his cheek and hat pushed back on his head. "Hey, Boss. You want two window frames in the front or four?"

"Two on the side with the dining room, one on the other. I told you twice." Tamping down his frustration, RJ strode over to the rising skeleton frame.

"Yeah, yeah, you can just never be sure with these lowlifes." Clive followed, spitting a stream of brown juice into the dirt.

Did he mean the other workmen or RJ? Trying to ignore the pain jabbing into his skull, RJ leveled a stare at his employee. "All you need to worry about is what I tell you."

"Sure, captain." Clive gave a mock salute.

RJ blew out a breath and rubbed the back of his neck. He needed to find some more workers, or preferably better workers. Those he had came from the crew who had built the train station, but most had moved on with the railroad as it continued westward. Many of those who remained seemed to show as much interest in frequenting the liquor and gambling tent as in keeping steady at their work.

A beam clattered to the ground, followed by a string of words that seared even RJ's ears.

"Hey!" he barked, striding over to the workers. "Careful with that lumber. It cost an arm and a leg to have it brought from Omaha. And watch your language, men, or you'll be off this job as quickly as I hired you on."

"Who're you gonna get to replace us, Boss?" Clive asked laconically.

RJ glared at him until he bent to help another man replace the fallen beam, and then he headed back to the shade of the cottonwood grove, sparse as it was in the noontime heat. Here he had set up a rough table with his plans and tools, along with a water bucket for the men.

"Mr. Easton, sir?"

At the unfamiliar voice, RJ spun around. "Yes?"

A powerfully built man with a red beard approached him, clad in simple homespun with his hat in his hand. "Name's Liam O'Rourke. I heard you were lookin' for workers on the boardinghouse here and wondered if you could still use an extra pair of hands."

"Perhaps." RJ sized up the man. He certainly had the muscle for the work. "Depends on your experience."

"I've worked many a construction job in New York City, buildin' warehouses and the sewer system. I know my way around a buildin' site and even supervised other men before."

"I hail from New York as well. Though upstate." RJ pondered. He'd need a foreman at some point unless he never wanted to be able to leave the building site. "When could you start?"

"Today, if ye like. But there's one thing. I can't work full days just now. I've a homestead also. And I'd need time off for harvest."

"We should be finished before then. It's a short-term contract." But RJ frowned. "Why take time away from your land?"

"We got hit hard by the grasshoppers." O'Rourke twisted his hat between his hands. "Lost half our corn crop, we did, and much o' the wheat. We've tried to replant some, but harvest will be slim. Me boys, they're helpin' in the fields as much as they can, but they're not strong enough yet for this buildin' work. But if ye can't take a man who can only work half days, I understand and will be on my way."

He stood, waiting.

RJ rubbed his forehead, fighting to think through the pain. Even afternoons would help, and he knew something of what it was like to feel like everything was against you. "Join us for the rest of the day and show me what you can do. If all goes well, I'll give you a full day's pay, and you'll be hired."

O'Rourke dipped his head. "I thank ye, sir."

"Easton is fine." RJ gestured to two men struggling with a roof beam. "Know your way around a roof?"

"That I do." He headed toward the building frame.

Well. That might have been a hasty decision, but O'Rourke couldn't be much worse than the crew RJ already had. Bracing himself for the sun again, RJ headed back to the hammers ringing against nailheads. He set to work helping Lars, one of the steadier workers, saw boards in proper lengths for the window frames.

At least the work here gave RJ something to do, something to occupy his mind and hands other than the pain or pining over all he'd lost. But what was he really doing here? Delphinium Nielsen's innocent questions at the celebration rankled in his memory. He'd never supervised the construction of an entire building before, let alone one as large as a boardinghouse. The only real plans he'd laid had been for Francine's millinery shop and the home he'd meant to build for them, those projects of his heart now crushed flat under ruined dreams.

What if he made a mistake, in his plans or his direction, and someone was injured? And once this project was complete, what was he to do next? Seek work in Lancaster—soon to be Lincoln—as Anders had suggested? Was he never to return to New York?

If he were still a praying man, he'd ask God what in thunder He was doing with the life of Robert Joseph Easton.

At the call of a female voice some time later, RJ looked up from a turn with the hammer to see Larkspur Nielsen atop the seat of her wagon. He hadn't even heard the vehicle approach.

"How goes it, Mr. Easton?" She climbed down from the wagon just as a burst of raucous laughter erupted from some of the men nailing the doorframe in place.

RJ whipped off his hat, hoping she hadn't just heard whatever ribald remark preceded that laughter. Not that Larkspur Nielsen seemed like a woman easily discomfited.

"We're making progress on the frame," he said. "Waiting for another load of lumber on tomorrow's train, but hopefully by the end of the week, we can start boarding in the walls."

"I like the look of it so far." Hands on hips, she surveyed her property. "You have enough workers?"

"I'd like more, but these are all I could get for now. Most moved on with the railroad." He nodded at O'Rourke up on the roof frame. "Had one new man just show up today, so I'm putting him on trial."

"Isn't that Mr. O'Rourke?"

"You know him?"

"They're a new family at church. From Ireland, I believe."

"And more recently New York. He said he's experienced with construction, so we'll see."

"Mr. Young is also putting an advertisement in newspapers back east for jobs for workmen in Salton, billing us as a 'booming railroad town.' I don't know how accurate that is, but hopefully that will bring in more help soon." Lark pushed back the brim of her sunbonnet. "I know my sister Del regrets that we've taken all the workmen for the boardinghouse instead of starting on the schoolhouse. But the new workers will need a place to stay, as do arriving families, and . . ." She raised her hands and sighed.

RJ kept his mouth shut. If anyone asked him, which they hadn't, her sister Del could stand to be taken down a peg about her precious school. It wasn't like she had no place to hold classes. Guilt niggled as he remembered the passion in her eyes when she'd spoken about her students during their dance at the celebration. When was the last time he'd felt that strongly about anything? And those eyes, their rich vibrant color. She'd fit nicely in his arms too. . . .

"Well, I just wanted to check in on you and also ask a question. We're looking to breed our mare and wondered about your horse, Captain, as a stud. Anders said he's a stallion?"

RJ's attention snapped back to the present. *What* had she just said? "I beg your pardon?"

"Your horse is a stallion, correct? Would you be open to his servicing our mare?"

His face flamed as if struck by a branding iron. "Uh, well, yes."

"Yes, he's a stallion, or yes, you'd be open to the idea? We'd pay you, of course."

"Uh." RJ blew out a breath. "Both, I suppose."

"Well, fine, then. I'm thinking she might be ready sometime toward the end of this week, from what we've observed. Could you come over for supper Friday or Saturday and bring Captain?"

RJ hardly knew where to look. "I suppose."

"Splendid. I'll let you get back to work, but do let us know if you need anything."

"I will." RJ watched her climb back in the wagon, willing his ears to cool. Were Lark's lips twitching? Things sure were different out in this territory—at least when four sisters took it on themselves to run a farm alone.

Just as Larkspur drove away, a scream rent the sweltering air.

"Boss! Over here."

Suppressing a curse himself, RJ ran over to where several men huddled at the corner of the boardinghouse frame. One worker lay sprawled on the ground, clutching his head. Blood spurted onto the dirt. Wonderful.

"Paddy didn't see him and swung back too far with his hammer just as Mike was bending down behind," Lars explained, stepping out of RJ's way.

Mike writhed on the ground, groaning and holding his forehead.

"He'll need stitches, that one." Liam O'Rourke yanked off his neckerchief and pressed it to the wound. The fabric swiftly stained red.

"I'd better get him to the doctor." RJ glanced back and saw Larkspur had pulled her wagon around and come back.

"Need a ride?" she called.

"Yes, please. I sure hope the doctor isn't away."

"I saw him entering his office when I drove by."

RJ and O'Rourke hauled the groaning, bleeding Mike to his feet and half dragged him to the wagon.

"Come on, man, pull yourself up. You're not dying." RJ bit his tongue at the sharpness of his own tone. Of course, the pounding pain in his eye socket didn't help matters. If he moaned whenever he felt like it, he'd be moaning all the time.

But Mike swallowed his next complaint and heaved himself into the wagon bed.

RJ faced his crew. "The rest of you, back to work. I'm leaving Lars in charge till I return. And I don't want to hear of any more careless accidents when I do."

The men nodded and stepped back to their tools.

RJ puffed out a breath and hopped into the back of the wagon to keep an eye on Mike, who was now lying quietly as if he'd fainted, though one hand still held the bloody kerchief to his wound.

One thing after another today. Maybe this incident would knock some sense into the men's heads. No pun intended.

Half an hour later, RJ watched as Adam Brownsville finished the line of stitches across Mike's forehead.

"You're fortunate, young man." Adam tied off the thread. "The claw of that hammer could have taken out your eye had it been half an inch lower."

RJ swallowed and averted his gaze from the angry gash, his stomach wrenching.

"I thank ye, Doc." Mike got unsteadily to his feet. "Don't got money to pay ye, though. Not till next payday."

RJ frowned. "Didn't you get paid for finishing the train station?"

The young man had the grace to redden. "I, uh, had me some debts to settle."

The gambling tent again. RJ shook his head and looked at Adam. "I'll see that you get paid."

"Don't trouble yourself over it." Adam wiped his hands. "Mike, see that you rest the remainder of the day. Come back to see me if you have any dizziness, severe pain, trouble with your vision—anything unusual."

"To be sure, Doc." Mike touched his fingers to his head and exited the house rather unsteadily.

"I'd best follow him back." RJ pushed to his feet, suddenly weary to the bone. He hadn't worked this hard since building bridges during the war. He hadn't realized how soft he'd become, but months in the hospital would do that to a man. He'd have thought the work he'd done on the train station when they first arrived would have started to toughen him up, though. "Thanks, Adam."

"Wait a moment, RJ." Adam finished washing up at his basin and dried his hands. "I wanted to speak to you. I was out visiting Henry Caldwell today."

"Is he sick?"

"No, no. But he told me something. Do you have a few moments?"

RJ hesitated, glancing out the door. "I really should follow Mike, then get back to the building site."

"Of course, you're right. We can talk tonight, don't let me forget."

RJ nodded and headed out. Who knew what other disasters the workmen might have created by now.

But no new crisis greeted him. In fact, things seemed to be progressing smoothly. The roof frame was taking fine shape—thanks to O'Rourke's quiet direction, from what RJ could tell. He examined the work, told the burly Irishman he was hired, then spent the remainder of the day checking and double-checking the stability of all the joists and connections of the building so far. He wouldn't move on to adding flooring and walls until he knew the frame was secure. But if progress continued on like this, they'd be well on the way to a boardinghouse soon.

RJ stayed at the site after his workers left, going over his plans until the twilight grayed toward darkness. Night fell sooner as autumn approached, however warm the days might be. He dragged himself up the Brownsvilles' steps long past suppertime, every muscle aching to the bone.

"There you are, RJ." Adam looked up from studying a medical

journal at the lamplit dining room table. "Forsythia left a plate of supper for you in the kitchen. She's upstairs putting the children to bed."

"I'd thought just to head up myself." RJ leaned one hand on the doorframe. His stomach rumbled, belying his words.

"Go on, don't let it go to waste. I can tell you my story while you eat."

Oh, right, Adam had wanted to tell him something. RJ sighed and headed on weary legs to the kitchen. The plate of ham, fresh beans, corn on the cob, and fluffy biscuits did water his mouth a bit, and he carried the plate and a glass of water to the table to join the doctor. He sank into a chair and downed the glass in one gulp.

Adam looked up from his journal again. "Long day?"

"You might say. Well, you saw part of it." RJ sighed and stabbed a bite of ham with his fork. "You wanted to tell me something about Caldwell?"

"Not Caldwell exactly." Adam folded his hands atop the journal. "More about his land. I remembered something he'd said once before and wanted to ask him more about it. When he first came out to this territory—he was among the earliest settlers, back before the war—an elderly Pawnee woman still lived on the large tract of land that he purchased. He lives a ways outside of town, and he owns a good portion, much of it still undeveloped. At any rate, he let her stay, acknowledging she had more right to it than he did, after all. Most of her family had died, and the few who remained had moved to the reservation, but she refused to go." Adam shook his head. "Said she had little time left to live and wanted to spend it at home, on her land."

"She just stayed out there alone?" RJ bit into a biscuit, drawn into the story despite himself. "In a tipi or something?"

"Pawnee only use tipis when they're traveling on buffalo hunts, I believe. Henry said she had some sort of earth-covered lodge. He and Beatrice would visit her now and then, take her some food or supplies. Over time, their conversations got longer—she spoke some English, they learned a little of her language—and she told them much about this land that few white people know."

RJ hadn't thought much about what this land was like before European settlers arrived, but it had already had residents. So where were they all now? Reservations . . . whatever that meant. He hoped they were better than the prison camps Anders and so many others had endured during the war. His gut twisted at the thought.

"Anyway, one winter this woman—they called her Atika for 'grandmother'—told them of a salt spring somewhere on Caldwell's land. She said the waters and mud held great potential for healing all sorts of stubborn ailments and that it would draw out poison from festering wounds. Atika promised to show them in the spring, but she died before that happened."

RJ watched the doctor, his guard rising.

Adam rubbed his hands on his thighs. "I wonder if this salt spring might help your eye. I've been reading about the benefits of mineral springs, and there does seem to be veracity to it. Henry has given me permission to search his land to find it."

A snort erupted from RJ's nose. He immediately quenched it, holding up a hand of apology.

Adam cocked his head, his eyes keen but without anger. "You find this funny."

RJ wiped his plate with the last bit of biscuit, then rose, shaking his head. "Forgive me, Doctor. I appreciate your efforts, I do. But spending time on a wild goose chase, looking for some magical saltwater for my missing eye . . . surely that's a waste of your time. I regret the time you've already spent on it."

"I know you hold out little hope for healing. But I believe we serve a God of hope." Adam's voice held steady. "And as I've been praying and pondering, this memory was what came to mind. You say it's a wild goose chase, and maybe so. But since it's my time to waste, as you put it, I'm going to chase it."

"Do as you wish."

A sudden stab of anger smote RJ's chest, matching a renewed knifing in his eye socket. Why did everyone seem to think they knew what he needed? Anders dragging him hither and yon, and now the doctor with this harebrained idea.

He snatched up the plate and shoved his chair back toward the table so hard it tipped forward, then righted itself. Shame burning his face, RJ headed for the kitchen to return his empty dishes. Coming back through the dining room, he avoided looking at Adam. "Good night."

He climbed the stairs without another word, then stood before his bedroom window for a long time. The cooling breeze caressed his face, and the opium bottle was clenched in his hand.

It beckoned relief like cool water to a parched man, but he didn't want to succumb to the drug's power. Why were the battles waged within him so much fiercer than any he'd faced in war?

Too weak to fight the weariness and pain any longer, he swallowed a pill. Then he fell into bed and let sleep swallow him.

15

What happened to you, child?" Del asked.

"H-he fell—over a log." Bethany spoke up for her brother, who had a black eye, a cut lip, and scratches on his arms. He favored his left leg.

The boy stared down at his hands, not willing to look Del in the eye.

Something was not right, but Del hesitated to ask more. How many logs were there around here to fall over?

"Ma took care of him."

Del looked to Bethany, who dropped her eyes immediately. "I hope your ma scrubbed those cuts good so he doesn't get an infection."

"Yes, ma'am."

Del patted John's shoulder and called the class to order. "Elsie, will you lead the flag salute today and the opening prayer? Then we'll sing 'America' and one song of your choice." She made her way to the piano and lifted the lid from the keys. "Please rise."

She wished Mrs. Caldwell or Forsythia were here to play the piano. But she knew the opening chords, and that led right into the singing.

When they finished and sat down, she smiled and nodded. "We need to sing more. I was so proud of you on Saturday when you helped us teach 'Battle Hymn of the Republic' to the townsfolk. Several people told me how pleased they were with your performance. I think you need a round of applause." She started clapping, and the children joined her.

"I wish we could sing every day," one of the little girls said. "My ma sings to us when we say our prayers at night."

Bless that mother. Del raised her voice. "How many of your families sing together? Do any play instruments?" Probably half the children raised their hands.

"My ma plays the dulcimer," Iris O'Rourke said.

"Do you think she would come play for us one day?" Del asked.

The little girl shrugged.

"I'll send her a note."

Iris shook her head. "Ma has a hard time reading. That's why she wants us to come to school, so we can read."

"Your ma is very wise."

Elsie raised her hand. "My pa plays the harmonica. He says it makes him happy."

"Music of any kind can help make us happy." Del paused. "Today we will begin with sixth grade and up on history. The textbooks are on the shelf. You will read chapters nine and ten and prepare for oral examination."

As always, groans met any phrase that meant *test*.

Del pointed to the blackboard. "Grades four and five will do the sums on the board on your slate. Two and three, read chapter two in the McGuffey Readers on the shelves. Grade one and primers, meet with me in the corner." As everyone settled in, she sat on her stool and shifted her papers in her lap. "We'll review our alphabet and the sounds." She held up a *D*. They all named it and made the sound. "What words begin with *D*?"

"*Dog, do, desert, dessert, down.*"

"Very good. Now give me a couple words with *D* in them."

Frowns met her.

"*David* both starts with *D* and has another one in it." Josie smiled. "My baby brother is named David. I saw his name."

"You are so right. Very good, Josie. Anyone else?"

When they finished the review, they all were smiling, even the older ones.

"Now, take up your slates and chalk and write each letter, both capital and small." While she paused for them to get ready, she looked around at all the others. So far, so good.

They went through the entire alphabet, and then she raised flash cards of words, going around the group one at a time and in unison.

"You are all doing well. Take out your reader, and we'll start on page fifteen. Clarabelle, you read first." When they finished, she stood and raised her voice. "Thank you all for working so well. Put your things away, and you are dismissed for recess."

The instant hubbub made her smile. She watched John Kinsley stand very carefully and follow the others out the door. He was definitely favoring that left leg. What, if anything, could she do about this?

"Good morning, Del, I brought some goodies," Beatrice Caldwell called from the doorway.

"Come on in. As you can see, they are out for recess."

"How is your day going?"

Del paused. "I have a situation where I'm not sure what to do."

Beatrice set her towel-wrapped plate on the desk. "What is it?"

"A child showed up injured today. Black eye, and something is wrong with his leg. His sister says he fell over a log, but I don't know. Something doesn't seem right to me."

A frown creased the older woman's forehead. "Which family?"

"The Kinsleys. I don't know them, have never met the parents. But the boy never speaks. I think he can; he just won't." Del's stomach knotted. Another way things didn't seem quite right.

"I'll speak to Henry, see if he knows who they are." Beatrice patted Del's hand. "In the meantime, at least we can pray about it."

"Yes. Thank you." The tension in Del's middle eased a little. Mr. Caldwell had lived here longer than most and seemed to know more of the goings-on in the area than anyone. *Thank you, Lord, for sending Beatrice just now.*

"How are things going otherwise?" Beatrice asked.

"Well, I think we made good progress toward reading with the little ones this morning. I would like to do more with music and wish I were better on the piano or that you or Forsythia were available."

"What makes you think I'm not?" Beatrice cocked a brow.

"Well, I mean, I didn't want to presume. . . ."

"Goodness, dear, what do you think I do all day? Why, I'd play for you every morning if you'd have me."

Del stared at her. "Truly?"

"We rent out much of our land, and I don't have any children of my own. There's only so much time I can fill with cleaning and gardening and cooking for two." A wistful note crept into the older woman's voice.

"Oh my." Del clasped her hands beneath her chin. "That would be such a gift." She glanced at the clock she'd brought for her desk. "I need to call the children in. Would you like to stay a bit and get to know them?"

Beatrice's smile bloomed. "I'd love to."

Del rang the bell, and the children laughed and chattered their way into the church. They settled back onto their benches, only quieting when Del fixed them with a look.

"Thank you. Now, children, I'd like you all to say hello to Mrs. Caldwell. She brought some cookies for you to have at our dinner break. What do we say to her?"

"Thank you, Mrs. Caldwell" came the dutiful chorus. Del smiled at the longing glances sent toward the covered plate on her desk.

"Mrs. Caldwell is going to join us in the mornings to help with music, so you'll all get to know her much better. Now, before we start science, I have another special announcement for you. On Monday, we are going on an outing to the salt marshes. We'll study the plant and animal life out there, and my sister Lilac will come along and teach you how to draw the specimens you find. Any questions?"

Thomas Dwyer raised his hand. "Will we be back for dinner?"

Del bit the inside of her cheek. "I believe we'll head out right after dinner and spend the afternoon there. We'll be back before your parents expect you home."

Excited whispers and rustlings.

"Now, primers through grade three, I want you to draw on your slates what kinds of animals and plants you think we might see at the salt marshes. Then Monday we'll see if you are right. Grades four and five, let me check your sums, and then you can do your reading. Upper grades, you check on the little ones if they need help, and I'll hear your history lessons next." Del had to stop for breath. Juggling so many levels still made her a bit dizzy at times.

"Miss Nielsen?"

Del looked up at the gentle touch on her shoulder some time later, just as she finished helping the last fourth grader correct a sum on his slate. "Mrs. Caldwell." She straightened, her face heating. "I'm so sorry. I didn't realize you were still here."

"Not to worry. I've been enjoying watching you work with

the children. But I'd best go see to Mr. Caldwell's dinner and just wanted to say good-bye."

"Thank you so much for the cookies and for your willingness to play for us." Del had another thought. "Also, I meant to ask you—your property borders some of the salt flats, doesn't it? I don't know just where the lines are, but I don't want to take the children onto your land without permission."

"Goodness, you're more than welcome, surely you know that by now. We do own some of that salt marsh area, but we don't do anything with it. Not yet, anyway—I believe Henry had notions of getting into the salt business once when we first moved out here, but nothing much has developed in that direction. At any rate, you're more than welcome to roam over our piece of it as much as you please." She hesitated. "Could you use anyone else along to help with the children?"

Del smiled. "If you're sure we're not asking too much of you."

The beam on Mrs. Caldwell's face was all the answer she needed.

Walking across the prairie toward home that evening, Del's heart weighed heavy again despite the satisfaction of finishing another week. What was going on with the Kinsley family? What horrors might Bethany and John be facing every day? Was there anything she could do? Wait to hear what Mrs. Caldwell could find out, that was the first step. But what if one of the children was injured again in the meantime?

She trudged up the lane to their homestead and stopped short at the sight of Lilac leaning on the corral fence with a man.

Of course—RJ was bringing Captain over for Starbright tonight. She'd completely forgotten. A prick of excitement quickened her step, and she hurried into the soddy to drop off her school satchel. The house was empty. Lark must be out doing chores.

Del changed into her work dress and checked the pots on the stove. Chicken stew simmering, potatoes fried. Supper seemed well on its way. She glanced out the small window and then, unable to suppress her swell of curiosity, headed outside.

"Good evening, Mr. Easton." She approached the corral. "How goes it?"

"They're still getting to know each other." Lilac leaned her arms on the fence, her sunbonnet pushed back off her flyaway dark curls. "I think Starbright's playing a bit hard to get."

Del stepped nearer, watching the horses. They circled each other, prancing and pawing. What a fine specimen of a stallion Captain was. His deep bay coat gleamed in the setting sun as he arched his neck and neighed after the mare.

RJ cleared his throat and shifted away from the fence. "I really think you ladies should go inside."

Del glanced at him. His neck shone red as a sunburn, and he couldn't look at her or Lilac. She ducked her head to smother a chuckle.

"Starbright is my responsibility and has been since she was born." Lilac's voice was firm. "I'm staying."

"This is the frontier, Mr. Easton. Things are a bit different here." Del exchanged an amused glance with her sister.

Captain whinnied again and shook his mane, then nipped at Starbright's flank.

RJ rubbed the back of his flaming neck, then glared at Del. "Miss Nielsen, go inside."

What, and Lilac was allowed to stay? He needn't order her around like one of her students. But at the miserable pleading in his eye, Del sighed and headed toward the garden. She'd best gather some of the new lettuce for salad and finish supper, since Forsythia and her family would be here soon.

Lilac joined her as Del was setting plates on the table beneath the shade roof.

"He finally got you to leave too?" Del asked.

"I figured I'd better help you. Lark is almost finished with the chores. Besides, the poor man looked about ready to squirm out of his skin."

"Well, he let you stay longer than me."

"Starbright is my horse."

"She's all of our horse—belongs to all of us—you know what I mean." Del sighed. "He just needles me at times."

"RJ? I think he's a mighty interesting fellow."

"Interesting, maybe. Taciturn, for certain."

"Well, Anders said he's often in a lot of pain. The last time you had a toothache, you weren't exactly personable either."

A fair point. Del glanced over at the corral, then quickly darted her gaze back to the table, cheeks burning despite herself. It looked as though things were . . . progressing.

Lark brought in the milk just as the Brownsville wagon arrived, providing a welcome distraction. Forsythia helped serve the food while Jesse and Climie kept the children occupied outside, well away from the corral. Jesse perched on a chunk of wood, carving something while Robbie watched with his usual fascination. Climie sat nearby and played a clapping and singing game with Sofie, eliciting squeals of glee.

"Shall we wait for RJ?" Adam asked as everyone headed toward the table. The breeze nipped cooler. They'd miss these outdoor meals with autumn coming fast.

Lark shook her head. "I think we'd best go ahead. He said he's going to stay as long as it takes."

"Look what Mr. Jesse is making, Mama Sythia." Robbie tugged Forsythia's skirt and held out the rough wooden carving.

Forsythia took the little figure and turned it gently. "A horse. Is it Captain, Jesse?"

The young man ducked his head and nodded.

"You have such a gift. Already I can see the spirited arch of the neck and the way he prances." Forsythia handed it back.

"It's a daddy horse, right, Mr. Jesse?" Robbie leaned against Jesse's knee.

Jesse nodded again. "Th-that's right."

"And you already made me a mama horse. Now maybe they can have a baby horse, right, Mama?" Robbie bounced on his tiptoes. "Mr. Jesse, will you make me a baby horse?"

Her ears pink beneath her golden hair, Forsythia picked Robbie up and plunked him on the bench at the table. "Time to eat."

Embarrassed chuckles faded into silence as Adam said the blessing, and then the dishes were passed around. Del forced herself not to look at the corral by chatting with Climie, who was seated beside her. She'd had little time to spend with their friend of late, with so much to do at school.

"Are you still thinking you'd like to run the boardinghouse?" Del speared a bite of fried potato and savored the flavor. No one fried potatoes like Lilac.

"I am." Climie gave a firm nod. "I like cooking and organizing things. And people . . . nice ones, anyway." A flicker of shadow threatened the new steadiness in her eyes. She'd certainly had plenty of experience with those who weren't so nice.

Del studied their friend's face and the scars there, visible and unseen. How could a man be so cruel to such a gentle soul?

The same way one could injure a child and scare his sister into lying. The thought hardened the potatoes into a lump in her stomach.

Del set down her fork. "Well, we'd certainly hire others to help you, but it would be nice to have someone we trust in charge. Lark thinks another woman or two to assist with cooking and cleaning and laundry, and a couple of men for the stables and such."

"Jesse said he's going to build the furniture for inside?" Climie glanced down the table at the quiet young man.

"There's none better."

"No. There isn't."

Del wondered at the soft sheen in Climie's gray eyes. Could there be—but no, surely not.

Jesse glanced up and met Climie's glance. He gave a shy grin, then focused back on whatever Robbie was chattering into his ear at the moment.

This was a new twist to worry about. *Lord, I sure don't know what to do with that one. I guess I'll leave that in your hands for now, as I should all things to begin with.*

Dusk fell, and Lark had lit the lantern in the center of the table by the time RJ approached from the shadows.

"Behold, the matchmaker returns." Adam lifted his tin cup in salute.

"Are we going to have a baby horsie?" Robbie piped up, sliding off the bench and running toward RJ. Del clapped her hand over her mouth.

RJ stared down at the child for a moment, nonplussed, then shrugged and grinned. "Well, maybe." He lifted his head and looked at Lark. "In round about eleven months or so."

At the scattered applause, Lark stood, beaming, and lifted the lid from the plate they'd kept covered for RJ. "Well, that deserves a full plate. And your fee, of course."

RJ took the plate, then looked about for a space to sit.

"Here, take my place." Climie stood, waving off his objections. "I'll start washing up."

"I'll help you." Del started to stand.

But Climie pushed her back down with a gentle hand. "You've been teaching all day. Sit."

Del couldn't deny that her limbs were weighted with weariness. But RJ, sitting next to her now, felt uncomfortably close. She scooted away an imperceptible inch on the bench.

RJ dug into his supper in silence.

Should she make conversation or just let him eat? Fireflies darted about in the darkness like elusive stars, Robbie and Sofie giving eager chase. Forsythia, Adam, and Jesse visited at the other end of the table. Lilac must have gone to help Climie.

"Sorry I sort of shooed you off earlier." RJ shifted on the bench beside her.

Surprised, Del glanced at him. "Sort of?" She quirked a brow.

He had the grace to wince.

She chuckled. "Never mind. I needed to get supper ready anyway. We do thank you for . . . coming today."

"The honor is mine." He dipped his head, unexpectedly gallant. "Starbright's a lovely little mare."

"Lilac adores her. She's special to all of us, the only one of our stock we brought from Ohio. Anders said you rode in the cattle car with Captain and Barker when you came out?"

"And Scamp, between Ohio and here. I tend to get along better with animals than people."

Had it always been so? Or just since whatever had turned him so bitter?

RJ took another bite, then chewed in silence, watching the fireflies. "This reminds me of the woods behind my parents' house back home. Well, my sister and brother-in-law's now. But when we were little, my sister and I would spend hours chasing fireflies. It seemed like those days would never end."

"They're gone, your parents?"

He gave a slight nod.

Then he had indeed known loss. "Ours too."

A quick glance at her. "Does it ever stop hurting?"

"I . . . don't know yet. I don't think so, somehow." Her eyes stung, catching her off guard. "But that doesn't mean there isn't healing. In time."

He nodded reluctantly. "Time."

They sat in silence as RJ cleaned his plate. Yet the awkwardness had fled, leaving the quiet companionable.

The tuning of a fiddle made them look up. Lilac stood nearby in the lanternlight, fiddle in hand, Forsythia and Lark bringing the other instruments out of the soddy. "Come on, Del, get your guitar."

Del quirked a brow at RJ and stood. "Ready for another Nielsen sing-along?"

"Sure." He smiled, a softness in his face she hadn't seen before. Or maybe the evening shadows made his eye patch seem less harsh.

Del headed for her guitar, a smile warming her face too.

His eye was killing him.

He'd enjoyed the evening until now, except for the awkward moments at the corral. He still thought women should keep well out of such sides of farm business. But the family, food, and companionship had loosened something deep within him tonight. Especially sitting and talking with Del. Talking and being listened to, as he hadn't with anyone in some time, especially a woman.

Who would have thought that woman would be Delphinium Nielsen?

Once the music began, though, the grinding pain began also. It seemed sometimes it had a fiendish mind of its own, starting its torturous tattoo whenever he let his guard down or dared even an inkling of hope for finding a place to belong out here in this territory. The more everyone sang and tapped their feet around the campfire, the more the agony drilled deep.

"'. . . Glory, glory, hallelujah! His truth is marching on!'"

At the rousing finish and burst of applause, RJ leaned his elbows on his knees and pressed his hands over his ears, hoping the darkness kept him from being too obvious.

As the sisters led into the gentler "Abide with Me," RJ rose and headed toward the wagon, sucking deep breaths of the cool evening air. Maybe being away from the smoke would help.

If only he'd brought some opium. He'd thought of it but resisted, blindly hoping he could get along without it for one evening.

More fool he.

He braced his hands on the side of the wagon and looked up at the sky. Stars upon stars, millions, billions of miles away. Bright as the fireflies and making him feel as small.

God . . . I know you're up there. I just kinda doubt you want to be bothered with me. But if you do, please . . . please take away this pain. He closed his eye and swallowed hard, feeling weak and childish. What did the Lord of Lords care for one injured soldier's eye? So many had been hurt worse.

"RJ."

He started at the voice behind him and whirled to see Adam's shape in the darkness.

"Here." Adam pressed a cool tin cup into his hand, the rim glinting in the moonlight.

RJ took it. "What . . . ?"

"Just drink."

Hardly knowing why, RJ obeyed, then nearly spat out the liquid. Cold tea, but another flavor laced it. His throat burning, he tried to push the cup back. "No."

"Take it." The doctor's voice came low, empathy without condescension. "For tonight."

RJ resisted a moment longer. Then, blinking back tears of relief mixed with regret at his own weakness, he downed the cup of opium and tea in one swallow.

The doctor gripped his shoulder in the darkness. "This isn't forever, RJ."

But what if it was?

16

Boys!" Del used her sternest voice. "Down out of the tree and into the wagons now. Josie, Clarabelle, what are you doing under the church steps? Get in, all of you, unless you want to be sent home and miss the entire outing."

That threat sent eighteen excited youngsters scampering into the wagon beds, the older ones boosting up the younger. Jesse perched on the seat of the Brownsvilles' wagon, Climie beside him. Isaac McTavish was helping out on the farm today, and Lark was harvesting seeds with Forsythia and her little ones, so she'd sent Jesse to help drive for the school trip. Lilac drove the Nielsen wagon, leaving Del free to supervise the children with the help of Climie and Beatrice.

"All right." Del counted heads once more. "That's everyone. Let me pray a blessing over our day, and then we'll be off." She bowed her head, needing the Lord's presence and focus for herself, not to mention everyone else. Why had she thought taking the entire school on an outing would be simple?

"Father, we thank you for this chance to enjoy and learn from your creation. Please cover us with your protection and peace, and let us listen to each other and especially to you. In Jesus' name, Amen."

A chorus of *Amens*, and then Josie piped up. "Let's go!"

Amid the chuckles, Del climbed up to sit on the back of the wagon beside Josie and Clarabelle. "I agree. Onward, drivers."

They laughed and sang as they rumbled over the rough grasses, strains of "Oh! Susanna" and their new favorite, "Battle Hymn of the Republic," ringing out amid the meadowlarks and dickcissels. An enormous flock of geese honked overhead, nearly covering the sky.

"Look, children." Del craned her neck and pointed. "They're going south for the winter. What do we call that?"

"Migration," called Elsie Weber from the other wagon.

"That's right. We'll see even more birds where we're going today."

The sharp tang of salt in her nostrils announced that they'd reached the salt marshes. Jesse and Lilac stopped the wagons, and the children tumbled out.

"Watch out for the mud," Del cautioned. From the dampness beneath her feet, she wished she'd cautioned the mothers to dress their children in old clothes today—not that many would have more than one set of everyday clothes anyway.

The children scattered along Little Salt Creek, voices ringing out. Lilac gathered several of the older ones by the water to study and draw cattails and saltwort, along with the waterfowl and shore birds that gathered. Del and Beatrice strolled along the creek's edge, keeping an eye on the younger ones.

Del breathed deeply of the salt-tanged air, the dampness of the earth. A killdeer started up before her and winged away. *Such a unique spot on your earth, Lord. Thank you for letting us know it.*

She saw John Kinsley perched on a rock near the creek, clumsily trying to draw a clump of saltmarsh asters with his paper spread on his knee.

"Aren't those pretty?" Del crouched beside him and brushed the delicate white petals with a finger. "What if you spread your paper on this flat part of the rock? That might make it a bit easier."

John sat huddled into himself a moment, then, with a stiff movement, shifted his paper to the rock. He bent over it with his pencil and added slender leaves to his clump of asters, still crude but recognizable.

"Lovely." Del smiled and touched his shoulder.

He flinched away.

She withdrew her hand, her middle clenching again. "Are you all right, John? Is your leg bothering you?"

He said nothing, just kept coloring in the leaves with his pencil.

Del lowered her voice. "John, did someone hurt you?"

He looked up at her, his eyes wide. Then his gaze darted away, and he pushed to his feet, the paper clutched and crumpling in his hand. Without a backward glance, he limped away, perhaps in search of his sister.

Del straightened, a shadow falling over the beautiful day. She shouldn't have asked that, not yet. She'd spoken before she thought it through. *Father, something isn't right, but what am I to do about it?*

She scanned the surrounding marsh, noting that the children had spread beyond the creek now. The little ones played in the muddy flats under Lilac and Mrs. Caldwell's supervision. Ah well, they were mud-smeared already. Let them have their fun, and she'd bear any ire from the mothers. The older students still roamed the nearby portions of the marsh or crouched in patches of reeds or cattails, sketching or pushing grasses aside to study something else. Del smiled to see Elsie Weber and Betsy Jorgensen point at a bald eagle soaring in the distance, then furiously add to their drawings.

On the wagon tongue nearby, Jesse perched with a stray branch in his hand, trimming off the excess leaves and twigs with his knife. What would he be carving now? The young man's creativity and skill with wood seemed to know no bounds. Climie sat nearby with a couple of the shyer children at her side. They watched as he held out the piece of wood and said something. Climie laughed softly, a smile touching her face.

Del swallowed. She loved seeing them happy. But what of this new closeness that seemed to be cropping up between the two? They'd both been through so much suffering in life, it made sense they'd be drawn together . . . yet Climie wasn't free, not as long as that snake of a husband roamed about somewhere in the country.

Del tried to push aside the worry snaking up her spine. She should talk to Lark about this. Or just go talk to Climie and Jesse. Maybe it was all her imagination.

Del scanned her charges again, making sure all students were accounted for, then headed over to the wagon. "Thank you both for coming today. It makes such a difference to have extra chaperones."

"Of course." Climie added another wildflower to the chain she was helping Clarabelle weave. "It's a joy."

Joy . . . something Climie's life had held so little of until now. *Lord, please provide a way for her to keep it.* "What are you carving, Jesse?"

"That eagle we s-saw." He held out the hunk of wood for her to see. Already she could see the beginnings of wings outstretched in flight.

Del shook her head. "You are amazing."

"Will you make me a horse and wagon like Robbie's?" Abel leaned on Jesse's knee.

"Sure."

"Miss Nielsen, how come Robbie don't come to school?"

"Doesn't. And he's not quite old enough. Next year, maybe."
She knew her sisters thought Robbie was ready now, but Del
still held that starting too soon could do more harm than good.
"How did you see Robbie's horse and wagon?"

"He showed me one time after church."

"Can you make *anything*, Mr. Jesse?" Clarabelle's eyes
stretched wide.

"Seems that way." Climie placed the flower garland on the
little girl's head. It slid over one ear, eliciting a giggle.

Del studied Climie's face, smiling as she adjusted the flowers. There was no untoward shyness when she spoke of Jesse.
Perhaps Del had been mistaken. It was so hard to know . . . and
was it really her business, anyway? Yet Jesse and Climie were
both like family.

"Miss Nielsen!"

At the youthful call, she turned to see Timothy O'Rourke
coming toward her, his thin face alight. He clutched his piece
of paper.

"Just back there." He pointed behind him. "We found a muskrat lodge."

"Oh my." Del peered and noted the brownish mound near
the pond bank. "What a special thing to see."

"Look at how they built it. Aren't they clever? I made my
drawing of it." He held it out to show her. "They weave grasses
and reeds and sticks all together, with a hole down under water
to get in by."

"Indeed." Del bent to examine his drawing. "They're regular
little architects. And this is excellent, Timothy. Wonderful de-
tail." He had captured not only the finer points of the construction but also a muskrat's nose poking up from the water nearby.

"I like to build things too." He glanced up at her, face shy.

"Do you really? What do you like to build?"

"Well, mostly I've helped my da build fences and things, and the barn. But I like figuring out how to put things together. I even came up with a new way to make the fence tighter, and Da said it was fine. And I made a dollhouse for Iris out of wood scraps from the dockyard back in New York City. Made wee dormer windows and a staircase and everything. She said it was like a grand lady's house." He nibbled his lip. "We had to leave it behind when we came west, but I'll make her another as soon as I can find enough scraps. There isn't as much wood lyin' around out here."

"No, there isn't," Del agreed. She hadn't known this quiet lad could say so many words at once. "You know, my family is having a boardinghouse built in town. Perhaps you could stop by the site sometime and see if Mr. Easton would give you some scraps." Not that she'd have considered RJ the genial type, but he seemed to have softened some at their home the other evening.

"I think my da has been working there." Timothy straightened, his eyes lighting. "That's a grand idea. Thank you, Miss Nielsen."

Mr. O'Rourke working on the boardinghouse? That was news to her. But between teaching and helping on the farm, it was little wonder Del wasn't up on all the news in town, let alone who RJ had hired on for the job.

A sudden shriek sent both her and Timothy hurrying for the creek.

Josie Jeffers stood knee-deep in a muddy sinkhole and was sinking farther. Lilac had her fast by the hand, her own boots sinking, while the children around shouted encouragement or admonitions.

Del ran toward them, holding her skirts away from the clinging brush. "Stay back, children. Lilac, how stuck is she?"

"It's a patch of quicksand. We didn't realize. Get a branch."

Del turned to dash for one and ran smack into Jesse, who

held out a branch bigger than the one he'd been carving. She snatched it and ran back to the mud. Keeping her own feet on firm ground, she held out the branch to Lilac.

Her sister reached it out to Josie. "Put it under your back, little one. That's it. Now lie back on it. We're going to pull you out."

Del steadied Lilac's waist while her sister tugged, the mud sucking and oozing as it gave up the battle. The little girl squelched free with a sudden burst, sending Lilac and Del tumbling in a heap, Josie landing muddily on top.

The children clapped and cheered. Jesse and Climie held out hands to help everyone up.

Del staggered to her feet, knees weak now that the danger was past. She knelt beside Josie and brushed back the child's muddy hair. Goodness, this little one was prone to crises. "Are you all right, Josie?"

Josie hiccupped a sob and nodded.

"That was frightening, I know." Del hugged her. "But you're safe now. And think what a story you'll have to tell from our outing."

A smile tipped the corners of Josie's mouth, and she ran to join her friends, safely on higher ground under Mrs. Caldwell's watchful eye.

"Well." Del blew out a breath, her hands still trembling. "I think that's enough excitement for one day. We'd better head back." She reached for Lilac's hand beside her. "You all right?"

"I am." Lilac squeezed back, her face pinched. "I'm sorry. I should have taken more care."

"Quicksand is so hard to see or predict. You had the presence of mind to keep hold of her and get her out. That's what counts." Del frowned. "Whatever are you doing, Jesse?"

Being careful where he stepped, the young man was poking with the branch under some brush near the sinkhole. "Q-quicksand forms where there's lots of water. I'm t-tryin' to see where it's coming from. We're not by the c-creek." He stepped onto a grassy hummock and bent to clear away reeds with his hands. "There." He sat back with a grin as water bubbled up through the mud. "It's a spring."

"Oh my goodness." Mrs. Caldwell hurried forward. "I wonder—we're not that far from where our friend Atika used to live. Could this be the salt spring she told us about? We've never been able to find it."

"What salt spring?" Climie asked.

"The native people used the waters for various ailments, and the mud too, I believe. Dr. Brownsville asked Henry about it, wondering if it might help that young man's eye."

"RJ—that is, Mr. Easton?" Del had heard nothing of this. But why would she? She bent close to the spring and ran her hand through the cool, muddy bubbles. "Perhaps we can take some mud back with us and see what the doctor thinks."

"A fine idea." Mrs. Caldwell nodded. "I believe I've got an empty jar in my wagon from the tea I brought."

"Or this." Climie appeared at Del's elbow, a small crock in hand that she must have fetched from their own basket in the wagon.

"Thank you." Del took it with a smile and shake of her head. "How do you always know just what we need?"

"She p-pays attention, that's how," Jesse said, sending Climie a shy grin.

Del bent to scoop up the mud, wonder and foreboding mingling in her heart. If only this could make a difference for RJ. But, oh, she was terribly afraid she wasn't mistaken about Jesse and Climie at all. And what could possibly come of that?

17

RJ could hardly believe what he was seeing.

Perched up on a roof beam of the skeleton boardinghouse, he stared down as Clive Johnson approached the building site. Or more accurately, staggered toward it.

Was the man dead-dog drunk?

Clive always tended to be late, but today RJ had given up on seeing him at all. Work started at sunrise—all the men knew that—and the sun was climbing toward midmorning.

Now here came Johnson, lurching along with an out-of-tune whistle as if he hadn't a care in the world. And maybe he hadn't, with that much alcohol in him.

Clenching his jaw, RJ twisted around and climbed down, calling himself all kinds of names for taking on a job where he didn't know the men he'd be working over. But this needed tending to, and there was no one to do it but him.

By the time he reached the ground, Clive had wandered inside the would-be dining room and picked up a hammer, passing it from one hand to another as if meditating what to do with it. As RJ approached, he found a stray nail and then, still whistling, pounded it square in the middle of a window frame.

He raised the hammer high, then brought it down smack on his thumb, based on the string of words that followed.

"Johnson!" RJ barked.

Clive jumped, lost his footing, and sprawled flat out on his back. Several other workmen guffawed.

"Get up, Clive." RJ nudged him with his boot. "And get yourself back home, preferably not by way of the liquor tent."

"Why would I go home, Boss?" Clive grinned up at him lazily, apparently already forgetting his thumb. "I come here ta work."

"You're under-the-table drunk, man." Disgust twisted RJ's middle, but he offered the man a hand. Clive ignored it. "And you're fired."

Clive blinked, the grin leaving his face. "You can't do that to me."

"I can and just did. It would be negligent to your safety and that of my other workmen to do otherwise." RJ sharpened his tone still further. "Now get up, and get out of here."

Hauling himself to a sitting position, Clive glared at RJ, lip curled. "You'll regret this."

"Not as much as I regret ever letting you on this site. Now go."

Muttering threats and obscenities, Clive stumbled to his feet and went, the venom in his words somewhat belied by the weaving of his gait.

RJ shook his head and blew out a breath. It was hard to believe some people thought that liquor tent worth the trouble it caused.

"Mr. Easton, sir."

"Yes, O'Rourke?" RJ turned to the burly man he had come to lean on as his foreman, at least during the hours O'Rourke could work away from his farm.

"One of the lads just realized he cut a passel of boards the wrong length. We'll have to cut more lumber, I'm afraid, and start that wall over again."

RJ sighed and glanced at the sun. "Do what you need to do."
And only half the morning gone already.

It would be a long day.

What was he doing with his life?

RJ dragged his feet up the steps of the Brownsvilles' home
that evening, bone-weary, as it seemed he ended every day. Light
and voices from within spoke of company. Just what he did not
need tonight. Perhaps he could slip past unnoticed and just head
up to bed. The pain in his eye socket lanced something fierce.

He eased open the door and stepped inside.

"Oh, RJ, you're here. Wonderful." Eyes alight, Forsythia hurried to meet him.

He forced a smile to greet his hostess and the portly woman
who followed from the sitting room. And Delphinium. Why in
tarnation was she here? She must have stopped by for supper
after school. "Evening, ladies. Doctor."

Adam stood back a bit, hands in his pockets.

"You know Mrs. Jorgensen from the mercantile." Forsythia
drew the woman forward as the children crowded around. "She
stopped by to share some good news with us."

"Really, you needn't make a fuss." Her face reddening, Mrs.
Jorgensen drew a shawl closer around her shoulders, though
the evening was still warm.

"Oh, but Mr. Easton will want to hear this." Forsythia turned
back to RJ. "We haven't had a chance to tell you yet, as you left
so early this morning. But Del had the schoolchildren out at
the salt flats yesterday, on the Caldwells' land—Mrs. Caldwell
was along, too, and Lilac and Jesse. They were drawing flora
and fauna and I don't know what all. But at any rate—tell
him, Del."

Del stepped forward, a small earthen jar in her hands. "We

think we came upon that salt spring Adam told you about, that the Caldwells had heard stories about from the old Pawnee woman. So we brought back some mud."

"And?" RJ resisted the urge to rub his throbbing temples. As it often did, the pain had spread from his eye into his very skull.

"Well, I brought it over today before school. And Adam tried it on Mrs. Jorgensen."

Adam spoke from the shadows. "She's been suffering from a cluster of carbuncles on her shoulder. She'd mentioned it to Forsythia when she was working at the mercantile."

"So this morning I convinced her to let Adam make an application of the salt mud to her boils as a poultice." Forsythia gently touched the older woman's arm. "Our mother used all kinds of poultices for healing, sometimes even mud. And Lucretia—Mrs. Jorgensen—just came by to tell us that it helped as nothing else has."

"I'd tried everything—bread poultice, onion poultice, castor oil." Mrs. Jorgensen shook her head. "It was keeping me up at night. Never would have thought I'd stoop to trying mud, but . . ." She looked at Adam, something in her eyes that RJ didn't understand. "I'm beholden to you, Doctor."

Adam met her gaze. "Many of the Pawnees' ways are older and wiser than ours, I think. And you're most welcome."

"RJ." Del stepped nearer, her gray-blue eyes searching his face. "We want to try this on your eye, or rather on your scar. To see if it will help you too."

RJ stiffened. "I don't think so."

"I was skeptical too, young man. But I'm a believer now." Mrs. Jorgensen adjusted her shawl once more. "I'd best get back to my husband. I just thought I should let you all know. Good night." With nods all around, she made her way to the door and down the steps.

Robbie and Sofie ran after her to wave good-bye on the porch.

"Come, it's getting dark." Forsythia drew her children inside and closed the door. "RJ, I know this might seem an odd treatment, but where's the harm in trying? For Mrs. Jorgensen—I didn't want to give details while she was here, but Adam examined her in his office before you came, and the majority of the boils had already opened and are now draining. And she was in such misery before."

"Does Mr. RJ have a boil in his eye, Mama Sythia?" Robbie clasped his arms around his mother's skirts.

"No, I don't have a boil in my eye." RJ's irritation spiked, and he slammed his hat onto the rack by the door.

"But the mineral salts in these waters can have so many healing properties." Del followed him. "Adam says he's been researching his medical journals about it, and people soak in the water for rheumatism, consumption, all sorts of things."

"Of which I have none." He knew his tone sliced, but he couldn't help it. He turned to face them all. "No miracle mud plaster is going to bring back my eye, and I don't wish to be a subject for experimentation."

Silence hung. Sofie whimpered. Del lowered her gaze, her thumbs rubbing the sides of the little crock.

Adam reached down and picked up his little girl. "No one is going to force anything on you, RJ." His voice was even. "Merely see it as an option, should you choose to try it."

"Right now I just need to *try* to find more workers for the boardinghouse. I had to fire one today for showing up drunk." RJ turned toward the staircase. "Let me know if you hear any word of response to Mr. Young's advertisement. I'm going to bed. Good night."

He stomped up the stairs, pain flashing in his head with each step.

In his room, RJ threw himself on the bed and flung his arm across his face. What a louse he was, speaking that way to the people who had taken him into their home. It would serve him right if they kicked him out onto the dirt streets of Salton.

An unexpected lump of homesickness rose in his throat. The Brownsvilles and Nielsens had been kindness itself, but he missed his family, missed Esmay and Emmaline, Jemmy and Jehosephat, and especially his parents. He'd written home, and Esmay wrote often, but it wasn't the same. He even missed Francine—or not her exactly, now that he saw more of who she was, but what he'd had with her, who he thought she'd been.

What was he doing out here, bumbling about on the Nebraska frontier, supervising a building project as if he knew what he was doing? Not that he didn't—he had the training and the expertise, but it wasn't like he'd imagined. Maybe the rest of the population of Salton was building a new life, but not him. He was just a sham, forcing his way through each day until he could take another pill from the opium bottle and forget everything in sleep for a few hours.

Moisture leaked from his good eye, trickling down toward his ear. He swiped at the tears with the back of his hand. At least no one was here to see his foolishness. Misery squirmed in his gut at the memory of the look in Del's eyes a few moments ago. Why was he always at his worst around her?

"Lord God, I'm a mess."

The words caught in his throat. There was no answer save the breeze at the curtains, the cooling dusk as light faded from the room.

At a tap at the door, he sighed and sat up. "Come in." No doubt it was Adam, either to remonstrate or to attempt to convince him to try the treatment.

But Forsythia slipped into the room, hesitated, then sat on the end of the bed.

"I want to apologize, RJ. I expect we rather overwhelmed you down there."

He rubbed his forehead. "No, it was me. Forgive me. This eye of mine—it makes me half-crazy at times."

"That's why we want so much to find something to help you. But not if you don't want it."

Silence rested over them for a moment, a comfortable one this time.

Forsythia gazed at the fluttering curtains of the window, face thoughtful, her golden hair silvery in the fading light. She reminded RJ of Del, if less discomfiting. Forsythia didn't have Del's eyes, though—those striking eyes that seemed to change color with what she wore, sometimes gray, sometimes blue. When he was around her, he seemed always aware of those lovely eyes.

RJ shook himself. What was Forsythia saying?

". . . wanted to explain a little more about Mrs. Jorgensen. When we all first arrived here a year ago, before Adam and I were married, he rented rooms next to the Jorgensens' store. But Mrs. Jorgensen would have nothing to do with him. The previous doctor in town was a charlatan, a terrible man by the sound of it. He dosed people with poisons or quack remedies and made several sick. But the worst of it was, when the Jorgensens' daughter was struggling in childbirth, he clumsily attempted a dangerous procedure. I'll spare you the details." Forsythia drew a long breath. "Both mother and baby died. The husband gave up and went back east—we actually took on his abandoned homestead. Mrs. Jorgensen didn't trust any doctor after that."

RJ nodded, moved with pity toward the woman he'd barely met. "Makes sense."

"It does. But in over a year, Adam still hadn't won her confidence, not even after he saved her grandson from a rattlesnake bite and even aided Mrs. Jorgensen herself when she was injured in our tornado last fall. He'd about given up hope of ever getting through to her." She turned toward him. "So today, when she was willing to let us try the mud, and then even came herself to tell us that it had helped—it was like a bright ray of healing and hope for us. And it made us so hopeful for you too."

RJ rubbed his hands on his knees. He felt even more a cad. "I'm . . . afraid." The words came out in a whisper, yet still shocked him. What made him confess such to this young woman? He couldn't imagine doing so to anyone else. Certainly not to Del.

Now, where had that thought come from?

But Forsythia just sat there, accepting. No wonder she made the perfect doctor's wife. "Afraid of what?"

"I don't know." Words even more ludicrous. He really felt the fool.

"How did it happen, your injury? Anders said something about a Confederate renegade."

RJ nodded. "He jumped me one night when I was traveling home after the war. He must have been trailing returning Union soldiers, I don't know. Or he just happened upon me, saw my uniform, and thought I was as good a candidate as any to take his revenge. He sliced at me with his knife. I wrenched it away and . . . killed him." He swallowed back the bile of the memory. "And I'd thought I made it through the war without taking a life."

"I killed a man on our journey west." Forsythia's voice was soft.

RJ reared back.

"I know. You'd never think that I'm a dead shot at throwing a knife." She smiled wryly. "He was a ruffian who surprised us in the night and was attacking Del. Trying to drag her away into the bushes, a knife to her throat."

A sudden rush of rage turned RJ's palms damp.

"So I threw my knife and struck home. It was over before I knew what had happened. It took a long time before I really came to terms with it, though, and felt forgiven."

RJ sat silent. He didn't know if he'd ever come to terms with any of this, really.

"I've been afraid plenty. More than the rest of my sisters, I sometimes think, even if they don't know it. But often it seems that when I'm afraid, it's partly because deep down I know what I should do, I just don't want to do it. And that's when I need to reach for strength greater than my own." She rose, the bed creaking softly from the ropes stretched beneath. "Just think about it, RJ. What do you have to lose?"

With a soft step and whisper of skirts, Forsythia was gone, doubtless to put the children to bed.

RJ pushed to his feet and undressed, washing at the basin and pitcher always kept clean and filled. At some point, if he was to stay in this territory, he really should find a more permanent place to live. Forsythia had mentioned Adam renting rooms from the Jorgensens at first—could those be available? Not likely, with all the newcomers to town, but it was a thought. He'd try to remember to stop in the store and ask tomorrow when he passed through town.

Clad in his nightshirt, RJ stretched back across the bed, letting the breeze from the window caress his skin. He stripped off the patch and let the gentle air cool his face. The pain had mercifully lessened for the moment. Maybe he could actually sleep without the opium tonight. He hadn't eaten but craved sleep more than food just now. He'd think more about the mud treatment in the morning.

Some hours later, he jerked awake from a nightmare, gasping for breath, the quilt beneath him damp with sweat. RJ sat up in bed and pressed his fists to his temples, willing away the pounding pain, the burning in his eye. He could still feel the bushwhacker's grip on his throat, the hissed epithets spat in his face, the foul breath. Then the blinding slash across his eye, the burst of red pain and rage that surged through his limbs and gave him the strength to throw the man off him, wrench away the weapon, and send it home. The cold numbness as he stared at the renegade's still body in the falling rain, a sudden awareness of the blood sluicing down his own face.

The pain that had never truly left him since, in body and soul.

"Oh, God." RJ ground out the words. "How long?"

Do you want to be made well?

The words came so suddenly, so quiet yet clear on his heart, that RJ lifted his head. He blinked, his breathing heavy in the darkness.

Stories, snippets of Scripture he hadn't remembered in years, suddenly filtered through his mind. Jesus' question in those very words to the man at the Pool of Bethesda. Another man, this one blind, whose eyes Christ anointed with mud, of all things. And a still older story, of Naaman the Syrian, who had scoffed at the command of Elisha the prophet to go and wash in the River Jordan to be healed of his infirmity, simply because it seemed a thing too small.

RJ would never presume to put himself into those biblical accounts. And yet . . . was he showing that same stubborn heart of Naaman of old?

If it was possible, did he want to be made well?

RJ glanced in the direction of the darkened bureau, where the small bottle of opium sat. After all, as Forsythia had said, what did he have left to lose?

"All right." He lay back and let out a sigh that seemed months in coming. "Have it your way."

Not a prayer that would go down in the annals of faith, and no audible answer. But as he lay there, for the first time since that awful night, RJ felt able to breathe again.

He slept so soundly he nearly missed making the building site by dawn.

That evening, RJ lay on the doctor's examining table, his stomach once more in knots.

"Try to relax, RJ. I don't know if this will help, but I truly doubt it will hurt." With gentle hands, Adam lifted the patch from RJ's missing eye and cleansed the scar with a damp cloth. "There. Forsythia, hand me the poultice."

The mud smeared on coolly, with an earthy, slightly tangy scent—the salt of it? RJ forced himself to breathe slow and steady. "How long must I keep it on?"

"I don't know, frankly. Let's try an hour to start, and I'd like to apply it every day for a while. After a week, we'll see if there's been any effect." Adam wrapped a loose bandage over the mud poultice and both eyes, bringing to mind memories of the hospital. "I'll help you to the sofa, and you can rest there."

RJ let himself be led, then fumbled himself into a lying position on the sofa. Adam and Forsythia left him with remonstrances to lie still.

He lay there, listening to the evening noises of dishwashing in the kitchen and children being admonished to tidy up. He hated the sense of being helpless, unable to see, of others having to care for him. Yet perhaps that had been part of his problem.

For tonight, he would merely try to trust.

18

The rooster crowing woke her.

Lark looked to the open doorway, stretching as she did so. Talk about an early bird. Dawn was still a promise beyond the horizon. Though it was no longer dark outside, even the pup at the foot of her bed—where he was not supposed to be—was not moving yet.

Her list for the day was short: start harvesting wheat. She'd sharpened the scythes last night, and with no school this week, all three of them could harvest. They had less than two acres of wheat left by the grasshoppers, which was ready now, and about the same of oats, which would be next even though it was planted late. Corn would be last. It was strange that the grasshoppers must not have liked the oats, while less than half of their corn had survived.

She thanked God every day for the amount they had been able to save, which would be food for them and food for their animals. At least the grasshoppers had not taken everything. She had to remind herself to be grateful for that.

Tossing back her sheet, she swung her feet over the edge of the bed, rousing the puppy, who jumped down, short tail wagging. He gave her toes a quick lick and headed out the door to do his business.

The rooster crowed again, this time in full form, waking Lilac. "Where's Scamp?"

"Just went out. How about you milk this morning? I hear Del is up too." The clanking of the stove lids announced Del was tackling her first job. "I'll split what wood is left until we saw up that tree you and the oxen dragged in. We can't cut the wheat until the dew is lifted anyway."

"You know when we were talking about needed businesses? We could use a flour mill, but there's not enough flow in that creek to power a grinder."

"There were advantages to living in a more settled region. I remember going with Pa to the mill on the river at home." Lark finished dressing. "It sounds like Buttercup is ready for milking."

The cow bellowed again, and Starbright whinnied. Scamp tore off around the house, ferociously barking as if he were a guard dog of giant size. Lark quickly wound her hair in a bun and clapped her hat on her head.

The barks changed to happy whimpers as she reached the corner of the house.

"Jesse, what are you doing here so early in the morning? I thought you were working on the boardinghouse." She paused. "What is that thing you're carrying?"

"Good morning to you t-too." He grinned. "Sythia and I de-cided you n-needed me worse out here."

"Oh, you did, did you?" She could feel her own face stretch into a matching grin. "Have you had breakfast?"

He shook his head. "Too early."

"You ever helped harvest wheat before?"

"No, but I b-borrowed one of your scythes to adapt to a cradle." He swung his creation off his shoulders. "See? This will m-make bundling the wheat easier. Someone told me about it, and Jorgensen had a p-picture in his catalog."

"Well, now we will have two workers with scythes and two bundling."

"Good morning, Jesse," Del said on her way to the woodpile. "Breakfast will be ready by the time Lilac is done milking."

As they sat down at the table, Lilac greeted Jesse. "What a surprise. How's life in town?"

"Busy. We're siding the b-boardinghouse now, and the windows should arrive sometime this week."

They bowed their heads for grace and passed the bowl of scrambled eggs around, along with the biscuits left over from the night before.

Jesse reached for the bowl and, after glancing around to see that everyone was served, cleaned the remaining eggs onto his plate, then did the same with the biscuits.

The three sisters exchanged eye rolls. There were rarely leftovers when Jesse ate at their table.

"May I ask you a question?" Lark said while he was buttering the remaining biscuit. Jesse shrugged. "How old are you?"

He paused and frowned. "T-twenty-one, I think. I guess no one was keeping t-track when I was little."

Lark swallowed. One more peek into the young man's shrouded past. Adam had said his nephew was handed around after his mother died and his father disappeared.

Lilac propped her elbows on the table to hold her coffee cup. "Who taught you woodworking?"

"Uh, I g-guess my uncle Edward. I thought I would live with him and Aunt Sonja until I grew up, but she died t-trying to have a baby, and he got the c-consumption.

"I whittled lots, but Adam really t-taught me to build things. He even found me a cabinetmaker so I could apprentice before he and Aunt Elizabeth decided to move west." He smiled at Del.

"Your d-desk is nearly finished. I watch for wood wherever I am. I used part of a b-barn door for your desk. It must have been dumped by the tornado. I know people are looking for wood all the time for stoves, but take that tree we were sawing on. Let it dry and age, and it would be good for a chair or maybe . . ." He shrugged. "I look at a piece of wood, and I see what it might b-become." He looked up to see all three sisters staring at him.

Lark's smile lit her face and danced in her eyes. "I've never heard you talk so much. You're an artist, you know."

Jesse shook his head. "Nah, I just like wood. It d-don't talk mean at you."

Like some people do, Lark thought. In his case, it sounded like many people. He and Climie had so much in common. No wonder they were drawn to each other.

She slapped her hands on the table. "I think the dew is dried, so let's begin. Jesse and I will do the cutting, then you two will rake the wheat into a bundle and wrap a couple of stalks of wheat around it. We'll shock it before we quit. The oats will probably be ready when the wheat is threshed." She looked at Jesse. "You ever seen a flail?"

He shook his head. "All this harvest stuff is new to me."

"Just like the rest of us," Del muttered as she picked up the dishes.

Lark and Jesse took the scythe and the cradle out to the field. "Just like we did with the hay, lay it flat. I'll start, and you come a couple of sweeps behind me so we get all the middle left standing."

"You use the cradle, see if it works better," Jesse said. "If it does, I'll do another for tomorrow."

Lark hefted the cradle. It was heavier. She pulled back and swung the scythe. The wheat fell smoothly into the cradle, then laid out flat when she swung it back. Step by step, she worked up the side of the field with Jesse four steps behind and beside her. "Can you tell a difference?" she asked as she kept the pace.

"The cradle makes the wheat lie more even."

They stopped to look back at where Lilac was bent over, gathering the cut wheat into a bundle, then laying it down to wrap several stalks around it and tying a knot. She set the bundle aside and repeated the process.

They stopped for a water break when they got back to the starting point. "You want to change places?" she asked of Lilac and Del.

"We can try. But let me tell you, bundling takes practice." Lilac let the water pour down her chin.

"Surely there must be an easier way." Del arched her back, kneading her waist. "I'll teach fifty kids any day rather than this."

"Even Silas Gruber from last year?"

"Ten of him."

By noontime they'd made progress, but still the field stretched on, seeming endless.

"And I thought haying was hard work." Lilac shook her head as they ate a quick, cold dinner.

By the time the setting sun sent golden fingers over the field, they had nearly a third of the wheat cut and bundled. Lark showed them how to stand one bundle on end, then lean two more into it so that it stood upright, the better for drying.

The shock tumbled over as soon as she released it.

They stared at the fallen shock, then at one another, and shook their heads.

"Well, here we go again." This time Lark stood the bundles up together and rammed them firmly upright. "Now stay there."

It did.

"Guess you showed it." Lilac snorted, trying to keep from laughing.

Lark felt a burst of disgust at her youngest sister, then shook her head. "Yep, I did. We are in charge here, not wheat bundles."

"Will you stay for supper, Jesse?" Del asked as they all stumbled toward the soddy.

"No, Forsythia and Adam are expectin' me. I'll s-see you ladies first thing in the morning." He touched his hat and headed off.

"How does he still have the energy to walk home?" Lilac shook her head.

"Just as well he does. That way we'll still have some food left for tomorrow."

Lark joined in the weary chuckle and headed to milk Buttercup. Her hands, sore and blistered from the scythe and sharp wheat stalks, screamed as she squeezed the cow's teats. Gritting her teeth, she pushed through. They'd worn gloves, but hers already had slits in them from this first day. She'd need to mend them tonight. If she could stay awake long enough.

Yawning, Lark leaned her head against the cow's warm flank. "Lord, thank you for this land and the means to harvest its fruit. Please help us through the rest of the way."

Perhaps a couple more days on the wheat, and then would come the threshing—another new experience. Then on to the oats and later the corn. Perhaps those would be easier? At least they would be more experienced by then.

All around them, other families were in the swing of harvest just the same, grasshoppers notwithstanding. The rhythms of farm life. Most had more menfolk to do the outside labor part, though.

The sisters barely spoke through supper, their cramping hands fumbling to lift the food to their mouths. After a brief Scripture reading, they fell into bed.

Jesse must have said something to the Brownsvilles, for Forsythia and Climie came out to help the next day, taking turns watching the children and working in the fields. Adam even came for a few hours in the afternoon, and by day's end, the whole field of wheat lay flattened in the evening sun, though not yet all of it was bundled.

The next morning, Lark visited the boardinghouse site with Jesse, leaving her sisters to continue bundling and shocking the wheat.

"You can see M-Mr. Easton's doin' a fine job." Jesse nodded at the building, the siding almost completed now. "Though he's still l-lookin' for a couple more workers."

Lark shaded her eyes to look up at the two-storied structure, a little thrill traveling down her arms. Yet another dream taking shape before her eyes. *Thank you, Lord.* "Do you know where he might be?"

"Usually b-back behind the building where he has his plans set up, if he's n-not up on the roof." Jesse headed around the corner.

Lark followed. She wanted to see how soon RJ thought they might be able to open. She'd thought not until closer to Thanksgiving, but with how nearly complete the building was looking, at least from the outside . . .

"Hey, Boss. I'm b-back today, and Miss Larkspur's here to see you." Jesse spoke confidently, making Lark glad. If he felt at ease around RJ Easton, that definitely spoke well of the man.

"Good morning." RJ met her gaze with a smile, a welcome change. Perhaps his eye socket wasn't paining him as much today. Could the mud Adam had tried be helping? "What can I do for you today, Miss Nielsen?"

"I just wanted to check on how things are coming." Lark scanned the half-shingled roof. "From all appearances, they seem to be progressing well."

"I'd say so, though I could still use a couple more men." RJ tipped back the wool Union army hat he still wore.

"I hear Mr. Young has had some responses to the advertisements he placed back east. Hopefully we'll get some more men coming in on the train soon." Though that could be a mixed blessing, with how some workers frequented the liquor tent. Lark's stomach curled.

"I'll keep an eye out. I had to fire another man for drunkenness on the job just the other day."

It was as if he'd read her mind. "Well, let's pray for a steady replacement. When do you think we might be ready to open?"

RJ adjusted his eye patch and bent over his plans again. "Depends how fast we can move, but I'd say another three weeks, maybe a month. Assuming you want the inside as finished as we discussed."

"I was thinking that the only room we really need finished is the kitchen, so we can fix meals. Folks can sleep on pallets on the floors upstairs and eat at a table in an unfinished room." Lark thought rapidly. A month gave them time to finish both harvest and the inside of the boardinghouse, if barely. "Jesse, could we pay you to get started on some furniture? We'll keep it basic to start, but we'll need a large dining table and benches. A couple of chairs would be good but not necessary. Cupboards and counters in the kitchen, along with a worktable. Anders has ordered us a cookstove. Oh, and a washstand or two."

"Sure thing."

She shook her head and blew out a breath. "There sure is a lot to do." With harvest not yet complete, her head spun from it all.

"One step at a time." RJ gave her a reassuring nod, then frowned up at the sky. "Clouds are rolling in. Think we'll get some rain?"

"Oh dear." Lark craned her neck to look upward. Sure enough, darkening clouds covered half the sky, though it wasn't yet noon. "I'd best get back and help finish getting the wheat shocked."

"Need me to come too?" Jesse asked.

"Hopefully Del and Lilac are nearly finished." She prayed so. After jogging Starbright all the way home, Lark ran out to the wheat field to join her sisters, the wind lashing her skirts and whipping her hair against her face. Del and Lilac bent over the cut stalks, working fast.

Lark paused to catch her breath. "What should I do?"

"Help Lilac start shocking the sheaves," Del called above the wind. "I've nearly finished the bundling, then I'll help."

Lark joined Lilac in grabbing several bundles of wheat and standing them together, heads up, then laying another sheaf on top to shield the grain as much as possible. It seemed hard to believe this would do much to protect it from the rain, but farmers had been doing it for generations, so there must be some value to it.

The first heavy drops of rain splatted as Lark spread the final sheaf over the last shock. The sisters grabbed hands and ran for the soddy, laughing as the rain chased them inside.

"Goodness, that came on fast." Under the porch roof, Lark smoothed back her dripping hair and peered at their field, nearly hidden now by sheets of rain. "Lord, please protect our harvest."

19

So Mr. Caldwell doesn't know much about the Kinsleys?" Mrs. Caldwell shook her head as she and Del stood outside after church the next Sunday. The September breeze finally nipped cool after the long summer, and Del tugged her shawl about her shoulders.

"No, he only met the husband briefly once when he came in for something about a legality regarding his homestead. He said Mr. Kinsley seemed quiet but nice enough. Their land is quite a ways out, so perhaps that's why we don't see them at church."

But nice could be deceiving. Not everyone showed their cards as flagrantly as Deacon Wiesel—and even he had kept some of their church members back home deceived.

Del fought a rising angst. "If I was somehow able to prove John is being abused, what could we do?"

"That's the other hard thing." Mrs. Caldwell winced. "Henry says legally there's really no recourse. Parents have the right to do what they wish with their own children and punish them as they see fit. Unless it actually amounts to murder, the law can do nothing."

Just as Wiesel's abuse of Climie to "keep her in line" did not qualify as criminal. A red blur swam across Del's vision. "That's purely evil. What is wrong with this world?"

Lark joined them. "A good deal, I'm afraid, as the Bible minces no words about. But fortunately, there are some things we can do about it, if we join together. I've just been talking with the other ladies, and we have at least a dozen who wish to meet and discuss the problem of the liquor tent. Mrs. Caldwell, you'll join us?"

"You may be sure of that. When and where?"

"We thought the church, this Friday evening. Any children can play in the yard if their mothers are in the meeting, and the older ones can help watch the younger."

"Good." Del drew a breath of hope. Even if she could do nothing else about whatever was going on in the Kinsley family, if liquor was involved, perhaps dealing with that problem would still help.

Lilac stepped up to the group, her voice more subdued than usual. "Did Reverend Pritchard give his permission?"

"He did." Lark nodded. "He's glad for us to use the space and to lend his support in whatever other way he can."

Del cut a keen glance at their youngest sister, but Lilac avoided her eyes. Del pressed her lips together. She'd given Rev. Pritchard no encouragement whatsoever, and so far nothing else had happened, but she needed to clear the air with her sister, and soon. Family ties were too precious to let misunderstandings get in the way.

"Well, I see Henry is looking for me. The man can wait only so long for his Sunday dinner." Mrs. Caldwell smiled. "I'll see you Friday, ladies."

A chorus of waving and good-byes, and then the sisters walked Forsythia toward her house, a sleepy Mikael in Climie's arms. It was good to see Climie able to enjoy church again. It had been such a traumatic place for her before.

"Miss Nielsen?"

Del turned at the low voice behind her. "Mr. Easton." Her heart quickened a bit. She was surprised to see him there, though she shouldn't be—he'd be heading home with the Brownsvilles. "How is your eye?" She bit her tongue as soon as she spoke. After his response the other evening to the mud she'd brought, he'd likely freeze her out now.

But he only gave a half smile and touched a finger to his eye patch. "A little better, maybe. I'm not sure."

"I hope so." Her lungs filled with relief, not just for his eye, but that he didn't seem angry at her. Though why should that matter? She pushed the thought away. "We all so want to see you free of pain."

He shifted his feet, removed his hat. "I wanted to apologize for my ill temper the other evening. You didn't deserve that."

"Who does?" She arched a brow but smiled at him. "Of course you are forgiven. You must have felt a bit swarmed."

He hesitated, then glanced over at her waiting sisters. "Well, I'd best let you go. See you later."

"See you."

Del watched him stride off toward the Brownsvilles' house ahead, then turned to join Larkspur and Lilac in saying goodbye to Forsythia.

"It still feels strange with only three of us, especially now that Anders is gone," Del said as their wagon rumbled over the prairie toward home. Would the Nielsen siblings continue to drift apart one by one? She shook her head to dispel the melancholy thoughts. At least RJ's eye might be improving. Thank the Lord for that. And there was definitely a softening in him of late. She actually enjoyed his company now—when he wasn't in one of his foul moods.

The next morning, school started again after a week off for harvest, but both John and Bethany Kinsley were missing at roll call. Del marked the absences and carried on with a smile for the other children, but worry wound a knot in her middle until she couldn't eat much of her dinner. By the last period of the day, she could barely concentrate on the older students' recitations. Timothy O'Rourke's fumbling through his lesson grated on her last nerve.

"Timothy." Her voice came out sharper than she'd meant it to. "Concentrate. You're stumbling over every other word."

"Yes, miss." The boy ducked his black-haired head. "Sorry, Miss Nielsen."

Del sighed. "Try it again, slower."

This time she listened closely, noting with concern that Timothy seemed to have difficulty with fairly simple words. Had he truly had so little schooling for a boy of his age? He and his sister had attended school in New York, and Iris read easily at the same level as the other Third Readers, or better.

"That's fine, Timothy. You may stop now." She gave him a smile she hoped atoned for her sharpness. "Thomas, will you please read the last page?"

It was not the best choice on her part to leave young Dwyer for last—though he pronounced competently enough, the drone of his recitation might put anyone to sleep.

With gratitude she rang the bell at the end of the day, then gathered her own books to take home and prepare for tomorrow. She should ask Lark's advice on what to do about the Kinsley family.

Turning from her desk, she paused to see Timothy O'Rourke still on his bench, studying his reader. His lips moved soundlessly, his face twitching every now and then as if with the effort to comprehend.

Del laid her books back on her desk and walked down the aisle. Easing into a bench nearby, she touched Timothy's reader. "Did you get engrossed in the story?"

He jumped and slammed the book shut, his thin face flushing. "Sorry, miss. I'll go."

"You needn't. I didn't mean to startle you. And I wanted to apologize for speaking sharply earlier. I was frustrated over something else, not you."

"But I'm a sad case at readin', I know that." Timothy traced the book's gilt border with his finger. "The schoolmaster back home said I hadn't the brain for it. Said no Irish did."

"That's not true." Indignation crackled up Del's spine. She'd like to tell that schoolmaster a thing or two. "Why, some wonderful writers have come out of Ireland. Have you ever read anything by Jonathan Swift?"

He shook his head, blue eyes wide.

"I'll have to lend you a copy of *Gulliver's Travels*—once you feel ready to read it. But for now, show me which words are giving you trouble."

"Them that don't follow the rules." Timothy opened his reader again. "Some of 'em I can sound out well enough, if I take the time. But others get my mind all tied up in knots, and then I feel like an engine stuck on the tracks."

"English is a cantankerous language, I admit. It doesn't follow its own rules very well, not like French or German." Del thought a moment. "Timothy, do you think your father could spare you a bit longer after school at times? Perhaps two or three days a week? I'd be glad to stay after and help you."

"I'll ask him." If Timothy's face could shine any brighter, he'd light up the church.

Del smiled. "We'll get you caught up in no time." At least she hoped so. She'd a notion Timothy's brain might process language differently than others, but she'd no idea how to deal with that. Nor had she read anything about it in any of the meager teaching materials she'd been given. "What about your other subjects? You seem to do well on your sums. I've yet to find a mistake on your slate."

"Oh, I've always been a good hand at figurin'. The sums you give are easy. I'd like some harder, if you have them."

"Really?" Del raised a brow. "I'm afraid mathematics aren't my forte, but I'll dig into my books and see what I can do. Perhaps you can help *me*. But for now, you'd best get home before your parents think you've been carried off by a catamount."

With another dazzling smile, Timothy snatched up his books and dinner pail and dashed out the door.

"Well, Father." Del blew out a breath and pushed to her feet. "What have I gotten myself into?" Two missing children to track down, and now she'd pledged to give up even more of her too-limited time to help Timothy. But wasn't that what her job was all about? And with interest like his, tutoring him would be more pleasure than burden. As long as she could find a way to help his mind and eyes better work together.

At least her appetite had returned. Del's stomach grumbled as she gathered her books and headed out for her daily trek home across the prairie.

The next morning, Bethany came to school but still no John. Del held her tongue until recess, then laid her hand on Bethany's shoulder just before the little girl hurried out the door.

"Bethany, where's your brother today? I was worried about both of you when you were absent yesterday."

"He's all right, miss. Just feeling a mite poorly." She kept her gaze down.

"Is it his leg? Or is he sick?"

"He's, uh, sick." The child wriggled under Del's hand.

Del crouched to Bethany's level. "I was wondering if I could come visit your family to see if there's anything I can do to help."

The little girl jerked her gaze up. "No, miss, please. Please don't do that."

"Why not?"

"It's . . . our ma." Bethany glanced away. "She's poorly too, got a baby comin' soon."

"Has Dr. Brownsville been to see her?"

"Pa don't hold with no doctors." The child bit her lip as if she'd said too much. "Please, may I go out to play?"

"Go on."

Del let her go and straightened with a sigh. Lark had been wary of Del visiting the family unannounced, but surely she had a responsibility to do something. No doubt it would be safer to take a man along again, as she had to the O'Rourkes, but she hesitated to ask Rev. Pritchard after last time. Who, then? Mr. Caldwell? But a lawyer might intimidate too much. *Lord, please show me what to do.*

John returned for the last few days of the week, still limping slightly but otherwise apparently none the worse for wear. No amount of gentle coaxing could get him to speak or give any indication what had happened.

Del met with Timothy on Wednesday and found him already nearly beyond *Ray's Mental Arithmetic*, though his reading still floundered.

By Friday, she had to set everything else aside to prepare for the women's meeting that evening.

Since they would meet in the church, she stayed after school to sweep and tidy, push the desks aside, and arrange the benches into Sunday-morning form for the ladies. She did a brief outline of lesson plans for the following week, then gathered her books and student papers into her satchel so she could try to catch up on grading tomorrow.

"There's our schoolmarm." Lark entered, basket in one hand and small notebook in the other.

"You're here early." Del hugged her sister.

"Brought you supper." Lark held out the basket. "Can't have you going hungry. Lilac is finishing the chores, and then she'll come."

Lilac. Del's stomach pinched at the aromas of cold chicken and hot corn bread coming from the basket. She took it and lifted the checked cloth covering for a whiff. Maybe after they got home tonight, she could find a quiet moment to talk to her younger sister. Or tomorrow. Or Sunday . . .

"Go ahead, sit and eat. You must be worn out from the week." Lark deposited herself on a bench and motioned for Del to do the same. "How was your day?"

Del sat down with a sigh, bowed her head for a quiet grace, then started to eat. It was amazing what a comfort good food could be. "It was all right. Nothing new with the Kinsley children. They were both present, but something's still not right with that family. Bethany said her mother is expecting another baby."

"Another family member to suffer whatever is going on. Maybe Adam can check in on the mother and learn something."

"That's what I thought, but Bethany said her pa 'don't hold' with doctors." Del sighed and caught a crumb of corn bread with her finger. "What are your plans for the meeting?"

"Actually . . ." Lark hesitated. "I wondered if you would chair it."

"Me?" Del stared at her.

"I know, I shouldn't spring it on you this late. I was planning to lead it, but then I thought, you're already something of a community leader, being the schoolteacher in town. You know all the families better than I do. But if you don't feel comfortable, I'll do it."

"No." Though her stomach churned, a certainty grew too. Del set aside the food basket. "I'll do it. As long as you'll step in as needed."

Lark grinned and squeezed her hand. "You can count on it."

Before Del was ready, the church began filling with women—more than she'd expected. But that was a good thing, as long as her heart would stop pounding. Speaking in front of a classroom of children was one thing, but before adults . . . Del surreptitiously wiped her damp palms on her skirt and turned to smile and greet Mrs. Dwyer and Mrs. Weber. These were the mothers of her students, after all.

Once most of the ladies were settled on the benches, if not quiet, Lark gave Del a nod.

Del stepped to the front near the pulpit and cleared her throat. "The meeting will now come to order." Schoolmarm indeed. She sounded like she was about to begin morning class. But how else did one start a meeting?

Amid rustling and whispers, nearly two dozen faces looked up at her.

Well, it had worked. Del smiled, hoping to belie her nerves. "Thank you all for coming tonight. I believe we are all here because we are convinced that while women may be known as the weaker sex, we nevertheless have a strength not to be trifled with. And we want to use that strength for the good of our town."

Lilac, who had slipped in and found a seat at the side of the room, caught Del's eye and gave her an encouraging nod.

Bolstered, Del went on. "We have a number of issues we'd like to discuss this evening, but first, I ask my eldest sister, Larkspur, to lead us in prayer."

Lark quirked a brow as she stepped forward, as if to say, *Fair enough. I sprang one on you, then you on me.* Del hid a smile and bowed her head.

After the prayer, she stepped forward again. "Thank you. Now, would anyone like to say anything to begin?"

Lucretia Jorgensen lifted a hand. "I thought the main point of this meeting was to deal with that infernal liquor tent outside of town. My Edgar says it's full of carryings-on, morning and night."

"And how would he know that 'less he's been in there himself?" asked Mrs. Dwyer, a sharp-nosed woman.

The storekeeper's wife glared at her. "Business, that's how. He has to go by the station regular to pick up supplies for the store." Lucretia sniffed. "My Edgar would as soon light himself on fire as touch a drop of liquor."

"And you're one to throw aspersions, Ellen Dwyer," Maybelle Young put in. "I hear tell your eldest son was seen comin' out of that tent last Saturday night."

"Well, I never—"

"Ladies, please," Del broke in. "I'm sure what we all want is to find ways to keep this saloon—for such it is, even if it's in a tent—from causing further harm to our families or community. Does anyone have any ideas as to how we might do that?"

Silence, and then Rebecca Weber put up her hand. "My mother used to belong to a women's temperance society when I was a little girl. Perhaps we might get some ideas from what they did."

"That's right." Lark nodded. "Our mother was part of one too. Most societies stopped meeting during the war or switched to focusing on abolition or helping soldiers. But we could certainly glean from their experience."

"Much of what they did was education, wasn't it?" Lilac put in.

"Yes." A prickle of excitement straightened Del's shoulders. "Maybe we could hold a rally on the dangers of alcohol, perhaps right here at the church."

Lilac nodded. "Dr. Adam could speak on the health side of things."

"Would the church really be the best place?" asked Mrs. Caldwell. "It's lovely for us, but if we want to reach folks most vulnerable to liquor, we might consider holding it outside. Perhaps have food and music—make it an event people will want to attend."

"Mrs. Caldwell, you are ever wise." Lark jotted in her notebook, making Del glad they could split the labor like this. She'd nowhere near the capacity to both lead and try to take notes, especially with these women proving harder to corral than her entire classroom of lively youngsters.

"We should ask Reverend Pritchard to lend his support too, maybe speak at the event as well." Lilac again.

Ideas continued to fly, from obtaining literature on the evils of alcohol—a step approved by a majority—to demonstrating its demeaning effects by getting a pig drunk as part of the entertainment—a notion soundly shot down.

"Well, I believe that's sufficient to get us started." Del drew a breath. "Mrs. Caldwell, would you speak to your husband about where we might obtain some temperance literature? And, Forsythia, you'll confer with Adam about giving a talk?"

Forsythia, who had arrived late due to something with her children, nodded from the back, where she stood bouncing a tired Mikael in her arms.

"And Larkspur or I will talk to Reverend Pritchard." Preferably Lark. Del glanced around the room. "While you are all gathered here, I also wanted to speak to you about our need for a schoolhouse."

"Isn't this your schoolhouse at present? What's wrong with it?" Mrs. Dwyer appeared determined to keep her tongue as sharp as her nose today.

Del bit the inside of her cheek. "Yes, the church is serving adequately for now. But I believe your children deserve a dedicated schoolhouse to replace the one destroyed by the tornado. One where we can settle and make it our own, not have to constantly shift around, setting up and tearing down." Why was this something she always had to argue for? "If our town can raise a train station in a matter of weeks, and now soon complete a boardinghouse, why not a school? Or is the education of our young people lowest on our list of what matters?"

"Hear, hear" came a hearty reply from the front row.

Del glanced in surprise to see Mrs. Jorgensen nodding in approval. She scanned the group, meeting the eyes of each mother there. "I know your sons and daughters, and I love them. I love teaching them, discovering the riches of the past and the glories of God's creation with them, seeing the world afresh through their eyes. I want a schoolhouse where they can have the space to flourish, to cover the walls with maps and charts and their own creative work. But I can't make it happen alone, and I can't seem to make it happen by appealing to the men of this town. And so I come to you. Will you help me?"

Everything was quiet for a moment, and then applause started from the front corner where Lark sat. Gradually, it spread through the gathering. Heads nodded, approving.

Del's face heated. "Thank you. But what I really need are ideas. How can we get this school built?"

Mrs. Caldwell lifted a hand again. "What about a school raising? We've had barn raisings often enough. If we got everyone together, surely we could raise a schoolhouse in a couple of days."

"You really think so?" Del glanced at the other ladies. "We'd need supplies as well as the labor for building."

"Don't we still have some money from the Thanksgiving fundraiser last fall?" Lilac asked. "Surely that could cover buying lumber, at least."

"And if it doesn't, I'm sure Mr. Caldwell would agree to help donate the rest." Beatrice gave a firm nod. "He believes in education for the future of this state—or he will, when I remind him trains alone won't build a nation."

Scattered chuckles.

"I'm sure Edgar and I could help with supplies too, nails and window frames and such." Lucretia Jorgensen shifted her heavy shoulders. "We've grandchildren in the school, after all."

"And our husbands and sons will certainly pitch in for the building, am I right?" Rebecca Weber glanced around, humor in her eyes. "If they still want three square meals a day and their washing done, that is."

The chuckles turned to outright laughter.

Del joined in, even while tears pricked her eyes. Was this really all she had to do—ask for help from her neighbors? Perhaps . . . or perhaps the Lord had needed to humble her first, show her she could be content with what she had while still persevering for what would be best.

"Thank you, ladies. You have given me much hope tonight." She drew a shaky breath. "I know you all need to get home to your families. Shall we work on these ideas and meet again, say, next Friday at the same time?" She caught the eye of Larkspur, who nodded. "Let me close us in prayer."

After the ladies left, Del stayed to straighten the benches with Lark and Lilac assisting. Darkness fell earlier now, and it was already pitch-black outside. She was grateful for the lamplight they had inside the church.

Once everything was ready for the service on Sunday, the Nielsens stepped outside and headed toward their wagon.

"Wait a minute, I'll be right back." Del ran back into the church and headed for the bookshelf to pick up a couple of books.

"How was the meeting, Miss Nielsen?"

She looked up to see Rev. Pritchard in the open doorway.

She glanced past him, wondering if he'd seen her sisters in the yard. Surely he had.

"It went well, thank you." She put the books she needed into her satchel. "I think we may actually be getting close to raising a new schoolhouse and getting out of your way here." She tried to lighten her tone.

He stepped down the aisle toward her. "You haven't been in my way at all. It's been a joy to share the space, and with my other church in Antelope Creek, I'm not here much. But I'm glad for you. I know how you've longed for that schoolhouse. What is the plan?"

"A school raising." Del adjusted her shawl. "Mrs. Caldwell suggested it."

"What a splendid idea." The young minister's eyes lit behind his spectacles. "Gather the community to build it rather than waiting for enough workers. I should have suggested that myself." He hesitated, then stepped closer, sobering. "Perhaps I would have if—if I didn't so much enjoy the chance to see you more often."

Oh dear. Del gripped the handle of her satchel. *Lord, show me what to say here.*

"Miss Nielsen." Rev. Pritchard cleared his throat and coughed slightly. "I've been wondering. Would you permit me to—to call on you?"

Del looked up into his eyes, so earnest, so full of goodwill. He was a good man, the best. Most young women would consider her a fool not to jump at this chance. And yet . . .

She shook her head. "I'm honored, Reverend, truly. You have my deep respect and admiration. But I'm not interested in pursuing a relationship at present. I hope you can understand."

His brow furrowed under the unruly shock of hair. "Not interested in general? Or not interested . . . with me?"

Del's heart twisted. But she must be honest. "Both, I'm afraid."

The light went out of his eyes. "I see."

They said awkward good-nights, and Rev. Pritchard snuffed the remaining lamps. Del stepped outside and headed to the wagon to join her sisters. They rode home under the starlit sky, Lark and Lilac chatting about the meeting. Del had trouble keeping her mind on the conversation, though.

She had been right to refuse the minister, she knew that. Not only for Lilac's sake but because Del didn't care for him as he desired. And yet, a part of her heart had warmed, knowing a young man could still show interest in her all these years after Everett.

And now, whatever chance had been there was gone. Interesting that she was more relieved than sad.

20

The pain was lessening.

RJ pounded shingles atop the boardinghouse roof, almost afraid to form the thought. Afraid if he actually put words to it, he would find the notion only his imagination, that the searing agony in his eye socket would rear its head once more, uglier than ever.

And yet it had been four days since he felt the need to take opium in order to sleep. Surely he wasn't making that up. Adam had been applying the salt-mud poultices to his scar each evening for more than a week, and implausible though he might have thought it, the stuff appeared to be as healing as the elderly Pawnee woman had said.

He swung his leg down to find a foothold and clambered down the side of the building to fetch more nails. The walls were all closed in now, the roof nearing completion. Soon they'd be ready to work on finishing the inside, at least to the degree the Nielsen sisters wanted before they opened. To welcome travelers before Thanksgiving—that was their goal.

The crisp October breeze cooled the sweat from RJ's neck, and he dipped a cup of water from the barrel. A beautiful day, a job he enjoyed, and a growing freedom from pain. Perhaps he could hope for a new life in Nebraska after all.

He scanned the building site and his men, working steadily. He had a good group now, after having to fire one more for drunkenness on the job, just not as large a force as he'd like. Not to finish the boardinghouse well in such a short time. He'd heard a number of potential workers had arrived on today's train in response to Mr. Young's advertisement but hadn't seen any yet. He needed to check that out.

At the end of the day, RJ stopped at the Jorgensens' mercantile on his way back to the Brownsvilles'. He kept forgetting to ask about the availability of the rooms next to the store, but now that he was feeling better, he might as well find out. Forsythia and Adam were nothing but gracious, but with Jesse and Climie also living under their roof, the place did get crowded at times.

The bell on the door jangled as RJ stepped inside. He breathed the scents of dry goods and tack, pickles, horse feed, and some sort of pastry—Mrs. Jorgensen must have had a baking spree again. This was the only mercantile he'd known where the storekeeper's wife sold fresh baked goods from the counter more often than not.

"Be right with you," the proprietress called over her shoulder. She was showing another customer some lengths of cloth.

RJ leaned on the counter and amused himself by examining the stock of candies lined up in glass jars. This was always his favorite part of a general store as a child. Maybe he should bring a small paper sack back for the Brownsville children.

"Well then, Mr. Easton." Mrs. Jorgensen approached, smoothing her apron over her ample middle. "What can I do for you?"

"Well, first off I'd like a piece of whatever that is." RJ nodded at the tray on the counter that emitted the tantalizing aroma.

Mrs. Jorgensen chuckled and lifted the cloth that kept away

bugs. "One apple fritter, then." She wrapped it in paper, making RJ's mouth water. "Anything else?"

"I need another box of nails for the boardinghouse, and I'd like a sack of peppermints and horehound candy for the children." He straightened and laid his palms on the counter. "Then I was wondering—I hear Dr. Brownsville rented rooms from you when he first came to town. Are those by chance available?"

"I'm afraid we've got several workers staying in them right now. You know space is in high demand in town these days." Mrs. Jorgensen pursed her lips. "However, one of them did say they might move to the boardinghouse once it's up and running, as long as it's cheaper. They grumble about not getting meals here, but I've all I can do with running the store."

"I see." RJ deflated slightly, but maybe there was still a chance. "Well, I'd be interested in the possibility of renting if they do leave. If you'd have me."

"I'll let you know, that's certain. I've a mind you're a lot tidier than those fellows." Mrs. Jorgensen shook her head. "We might have quite a cleaning job to deal with when they leave, I'm thinking." At the bell's jangle, she looked over RJ's shoulder and stiffened. "Can I help you?"

Struck by the woman's change in tone, RJ turned to see who had come in.

A short, wiry young man stepped farther inside. He removed his hat, revealing close-cropped black curls above the smooth dark brown of his face. "Good evenin'. Just hopin' to buy a bit of supper. I came in on the train today, lookin' for work."

"Foodstuffs are that way." Mrs. Jorgensen nodded stiffly to the far wall.

"Thank you, ma'am." The young man moved quickly to the shelves of canned goods.

Mrs. Jorgensen kept her gaze on him, tight-lipped.

RJ cleared his throat, trying to turn her attention away. Did she think the fellow was going to abscond with a can of beans? "Shall I go fetch those nails, Mrs. Jorgensen?"

"Oh. No, I'll get them." With one more glance at the young black man, she hurried back to the storeroom. Returning in record time, she rang up RJ's purchases. "Will that be all?"

"I believe so. Thank you." RJ took the box of nails, the wrapped pastry, and the bag of candy. He stepped aside for the newcomer as he brought his purchases to the counter.

Mrs. Jorgensen scanned the pile of canned fruit and beans, crackers, cheese, bacon, a sack of dried beans, and one of cornmeal. "This comes to four dollars. Can you pay?"

RJ winced. He hadn't known the storekeeper's wife was so prejudiced, but then, he'd never seen anyone in Salton besides white folks. He nearly stepped in to offer to help, but the young man leveled a smile at the woman.

"There you are, ma'am." He pulled out a worn pocketbook and counted out a pile of coins.

Mrs. Jorgensen counted it again and then, appearing slightly mollified, wrapped his purchases and handed them over.

"Thank you, ma'am." The man spoke with a soft Southern drawl. Was he a freedman? Yet his speech didn't seem quite what RJ would expect from a recent slave. "Might you know where a fella could find work around here?"

"Not sure about that. You'd have to ask around." Mrs. Jorgensen turned closemouthed again. Never mind that there were at least three building projects going on around town. In addition to the boardinghouse, Mr. Young was adding on to his bank, and RJ had heard something about the schoolhouse moving forward.

But the young man just nodded and turned, nearly bumping into RJ as he headed for the door.

"Sorry, sir." He ducked his head and hurried past.

RJ's neck heated at being caught watching the small drama play out. He turned and followed the young man out of the store.

"Forgive me." RJ's voice halted the man as he stepped into the dusty street. "But you said you're looking for work. What kind?"

The young man turned, his face wary. "Most any kind I can put my hand to, I reckon. I can dig, farm, work with horses. I'm best at workin' with wood. That advertisement for construction workers is what brought me out to these parts."

"Really?" RJ cocked his head. "I'm heading up a construction project and looking for good workers. If you show up tomorrow morning at the building site on the other side of the church, we'll see."

A smile flashed across the young man's face. "I'll do that."

"RJ Easton." RJ held out his hand.

The young man hesitated an instant, then gripped it warm and firm. "William Washington Thacker."

RJ pressed William's hand between both his own. "Welcome to Salton, Mr. Thacker."

The next morning, William Thacker was waiting at the boardinghouse site when RJ arrived, the sun just peeking a sliver of rosy gold above the horizon.

"You're here early." RJ greeted him with a nod. Had the young man found any place to stay? He hadn't thought to ask yesterday. There was a good chance the man had camped out under the stars. "Had breakfast?"

"I ate." William tipped his hat back and scanned the building. "What's this to be?"

"A boardinghouse run by a family of sisters who homestead outside of town, the Nielsens. Good folks. You'll get to know them if you stick around." RJ cast a glance at Thacker as he unrolled his tool belt for the day.

"Well, that depends." William took the hammer RJ held out.

"Depends on what?"

William hesitated, then gave a half smile. "On a lot of things. So what needs doin' today?"

RJ wanted to press but held back. William deserved his privacy. "As you can see, the roof still needs to be finished. Once we have the outside all secure, we'll begin on the interior. They hope to open in a few weeks." He rubbed his chin. "Comfortable on a roof?"

"As if I was born there." William scrambled up the ladder and set to hammering shingles like he'd been on the project from the beginning.

RJ turned to greet the rest of his arriving workers with a lifted spirit. This was a good start to the day.

At noon, he headed over to the church to take a book to Del. Forsythia had asked him to drop it by, seeing as the building site was so close. RJ passed through the scattering of children outside running and hollering in a game of crack-the-whip and mounted the church steps. He knocked, then pushed in the church door.

Del sat bent over her desk at the front of the room, so intent on a book that she didn't appear to hear him. RJ walked softly up the aisle and cleared his throat.

She startled and looked up, fluttering the pages before her. "RJ—I didn't hear you."

"That's evident." He quirked a brow. "Studying at noontime, huh? I've brought you more material. At least, I think so."

"Oh, thank you." She reached for the book eagerly. "Forsythia said she'd send it. It's a volume of Adam's. I suppose doctoring requires a higher knowledge of all the sciences, including mathematics."

"You're studying higher mathematics?"

"Not by preference." She gave a rueful laugh. "One of my students loves figures, and he's already through nearly all that *Ray's Mental Arithmetic* can teach. I'm trying to learn more to help him. I tutor him after school some days. But I'm afraid calculations at this level put my brain in such a muddle that I may be more hindrance than help. My sister Lark is so much better at mathematics." She opened the new volume and flipped through the pages, brow creased.

"May I see?" RJ stepped closer. He'd barely glanced at the book's cover when carrying out the errand.

She handed him the book.

He opened it, scanned a beginning chapter. "Ah, I remember this from the start of engineering studies." Memories washed in. "My friends and I used to try to stump one another with equations for fun."

"For fun?" She stared at him as if he'd dropped in from another continent.

His mouth quirked. "To each his own. I suppose you find wrangling that group of young scamps out in the yard fun?"

A smile touched her lips. "After a fashion. And actually, I should call them in."

"Well, I'd best get out of the way before they trample me, then." He closed the book and handed it back. "When do you meet with this boy? Perhaps I could stop by and help."

"Truly?"

He'd come every day if it meant seeing that kind of light in her eyes. "As long as I can manage it along with the boarding-house, sure."

"I'm meeting with him today, and I promised him we could do a bit of figures once we finished working on reading. To him, mathematics is a treat." She lifted her hands and shook her head.

RJ held back a chuckle. "I'll stop by before suppertime, then, and see if he's still here."

RJ ended the day for his men a bit early; they'd made such progress. Thanks in part to the steady work of William Thacker, whom he'd now officially offered a job. So far his presence didn't seem to be causing any trouble among the men, thankfully.

With an eagerness in his step he couldn't fully account for, RJ headed to the church and slipped in quietly, not wanting to disturb teacher and student. Del sat next to a young boy, who was pushing toward manhood but still with a child's slight frame, her snood of pale brown hair bent next to his tousled black head. A few wisps slipped from the snood, catching the last rays of afternoon light from the window.

RJ leaned against the back wall, listening to the boy read aloud. He stumbled slightly over the words.

"It was the best of t-times, it was the r—worst of times . . . it was the age of wisdom, it was the age of foolish . . . foolishness . . ."

On he read, with Del gently prompting him as needed, until the paragraph concluded.

"Well done, Timothy. Now you have read the opening of one of the greatest novels of recent years. We'll make our way through the book together bit by bit, and I hope you will come to love it as I do." Del looked up and caught RJ's eye with a smile. "But now I have a surprise for you. This is Mr. RJ Easton, and he's come to help us with mathematics today—far better than I can do for you on my own."

Timothy jumped to his feet and gave a little bow.

RJ stepped forward and shook the boy's hand. "Pleased to meet you, Timothy."

The lad stared at RJ with wide blue eyes. "Please, sir, is that a war wound?"

RJ touched a finger to his eye patch. "You might call it that."

"Come, Mr. Easton." Del rose to make room on the bench. "Have a seat. We don't want to take advantage of your time. I'll just do a bit of preparation for tomorrow while you gentlemen confer."

Feeling a bit out of his element, RJ sat on the bench, Timothy sliding in next to him. He opened the book. "Let's see, now. Have you heard of geometric proofs?"

"A bit." Timothy leaned in, eager.

RJ began to explain, demonstrating on the slate Del had provided. Soon he forgot about trying to fit into the role of teacher and student, and he and Timothy just became two lovers of numbers, logic, and the beautiful way both came together. He started when Del finally interrupted them to say dark would soon be falling, and Timothy must get home.

"Sorry." RJ pushed to his feet. "Guess I lost track of time."

"You both did, by the look of it. Timothy, would you like to take *A Tale of Two Cities* home with you?"

"Yes, miss, if I may." The boy tucked the novel under his arm and cast a longing look at the book of mathematics.

"I can't lend that one, I'm afraid, as it belongs to Dr. Brownsville. But perhaps Mr. Easton might come again another time to do a bit more?" She raised a brow.

"I'd be glad to."

"Thank you so much, Mr. Easton. Miss Nielsen." Timothy bobbed his head at both of them and fairly jigged out the door.

"He's an unusual boy." RJ rubbed the crick in his neck. How long had they sat there, bent over the makeshift desk?

"Thank you for doing that." Del rubbed her elbows. "I can tell it meant so much to Timothy. I can't meet him on the same level you can."

"I didn't do much." RJ shrugged. "But I'm glad if it helped." He scanned the inside of the church, darkening now with shadows. "I hear you may finally get your schoolhouse soon."

"It's looking hopeful that we can have a school raising before the snow falls." She began gathering her things to leave. "It appears all I had to do was talk to the women." She smiled archly.

Guilt twisted his gut. "You asked me for help long ago, and

I'm afraid I dismissed you rather rudely. I do apologize. I wasn't
. . . quite myself then." Though that was no excuse. He seemed
to have a lot of apologizing to do lately.

She gave a graceful dip of her head. "Accepted."

"If you need any help still, I'd be glad to assist in any way I
can."

Del looped her satchel over her arm. "It would be nice to
have someone in charge at the raising who knows what he's
doing."

"Consider me at your service then, Miss Nielsen." He gave
a gallant bow.

She laughed. "Thank you, I shall."

He walked her out the church door, and they stood for
a moment in silence in the darkening yard. He might have
missed supper at the Brownsvilles by now, but Forsythia
would keep back a plate for him to devour before his nightly
mud poultice treatment—one he welcomed now rather than
dreaded.

He glanced at Del, who stood with her head tilted back to
see the rising moon. Watching her serene profile in the falling
twilight, RJ suddenly found his mind blank of anything else
to say.

"Well," she said at last, drawing her shawl closer with a shiver.
"It feels like a hard frost tonight. I'd best get home."

"Can I drive you?" RJ blurted. Somehow he didn't want to
let her go. Not alone in the cold all the way home.

She glanced at him askance. "In what?"

His neck heated. "Uh, your wagon, I suppose." Belatedly he
saw it parked beneath the lone tree by the church.

"I bring the wagon on days when I stay afterward to help
Timothy. So no, I'll be perfectly all right. But thank you, just the
same. Good night." With a parting smile, she was off.

He echoed the good-night and watched her drive away. At

last he shook himself and headed on foot down the dusty street, quiet sounds of evening coming from the scattered houses.

Has it been so long, Easton, that you've clean forgotten how to talk to a pretty woman? Let alone woo one?

The thought halted his feet and set his mind awhirl. Where in thunder had that idea come from?

21

She was finally going to get her school.

Del breathed deeply of the crisp autumn morning as she strode through the drying prairie grass toward town. A sparse flock of geese honked overhead, stragglers following late after the wiser birds already headed south. She tugged her coat collar about her neck against the frosty chill.

In only a few more weeks, she'd be walking not to the church but to her own new schoolhouse, if plans for the school raising continued to be promising. Now that the families were banding together and RJ had offered to oversee the building itself, she didn't see why they wouldn't. RJ had even said he'd bring some simple design sketches for her to look at later, when he stopped by to help Timothy after school.

Such a change in that taciturn former soldier lately. Del smiled at the thought.

She walked down Main Street, greeting Mr. Jorgensen as he opened the mercantile. Reaching the church, she let herself in and breathed the comforting fragrance of books and chalk dust.

A new week. Always a bit daunting but also full of promise.

Del sat at her desk and opened her notebook to review her

lesson plans for the day. Soon the whoop and chatter of children, the stomp of feet, and the clatter of dinner pails outside let her know the time as well as the clock did. She jotted down one more idea before she picked up the bell and opened the door to ring in the school day.

Boots and some bare feet despite the cold stampeded in through the door, her students laughing and jabbering like magpies.

"Teacher, Teacher—I mean, Miss Nielsen." Josie tugged at Del's skirt. "Look, I got new shoes. I mean, I got 'em from somebody else, but my mama fixed them up for me. Ain't they nice?" She gazed at the worn but newly blacked boots on her feet in delight.

"*Aren't* they nice. And yes, they most certainly are." Del smiled and gave Josie's shoulder a gentle squeeze.

"Miss Nielsen, why does Bethany have a purple eye?" Josie gazed up into Del's face, her wide eyes guileless.

Del's face froze, but she stroked the little girl's hair. "I'll check on Bethany, all right? Why don't you go and find your seat? It's almost time for class."

A cold knot in her stomach, Del spotted Bethany Kinsley's familiar shabby pinafore and blond braids in the second row, as usual. She couldn't see her face from this angle. Oh, if only Josie were mistaken.

Del stepped to the front of the room and scanned her students, trying to be surreptitious. "Good morning, everyone. Class, come to order." Only for a fleeting instant did she let her gaze rest on Bethany's face—enough to register the purpling bruise around the child's eye and for the cold in her stomach to burn hot. "Mrs. Caldwell will be here shortly to lead us in music, so let's begin with prayer and the Pledge of Allegiance."

It was a good thing those words were familiar, for she could barely keep her mind on them. Only the Lord knew what she prayed, other than the *Please, God, help* that tumbled through her heart.

Mrs. Caldwell's comfortable form filled the doorway as soon as the words of the pledge finished, and Del beckoned her forward to the piano. They'd need to figure out what to do for music once they moved to the new building. Having a piano was one thing she would miss.

Del stepped aside while the attorney's wife led the morning singing, her mind in a whirl. Why did Bethany have a black eye? Her brother stood beside her, head down and not singing, nothing unusual for him. Perhaps Bethany had fallen or run into something, but Del's heart urged there was more. Why had she not acted sooner? Had she really thought she was imagining all this?

After the music finished, Del stepped forward again. "Thank you so much, Mrs. Caldwell. Now, primer class through second readers, I'd like you to read the next lesson in your readers aloud to one another. Older ones can help the primers as needed. Third and fourth readers, review the spelling words from last week, and we'll have a team spelling contest before the end of the day." A giggle or two followed her announcement. "Fifth readers and up, work the grammar lesson on the board in your slates, and we'll go over it together before recess."

With the low hum of the younger children behind her, Del worked her way through the rows of spellers and finally approached Bethany Kinsley, who was bent over her book with her brother.

"Bethany?" Del touched her shoulder.

The child flinched away and looked up, the bruise dark on her small face.

Del drew away her hand and crouched to the children's level. "I didn't mean to startle you. How are you two doing with the spelling words?"

"I think I have them all." Bethany angled her face away. "I don't know about John."

"Good. You'll be ready for the contest, then." So far she'd only been able to get John to spell on his slate, never aloud. "But, Bethany, what happened to your eye?"

Bethany glanced at her, then away again. "I-I fell—onto the corner of the stove."

"Oh dear. Did you get burned also?"

"N-no." The little girl's ears reddened. "I mean, it was the corner of the table, actually. We don't have a stove." She caught her lower lip between her teeth.

Del's own lips thinned. She scanned the classroom to ensure the other students were occupied and lowered her voice. "Bethany, John. I need you to tell me. Is everything all right at your house? With your family?"

"Yes." Bethany scooted closer to her brother, her voice firm. "Everything is fine."

"John?" Del waited. "John Jacob, look at me."

The boy slowly raised his head.

"Is there anything you want to tell me, John?"

Something flickered in his gray eyes. Then he lowered his head and shook it once.

Frustration tightened Del's shoulders. What was she to do if the children wouldn't speak?

"Miss Nielsen," piped up a small voice, "we finished reading our lessons. Now what do we do?"

Del sighed and went to help the little ones.

She had intended to try again to speak with the Kinsley children at the end of the day, but Elsie Weber had a history question just after school, and by the time Del looked around for Bethany and John, they were gone.

Nor did they appear the next morning, or the next. By Wednesday afternoon, a growing lump of dread weighed in her chest. Come what may, she was going to visit the Kinsleys today. Even if she had to cut short her session with Timothy to do it.

Timothy, though, came up to her as soon as she set down the dismissal bell.

"I'm sorry, Miss Nielsen, but my da wants me to come straight home after school today. And the same till we finish the threshing. He says I got to earn my keep same as the rest of 'em."

"Very well." Her heart sank a bit. Timothy had started to bloom in these after-school sessions, especially when he worked with RJ on mathematics. Would Mr. O'Rourke really let him resume after this? But that wasn't up to her. And today, it would help. "Thank you for letting me know. I'll see you tomorrow?"

"Yes'm." And he was out the door, dinner pail swinging.

Del walked between the rows of benches and desks, gathering slates and slate pencils—she kept them at school to guard against the children losing or breaking them. She thought of John Kinsley's clumsily spelled words on the slate the other morning when she had finally returned to quiz him. *Lord, perhaps I'm magnifying this out of proportion in my head, but I don't think so. Please go with me this afternoon, show me what to do.*

Her sisters would say she shouldn't go alone, but whom could she ask? One of them? They were still pressed to finish harvesting the gardens and missing her help as it was. Rev. Pritchard was in his other circuit town this week. Maybe Adam. Mr. Kinsley might not hold with doctors, but surely he wouldn't throw one out of his house. At least she hoped not.

Del wet her rag and rubbed at the sums on her makeshift blackboard, trying to rub the nerves from her middle at the same time.

"Where's our young Irish scholar?"

She jumped and turned to see RJ standing in the aisle, felt hat in hand and a quizzical lift to the brow over his good eye.

"Oh, I'm so sorry." She crumpled the rag in her hand. How

could she have forgotten? "I should have sent word. Timothy didn't stay today. He won't until their threshing is complete. I hope you didn't cut your workday short."

"Oh." RJ's face sobered. "That's a shame. When will that be done, next week?"

"It depends on how much they have to harvest. I know the O'Rourkes were hit harder by the grasshoppers than some."

"Liam mentioned that." RJ nodded. "And he's had to be absent from the building himself lately for the same reason. Well, I already sent the men home for the day, so I might as well head home myself. Here are the sketches for the school I told you about." He laid a few sheets of paper on her desk.

"Thanks. But could I go with you?" Del grabbed her coat and satchel. "I want to ask Adam if he might go with me to visit a family I'm worried about."

"Sure, but I doubt you'll find him. Jesse went home for dinner, and when he came back, he said Adam had been called out to a farm where someone got injured with a scythe. It sounded pretty serious. I think he'll be gone awhile."

Del's shoulders slumped. "Oh."

"What's wrong with this family?"

"I'm not entirely sure." She hesitated, then pushed forward. RJ would have found out anyway if she'd gone for Adam. He was part of their family circle now. "I've never met the parents, but I'm concerned the children are being mistreated. Both have come to school with strange injuries. And now they have been absent since Monday. Which has happened before, with no explanation."

RJ eyed her. "That doesn't sound good."

"I know." His validation tightened her resolve. "I should have gone before this, but I'm going now."

"Whoa." He raised his hand, palm out. "Not alone?"

"As I said, I hoped to take Adam. But I'm not going to wait."

Now that she'd determined to go, the urgency pressed on Del's shoulders until she could hardly keep her feet still.

"Then I'll go with you."

"You?"

"You need someone, and I'm available. And I can't stand a kid getting beaten." A hardness shone in the dark brown of his eye, but then one side of his mouth tipped up. "Besides, I'm rather a teacher's assistant now, aren't I?"

Del smiled despite herself. "I suppose you are, at that. Well, if you're sure." The pressure in her chest lifted a bit at the thought of his presence. And she'd avoid a tongue-lashing from Lark for going alone.

RJ gave a quick nod. "Shall we get the Brownsvilles' wagon?"

"Adam didn't take it?"

"No, he took the gig. It's faster."

Del nodded. "Let's do, then. Mrs. Caldwell says the Kinsleys live a ways out."

After fetching the wagon from the Brownsvilles'—along with the promise of Forsythia's prayers—they drove out across the prairie. Evening shadows already stretched long, the grasses sere and gilded in the lingering October rays.

Since RJ had insisted on driving, Del tucked her mittened hands in her lap to shield them against the chill. "So what really brought you out here to Salton?"

He shot a glance at her. "Anders invited me."

"I know that. But why did you stay after Anders left? Don't you have family and a life back in New York?" Now that she'd begun, the questions bubbled up. Funny that she'd never thought of them before. Of course, only lately had she and RJ been getting along.

RJ blew out a breath. "You really want to know?"

"I do."

He shifted the reins to one hand and rubbed the back of his

neck. "I was in the Army Corps of Engineers during the war—maybe you know that."

"Building bridges and such?"

"Yes, among other things. That's how I met Anders, when our companies intersected for a time." He seemed to debate how much to say. "Do you know how I lost my eye?"

"Anders said something about a Confederate renegade."

"Yes. I guess there's a number of them around even now, disgruntled Southerners who can't let the war go. Or just use that as an excuse for stirring up trouble. At any rate, I ran into him when I was on my way home. I only lost an eye, but he lost his life." RJ's jaw shifted.

"That must have been difficult." Del tried to imagine going through life with one eye missing. She'd heard the body would compensate, but even so. "Does it still pain you a great deal?"

"It's improving since Adam started using that salt mud on me. I was skeptical—well, more outright disbelieving. But you might say God got hold of my stubborn hide long enough to sit me down to try it." He drew a long breath. "It's brought a relief I didn't think possible, though pain still flares up now and again."

"I'm so glad." Del's throat tightened. And all from their school excursion to the salt flats. "So you came to Salton because of your injury? Were you not able to continue the work you'd had before the war?"

"I was in the hospital for months, but I could have returned to engineering school if I really wanted. I didn't feel the need. And after I finally got home . . ."

Something in his voice made Del look up. His face had turned hard, set straight ahead. "Did something else happen?"

A muscle in his jaw twitched.

"I'm sorry." She glanced away. "You must think me quite the nosy schoolmarm."

"No. It's just . . ." He breathed out hard through his nose. "I had a sweetheart back home, a fiancée waiting for me through the war . . . I thought. I finally came back from the hospital to find she'd up and married someone else."

"What a horrid thing." Del's heart hurt for him. How could a woman do that? But then, many did.

He shrugged. "Not as horrid as what many have endured."

"I lost my fiancé in the war too. But at least that wasn't by his own choice."

He shot a quick glance at her. "I'm sorry."

"It was years ago." Yet something stretched between them, a warming thread of understanding. Del nodded at the homestead appearing on the horizon. "That must be the Kinsleys'."

The sod house and barn stood silent as they drove up, seeming to hunker against the chilling prairie for warmth. A few chickens scratched in the yard, unshielded from hawks or coyotes. RJ set the wagon brake and jumped down, then offered a hand to Del.

Leaning on his strong grip, Del scanned the farm as she climbed down. Where was everyone? A field of grain stretched to the west, some still lying cut in haphazard swathes, the rest in slipshod shocks. Squinting against the setting sun, she saw a slender figure bent out there, attempting to bundle some of the fallen wheat into a sheaf. A few clumsy shocks behind him told of his effort. He was too small to be the father. Was it John? Harvesting all by himself?

"Miss Nielsen?" At the childish squeak of surprise, Del turned.

Bethany had emerged from the sod barn, a foaming milk pail straining her small hands. "What—what are you doing here?" She glanced between Del and RJ, the surprise on her face shifting to fear. The purple bruise around her eye was fading to yellowish-green.

"Bethany." Del put on her gentle teacher smile and stepped forward. "This is Mr. Easton. He helps me at the school. We just came to check on you and your family, since you and John haven't been to school for a few days."

Bethany shifted the pail between her hands, a milky splash wetting her bare feet. "My ma's been sick, and Pa—needed our help."

Did Del detect a flinch? "I'm so sorry to hear that. Would you take us inside to meet your folks, please?"

Bethany hesitated and glanced to the fields where her brother had stopped bundling and stood motionless. Then she gave a slight nod and headed toward the soddy, the weight of the milk pail leaning her to the side.

At first Del could barely see a thing within the darkness of the soddy, as there was no lamp burning within. The stench of sickness hit her hard, making her gag. She pressed a hand to her mouth. *Chin up, Del.* She could almost hear Ma's steady voice from when she'd accompanied her on sick calls as a girl.

Del lowered her hand and made out the form of a woman struggling to rise from a chair where she'd been watching a pot of something over the dying fire.

"Ma." Bethany set down the milk pail, the handle clanging, and hurried to support her mother. Mrs. Kinsley leaned heavily on her daughter's shoulder, the bulge of her belly evident even in the firelight. "My teacher's come."

"Miss Nielsen." The woman shook her head with a half sob. "I—I'm sorry. I wouldn't want you to see—we're in such a mess. . . ."

Del stepped forward to steady her and eased her back into the chair. "Please, Mrs. Kinsley, don't trouble yourself. We're here to help."

The pregnant woman leaned back against the roughhewn chair, her breath coming in shallow gasps. As Del tucked the shawl closer about her, she could feel the rapid thunder of her pulse. Yet she didn't sense fever, nor smell the sickness on her.

She glanced around the cramped room, now more distinct as

her eyes had adjusted. A table shoved in the corner, still covered with dirty dishes. Discarded rags on the floor, as if attempts to clean up some mess had been abandoned. Pallets in the corner where the children must sleep.

And on the other side, a rope-strung bedstead where a man lay sprawled and snoring atop rumpled bedding, still wearing his pants and boots, though his shirt and coat had been shed. Del could smell the noxious odor from his union suit and bedding, and her stomach roiled.

So that was Mr. Kinsley. Passed out drunk.

Del turned to RJ. "Go get Adam. Or Forsythia, if he's still not back. In that case, bring Reverend Pritchard—no, never mind, he's in Antelope Creek. Mr. Caldwell, then, or whoever you can find."

He met her gaze. "You'll be all right?" His eye flicked a hard glance at the man on the bed, then at the rifle over the doorway.

"I don't think he's going to cause trouble any time soon. But yes, I know how to shoot."

RJ gave her one more look, then reached out to give her hand a brief, unexpected squeeze. "I'll hurry." And he was out the door into the creeping dusk.

Del found a lamp and helped Mrs. Kinsley into a nightgown, then onto one of the children's pallets, since the bed was rendered unusable for now. After tucking an extra quilt around the woman, she set Bethany and John to bringing in wood, stoked the fire, then swung a kettle of water over the snapping flames.

Once it boiled, Del dipped some water into a basin and set to cleaning the table. When it was as decent as she could make it, she washed some bowls and ordered the children to serve themselves some stew, then took the pan outside to dump the dirty water.

The evening star winked above her in the darkening sky. Del's throat ached, her heart whispering more prayers than she had strength to voice.

Lord, please bring help soon.

22

Anger burned in RJ's chest.

What a despicable excuse for a man, laid out drunk while his wife and children suffered. Directly by his hand, from what Del had said and from what he could see in that little girl's bruised face. Having unhitched the Brownsvilles' horse from their wagon, he urged the mare forward over the darkening prairie toward Salton, riding bareback as the sun set in streaks of vermilion and orange.

Yet that fire in Del's gray-blue eyes, mirroring the feeble firelight in the Kinsleys' soddy. The firmness in her voice as she took charge. He hadn't seen strength like that since his ma died. He'd hated to leave her in such a place, but the command from Del's lips brooked no question. That, too, was like his ma.

After far too long, he reached the Brownsvilles' and swung down from the horse. "Adam? Forsythia?"

He noted with relief that the gig stood in the yard. Looping the mare's reins to the rail, RJ bounded up the porch steps.

Adam met him at the door, face weary and questioning.

Regret twinged. RJ could only guess the grueling day the doctor had already known, and now he was dragging him out for yet another crisis. But such was a physician's life, especially on the frontier.

"Sorry, but Del needs you."

He explained as quickly as he could, then headed to the stable while Adam fetched his bag and Forsythia packed up some food. No telling when they'd be back. He gave the mare a quick brush down along with oats, then led Captain out of his stall. Barker wagged his tail beside them, no doubt hoping to come along.

"Ready to give us some help tonight, fella?" He ran his hand down the stallion's broad nose and chuckled at the answering snort. Captain hadn't been getting enough riding lately, not with RJ so tied up at the boardinghouse. Well, tonight should make up for it. He'd ride his mount out while the doctor drove the gig pulled by another horse, then hitch Captain to the wagon coming back.

"Ready?" Adam appeared in the barn door.

RJ nodded and cinched Captain's saddle, then led the horse outside. "Sorry, Barker, you're going to have to sit this one out." He rubbed the dog's head between his hands, then sent him to the porch, where Forsythia let him inside.

She lifted a hand. "Go with God."

They started out, the lantern on the gig bobbing its light across the darkening prairie.

"Your patient from this afternoon going to be all right?" RJ trotted Captain alongside the doctor.

Adam shook his head. "I pray so. He missed with his scythe and sliced his leg to the bone. I cleaned, stitched, and stabilized, so now they've just got to keep him off it. Easier said than done for a farmer at harvesttime. Infection is the big danger." He flicked the reins. "This Kinsley fellow—you think he's ill or merely drunk?"

"I wasn't there long enough to tell. My guess would be just passed out drunk, but you'll know better. I think Del's more concerned for his wife. She's, uh, in the family way." Heat crept up RJ's neck. No doubt the doctor was accustomed to discussing such things, but he wasn't, even after that evening with Captain and the Nielsens' mare.

Adam nodded and urged the horse to pick up its pace. "Perhaps you should ride ahead? You'll get there faster than I will."

RJ nudged Captain with his heels and let him fly.

When he stepped back into the Kinsleys' soddy, he found the floor and table cleared and the children finishing bowls of stew, their appetites seeming hearty enough. Del knelt by the pallet, spooning bites of stew into the mother's mouth.

RJ cast a quick glance at the bed with its hefty inhabitant. No apparent change there. His shoulders eased. He'd been hounded by dark thoughts of the man waking with Del there alone.

"You're back." Del glanced at him, relief in her voice though he couldn't clearly see her face. "Is Adam coming?"

"He is." RJ crossed the floor to crouch beside her. "He's in the gig, so I rode ahead."

"Thank you. For going to get him." She turned back to feeding the mother.

"Of course." RJ crouched there a moment longer, then rose to peer out the single window. A faint bobbing light heralded the doctor's gig drawing near. "I see him."

"Tom don't . . . trust doctors." Mrs. Kinsley's voice came weak from the pallet.

"Tom doesn't get much choice here today." RJ's words came out harsher than he meant. After all, this wasn't the woman's fault. But how did she end up with such a man? Or maybe he hadn't always been this way. RJ had seen in the war, and even more so after it, the havoc drinking could wreak on decent men.

A soft rap at the door, and RJ opened it.

Adam stepped inside with a doctor's instant familiarity, bag in hand. At a glance he took in the scene, then crossed to Del and the woman on the pallet, bestowing a nod and smile on the children. They stared up at him soberly, no doubt waiting for whatever made their pa regard doctors with such suspicion.

Del scooted back and rose to make room for Adam. "I've gotten her to eat a bit, and her pulse has steadied some. No fever that I can tell."

Adam felt the woman's wrist, then listened to her chest. "Still rapid, and shallow breathing. Do you have trouble drawing a full breath, Mrs. Kinsley?"

She nodded. "I had that with . . . John and Bethany at the end too. But it seems worse . . . this time, though I'm not as far along."

"When do you expect your baby?" Gently the doctor drew back the quilt and palpated the woman's abdomen. RJ averted his eye.

"Maybe January, I think."

The doctor felt Mrs. Kinsley's hands and feet and examined her face in the light of a lamp drawn near, then tucked the quilt back around her and stood to confer with Del.

"She's weak, and her skin is cold and a bit yellowed, though it's hard to tell in this light. But I agree with you, no sign of infection. She needs nourishment more than anything, greens and beef and liver, if she can get it. That and rest."

"That's hard to find on a farm and with a husband like that." Del's lips pressed in a thin line.

The doctor sighed. "I guess I'd better see to him next."

"Would you take a look at the children first? Bethany has a black eye, and John's leg has been troubling him." Del gave a significant tip of her head toward the bed.

Adam's jaw tightened under his beard. He turned to the children. The boy sat slumped in his chair, eyes on the table, while the little girl stared up at him with an unveiled mixture of curiosity and suspicion.

The doctor examined them, his voice low and reassuring, as

best he could by the dim lamplight. Del stepped close to RJ by the door, rubbing her arms.

"Cold?" RJ touched her shoulder.

"I'm all right." A shiver belied her words.

RJ found her coat thrown over a chair and draped it around her. "There."

"Thank you." Her brief smile did something strange to his insides.

Adam had moved on from the children to the man snoring on the bed. None too gently, he used his knee to prod the man's extended leg.

"Tom Kinsley? Wake up."

The man snorted, groaned, and rolled over—completely off the bed, landing with a thump on the dirt floor. Both children flinched. Cursing, Tom pushed himself to a sitting position and scratched under the arm of his wool union suit.

He peered at the assembled gathering, squinting against the firelight. "Wha's all this?"

"Are you ill, sir?" Adam's voice was sharp.

"Ill—me—ne'er sick a day in m'life. Tha's my woman, she's always caterwaulin' about somepin don' feel right." He glared around the room, apparently trying to focus, then pointed a shaking finger at his two offspring. "You'uns—why ain't you out doin' the chores? Good for nothin' boy, din't I tell you—"

"John already worked in the fields a long time today, Pa," Bethany protested, her voice quivery but brave. "It's plumb dark now. And I did the milkin'—"

"Did I ask you?" He glowered at her.

Bethany lowered her eyes but kept a firm grip on her brother's arm.

Was that how she'd gotten the black eye? Sticking up for her brother? Flames smoldered in RJ's chest again, his fists aching to swing at Tom Kinsley's florid face.

"Mr. Kinsley." Adam's words could cut steel. "You appear to be inebriated, sir, and in no condition to care for your family. Your wife is not well, and I fear for both her and the child she carries if she does not receive better rest and food."

"You one of them quack doctors?" Tom Kinsley's lip curled.

"I am a doctor, though I hope no one who knows me would consider me a quack. I am a trained and experienced physician, and I urge you not to take my words lightly."

Tom staggered to his feet. "Get out o' my house."

Even in his lurching state, Tom Kinsley wasn't a man to be trifled with. He wasn't overly tall but had powerful shoulders and fists and easily fifty pounds on the doctor.

But Adam stood his ground, staring the other man in the eye. "You have the right to order us to leave your home. But I urge you to dispose of whatever alcohol you have hidden about it. Your wife's health is in danger, and your children both bear the marks of your drunken lack of self-control. If things grow worse, I will have no choice but to inform the legal authorities."

"Get out." The words rumbled low and were filled with warning.

"I will be back to check on Mrs. Kinsley when you are in a more amiable mood." Adam turned and gave a quick nod to Del and RJ. "Let's go."

"Is there nothing more we can do?" Del asked when they paused by the wagon for RJ to unsaddle and hitch up Captain. "The children, are they seriously injured?"

"They'll live. At this point." Adam set his bag in the gig and sighed. "Bethany's eye is healing, and the best I can tell, John's leg is only badly bruised. What might come of further drunken rages, I cannot predict."

Del gripped the edge of the wagon bed so hard the boards rattled. "We *must* get that liquor tent abolished."

"What about the legal measures you mentioned?" RJ asked.

Adam tugged on his gloves and shook his head. "I spoke hastily in my own anger, I'm afraid. From what Henry says, we've no real legal recourse in these cases unless there is egregious injury or death. I only hope Tom is too ignorant to know that."

"So we can do nothing?" RJ yanked the last harness straps into place. "In New York this year, a man founded a society for the prevention of cruelty to animals. But we can't prevent cruelty to children?"

"I'll check in on the mother as long as he'll allow and use that to keep an eye on the children too. As Del will at school. That's about all we can do now besides pray." Adam's shoulders sagged wearily. "I don't suppose they have any family around?"

"While I was waiting for you tonight, Bethany told me they have an older brother. I'd never heard that before." She paused and shook her head. "I asked Mrs. Kinsley, and she said he left some time ago. He promised to send money back to pay the chit at the store but for her not to let the father know. I guess he tried to talk her into coming with him with the younger children, but she insisted her place was by her man. He was a good man until the liquor got him. So she says, anyway."

"Who knows where that son is now." Adam heaved a sigh. "RJ, perhaps you could drive Del home?"

RJ did, wanting to say something to comfort her, but the cold weight of the night rendered them both silent. At last he helped her out of the wagon, the door of the Nielsens' soddy immediately spilling light and anxious sisters.

"RJ?" Del's voice, soft with fatigue, caught him as he lifted the reins to drive home.

"Yes?"

"Thank you. For going with me today." She laid her hand on the wagon side by his foot.

His spontaneous offer in the schoolroom seemed a week removed from them now, a somehow more innocent time. But he nodded, his throat suddenly thick in the darkness. "You're welcome."

RJ slept until the sun's rays woke him, then dashed for the boardinghouse site without breakfast, berating himself for sleeping so late. His workers all arrived before he did—no lazy good-for-nothings like Clive Johnson in this bunch— and had gotten started on the day's labor. A good thing too, for RJ's mind stayed blurry, his hands fumbling the tools with exhaustion. His eye socket bothered him, probably because he'd missed his mud poultice last night.

"You all right there, Boss?" William Thacker's young brow wrinkled with concern.

"Yeah." RJ shook his head and focused on driving a nail straight. They were building walls and stairs inside the board-inghouse now. "Just—there are some rather awful people in this world."

"Ain't that the truth?" William sent a ringing blow with his hammer.

Something twisted in RJ's chest. "I'm sure you know that better than I."

The young man shot him a quick glance.

RJ swallowed. He'd said that before he thought. "Forgive me, I didn't mean to pry."

William hammered for another moment in silence, then reached down for a new handful of nails. "No matter. Expect you've been wonderin' if I was a slave."

RJ glanced about the building, seeing the other workers bus-ily occupied. "It's no business of mine."

"Maybe not. But I don't mind tellin'." William positioned a

nail. "I was enslaved down in Maryland but got free some years ago. Several other slaves and me, we managed to write ourselves passes and paddle a canoe up the Chesapeake Bay."

"How did you write your own passes? I thought . . ."

"That slaves couldn't read or write? Not legally. But there are ways. You ever read that book by Frederick Douglass?"

RJ nodded. "My parents were great admirers of his." It was through their involvement in the New York Manumission Society that Jemmy and Jehosephat had come to them years ago when they needed a safe place to live after reaching freedom.

"Well, then you know how he taught himself to read as a boy there in Baltimore and then taught other slaves in secret. One of them ended up bein' sold to my master later on, after they failed to escape and got separated. He was an old man by the time I knew him, but he taught me, so's I could write those passes."

RJ shook his head. "You are a braver man than I, my friend."

"Courage ain't so hard to come by when the alternative is staying in chains." William pulled a nail from his mouth. "Now I just need to find my little brother."

"Where is he?"

"I didn't know, not for the longest time. We were separated when he was just a baby." His eyes darkened.

"You mean he was sold?" RJ's gut clenched.

"He and my mama were sold farther south when our master fell on some hard times. After the war, I got news my mama had passed on, but my little brother had been taken under another family's wing, and they was makin' their way north." He paused. "He'll be near on ten years old now. I sure would like him to get some schoolin'. But that'll come later, once we're together. I'm savin' up for enough to bring him out here on the train as soon as I find him."

RJ shifted the hammer between his hands. Here he'd thought

he had a bum deal on life. When he got even a hint of what some people went through . . . Shame tasted bitter in his mouth.

"If there's ever anything I can do to help," he said, the words seeming inadequate, "let me know."

"You givin' me a job is already a big help." There came William's quick grin again. But then he sobered. "There's one thing I should say, though. This mornin' as I was heading here to work from where I camp a ways outside town, had the feelin' somebody was followin' me."

RJ frowned. "What?"

William shook his head. "Could be I'm imaginin' things. Just thought I heard rustlin' or footfalls behind me at times, and once when I turned 'round real quick, I thought I saw someone slip behind a building. My ears got mighty sharp evading slave catchers when we made our way north. But again, maybe it's nothin'."

A prickle ran down RJ's legs. "Is this the only time you've noticed anything?"

"Maybe one other day. Then one night, I heard some rustlin' and heavy breathin' in the grasses. Lit a fire, and whatever it was moved away. Coulda just been a coyote."

Could have. But . . . "If it happens again, let me know. I'll keep an extra eye out, regardless. Maybe you should start sleeping in town."

"I'd move in here soon's this boardinghouse is ready." William shrugged. "If they'd have me."

"If I know these Nielsen sisters, they will." At least he could be confident about that. A thought struck, and before he could think, he added, "How about you move your stuff in here now? It'd be good to have someone always on site."

"You mean that for certain?"

RJ nodded, at the same time wondering what the sisters would say to that. He guessed he'd find out.

When he stepped outside the near-complete structure and scanned the surrounding area, a foreboding in his belly chased away the tiredness, at least for now.

There was nothing to see, only the autumn wind blowing dry leaves about the bare yard. Maybe William had just imagined whatever happened. But RJ didn't like it. Not at all.

23

Who around here has threshed their wheat?" Lark smiled at Mr. Jorgensen, who had become her repository of information on farming and local farmers.

He twitched his nose, a sign he was thinking hard, and nodded at the same time. "Martin Huckstep planted wheat the last two years and fixed hisself some kind of threshing floor or something. The Hucksteps live some south of here, but we're still the closest town. And now that the train goes through here, I've seen a bit more of him."

"But you don't know exactly what he does?"

"Sorry, shoulda asked more questions. I know some people use a sheet to throw the threshed wheat in the air so the wind can blow away the chaff. Wheat head is heavier and falls back to the sheet. You can get it pretty clean that way. Someday when we get fields of wheat growing here, perhaps someone will build a mill. We're going to need a granary to hold the harvest before it can be loaded on the train too."

Lark stared at him. "I'd no idea how much there was to all this."

"People have been growing wheat for hundreds of years. They had to figure a way to get the grain from the stalk." He scratched his head. "You oughta talk to Caldwell. He digs into anything he might find useful or even just interesting. He might know if there are any new methods." Head shaking this time, he shrugged. "Yup, that's what I'd do."

"Thank you, I'll do that." She picked up her purchases, including flour so Del could keep on baking. Good thing they'd learned to put bay leaves in the flour barrel to keep out the weevils. "Have a good day."

"You too." He paused. "You know, that sister of yours sure is doing a good job with those kids."

Lark paused, mostly in shock. "Why, thank you. You might want to tell her yourself. It would mean a lot." She noticed the red creeping up his neck. "By the way, your granddaughter is one smart little girl. Del said she knows the answers sometimes before the question gets finished."

Jorgensen almost grinned. "She's a pistol all right."

Lark climbed up in her wagon. All the way home, she pondered threshing the wheat. What if she built a wooden frame with slats close together, raised a couple of inches off the ground with a canvas under it, and they all walked on it? She turned the wagon around and headed back to find Jesse at the boardinghouse.

She parked the wagon, tied Starbright to a post, and hailed RJ. "You know where Jesse is?"

"Good mornin' to you too," he said with an almost-smile, eliciting an answering smile from her. *He sure has changed.*

"It sure is. My land, but this building is coming together fast."

"It takes a good crew, and now we have one." He looked over her shoulder. "Here comes Jesse now." After waving the young man over, he turned to answer a question from one of his workers.

Lark greeted Jesse. "Am I ever happy to see you. I have an idea, and only you can help me with it."

Jesse leaned against her wagon, obviously waiting.

"You know we're needing to thresh our wheat?" At his nod, she described her idea.

Watching him ponder something always made her marvel. "*Patience is a virtue*," her mother had said so often, especially with her eldest daughter. When he took a pencil nub out of his pocket and picked up a piece of wood, she knew he was into the idea.

RJ approached, eyebrow raised. He paused to see what Jesse was drawing, then cocked that eyebrow again at Lark. "When you get done here, come and look at the cabinets Jesse's been building for the kitchen."

Lark nodded. How could she take him away from that job to work on another? But usually Jesse did his other woodworking at night.

"We need to build you a shop of your own, Jesse, with tools," she said.

He glanced at her and snorted.

"Don't give me that. I'm serious."

He held out a rough sketch.

She studied the piece of wood. "Generally." Amazement made her more anxious. "Do you think you could build it in time for us to use this year?" As she spoke the words, she knew the answer.

Jesse matched her shake of the head. "Not with the b-boardinghouse. Next year?"

Lark nodded acquiescence. "Next year."

They'd go ahead with using a sheet. The oats were ready to be cut too. And the corn was drying. What they had left of the garden produce was ready to haul into the root cellar—at least what they'd not dried or canned or pickled. The replanted beans were growing well, and they prayed daily for a late frost so they'd have beans to can or dry.

"Thanks." Lark climbed back up on the wagon seat and backed Starbright enough to turn around.

Back home, after letting Starbright out in the field, she joined Lilac at the packed earth spot where they would thresh the wheat. Lilac was hardening a floor similarly to how they'd done it in the sod house, with repeated coats of water and letting it dry, then sprinkling on water again.

Lark told Lilac what she'd learned from Mr. Jorgensen. "I should have brought Robbie and Sofie out. They would enjoy walking on wheat."

"I think there will be plenty of chances for them to join us," Lilac said as she sprinkled.

"We'll toss the grain with a sheet here too. The hard floor will help us avoid missing any fallen grains. We can't afford that. We've got to save every kernel. I showed Jesse an idea I had for the threshing floor, and he figured it out but said there's no time to build it this year. Next year he'll have it ready."

Lilac nodded. "There must be an abundance of ideas popping up. I read the story of Ruth again. They were harvesting wheat. It sounds like the same way we are doing it. Not much progress in these hundreds of years."

Lark watched her baby sister, amazed as always at how her brain worked and remembered things. Putting puzzles together had always been one of her favorite pastimes. Along with drawing and dreaming and music and animals and . . .

"I better get moving. I'm going to yoke up the oxen after we eat. We can haul up a wagon of shocks and get started."

By the time Del came home from school, they had begun a straw pile from threshing their first shocks and then moved on to throwing wheat in the air with a sheet. They had a bucket of almost clean wheat and were both sitting down, puffing.

"You started threshing!"

They nodded and sucked in matching deep breaths. "Tossing wheat in the air with a sheet is a bit tricky," Lark admitted.

"Why do I get the idea that teaching school is far easier?"

"You want to swap?"

Del shook her head. "I'll go start supper. RJ asked if you would come to the boardinghouse again tomorrow."

"I think Lilac ought to come too. We all need to be in agreement on the boardinghouse."

Lilac rolled her lips together. "I guess I'll go milk Buttercup. What can we dump the wheat in so I can have the milk pail?"

"That burlap feed sack. Make sure there are no holes in it."

Lilac fetched the sack from the storage room and held it open while Lark poured in the wheat.

"Let's see, we worked most of the afternoon, and this is all we managed to thresh and winnow," Lilac said.

"True, but we're getting better at it, and we'll get the children and anyone else we can to help." Lark scratched her shoulder and wiggled to shed some of the wheat spears that easily penetrated clothing. It was itchy, tedious work, but they had just proved they could do it. They had grown and harvested their own wheat.

Thank you, Lord, for a successful harvest.

In the morning, while waiting for any dew to lift, Lark and Lilac finished the chores and rode Starbright into town to the boardinghouse.

"You wanted to show us something?" she asked after greeting RJ.

He nodded, his eye darker than usual. "I want your opinion on the kitchen. But something happened last night that's more urgent."

Dread laced Lark's chest at his tone. "What?"

He started to speak, then hesitated and tipped his head toward the boardinghouse front door. He scanned the street once more, then turned and led them inside. "Come into the dining room."

They found Jesse and William building a long table.

Both Lilac and Lark stared from the size of the table to the two young men working on it. "How many are you planning on seating?" Lark asked.

"Fourteen to sixteen, wouldn't you think?" Jesse looked from the table to Lark and back. "I mean . . ."

"No, no, you're right. It just looks huge."

William straightened. "We could make it slide together or add boards when needed, but that would take a lot more time."

Lark froze. A bruise circled the young man's eye, dark against his brown skin. His nose swelled purplish with a cut on the side, though it had obviously been treated. "What *happened*?"

RJ's face was set like stone. "That's what I wanted to talk to you about. You know Jesse and William started staying here at the boardinghouse last week."

"And?"

"Well, last night . . ." He gestured for Jesse and William to continue.

William bent over the table, smoothing a rough edge.

"A rock came through the w-window." Jesse pointed to the broken glass on the back of the building, now patched with brown paper. "W-William went out to see, and somebody jumped him."

"What?" Lilac sounded near tears.

"I ran outside, b-but he'd already fought the fellow off, and I just saw a shadow darting down the street. Maybe more than one."

William glanced up and shrugged, though something flickered in his warm brown eyes. "No real harm done."

"I disagree." Anger reddened Lark's vision. "William, did I hear something about some ruffians slinking around before you moved into the boardinghouse?"

"Yeah, you did." Jesse's talkativeness surprised her. Clearly the two young men had formed a bond.

"Remember you told me you thought someone was following you? Did you notice anything else?" RJ waited until William met his gaze.

"Not till last night."

Jesse watched his friend, then shrugged. "I'm thinkin' it might be those men you f-fired."

"Hmm." Lark watched RJ's thoughts flicker across his face. "I thought they left town."

"They're campin' out by that other camp," William said.

"The liquor tent?" RJ asked.

William nodded.

"You followed them?"

"General direction. Stayed hidden."

RJ had shifted back into military officer mode as naturally as breathing. "Do you both have rifles?"

They shook their heads.

"Can you both shoot?"

Nods this time.

"I will bring you a rifle to keep by the door or window, loaded."

Jesse nodded. "Good."

RJ sucked in a deep breath and turned to Lark. "When are you having that women's meeting?"

"Monday night."

"It looks to me like we have a lot to talk about. Do you mind if I invite Caldwell and a few others?"

Lark and Lilac exchanged looks. "This is a meeting for the women." *And they won't talk if the men are there. Some won't even come.*

RJ studied her. "I'll talk with Caldwell and a couple of others. Sooner might be best anyway." He scrubbed a hand over his hair. "I'd better show you the kitchen."

Lark blinked as soon as they stepped through the doorway.

"I've never seen so many cupboards and shelves. All the walls are covered." Lilac turned in the middle of the large room, her voice lifting though still a bit shaky. "And the stove will go there." She pointed at the brick chimney.

"That will help heat the upstairs along with reducing the heat in the kitchen." RJ pointed at the square hole in the ceiling. "We've ordered a register, and it should arrive anytime." He stepped back and nodded to a smaller room. "That's the pantry, and the room behind the stove will be for Climie, right?"

"As far as I know she still wants to run it." *If last night's developments didn't change her mind.* The worry strand in Lark's chest wound tighter.

"The back porch will be for doing laundry."

Lark stared at RJ. "Did all this show up on the plans?"

He shook his head. "We kind of figured things out as we went. A couple of the workmen had suggestions too. William worked for a short time at a hotel, so he was a big help."

"And you still have enough funds in the account to pay your workers?"

"We do, thanks to your brother."

As much as Lark liked doing bookwork, she had gotten behind of late. There was too much to keep up on, always too much. At least God had sent her others to share the load. She needed to remember that.

And now they needed to share William's. "Thank you for

bringing what happened to our attention. I don't know what we'll do, but we've got to do something."

"I'll bring the rifle tonight and camp out myself too, for a couple of nights."

"Thanks."

Who would have thought RJ Easton would be such a godsend when Anders first brought him to town?

The two sisters mounted their horse and waved good-bye. *All this because we offered a young black man a place to stay.*

24

R J Easton was truly remarkable with Timothy.
Del sat at her desk in the church late Friday afternoon, watching him work with the boy. She should be
grading the stack of essays before her, but the excited murmur
of their voices had drawn her attention like a moth to flame.
She leaned her chin on her hand, marveling as they held an
animated discussion about algebraic geometry, the concepts
of which she could only vaguely grasp.

RJ's tutelage had made an enormous difference, even if they'd
only recently been able to resume their sessions. Timothy's reading had improved too, but digging deep into the mysteries of
mathematics lit his soul until his blue eyes sparked and his shock
of black hair fairly stood on end, his fingers dancing equations
across the slate nearly as fast as did his tutor's. RJ was patient,
engaging, and treated him as an equal. Little would she have
thought it when she and the surly former soldier butted heads
a few months ago. Only one of many areas where she'd been
wrong.

Del rubbed her temples, a weary ache pulsing there. How
overwrought she'd been at holding classes in the church for

another term, how righteously indignant at having her wishes ignored. Now, with the scene at the Kinsleys' a raw mark on her soul, it all seemed so petty.

Del pulled Elsie Weber's essay from the stack to begin marking. The assigned topic—the injunction in James that to him who knows to do good and does not do it, to him it is sin—made her swallow. Yet what more could she have done about the Kinsleys? As the doctor said, there was little they could do even now.

Lord, if there's something else I can do, please show me. Otherwise . . . please take over. You're the only one who can. Take care of those children and their mother, please.

"Miss Nielsen, did you want me to take any readin' home today?"

She looked up and smiled into Timothy's eager face. "You finished *A Tale of Two Cities*, correct?"

"I did—well, Iris and I read it together." He held the book out to her. "In bits and pieces before bed when we could. Mam even had us read some parts aloud, though Da said it just sounded to be about a bunch o' Englishmen."

"Well, Englishmen and French. But I'm glad you enjoyed it." Del reached for her satchel. "I was able to get a copy of that book by an Irishman I told you about. There you are, *Gulliver's Travels* by Jonathan Swift. Perhaps your da will like that better. And it's another adventure story, so I think you and Iris will enjoy it."

"Thank you, Miss Nielsen." Timothy took the small volume reverently. "I'll take good care of it."

"I know you will." Del watched the boy pull on his coat and hurry out the door. Students like Timothy made teaching worth all the headaches and heartaches. Her chest heaved again, thinking of Bethany and John. They'd been in school all week, but Bethany had hardly spoken more than her brother.

RJ joined her at her desk. "He'll soon be ready for more

advanced mathematics books. I've some at home. Would you like me to send for them?"

"Could you?" She looked up at him. "I hate to put you to the trouble. Perhaps we can help cover the expense."

"No need. Your family is paying me amply to build the boardinghouse, after all."

"How is that coming? Lark says we are nearing ready to open."

"I believe it should be finished enough by next week for you to start setting up the rooms. Jesse and William have been hard at work on the furniture. Those two make quite a team."

"How is William? Has there been any further sign of those ruffians?"

"Not since I've been spending nights there. And Jesse barely lets him out of his sight when they go about town."

She smiled. "That's a really good thing, isn't it? Those two young fellows working together. I don't remember Jesse ever having a friend like this before—not that I've known him that long. Lark told Jesse we need to build him a workshop where he can have all his tools about him, all he needs to build cabinets and furniture. Maybe that would be good for William too." She stared unseeing at the stack of essays.

"You have to do all those today?" RJ ran his finger down the edge of the paper pile.

"I should—tonight, anyway. Or tomorrow, but I think Lark wants me to help her at the boardinghouse for a while in the morning, since it's Saturday."

RJ raised a brow. "We won't be finished by then."

"Tell that to my older sister. I think she wants to figure out how to arrange the kitchen, that sort of thing. Don't worry, I'll try to keep her out of your way." Del gathered the papers and slid them into her satchel. "I'll just take these home to grade. I can't seem to keep my mind on them just now."

"Miss Nielsen . . . Del." RJ laid his hand on her arm.

She stilled.

"The Kinsley family—it's not your fault. You do know that."

Del bit her lip, tears suddenly pricking from nowhere. "I should have checked on them sooner."

"And done what? What good did our going do even now?"

She gave half a laugh and dashed her hand against her eyes. "Some comfort you are."

He grimaced. "I don't mean it like that. Hopefully we did something. Adam is able to check on the mother for now, and Kinsley knows someone is watching him. I just mean . . . this isn't under your control."

Del clenched her jaw against more tears. "I don't do well with that."

"Nor do I. But my ma would say we're not supposed to be in charge anyway. That's what God is for."

She blinked. "Sounds like our mas would have gotten along."

"And I wish we still had them. But since that too is something I cannot control . . ." He took her satchel with a gallant sweep and held out his other elbow. "Might I have the honor, Miss Nielsen, of escorting you to the mercantile?"

Del stared. Had he lost his senses? "The mercantile?"

"Indeed." RJ bent his head conspiratorially. "It's near four o'clock. That sacred hour when, without fail, Mrs. Jorgensen deposits a new batch of some heavenly baked goods on the counter. And it is a scientifically proven fact that sweets can alleviate one's cares in a truly magical way." He waggled his one visible brow.

Del couldn't help a smile, which spread into a chuckle. "A treat does sound rather nice."

"Well then, fair lady." He set his felt hat on his head at a jaunty angle, which combined with his eye patch to give him a rakish look. "Let us be off."

Inside the Jorgensens' mercantile a short while later, Del bit into a fresh apple turnover, savoring the warm pastry and sweet, cinnamony chunks within.

"Mmm." RJ closed his eyes and chewed. "That must be pretty close to heaven."

"Thank you for this." Del caught a crumb from her chin with her thumb. "I must admit this day just decidedly improved."

"You're welcome."

The dark brown of his eye warmed. She'd never noticed it being such a rich color or the depth and feeling there. And just now, it was focused entirely on her. Her coat felt too warm inside the store, the air between them too close.

Del took a step back, her cheeks tingling. "I'm . . . going to see if there's anything I should pick up for home while I'm here."

She hurried over to the dry goods section, scanning the bolts of fabric with unseeing eyes and trying to breathe. What was the matter with her? One moment it had seemed perfectly natural to walk down the street on RJ Easton's arm, two colleagues off for an after-school treat. Then they were standing there munching pastry together, and suddenly she'd been all too aware of his closeness, his manliness. Del lifted a hand to her throat, her pulse pounding.

"I hear they let him move right in before the boardinghouse is even finished. And then he got into some fight in the middle of the night."

The murmur of women's voices caught Del's ear. She glanced over to the counter.

Mrs. Jorgensen and Mrs. Dwyer, the speaker, bent their heads together over a length of cloth.

"I heard that too. Could be that more and more of 'em will be coming to these parts now they're freed. Not that I begrudge them that. Slavery was a terrible thing, but . . ."

"That's all well and good, but I wish they would keep to their own place and not bring trouble here."

"And what place would that be, Mrs. Dwyer?" Del stepped up to the counter, a cool smile in place.

"Well, not having first choice of our town's new boarding-house, for one thing. Begging your pardon, Miss Nielsen"—Mrs. Dwyer peered down her nose at Del—"but your family ought to know how the folks of Salton feel about your letting that boy stay in your building and bring disorder into our community."

"I believe Mr. Thacker is a young man, actually. And the disorder came from our town to him, not the other way round." Heat pounded in Del's ears. "If the fine people of Salton have some problem with our decision, they are free to speak to my sisters and me about it. As long as they give their reasons for not wishing to welcome and defend a new citizen and hard worker of our town." She brushed the last crumbs off her fingers, not caring if some hit the floor. "I trust I'll see you ladies at the meeting on Monday?"

She turned and rushed past RJ to the door.

"I'm sorry, I need to go."

"Right behind you." He touched a hand to her elbow and followed her.

A cold wind hit her hot cheeks when she stepped out on the porch. Del paused to wind her scarf about her head. "Thank you for the treat. Forgive me. I'm afraid two fine ladies of our town nearly made me lose my temper."

"I overhead something about William."

"I don't understand people. Didn't we just spend four years in an awful war over this?" Del fought with her scarf, the wind determined to blow it over her face.

RJ stepped in front of her to block the gusts and tucked the scarf under her chin, then over her shoulder. "People were fighting for all different reasons in that war, believe me. Not as many for equality and freedom of the slaves as we might like to think, I'm afraid."

She stilled, looking up at him. "I suppose you would know better than I."

His face appeared older now, the eye patch and dark hair clubbed back reminding her of all he'd seen, things she couldn't even imagine.

He lowered his hands from her shoulders and shoved them into his pockets, hunching against the wind. "See you Sunday?"

"Yes." Del forced her gaze from his face. She shouldn't stare. "At church, then. And thank you again."

He nodded and strode away from her, his figure somehow lonely. And leaving her bereft.

She was glad for the long walk home, despite the bitter wind. Pale gray clouds blanketed the sky over the sere expanse of grasses. Would they bring snow soon? She'd so hoped to get the school raised before then. She'd forgotten to ask RJ if everything was in place for next week.

She had too much on her mind. Too much of it RJ himself. How had he suddenly come to occupy so much of her mind—and, if she dared to admit it, her heart?

She arrived home in time to help with the chores, grateful for a turn at the evening milking. Buttercup's supply was dropping since she was with calf again, only yielding half a pail. But it was comforting to sit beside the cow, listen to her chew her cud and swish her tail, and lean her head against the warm flank. Things were uncomplicated here in the barn, away from horrid prejudice and abused children and rakish one-eyed soldiers who did unexpected things to her well-guarded heart.

Del closed her eyes. *Lord . . .* She was too weary to think of more words, thankful God didn't need them.

After supper, she and Lilac continued sorting the dried seeds they'd saved from Leah's Garden while Lark washed the dishes. Carefully they poured the precious seeds into brown paper packets, sealed them, then labeled each by flower variety and date. The fire crackled comfortably in the stove, and Scamp curled at Lilac's feet with his fluffy head on his paws.

"I think he's snoring." Lilac leaned down to give the puppy's head a rub. He was hardly a puppy anymore in size, though certainly in spirit.

"What did you get done today?" Del carefully penned *zinnia* on another packet.

"We finished filling the root cellar from the vegetable garden. And threshed more wheat, so the pile of shocks is near to gone. We still need to shuck the corn."

"How is our wheat crop looking? Now that we can measure it?"

"Not as much as we'd hoped. But Lark thinks we'll still be able to sell some after setting aside what we keep for flour. We scrounge for every kernel that falls, which takes more time, but we can't afford to lose any."

"Is nothing left in the garden now?" Sometimes Del felt so distant from goings-on at the farm, being at school so much.

"Only a few hardy greens. We got the last of the root vegetables in. Between that and the canning we did, the cellar is nearly stuffed full. We'd better not have another late tornado like last year, or we wouldn't fit."

"I doubt it. That was highly unusual, from what I understand, and we're later in October now anyway."

"I know. I was merely joking."

At the slight edge in Lilac's voice, Del looked up. But her younger sister was concentrating on pouring seeds into another packet, dark curls shadowing her face in the lamplight.

"Where are we on the temperance rally?" Those plans had fallen by the wayside of late, but the Kinsleys made the need all the more urgent.

"We need to decide on a time and place still. Maybe the boardinghouse, once it's ready. I went into town this afternoon after we finished with the garden and picked up some pamphlets Reverend Pritchard ordered from back east. They look helpful, with details on the damage liquor does to individuals, family, and society."

Del nibbled her lip. "How is the reverend? I haven't seen him lately."

Lilac shot her a quick glance. "I thought he must be at the school often."

"Not really." Del drew a breath. "Not since I let him know I'm not interested in having him call on me, that is."

The seeds in Lilac's hand spilled across the table.

"Oh no, no, no." Lilac dropped the packet and scrambled to save them.

"It's all right." Del moved the lamp and her own packets out of the way. "Take it slow. We'll get them. Fetch that little broom. We can use it to sweep out any that catch in the cracks of the table."

Together they managed to salvage the seeds, at least all they could see in the lamplight. Finally, Del trickled the last few she'd gathered into the packet.

Lilac sealed it shut and labeled it, then sank back in her chair and covered her face with her hands. "I'm sorry. We have so few seeds as it is from this year, I can't believe I—"

"Lilac. It's all right. " Del scooted her own chair near, drew her sister's hands down from her face, and held them in her own. She waited until Lilac relaxed and drew a longer breath. "Did you truly think there was something between Reverend Pritchard and me?" Her heart smote her. With all that had been happening, she'd never spoken to Lilac as she'd meant, but since she'd had so little interaction with the pastor over the last month or two, she'd thought any ideas would have blown over on their own.

Lilac kept her eyes down, but tears trembled on her dark lashes. "I—didn't know. I thought maybe, after that dance. . . ."

Del sighed. "He was interested for a time, probably because I was convenient more than anything. But I wasn't interested, sister mine—certainly not once I realized how you felt, but not even before then."

Lilac flicked up a glance. "Truly?"

Del touched her sister's cheek. "Truly."

Lilac sniffed hard and swiped at her eyes. "I'm such a fool."

"No, you're not." Del reached over and hugged her hard. "You're a fine beautiful woman. And he's a good man."

"But he never even notices me." The tears spilled over, dampening Del's shoulder. "Even today, all he would talk about was the rally, except for asking after you."

Del's heart sank. She'd hoped his fancy would have passed by now. "Well, he'll just have to get over it. And he's passionate about causes, so no wonder the rally takes precedence." She sat back. "Take courage, dear heart. Some man someday will discover the treasure that you are, whether Reverend Pritchard ever gains the wisdom to see it or not."

"You girls all right?" Lark stepped between them and laid a hand on each shoulder, her fingers still damp from dishwashing.

"Oh, you know." Lilac looked up, her smile back despite a final sniffle. "Just solving all the problems of the world and the female heart."

"Typical day in the life of the Nielsen sisters, then." Lark sat down with a sigh. "Digging rutabagas from the ground uses a whole different set of muscles than threshing, I find." She stretched her arms over her head with a wince. "I wanted to tell you both—I talked with Climie today while Lilac was in town."

"You went to Forsythia's?"

"No, she sent Climie out here with the bread we had for supper. They'd had a big baking day. Anyway, she's ready to start managing the boardinghouse, though I think she should wait to move in until we're sure those ruffians won't be coming back, whoever they were."

"Does she seem excited about it?" Lilac passed another handful of paper packets to Del and resumed sorting herself.

"She's a bit intimidated, but yes, I think so. I see her courage growing since she's been out here, with the agonies of the past receding further away. I do think she'd be good at it, once she finds her footing."

"And that will lift such a burden off us." Del didn't see how they could possibly manage to run a boardinghouse, seed business, and farm all at once, especially with her teaching school.

"Yes. Of course, we'll still be closely involved, but she can cover much of the day-to-day details." Lark folded her hands on the table. "We also spoke about Jesse."

Del and Lilac both stilled.

"What did she say?"

"She admitted to caring for him. Not that that's a surprise to any of us." Lark blew out a breath. "She said Jesse hasn't said anything yet. Not that he says much to begin with."

"Jesse cares too," Lilac said, her voice low. "I can see it in his face."

Del's heart twisted. "What are we to do? Climie isn't free, not as long as that weasel Wiesel is alive and kicking—and biting."

"I'm sure I don't know." Lark shook her head. "Part of me wishes he would show his ugly face here, and we could just shoot him. It'd solve a lot of problems."

"Lark!"

"I know, I know." Lark lifted her hands. "Love thine enemies and all that. It's just easier said than done."

"Maybe Adam could talk to Jesse. We could ask Forsythia to ask him." Lilac pushed back a stray curl.

"Is it really any of our affair?" Del's head ached. She no longer felt sure of when to intervene in others' doings or when to mind her own business.

"Ma would say to pray on it. I'm afraid a miracle's the only hope for Climie and Jesse, but as she would also say, 'Is anything too hard for the Lord?'" Lark reached for a bag of seeds. "Let's finish this batch, then head to bed. I'm so tired I can hardly see straight."

They packaged seeds until the fire burned low, then banked it, shivered into their flannel nightgowns, and slid into bed, thankful for heavy quilts and the thick sod walls.

But Del lay awake a long time, despite the weariness weighting her limbs, listening to the wind and praying against snow before the school raising. And for the Kinsley family. For Climie and Jesse, two wounded souls drawn together against the cruel reality that would keep them apart. For Lilac, for Rev. Pritchard, even for herself. Why did love have to come with so many heartaches all the way round?

When RJ's pensive face filled her mind, she squeezed her eyes shut and rolled over, new emotions tangling her heart that she didn't feel fit to untie.

25

W e'll see you here at the church tomorrow night." Lark nodded to a group of ladies after Sunday service. The cluster of women nodded. "About time," someone muttered.

Lark wondered who had spoken. Why did she get the feeling there was more going on in town than she suspected?

Beatrice Caldwell walked with her to the Nielsens' wagon. "Can I do anything for the meeting tomorrow?" she asked.

"Del is going to stay after school and help Forsythia get the coffee going. We thought it'd be nice to have some kind of dessert."

Beatrice arched an eyebrow. "Trying to mollify your audience?"

"I hadn't thought of it quite like that, but it might be a good idea." Lark paused by the wagon wheel. "Is there something going on that I'm not aware of?"

Beatrice shrugged. "Mrs. Jorgensen has a bee in her bonnet of some kind, but I'm not exactly sure what is going on."

Lark nodded slightly, her tongue digging at her teeth. "Was there unrest before William Thacker came to town?"

"I hope that's not it. Mr. Caldwell says he's a fine young man and a hard worker. And he can read, write, and do sums."

"How does he know?"

"RJ, I imagine."

So she calls him RJ too. Isn't that interesting? "Well, I hope to get to the bottom of whatever is stewing tomorrow night." Lark climbed up the wheel to sit on the wagon seat. Del and Lilac saw her and came immediately.

"We just got the schoolroom all set up. Jesse and William helped us." Lilac climbed up to sit in the middle. "Sythia said she might bring the children out later. Mikael needs a nap right now."

"They can help us thresh the wheat."

"Lark, it's Sunday. We're not supposed to work on Sunday. Besides, I think she wants some sister time."

"We can always talk while we thresh. How would that be different than going for a Sunday walk?"

Lilac and Del both looked heavenward as if in supplication.

Once home, Lilac released Starbright into the pasture. While they'd not had a heavy frost yet, the grass was already turning brown, and the five animals had the pasture chewed short. They needed to move to the other pasture, and hopefully this one might grow a bit yet.

At the house, Del pulled a pan from the still-warm oven. She had already fired up the stove, so the burning wood could be heard crackling,

Lark strolled out to check on any remaining seeds in the garden. There might be a few more if the frost held off. The dried corn husks hung on the last stalks of field corn that had survived.

Lilac fell into step beside her. "We need to finish that last stretch of fence so we can move the animals into the other pasture for the winter."

"Between the threshing and the corn? We can't ask Jesse to take on any more. The fence will just have to wait." Lark turned to return to the house.

Del appeared in the doorway. "Dinner is ready."

The three of them gathered around the table inside, since the wind outside blew too cold. Lilac said grace, and they passed the stewed chicken with rutabagas, onions, carrots, and potatoes around, then the biscuits.

"This is a far cry from last fall." Lark nodded as she chewed. "Although that was pretty good, considering how late we got it in."

"We've come a long way in a year. Grasshoppers or no." Del sipped her coffee.

"That we have. And yet there's so much more to do. I wish we could bring Jonah out here. We could use that able body."

"I'm sure he'd be pleased to know you value his muscle."

Lark shook her head, chuckling with the others. "We'll do chores early tomorrow so we can grab a quick sandwich and leave." She nodded to Lilac. "Are you feeding that dog at the table?"

Lilac flinched. "Just a bit. He's a growing boy."

"Tell him he's going to have to get along with a cat too, one of these days."

The next evening, they set up the church for the meeting by pushing all the desks off to the side away from the benches. Del had kept the fire alive and stoked it up when her sisters arrived. Forsythia brought a pot of coffee and set it on top of the stove to stay hot, and Mrs. Caldwell brought cookies she'd baked that afternoon.

"Square cookies," one of the ladies said with a chuckle. "Easier to do."

Beatrice smiled. "That's right. Besides, I've misplaced my cookie cutter." She shook her head. "No idea where it went."

As the women arrived, Forsythia poured coffee while Beatrice passed around the cookies.

"Ah, such a treat." Rachel Armstead, Mrs. Jorgensen's daughter, smiled in delight. Lark sometimes wondered if Mrs. Jorgensen had lost all her smiles behind the counter at their store.

As soon as everyone was seated, Lark called the meeting to order. "Reverend Pritchard will now lead us in prayer."

"Welcome, ladies, it's good to see so many of you here. Let us pray." He paused. "Lord God, our heavenly Father, we thank you this night for the opportunity to gather here in your house. We ask that you guide the discussion so that your will might be known unto us. Bless us all in Jesus' precious name. Amen."

"Thank you." Lark watched him bid them good evening and leave to head back to Antelope Creek, where he boarded. "Now, ladies, we need to pick up from our last meeting about the temperance rally. Some families in our community are suffering greatly thanks to that liquor tent."

"I heard about that Kinsley family." Mrs. Young had a strong voice for one so tiny. "Terrible shame."

Lark hadn't necessarily meant to name names, but . . . "Perhaps if the tent was forced to move on and liquor wasn't so convenient, this situation at least might be helped. Plus, some ruffians have been hanging around our boardinghouse and assaulted William Thacker, one of Mr. Easton's workmen. We're hoping they've now left Salton." She looked up to see another woman shaking her head. "You have something to tell us?"

"Someone is camping in that grove over on the river not far from our house. I hesitate to let the boys go fishing, even. That camp can get pretty rowdy."

Lark's middle sank. So those men were likely still around.

"My husband says there is gambling out at that tent too."

"How does he know?" someone else asked.

Beatrice raised her voice. "Can we get back to our discussion, please?" Several mumbled, but all looked to Lark again.

"In other parts of the country, primarily the cities, where drinking problems are much worse—"

"And booze more accessible," someone chimed in.

"True. Women have been forming temperance leagues to educate people and bring about political reform. And since women are the primary sufferers when a husband gets drunk, we are the ones seeking help. The Bible castigates drunkards and preaches against violence, but most times people drink privately, and men are not the only ones who imbibe until they can't stop."

"Can we deal with the situation here in Salton rather than in generalities?" Beatrice asked. "I know the rally is important, but I want to know about the family we might be able to help. Can you tell us what the situation is?"

"A stain upon our town is what it is." Mrs. Jorgensen stiffened her spine and glared at Beatrice.

"Lark, can you give us more information, please?" Rebecca Weber asked.

Lord, help me. Lark nodded. "The children are missing school and have come to school with various bruises and injuries. The older son has already left home, and the mother is ill and pregnant with another child." She sucked in a breath. "The children are trying to keep up the chores and harvest their crops."

"And the father?"

"Passed out on the bed." Del added the last line.

Mutters darted around the room.

"This is gossip, pure and simple. The Bible speaks against that too."

"What can we do for them? There is no jail to throw him in. Not that being drunk is a crime, anyway."

"No wonder the older son left."

"Well, I never. Who are you to judge?"

"Ladies, ladies." Lark raised her hands. "I know this is a volatile topic. But that's why we all need to work together."

"Excuse me."

At the soft voice, heads turned.

Climie stood up from a bench, her face pale but resolute. "I have the misfortune to—to have experience being in this kind of . . . situation. And, well, I just want to say I'm grateful the Nielsens didn't dismiss me as none of their business. And I don't think we should do that to this woman and her children either." She sat down and wound her hands in her lap, but Lark could see them trembling. Lilac, sitting beside her, reached to cover Climie's hands with her own.

"Well." Mrs. Jorgensen gave a firm nod toward Climie, then glared at the rest of the room. "I'd say that makes our path pretty clear."

Nods and murmurs, a softening on the faces of those who'd been contentious. Lark's throat swelled. *Oh, Climie, good for you.*

Beatrice stood up. "What if we did something truly unusual?"

The others turned, listening.

"One of my mother's favorite sayings was to kill someone with kindness. And another saying works all the time: 'A soft answer turneth away wrath.'" She paused. "What if we took God at His word and did just that?"

Every eye stared at her, confusion coloring all their faces.

Lord, I have no idea where we're going with this. If this is from you, please make it clear. Lark swallowed and nodded slowly. "What might we be able to do to help them?" She figured her face was as confused as everyone else's.

"What if we pray about this?" Rebecca Weber asked.

They all bowed their heads.

"Help us, Lord." Lark recognized Lilac's voice. "Please."

Someone cleared her throat. "You said the children were doing the chores and trying to bring in the harvest?"

"Yes," Del said.

"Couldn't some of us do that?"

"Amen! It'd be much faster, depending on how many help."

"We'll get our menfolk to pitch in."

Lark looked at Del, whose grin stretched from ear to ear. The other women looked at one another, and a couple even shook hands.

The discussion turned to planning for the temperance rally, now postponed until after the school raising, and then to specifics of when to gather at the Kinsley farm in the coming days.

Well, Lord, at least we're in agreement. Now to see what Mr. Kinsley has to say when we descend on his farm and take over his harvest.

Mr. Kinsley was nowhere to be seen when eight men showed up to bundle wheat and toss it into a wagon early one morning a few days later. Adam, Jesse, William, and RJ were there. Anthony Armstead and a couple of the other fathers from the school as well. Even Rev. Pritchard joined in, as little as he was used to farm labor. They forked the sheaves into a pile between the house and the barn, ready for threshing. Some of the women brought out big pots of soup to feed everyone at noon.

Del and Lark, along with Beatrice, knocked on the door while the others returned to help finish in the field. "May we come in a bit? We brought you some soup."

Bethany, eyes round as saucers, stepped back and motioned them inside. It was all Lark could do not to cover her nose.

Mrs. Kinsley was struggling to sit up in the bed. "Please come in, I—I'm sorry, I . . ." She paused to breathe.

"Oh dear, we should have come to see you earlier." Del set the pot over the hook in the fireplace.

"H-how can I thank you? The children told me what you're doing."

"We're glad we could do something. Where is your husband?"

"Tom left two days ago and hasn't returned." She drank from the cup Lark held for her. Her hands shook so, she couldn't have held it herself. "Thank you."

"Were you this weak when he left?"

She half shrugged and shook her head. "The children have been caring for the animals."

Bethany sat on the foot of the bed. "We're almost out of wood. John and I sawed chunks off the tree out there."

"I'll get someone to split those," Lark said.

"Do you have a way to contact your older son?" Del asked.

Mrs. Kinsley heaved a sigh and shook her head. "But Tom said he'd be back. He went to buy supplies."

Went where, Chicago? But Lark kept her mouth shut. She had an idea that if they raided the liquor tent, they'd find him.

"Bethany, can you feed your mother?" Del asked.

The child nodded. "I been helping her."

"And, John, you've been doing the barn chores?"

He nodded.

Lark could hear the harnesses of the horses pulling the wagons out. The men must be finished. Should they leave the family alone or ask someone to stay with them?

"He'll be back tonight," Mrs. Kinsley insisted.

"You said that last night, Ma." Bethany stared at her mother, tears running down her face.

"You go gather the eggs. John, time to milk?" Mrs. Kinsley's voice faded, but after another sip of water, she looked at Del. "We'll be . . ." She nodded, her eyes drifting closed.

"We'll be back in the morning." Lark patted the woman's hand. As the three of them left the house, they saw the two children on the way to the barn. "Lord, keep them safe." She waved down the wagon holding Adam and RJ. "Could you split some wood before you leave? The mister left two days ago for supplies. His wife believes he'll return yet tonight or tomorrow. We'll see."

RJ halted the horses and set the brake. "I'll split wood if you want to check on the woman."

Adam nodded as they both stepped down.

"We'll be back in the morning with more food and to clean the filth out for them," Lark said.

"If he's here, promise me you'll leave." Adam stared at the three women.

Lark nodded. "We will."

Adam and RJ stopped by the Nielsen place on their way back to town, Adam shaking his head. "Unless we can get some nourishment into her and keep her off her feet, she and that baby will not make it. Lord God, please send us a miracle."

I'm afraid we need more than one, Lark thought.

26

Someone banged on the door.

RJ stumbled to his feet and down the stairs, snapping his eye patch in place. "Coming." This was his first night back at the Brownsvilles', and it must be someone for the doctor.

He pulled open the door just as Adam came up behind him. He had to look down to see the boy.

"Come! Come quick. Pa is on the floor. Ma said hurry, he's been hurt." Tears bubbled between the words.

The Kinsley boy—the one Del said never spoke, at least to her.

"RJ, you can ride out there faster than I can." Adam laid a hand on the boy's shoulder. "Come wait in here. Is he bleeding?"

John shook his head. "I-I don't know, not bad."

RJ took the stairs two at a time and dressed fast as he had when they were being attacked in the war. He grabbed his pistol in its holster off the bedpost and slammed his feet into his boots. Downstairs, he lifted his jacket off the coat-tree and clapped his hat on his head as he ran back through the kitchen to get to the barn.

Forsythia met him at the door with a packet. "Supplies. Go with God."

"Thanks," he called over his shoulder.

Captain heard him coming and met him at the fence. RJ had him saddled within minutes, then brought the horse through the gate and swung aboard, stuffing the packet in his saddlebag. They pounded down the westbound road and then north. *Lord, please keep us safe.* He banished thoughts of the injured man, focusing instead on Adam's request to hurry.

Keeping a firm grip on the reins, he slowed down as the road narrowed and roughened. A light ahead invited him onward. Captain skidded to a stop and, head down, fought to breathe. RJ swung off, grabbed his saddlebags, and got to the door as it opened.

"He's over there." Bethany pointed to a form flat out on the floor and covered by a quilt. "We couldn't get him up on the bed." She sniffed back tears.

"He fell off his horse, and . . . the children dragged him inside." Mrs. Kinsley laid her hand against her chest as if it might ease her breathing.

RJ dropped to his knees beside the man. He tossed the quilt up on the bed and glanced up at the little girl.

"I c-covered him. He's so cold."

"You did well. Bring the lamp here, please."

She had set the kerosene lamp on the floor beside him but picked it up again when he motioned.

"Is—is . . ." Mrs. Kinsley tried to ease closer but failed.

"He's still breathing." *But I don't know for how long.*

A large bump on Kinsley's forehead might have come from the fall. RJ felt for other injuries. A messed-up face, arms, and legs. *Lord, what, if anything, can I do for him?* Memories flashed of trying to care for wounded soldiers in the war, often to no avail.

Kinsley's breathing was growing more ragged, his belly distended. His hands looked like he'd been in a brawl. One foot swollen clear to his knee.

Put him up on the bed, or leave him on the floor? What could RJ do?

Running to the door, Bethany announced Adam had arrived.

Adam set his leather bag down on the floor beside his patient, his gaze seeking out the trouble spots. He flinched when he saw the distended belly, the flinch noticeable only to the man who was looking for one. Adam raised his gaze to RJ with not a trace of hope.

"Let's put him up on the bed." He looked up at Mrs. Kinsley. "Would you like us to help you move to a pallet?"

The look in her eyes told RJ she clearly understood what was happening.

Both men stood and hoisted the patient to the pallet covering the rope-strung bed. The children clung to each other at the foot of the bed, as close to their mother as they could get.

Adam bent over and laid his ear first on Kinsley's chest, then his belly. The stench of liquor mixed with unwashed body, urine, and excrement made RJ nearly gag. The body releasing early, that he remembered too. They should have left the body on the floor, but he knew why they'd lifted him. To make it easier for his wife to touch him.

RJ stared at Adam, who looked back, compassion showing in spite of the shadows. RJ shifted his gaze to the door and back, asking if he should take the children away. Adam's head gave the tiniest of shakes.

RJ crossed the room to the fireplace and poked the embers with a narrow chunk of wood. Sparks flared, still hot enough to attack the wood, so he tucked that piece in and added a couple more. The stack of wood by the fire was down to three or four pieces.

"Do you have a cloth and a basin?" he asked softly.

The girl nodded and left her mother to get it. "There's hot water in the teakettle."

Without asking, she took the basin to the bucket of water near the door, dipped some into the basin, and brought it back to him.

Ah, child, you should not have to watch your father die. He added hot water to the basin and knelt down at the side of the bed. Basin on the floor, he wrung out the rag and gently wiped Kinsley's beat-up face.

"I can do that." Bethany appeared beside him and reached for the cloth.

Fighting back tears of his own, RJ allowed her to perform this loving service for the man who had abused wife and children. What was she humming? A familiar tune, but at the moment, he couldn't recall the name. A lullaby his mother had sung to him? Surely not. He glanced at the mother to see tears streaming down her face as she bent over her husband. Bethany had started on the backs of his hands when he convulsed and breathed his last.

Adam laid a different cloth over his face. "Rest in peace."

RJ stared at his friend. Rest in peace? A blessing of sorts, at least.

Adam packed his things back into his bag. "Mrs. Kinsley, let me help you move to a pallet with your children."

She barely shook her head, her hand still resting on her husband's chest. "I will be fine here."

"But you—but the . . ." Adam motioned to the body. But when he met her gaze, an understanding seemed to pass between them. "I will send help in the morning. Please—"

RJ interrupted him. "I'll stay. I know it's not proper, but I'll stay."

"But . . ." Adam shrugged. "Walk me out."

Both horses roused as the men drew near.

RJ raised a hand. "Dawn will be here soon. I assume you'll tell Reverend Pritchard, and he'll come right after the church service. I figure we can get that body in the ground this afternoon and help this family begin to heal."

"I'll send someone back out right away." Adam stepped up into the gig, clucked his mare around, and trotted down the lane.

"Mister?"

RJ turned at the voice behind him.

"I can take care of your horse," John said.

"Shouldn't you try to sleep some?"

John shrugged.

RJ handed the boy the reins and watched him lead Captain toward the pasture. *Tom Kinsley, you must have been a good man at some point to have children like these.*

They buried Mr. Kinsley later that afternoon after RJ and Jesse dug the grave. Rev. Pritchard read the service with the four Nielsen sisters, Climie, and the Caldwells in attendance. Afterward, Climie offered to stay behind to help, but at first Margaret Kinsley refused.

"We've managed this far, my children and I." Her smile spoke courage.

"And you are so strong, we all know that." Climie pressed the woman's hand, looking into her eyes. "But sometimes it's good to let others help carry the burden for a while. I know."

Something passed between them, and Margaret's mouth trembled. She gave a quick nod and squeezed Climie's hand, a tear trickling down her careworn cheek.

"Lilac and I will be back after chores in the morning, then," Lark said.

"You always have a place to stay at our house." Beatrice spoke softly, making Margaret nod.

"Thank you." Margaret stopped to get a breath. "I will . . . be stronger soon. I want our baby born in this home, the home Tom built for us here. He . . . he wasn't always like what you saw."

RJ stood beside her. "If you are afraid of the drive to the Caldwells' . . ."

She shook her head. "Our Father has always watched over us. Why would He . . . leave now?"

They left Margaret and Climie standing in the doorway side by side, arms intertwined.

Three days later, RJ couldn't stand it anymore. Leaving O'Rourke in charge of the building site, he left the boarding-house and headed to the law office to confront Henry Caldwell.

"We've got to do something about that liquor tent." His words came out abruptly, but he was past caring. "I'm coming to you first, sir, or else I'll go out and shoot up the place myself."

Mr. Caldwell set aside the letter he had been writing and corked his inkwell, then regarded RJ evenly. "What do you propose? The women have been planning a temperance rally—"

"Rallies be hanged." RJ flinched. "Forgive my language, sir. But the women of Salton have been doing that because we men—I include myself—have refused to take any action. I'd guess they hope to rally us more than anyone else. And now a man is dead, a family wounded, my employee attacked, and that liquor tent still stands. We can't wait for more talk. We've got to take action before anyone else gets hurt."

"Well." Mr. Caldwell stood and reached for his cane. RJ wasn't the only wounded veteran in Salton. "I must say you make me rather ashamed of myself, young man. But again I ask, what do you propose?"

"That we go out there and confront them, sir. Tell them they aren't welcome in our town anymore."

"Technically, they've always been beyond the town limits."

"Anywhere near it, then. I don't know, but we've got to say and do something."

"*We* meaning who? Just the two of us?"

"Adam will go, I think—and at least a few more I can round up. But I wanted to speak with you first. I figure you're the closest thing to a sheriff we've got just now."

"I'd hardly call myself that. But very well, then." Caldwell leaned on his cane and met RJ's gaze. "Go and get them, son. I'll meet you on the way. And tell them to bring their guns."

By the time they headed out of town toward the liquor tent, their group numbered eight. Henry, Adam, RJ, Mr. O'Rourke, and Isaac McTavish—the drifter had just returned after working on the railroad a spell—and Jesse and William. Though RJ had balked at letting the young men along, they would brook no argument. Mr. Young came too, although RJ could tell the banker hesitated at anything that would drive away folks who might bring business to the town. But an appeal to his sense of leadership and responsibility for the community worked its charm.

A motley group, but a determined one. And mounted on horseback, rifles at the ready, they presented an intimidating posse. At least RJ hoped so.

They reached the liquor tent on the banks of the creek. Several rough-looking characters lounging outside the tent regarded them suspiciously. Were any of these louts those who had jumped William? RJ nudged his horse slightly ahead to shield his friend.

"We'd like to see your proprietor," Mr. Young announced with an authoritative air.

Guffaws, and then one of the men hollered over his shoulder. "Hey, Powell. Someone here to see ya."

The tent flap lifted, and a small, wiry man with sleeves rolled up and a dirty apron stepped out into the setting sun. "What can I do for you gents?"

Mr. Caldwell dismounted. "Your establishment is no longer welcome near our town. We are here to inform you that you would be wise to vacate this region entirely."

Powell snorted a short laugh. "Or what?"

RJ swung off Captain and stepped closer. "Or you'll regret it. All of you."

The owner bristled like a banty rooster. "There ain't no law says you can just tell us to clear out."

"Maybe not." RJ stood his ground. "But there are laws against murder. And we've reason to believe one of your customers here"—he raked the men outside with a scathing glance—"is responsible for the death of one of our citizens, Tom Kinsley. The victim of a brawl, beaten well nigh to death three nights ago."

"Brutal internal injury, by my examination," Adam added. "Perhaps by means of a booted foot repeatedly to the abdomen?"

One of the men, shifty-eyed with muscular limbs, suddenly scrambled to his feet and scuttled off down the creek. RJ's grip tightened on his rifle. Another man, who'd had his face hidden beneath his hat brim, raised his head a touch, giving RJ a jolt of recognition.

Clive Johnson, the first man he'd fired for drunkenness on the job.

"You," RJ barked, stepping toward Clive. "Johnson. Is it you who's been hanging around throwing rocks through the boardinghouse window? Following and attacking my employees?"

"Well," Clive growled, pushing to his feet, "when folks go about firing honest workers and replacing them with Irish and colored boys, one might say they get what they deserve."

RJ saw red. He started to raise his rifle, only held back by Adam's warning hand on his arm. He glanced back to see Jesse had moved his horse in front of William, gun ready.

"Now, now, gentlemen." Mr. Powell raised his hands, voice deprecating. "I'm afraid there's nothing anyone can prove."

"Mebbe not." Isaac McTavish's voice came soft as the hiss of a rattlesnake. "But there also ain't nothin' to stop us from using those rows of whiskey you got back there for target practice." His movements easy, Isaac walked forward and lifted the tent flap, flipped it over his shoulder, and sighted down the barrel of his rifle with a low whistle. "Would you look at those glass bottles, now? Wouldn't those make a right purty little fireworks show?" He cocked the gun.

RJ stepped up beside Isaac, his own rifle ready. He was liking this fellow soldier more by the minute.

"Wait! Stop, please." A note of panic entered Powell's voice, and he hurried to squeeze in front of RJ and Isaac, jerking the tent flap back down. "There's no need to get violent."

"Precisely. That's why we're requesting that you move your little establishment far away from our town." Adam's voice was flinty.

"And all your men with it," RJ added.

The proprietor's nostrils flared. "You got no right to order us to leave."

"We'll just take care of the problem ourselves, then." RJ took another step toward the tent.

Behind him, all the men from town put their hands on their guns, as if linked by a commander's word.

Mr. Powell stood in front of his tent door, arms spread as if he could stop the group like Moses and the Red Sea. His chest heaved, and beads of sweat lined his scant hairline despite the cold. He scanned the group, eyes resting on each face before landing on Isaac McTavish, who still stood with his rifle cocked.

Powell's mouth hardened into a grim line. "You'll be sorry."

In one quick motion, he spun on his heel and ducked under the tent flap, dropping it behind him.

"All right, boys, you heard 'em." A crash of breaking glass, and the owner swore. "Don't give me that. Get off your backsides and help me pack up."

The men lounging outside eased to their feet, eyes on the group, then slipped inside the tent. Clive Johnson flicked one last look of loathing at RJ and William, then followed.

Suddenly aware of his pounding pulse, RJ stepped back and reached for Captain's bridle, stroking the horse's neck. "Good boy," he murmured.

They all waited in silence a few moments, and then at a nod from Mr. Caldwell, those who had dismounted mounted up, and the horses turned as one. The group rode in silence back to town.

RJ reined Captain over to ride beside Adam. "Think that actually did it?"

The doctor shook his head. "Time will tell."

27

L ark sliced open the envelope and read aloud.

My dear sisters,
This is a letter I hoped I would not have to write,
but Wiesel is back in town. He went on a rampage like
you would not believe, even when we showed him the
grave in the cemetery. I know we did not tell you this yet,
but we planted a rock in the cemetery with Climie's name
on it.

Lark stared at her sisters, and they all burst into disbelieving laughter. They'd pretended to bury Climie so that so-called
husband of hers would never come looking for her? Del nearly
choked. Never would she have dreamed her straitlaced brother
might think of such a thing, let alone do it.

Of course, there is nothing beneath it, and it is not
a true headstone, but when Josephine suggested it, I
couldn't help but comply. I truly believed he would never
return to town. It took some scratching to get a semblance

of her name on it. I am letting you know this since he left town again, threatening—as always—to get even.

Jonah is getting restless to come out there, saying he would be of more use there. We are thinking nearer to spring, when he can bring seeds and starts like I did. You've not mentioned how well the starts did. Those we kept here have done very well. Even Ma's rosebush. I think we should name it Leah's Rose and make it the emblem of our products.

Lark looked up, shaking her head. "Is this our Anders?"

Lilac chuckled. "What I can't believe is that Wiesel actually had the nerve to show his face back in town."

I must get this in the mail. Congratulations on your progress with the boardinghouse. RJ must be working miracles or have an amazing crew or both.

We are all well, and our little dandelion is sprouting up, all bright and cheerful, although her hair is just now growing in. Her mother has tried to tie a ribbon on top, but that is not yet possible. We send you our love and always our prayers.

> *Your brother Anders and*
> *family*

Lark laid the letter on the table in the circle of lamplight. "I hope their façade holds and the weasel doesn't try to come here."

"Don't even think that. This has to be one of those trust-God situations. Climie is still out helping the Kinsleys, isn't she?" Del rubbed her eyes. It had been a long day, and she had a stack of papers to grade. But Anders's letter had been more important.

"Yes, but Margaret is gaining strength. I so wish we could find her older son."

"Mr. Caldwell is looking into it. Mr. Jorgensen received money from him once to apply to the store account." Del had heard that from RJ when he stopped at the school today. Something he was doing more and more lately, which fed a gentle warmth in her middle.

"That poor woman deserves some good news." Lark closed her eyes.

Del nodded, her heart aching for Margaret Kinsley. Her husband dying nearly in her arms and buried not far from their sod house. Now she and the children had to learn how to go on without him. At least Bethany and John were attending class again, and she could read a burden lifted in their eyes despite the grief.

Once October had rolled into November, Del met Lark at the boardinghouse one day to find the cookstove being delivered. They stood in awe at the crates that filled two wagons.

"It finally got here," RJ called to them as the men leaned against the wagon to catch their breath. "What brought you to town?"

"Just my usual visit to the boardinghouse." Lark shook her head, staring. "I was beginning to fear the stove had gotten lost—or worse, stolen. It's been so long since we placed the order."

Del poked her. "I think this might be a bit difficult to steal."

They backed the wagon as close to the boardinghouse door as possible, and four of the men hefted the largest crate inside first and then the others. As they pried the crates apart, the shiny black-and-chrome stove body emerged.

Lark clasped her hands to her chest, shaking her head and

chuckling. Del couldn't stop the grin stretching her face. She'd never seen such a large cookstove in her life—not that she'd been in hotel kitchens before. Wait until Climie saw this. She glanced over to see the men staring at it as hard as she was.

"We'll have to cook a special meal on it once you men get it all connected. Inaugurate both the stove and the boardinghouse. What do you think?" Del asked.

Jesse nodded. "We c-could invite all the men who've worked on it."

"A splendid idea." Lark smiled at him. "RJ, please spread the word."

The next evening, they gathered in the dining room of Nielsen House, as the sign Jesse was carving would soon proclaim for everyone to see. Forsythia, Adam, and their children came, along with Jesse and Climie. The guests of honor were RJ and William, Lars, Mike, Paddy, and the rest of the workers who'd stayed sober and worked so hard to build the boardinghouse to completion. Or at least, as close as it would get for now. No doubt they would be adding to it and improving it for years, and the upstairs still remained one long room.

The O'Rourke family had been invited but sent their regrets, as Iris had a cold. It was just as well, as it would have been a tight squeeze to add six more.

Lark, Del, Lilac, and Climie bustled between the kitchen and the huge table in the dining room, bearing steaming platters and bowls.

"I just can't get over this stove." Climie gazed at it again in awe, wiping her hands on her apron. "Six big pots going at once and room to spare. Can you imagine?"

"I like the hot water reservoir best." Del poured dried green beans stewed with salt pork into a bowl. "Plenty of hot water right there whenever we need it." Maybe someday they'd have one like this in their home.

"As long as we keep it filled." Lark drew the roast out of the oven. "I believe we could cook two turkeys at once in here, and maybe a ham too."

"Just in time for Thanksgiving." Holding a platter of carrots, Lilac backed through the swinging door to the dining room and held it open so Lark could carry the roast through.

The table was full when they all sat down.

"Good thing you men made this table to fit a few more people than I thought we'd need." Lark nodded at RJ. "It looks like we could squeeze twenty around it, at least if some of them aren't very big." She smiled at Robbie and Sofie, who stared round-eyed at the loaded platters. "Adam, would you say the blessing, please?"

Adam took his wife's hand on one side and his son's on the other. Everyone else reached to join hands around the table too, a circle of family and of strangers becoming family.

Del's breath caught as RJ's fingers touched hers. She slid her hand into his, and the warmth of his fingers enveloped hers, gentle and firm. She bowed her head, her heart full.

"Father, we thank you," Adam began.

Thank you, Father, she echoed within.

"We thank you for this place you have given to shelter those you bring to this town, for the creativity that brought the idea to the Nielsen sisters, and for those who have so skillfully executed it. We thank you for all our friends around this table and their faithful work to make this dream happen. We thank you that the liquor tent has left our town and for your continued protection and grace. We thank you for this food, for each other, and most of all, for your presence and love through Jesus our Lord. Amen."

Conversation flowed as plates were filled, passed, and emptied.

"I think the big stove cooks lots better," Robbie announced, holding his plate out for thirds.

Everyone laughed.

"I might have to agree with you there, my friend." William pierced a carrot with his fork. "That or I'm just too plumb tuckered of my own cookin.'"

"Me too." Jesse punctuated his words with another helping of roast, sparking more chuckles.

"So you really think the liquor tent is gone for good?" Lilac asked.

"I believe so." Adam buttered one of Climie's melt-in-your-mouth rolls. "Isaac rode out there today and said there's no sign of it but a bare patch, some broken bottles, and other refuse."

"We should get a group out there to clean up." RJ glanced around at his men. "Maybe tomorrow, if you can spare us from the boardinghouse?"

Nods all around.

"Shall we just postpone the temperance rally for now, then?" Del asked. "It seems we've got plenty to do, getting ready for the school raising and opening the boardinghouse."

"I hate to let it go, though." Lilac's brow puckered. "The abuse of alcohol isn't going to stop hurting families just because it's harder to find. People make liquor out of whatever they have at hand if they want it. Even Mr. Jorgensen stocks some liquor in his store."

"Only for medicinal purposes."

"So he says. But he can't control how people use it." Lilac leaned forward. "I'd like to start a women's temperance society in Salton, like Ma used to be part of back home."

"Maybe you will." Lark reached across the table to squeeze her hand. "But I think Del is right. Let's at least get the schoolhouse up first."

"Speaking of the schoolhouse, is there anything else you need from me for the raising next week?" RJ cocked his head and speared a bite of roast.

"I think we're just about set. The women are bringing food, and the supplies are almost all here. You'll organize the men and supervise the building, for which I'm ever grateful." Del smiled at him.

"Anything for you, Miss Nielsen." His mouth tipped up, and her pulse quickened at the warmth in his brown eye. Did he mean it?

A sudden explosion shattered the glass in the window behind William's head. As he leaped out of the way, a lit torch landed in the middle of the table.

Screams, shouts. Some men jumped up, others dropped low. Adam shoved Forsythia and the children to the floor, Robbie and Sofie wailing.

Lark and RJ leaped to douse the flames spreading over the tablecloth. "More water!"

Del dashed for the kitchen, coming back with a sloshing water pitcher. She splashed it over the smoldering fire just as a second shot ran out.

RJ threw himself over her, pushing her to the floor.

"Get out here, RJ Easton!" a raucous voice hollered. "I know you're in there, you son of a—" A spew of cursing followed.

"W-what's g-going on?" Jesse shielded Climie, who cowered in the corner.

RJ's face hardened. Without a word, he leaped off Del, grabbed his rifle, and ran for the entry.

"RJ, wait!" Del cried out, scrambling to her feet. She lunged after him, Adam right behind her, but RJ was already out the door.

Lark snatched Del back, holding her tight. She fought her sister's grasp, then pressed her hands to her mouth.

RJ, no!

A heavy body tackled RJ from the side as soon as he rushed out the door.

Realizing his rashness too late, RJ rolled with the attacker across the boardinghouse porch and down the steps. His rifle fell uselessly to the side.

The man pummeled RJ's shoulders and back, and RJ struggled to turn over, kicking at his assailant. Memories flashed—the Confederate renegade, the knife, his eye. Did this man have a knife?

With a sudden burst, RJ wrenched himself over onto his back and kneed the man in the groin. Howling with pain, his attacker rolled off for an instant, and RJ scrambled to his feet, bent to attack, breathing hard.

Another howl, this time of rage, and Clive Johnson flung himself at RJ again, catching him around the waist and trying to drag him down. RJ grasped Clive's shoulders, straining to wrestle him to the ground.

"You," Clive spat into his face, his breath putrid. "You took everything. Wasn't enough to take one job away. Now you got me fired from the only other place that would have me."

The liquor tent? Had Johnson been paid as a bouncer there or something? RJ struggled to think, using all his strength to stay upright. Clive didn't look like a powerful man, but liquor evidently gave him liquid strength as well as courage.

Shifting his weight, RJ pushed his foot against Clive's ankle, knocking him off balance, then threw him to the ground, kneeling on his arms. "When a man attacks innocent people and destroys a family"—RJ snatched a breath—"I say he gets what he deserves."

Clive stared up at him, blinking hatred. "I woulda killed that boy if'n he hadn't been so feisty."

RJ slammed his first into Clive's face.

Clive spewed blood and foul words. He yanked his arm from

beneath RJ's knee and thrust upward with a small blade he must have had hidden in his belt, slicing RJ's arm.

RJ caught Clive's wrist before the knife reached his face, but Johnson pushed against him, their strength matched. RJ strove to force the other man's arm back down, the blade winking at him in the moonlight. His breath came in gasps.

Lord, help. Everyone in the boardinghouse—please, please, don't let anyone else get hurt.

"You can freeze right there, mister." Not far above them, a rifle cocked.

Clive Johnson glanced up to see Larkspur Nielsen standing a few yards away, rifle poised and aimed.

"You have three seconds to drop that knife and leave these parts, never to show your face here again." Her words sparked fire. "Or I will shoot. And as anyone around here can tell you, I do not shoot to miss."

RJ took the instant of distraction to wrest the knife from Clive's grip and fling it away. Clive stared from Lark to RJ for a moment, chest heaving. Then he scrambled out from under RJ and took off into the darkness so fast that all they could hear was the sigh of the night wind in the dry prairie grasses.

"RJ." Del came running from the porch and fell to her knees beside him, lifting his arm. "You're bleeding."

Light-headed, he let her and Lark help him up the steps and onto a chair in the dining room, where Adam examined his bicep.

"Only a flesh wound, but it's deep and will need stitches. Del, keep the pressure on it, and I'll run back to get my bag. I'll only be a few minutes. Forsythia, I think he'll be all right, but watch him for shock." Adam stood. "Everyone else, clear out. Give him room to breathe."

Lark and Lilac shepherded out the children, the workmen following with sober faces. RJ leaned his head against the back of the chair and closed his eye, his heart still pounding, the gash on his arm burning like fire.

But more than the receding fear, more than the pain, a deep thankfulness throbbed through him. He hadn't had to take another life. And Clive wouldn't be back, judging by that look of terror on his cowardly face.

Del adjusted the dish towel on his arm. "You foolish man, you could have been killed." Her voice caught.

RJ opened his eye and smiled at her. "But I wasn't." And he had been able to protect those he cared for—no, those he loved. The Brownsvilles and Nielsens, William and Jesse.

And having Delphinium Nielsen's gentle hands pressing the dish towel to his arm made a knife wound seem a petty price to pay.

The look in her gray-blue eyes, so near his own, made him swallow. Might she feel the same way?

28

Lord, please. Not snow.

Peering out the soddy window the morning of the school raising, Del felt her heart sink. The falling flakes were tiny and scattered, but a thin dusting already veiled the ground. She'd so hoped and prayed against this.

"Don't look so glum, Miss Schoolmarm." Lark rattled the stove lids as she got the fire going for breakfast. "I don't think it'll stick."

"I hope not." Del shivered and held out her hands to the growing warmth. "This is only one reason I wanted the school built months ago." Old resentments threatened once more.

"Ah, ah." Lark held up a warning finger, but her eyes were gentle. "Let's not get into if-onlys today."

"You're right." *Forgive me, Lord.* Del straightened her shoulders and drew a breath. "Shall I mix the biscuits?"

"Yes, and then we'll tuck the ham inside and eat in the wagon. I know you want to get there early."

"How many children should I bring drawing supplies for?" Lilac held a stack of precious paper and a basket of pencils. Lilac and the children were planning to draw pictures to decorate the walls of the new school, and when they grew restless, there would be games or she would read to them.

"Well, some of the older boys will be helping with the building, and the girls with the food. We've got over twenty students all together now, though, so I'd say enough for twelve to fifteen."

"I think I've got enough, then."

"I'd love you to do more art with the children this next term." As Del hoped to do with music and botany in the spring. The new goals seemed endless. But exciting.

True to Lark's prediction, the scattered snow flurries had mostly stopped by the time their wagon pulled up at the school site a short ways off Main Street but not far from the church and center of town.

RJ was already there, checking the placement of the stones, which his workmen had found and laid last week to be ready to hold the joists today. Straightening, he waved at them with a grin. He wore his felt hat pulled down low over his ears and the collar of his overcoat turned up against the November chill.

Del climbed down from the wagon and hurried toward him, gladness warming her at the sight of him. "You're here even before the schoolmarm. How is your arm?" She couldn't see the bandage bulge under the thickness of his coat sleeve.

"Healing well, the doctor says." RJ flexed it and winced. "I just have to be a bit careful using it. But I think everything is in order." He nodded at the lumber stacked off to the side. "I've made note of how many we have of the different pieces and what goes where, so we can divide into teams and get it done faster."

"You really are an engineer, aren't you?" Del pressed her mittened hands together. "I can hardly believe this is really happening."

"You deserve this." He stepped nearer, his breath warming the air between them.

Del gazed up at him, memorizing the lines of his face, the

breadth of his shoulders under the woolen coat. She'd only seen him twice since that dreadful night at the boardinghouse. The memory of the choking fear when Clive Johnson raised his knife shook her again, and she clenched her fingers to keep from reaching for him. That wouldn't be proper.

RJ stepped back, nodding over her shoulder. "Looks like our workers are arriving."

Del hurried off to greet the wagons of parents and children, willing her pulse to calm. She really must sift through all these feelings, and soon.

Mothers left towel-wrapped dishes nestled in quilts in wagon beds. They would be set upon plank tables that the boys would put together later. Isaac McTavish cleared a spot bare of grass and started a fire to heat the coffeepots, not to mention serve as a place to warm hands. Children dashed about, the excitement of the day bursting forth in whoops of laughter and the occasional tumble from the little ones.

Del scanned the gathering. With all the rushing about, it was hard to keep track, but she saw no sign of the Kinsleys anywhere. Not that she should be surprised. But how were they faring? Climie was still going out every day for a while to help Margaret, the two women doubtless finding much in common. Hopefully healing as well as heartache.

"Perhaps I should take the children over to the church?" Lilac asked.

"After the blessing." Del drew a breath, her lungs cramped from the cold air and so much happening so fast. She nodded to Mr. Caldwell.

The attorney raised his voice and hands to get everyone's attention. "Let's get gathered together."

The men turned from joking and exchanging reports on their harvests, and mothers shushed babies and grabbed stray children.

"This is a special day for Salton." Mr. Caldwell smiled out over the gathering. "Our teacher, Miss Delphinium Nielsen, has tirelessly persevered in teaching our students since the destruction of our schoolhouse over a year ago. And she has just as tirelessly campaigned for a replacement to that building, even if at first we didn't listen to her as well as we ought."

Chuckles of acknowledgment ran through the crowd. Del's cheeks warmed, but she kept her gaze on her students, gathered near and listening now. They had made it all worth it.

"But dedication and perseverance can accomplish much. Especially when we come together, as our womenfolk have shown us. So today it is my great joy to commence the raising of the Salton school. Reverend Pritchard, would you open us in prayer?"

The slender young preacher stepped forward. "Let us pray. Father in heaven, we thank you for the gift of education, for providing a place for that education for the children of this town, both in our church and now here in our new schoolhouse. Bless us as we raise it today, give skill to our hands and protection as we build. Bless each child who comes to learn under this roof. Let them gain not only knowledge and skill but also understanding of your love. And bless Miss Nielsen for her dedication and service. In the name of Jesus Christ we pray, Amen."

Amens, then scattered applause and a cheer or two.

Rev. Pritchard met Del's eyes for a moment, and his mouth tipped in an understanding smile. She smiled back, believing he now read friendship and respect in her gaze. Then he moved back to join the gathering, and at Mr. Caldwell's nod, RJ stepped forward to stand before the laid foundation.

"We'll begin with one team framing and laying the plank floor while two teams of three build the framework of the walls on the ground. We plan to raise the walls before dinner, then some workers will start on the siding while others frame the roof. Getting it shingled . . ." He shook his head. "The finishing work may have to be done next Saturday, but we'll do the best we can today."

"Let's get movin', then." From the back of the crowd, Anthony Armstead raised his hammer in the air, grinning.

RJ grinned back, then divided the men into teams, placing Mr. O'Rourke, Jesse, William, and several of his other workmen in charge of the different groups. Soon the music of hammers and saws rang out over the gathering, sending a thrill through Del's limbs. Her school . . . finally.

While the men were getting started, the women gathered the children together and walked the school-age ones to the church, then took the little ones to the Brownsville house. The nursing mothers stayed there to assist, and the others returned to the church, both to help Lilac and the children and to form a sewing circle in one corner.

Del and Lark remained at the building site to maintain the fire, pass out hot coffee when needed, and settle the pots of stew into the coals.

"I think I'd better go help Lilac," Del said when all was running smoothly.

Lark nodded and set another chunk of wood on the block to split.

Inside the church, Del hung up her coat and rubbed her hands on her upper arms. It was too cold outside to be standing around. She smiled at the hum of voices—the children talking with Lilac, and the women visiting as they stitched on whatever handwork they brought.

Del made her way between the rows of tables and benches, admiring what the children were drawing. "Oh, Betsy, what a lovely dragonfly."

Betsy Jorgensen swung back her pigtails. "It's like one I drew on our trip to the salt marshes, Miss Nielsen. But I want to add colors to this one, purple and blue and green and gold. Miss Lilac said she's going to get colored paints for us soon."

"That's the dream." Del smiled over the children's heads at her sister.

"I want to add flowers around it too, and maybe a rabbit. Is that all right, even though I didn't see any at the salt marshes?" Betsy craned her head to look up at Del, a frown pinching her freckled nose.

"Using your imagination is perfectly all right." Del squeezed Betsy's shoulder. "These pictures will be like beautiful stories covering our walls."

"Look, Miss Nielsen." Across the table, Iris O'Rourke looked up, her piquant little face alight. "I'm drawing a scene from that storybook you lent Timothy and me." She turned her paper to show a lively sketch of a tall man bent over a castle peopled with tiny Lilliputians.

"That's delightful, Iris. You seem to have quite the artistic eye." It was always a new surprise with the O'Rourke family. What a mercy their father had let Timothy resume his extra studies after harvest. Under both her and RJ's tutelage, he was progressing well.

One of the boys heard shouting and ran to the window. "Come look. Come look."

All the children ran to peer outside. The women snatched their shawls and headed outside to set up dinner, followed by the children as soon as they bundled up.

With RJ calling commands to keep them in unison, four teams of men raised the four framed walls of the school. The women and children cheered as the frames settled onto the plank floor. With long braces pounded into place, the corners were nailed together and braces placed across the upper corners to keep the frame secure until the beam and rafters were hoisted. Above them, the sun broke through the clouds, touching the wooden beams with its rays in blessing. Several men threw their hats into the air and clapped one another on the shoulder.

"Good work, men." RJ squinted up at the sun. "It looks to be close to noon. Let's have dinner."

Talking, laughing. The pale sun warmed everyone's shoulders as they filled their plates and found places to sit down to eat, piles of lumber doubling as chairs.

Del, sitting on their blanket with her sisters and Forsythia's family, kept glancing at the half-built schoolhouse, where RJ and several of his workmen ate cross-legged within the open-framed walls.

"Shouldn't we invite them to eat with us? Jesse, William . . . RJ." Her tongue caught on the last name. Del dropped her gaze to her plate and hid her heating face by taking a bite of beef stew.

"Maybe they don't want to cause more trouble," Lark said.

"About William, you mean?" Lilac passed the basket of bread and cheese they had brought. "Surely not now."

"Ah, little sister." Lark shook her head. "I wish I still had your optimism about human nature."

"But look." Del nodded at Curtis Jeffers and Thomas Dwyer approaching William and Jesse, ball in hand. The boys said something, and Jesse shook his head, but William grinned and pushed to his feet. Soon the three of them were tossing the ball back and forth in the soon-to-be schoolyard, William proving to have quite a good throwing arm.

"See?" Lilac nudged Lark's arm. "There is hope."

"Hope for what?"

Del looked up to see RJ standing beside them. She pushed to her feet, hoping she didn't have gravy on her chin. "The school is looking wonderful."

"We'd best get back to work." RJ glanced at the sky. "This time of year the day will be gone before we know it, and we've still got hours of labor to get the roof on." A shy grin snuck across his face. "But I'm glad you like it."

"Del." Lark laid a hand on Del's arm. "Look."

Another wagon had pulled up, stopping a short distance away. A young man climbed down, then a woman who Del realized was Climie. They both reached to assist a quilt-wrapped woman out of the back of the wagon. Two children jumped down from the back, and then together—slowly, as if unsure whether they were welcome—the group approached the gathering.

Tears blurred Del's vision. She pressed her hand tight over Lark's, then hurried to welcome them.

"It's so good to see you, Margaret." Gently, Del embraced Mrs. Kinsley, the ponderance of her belly between them.

"Sorry we're so late." Margaret pulled back with a faint smile, then took the arm of the lanky young man beside her. "Miss Nielsen, this is my oldest son, Alexander. He was workin' way west of here on the railroad and finally got the telegram the doctor sent to one of the towns along their way."

"It's wonderful to meet you," Del said.

Alexander shook her hand. He was quiet, but he met her eyes frankly. She liked him.

"Home again, thanks be to God." Margaret glanced up at him, pride mingled with the grief lining her face. "I'm hopin' he might find a job closer to home, but we got all the fall work to do on the farm first."

"I'm sure some of the men in town might be able to help again. In the meantime, please come get some dinner." Del gestured toward the tables. "There's still plenty left."

Bethany and John looked at their mother and, at her nod, ran for dishes.

Del helped fill a plate for Mrs. Kinsley, then Alexander. She scanned the gathering for a welcoming spot. There, the Weber family, sitting on another lumber pile. She'd never seen Rebecca Weber be anything less than kind to everyone.

"May we join you?" Del smiled at Rebecca, who held her littlest one on her lap. Her other children were off making a game of picking up chunks of leftover lumber and tossing them on a growing pile. Her husband and all the other men were back to working on the schoolhouse.

Rebecca looked up, smiled at Mrs. Kinsley, and stood. "Of course. Here, you sit in my place on that blanket."

Together, she and Del settled Margaret with another folded blanket behind her so she could lean against the Webers' picnic basket.

"Sorry to be such trouble," Margaret murmured, her pale face flushing from the effort.

"No trouble at all. Goodness, with this last one, I felt I needed a locomotive to haul me around at the end." Rebecca held corn bread crumbs on her hand for her toddler, who picked up the crumbs, stuffing them in his mouth. "When are you expecting?"

"Was thinking late January, but I must have misjudged." Mrs. Kinsley put a hand to her belly and shifted herself back, wincing. "I don't think this one will wait that long."

"And how have you been feeling lately?" Del handed her the plate.

"A little better these last few days. The doctor gave me some sort of tonic, told me to eat more beef and greens. I wasn't sure how we'd manage that, but the doctor's wife sent some, and everyone has been so kind. It seems every day or so, someone shows up with a basket, ever since Tom . . ." Her chin wobbled, but she clenched it firm. "I still don't know how to thank everyone for gettin' in our harvest like you did."

Del's throat tightened. "That's what neighbors do."

"I know what everyone must think of Tom." Margaret's thin cheeks quivered. "But he wasn't all bad . . . not always like there

at the end. He used to be good to me and the children. It's just
. . . ever since we came to Nebraska, our troubles never stopped.
And when we got hit by the grasshoppers this summer, it about
broke him. Then with the liquor tent so handy . . . he never had
much willpower, my Tom."

Yet his family had loved him. Del saw that now and had heard
it in Adam's account of Bethany washing her father as he died.

She squeezed Mrs. Kinsley's cold hand. If only she knew what
to say. "Glad we can be of help." The words broke around the
tears clogging her throat.

"Thank you." Margaret dashed her hand at the tears slipping
down her cheeks, then managed a smile and lifted her fork. "I
guess I better eat some of this before I drown it."

"Del!"

At Lark's call, Del excused herself and headed over to her
sister, sniffing hard. "What is it?"

Lark motioned toward the school. "They need to ask you
about something with the building."

Jesse appeared in the open-framed doorway. "M-Mr. Easton
just wanted to check—you want one room or t-two?"

"One big one is fine for now." Del peeked inside, excitement
pricking her middle again to see the classroom taking shape,
even if the walls and roof had yet to be filled in. "We could
divide it into two later on, right?"

"Should be able to." Jesse nodded. "Thanks, we just wanted
to be s-sure."

"How does it feel to see it finally coming together?" Lark
linked her arm through Del's as they headed back to the church
to check on Lilac and the children.

"It's . . . rather hard to believe, I suppose." Del paused as she
opened the door. "Look, the Kinsley children are joining in.
They must have eaten fast."

She walked over to the table where Lilac had supplied the

newcomers with pencils and paper. Bethany looked up with a shy smile.

"Hello, Bethany. It's so good to see you." And to see no remaining trace of the bruise around her eye. *Oh, Lord, may the wounds inside heal as well.* Del moved closer and gave the little girl's shoulders a hug. "What are you drawing?"

"It's a windmill. Pa told me about them once and said maybe we could have one someday."

Del's throat tightened again. "Very good. And, John, is that a field of wheat?"

The boy nodded, eyes on the paper. "Yes."

Del gripped the edge of the table to steady herself. Adam had said he'd heard John speak that night when he came to get help for his father, and of course she knew he spoke to his family. But she'd never heard his voice before herself.

"It's lovely." Del forced her own voice to stay even. She bent to John's level. "Are those men harvesting it?"

John nodded. "Like those 'uns who came and helped my pa."

"You worked that day too. I saw you." Del touched his shoulder gently, and he didn't flinch away. Much. "You both have been a wonderful help to your family."

John hung his head a moment, then looked up and met her eyes, tears in his. "I miss my pa. Even though he was mean sometimes."

Del swallowed hard. "I know."

"I prayed Pa would stop drinking," Bethany said, her voice small. "Do you think that's why God made him die?"

"Oh, dear one." Del covered the little girl's hand, still around her pencil, with her own. She bent to look into Bethany's eyes. "No, no, my dear, none of this is your fault. There's so much in this world we don't understand and won't until heaven." Her voice caught. "All I know for sure is that the Lord promised to be right with us through it all."

"He was there that night Pa died." Bethany nibbled her lip. John stared at his sister. "Who? Pa?"

"God, silly." Bethany shook her head at him. "I didn't see Him, but I knew He was there." She looked up at Del. "You know what I mean, Miss Nielsen?"

Del managed a smile. "I do." *Oh, Lord, I think I do. I pray I do.* With a final touch to each of the children, she hurried away.

Lark found her a little while later in the cloakroom while Lilac was reading to the children. Del had her head buried in her coat sleeve as she leaned against the wall.

"There you are." Lark tucked a handkerchief into the damp crook of Del's arm. "What's wrong? Del, what is it?"

"John spoke." Del sniffled and mopped her face with the handkerchief. "Did you hear?"

"I did." Lark rubbed her shoulder in small soothing circles.

"It's just . . . so hard." Del blew her nose and drew a long breath. "Life, sometimes, you know?"

Lark hugged her. "That's why we need the hope of heaven. Oh, my dear sister." She blew out a tear-tinged breath. "I know something else: they've almost finished framing the roof. Want to come see?"

"Already?" Del wiped her cheeks and followed Lark out the door toward the schoolhouse site. The sun was heading fast toward the western horizon, already starting to gild the gray autumn clouds with crimson and gold.

"There you are." RJ climbed down from nailing a rafter to the center beam. "We were wondering what happened to the teacher." He came to stand by her and surveyed the building. "What do you think?"

Del shook her head, swallowing back tears again. "It's wonderful." The walls were in various stages of sided in with an open doorway and spaces left for the windows, which would soon be set with glass panes donated by the Youngs.

"I'd like to build you a bell tower, but that might have to come later." RJ shoved his hands deeper into his coat pockets as the air chilled. "But we should be able to get the roof on next Saturday."

"So we can move into the school in time for our Thanksgiving program the following week." Del rubbed her arms and shook her head again in wonder.

"The interior won't be completed."

"It doesn't matter." She paused to swallow again. "RJ, I can't tell you how grateful I am."

He shrugged, still scanning the structure with his critical engineer's eye. "It was all of us. I didn't do much."

"Yes, you did." She turned toward him, willing him to hear how much she meant it. There was so much this man had done for them all since he came to this town. How could she have ever thought him heartless and cold?

He looked at her then, a depth of feeling in that warm brown eye that caught her in the chest and sent a thrill down her arms. Something trembled between them, fragile and precious. RJ drew a breath as if about to say something more. He reached to take her mittened hand in his.

"Hey, Boss, anything else you want done tonight?"

The tender thread between them broke. Lowering his hand, RJ turned to answer his workman's call.

Del's shoulders slumped. What had he been about to say?

Shivering as the evening breeze rose, she hurried to the remaining wagons to thank the adults and bid her students good-bye. She hugged Forsythia and the children, promising to see them at church in the morning, then looked around for the Kinsleys, but they had already left. *Thank you, Lord, for bringing Alexander back to his family. Please bring your healing and provide for them.* So much abuse and heartache they had to overcome.

She had to pause and nod. Her mother's voice rang as clearly as if she were standing right there. *"Nothing was or is or ever will be impossible with God."*

She searched the falling darkness of the empty schoolyard for RJ, then saw the shadow of Captain riding away with a familiar figure on his back.

Disappointment panged sharp. But he had no reason to stay to say good-bye. They had no understanding.

Another thought blasted her. In her contract as a school-marm, she couldn't even consider marriage as long as she was teaching. She puffed out a breath and headed for the wagon where her sisters waited. The idea probably hadn't even crossed RJ's mind.

But logic did little to ease the longing ache in her heart.

Lord, do I . . . do I love RJ Easton?

29

He was in love with Delphinium Nielsen.

RJ let Captain have his head across the darkening prairie, hardly feeling the November wind whistle past his ears and beneath his eye patch. He'd told Adam and Forsythia he needed to let Captain get some exercise after the school raising tonight, but in truth, it was RJ who needed the ride. Time alone with only his horse, the night air, and God. To think, to pray—he was glad he'd learned to pray again in this healing little town amid the wilds of Nebraska.

To try to make sense of the emotions swirling around his heart.

When had it happened? He reined Captain in a bit, not wanting the horse to stumble in the darkness. When had she gone from being an infuriating woman whose mind he couldn't make heads or tails of to one who seemed the very heartbeat of his soul? With Del he felt like himself again, whole despite his missing eye. He had gotten to know her, that's all—the real Del, who poured herself out for her students, who gave selflessly to others, whose passion for teaching went far beyond that required by her job. The Del who stayed after school to help Timothy when she had twenty other students' work to grade and two family businesses to help run. The Del who cleaned up a drunken father's mess and spooned stew into his ailing wife with as much care as she gave to each of the children entrusted to her teaching.

The Del who had looked at him tonight with her heart in her eyes and tears on her cheeks, until it took all that was in him not to catch her in his arms and kiss those tears away.

He'd never known Francine like this, he realized with a twist in his chest. Odd, since they'd grown up together. But it was a parallel life, not one that entwined minds and hearts. They hadn't eased the suffering of others together or even shared their own. Francine hadn't *had* suffering, far as he knew. Perhaps that was why she hadn't been able to handle the news of his injury and shifted to something easier—someone easier. And thus showed him he'd never really known her at all.

Not that he'd pretend to know Del fully yet. The mysteries of a woman weren't to take lightly, his pa had told him once. But he wanted to . . . *Lord, I want to.*

Stars pricked cold overhead, the wind shifting and temperature dropping still more. RJ wheeled Captain around to head back toward town, wisdom dictating he shouldn't stay out too long in this weather.

What to do, then? Custom would dictate approaching her father, but she didn't have one. Anders, then—if only he weren't hundreds of miles away.

RJ sighed and bent his head over his horse's patient neck. *Lord, I've spent enough time following my own stubborn head over things. Show me the way here. And if this is my will only and not yours . . .* He paused, swallowing back the rebellion. Surely he'd learned by now it wasn't worth it, not in the long run. *Then your will be done. But if you would make a way for Del and me, please, show me what it is.*

That Saturday, while finishing the roof of the schoolhouse with William and Jesse and some of the others, an answer came so suddenly that RJ dropped his hammer, which clattered down the shingles to fall to the ground below.

"All right up there, Mr. Easton?" William craned his neck to look up at him.

"Sorry." RJ's neck heated. He never dropped his tools. It was a pure mercy it hadn't hit anyone. "I guess I'm getting clumsy." Or woman-addled. If this was a sample of his brain on love, heaven help his employees.

As evening approached, RJ headed to the train station. He stepped into the telegraph office operated by Edward Owens, a lanky man who had been a supervisor on the railroad but decided a quieter job was more to his taste. He managed the mail now too.

"To whom?" Mr. Owens asked, peering at RJ from behind the counter.

"Anders Nielsen, Linksburg, Ohio." RJ hesitated. "You have paper I can write the message on?"

Mr. Owens pushed a small sheet across the counter to him. RJ chewed his lip a moment, then bent over and wrote.

Dear Anders STOP I want to marry your sister STOP

He halted. He better specify which one.

Delphinium STOP Requesting your permission to court her STOP
Please reply immediately STOP Robert Joseph Easton

There. RJ blew out a breath and passed the paper over, grateful Mr. Owens appeared to be a discreet fellow—or at least largely uninterested in anything but his own affairs.

Now he had only to wait for Anders's reply.

It still had not come Monday, when RJ helped the Nielsens and a number of other Salton families move the desks, benches, and books into the new schoolhouse, ready for their first day of classes in the new space.

Wednesday afternoon, RJ stopped again at the telegraph office before the Thanksgiving program. It would be held at the school in honor of tomorrow's holiday and in celebration of the new building.

But the office stood empty, the telegraph machine silent. RJ drummed his fingers on the counter for a few minutes, waiting, then gave up and stopped back at the Brownsvilles' before heading to the school. Wherever Edward Owens was, RJ wouldn't let his own impatience make him miss the presentation Del and the children had worked so hard to prepare. But why hadn't Anders replied? Did he think RJ unworthy of his sister? He wasn't wrong, if so.

Warmth and laughter swelled the school building along with the scent of fresh-cut wood. The benches were filled so tightly with parents that RJ barely found a spot to stand against the back wall. He smiled to see Del up front, reassuring nervous students, fixing the untied hair ribbon of an eager little girl, whispering last instructions to the older ones.

He glanced over the gathering. Forsythia and Adam sat near the front, Robbie and Sofie beside them, Mikael on Forsythia's lap. Nearby sat the Caldwells, Youngs, and Jorgensens, and near the middle was Mr. O'Rourke with his wife. RJ had spoken with him about Timothy while they were doing finishing work on the boardinghouse the other day, and while O'Rourke was still cautious, he seemed more open to Timothy pursuing his passion for mathematics and even possibly going to college . . . someday. Near the back sat Mrs. Kinsley and her older son. RJ hoped she was well enough to be out, but doubtless she'd push through just about anything to see her children tonight.

Other single men stood with RJ in the back, along with some late-coming parents. He caught William's eye and nodded, grateful there seemed to be no fuss about his presence here today. Next to him stood Jesse and Isaac McTavish, a man RJ wanted to get to know better. Yet already, it seemed, he knew more friends and acquaintances in this little town than he had in a long time—since the war for certain, perhaps even since he lost his parents.

"Welcome, everyone." Ever the schoolmarm, Del clapped her hands to gain the attention of the room. Murmuring and rustling stilled. She smiled over the gathering, neat and proper in a gown of gray-blue wool that brought out the startling color of her eyes, wisps of pale brown hair escaping from her snood and curling about her face.

RJ swallowed hard at the loveliness of her.

"What a joy it is to gather here today in our new school building, made possible by the hard work of so many of you. I've asked Reverend Pritchard to open us in prayer, and then our program will begin."

The minister stepped forward, and all bowed their heads, but RJ couldn't concentrate on the words. All he could think of was Del, how he loved her, and the telegram that hadn't come. He squeezed his eyes tight, feeling the pull of the scar. *Lord, if this is not what you have for me, help me be content. Let me not turn away from you again just because I don't get my way.*

At strains of music, RJ jerked his head up, having missed the *Amen*. The schoolchildren filled the front of the room, a choir in two lines, little ones in front and taller behind. Lark and Lilac led off to the side with fiddle and guitar, since the piano remained at the church, though he'd heard talk of the Caldwells shipping one out for the school. Del conducted with simple hand gestures as the children launched into "We Gather Together," their voices high and clear.

"We gather together to ask the Lord's blessing;
He chastens and hastens His will to make known;
The wicked oppressing now cease from distressing;
Sing praises to His name; He forgets not His own . . ."

A rather fitting summing up of this fall in Salton, RJ thought.
They sang all three verses, ending with a final harmonizing
note and a burst of applause from the parents. Beaming, Del
nodded for the children to bow, which they did in tolerable
unison.

"Now we will have some demonstrations of all we have
learned this term. First, our older students will give us an ex-
hibition of mental arithmetic."

Timothy O'Rourke stepped forward, dark hair slicked back
with water and collar stiff with starch, along with Elsie Weber,
Henry Crawford, and a couple of sixth-reader students RJ
didn't know. Del posed a dozen complicated conundrums to
the students, and while all did well, Timothy shone. When he
finished with no errors and received the prize for top marks
in mathematics this term, the boy caught RJ's eye and smiled.
RJ grinned back, feeling his chest expand. He'd be dashed if
Nebraska wouldn't hear of Timothy O'Rourke someday.

Next the middle grades held a spelling bee, with first prize
earned by Bethany Ann Kinsley. She scampered back to join
her mother, a shy smile lighting her face. So much heartache
that little one had borne already in her short life. Hopefully this
would be the beginning of a new season.

By the time the littlest ones had all taken turns reciting poems
and the students closed the program with "Now Thank We All
Our God," RJ was ready to step away from the wall where he'd
been leaning and stretch his legs. As the schoolroom swarmed
with children and parents, he headed outside where others also
snatched a breath of fresh night air, even if cold. The clouds that

had gathered all day hung silent and heavy, perhaps bringing the long-awaited snow.

Isaac McTavish joined him and held out a cup. "The ladies are servin' hot cider inside. Thought maybe you could use some."

"Why me?" RJ accepted the tin cup with a nod of thanks.

"Just had that look about you." Isaac gave his enigmatic smile.

RJ didn't press the point. He sipped the hot brew, sweet and spicy. "Good to have you back in these parts. Thanks for your help with that liquor tent business. I've been meaning to ask, how was it working on the railroad?"

"Hard work, good pay. I helped lay the Union Pacific nigh clear to North Platte. But I decided I didn't want to be snowbound in a railroad car all winter, so I headed back this direction." Isaac tipped back his felt hat, his eyes pensive. "These parts have the nearest I know to kin anyplace in the country."

Strange that RJ was beginning to feel that way too. Little would he have guessed it six months ago.

"Ah, there you are, Mr. Easton." At the nasally voice, RJ turned to see Edward Owens approach. "You didn't stop at the telegraph office today."

"I did, but you weren't there."

"Well, since you've been so impatient, I took a guess you'd be here tonight and brought it with me." Mr. Owens held out a slip of paper.

RJ snatched the telegram, then hesitated, suddenly aware of the two men watching him. "Excuse me." He hurried around the corner of the schoolhouse.

Alone in the darkness, he closed his eye for a moment. Drawing a long breath, he held the paper up to the square of yellow light from the nearby window and read the neatly typed lines.

Dear RJ STOP Del knows her own mind STOP If you hurt her you'll
answer to me STOP But permission granted STOP Godspeed my
friend STOP Anders

RJ released the breath and leaned his head back against the
fresh plank wall of the schoolhouse. His heart pounded against
twin waves of exhilaration and terror.

He had his answer. Now he had to do something about it.

It had gone so well.

Del surveyed the schoolroom now that everyone else had
left save her sisters, who waited for her in the wagon outside.

Her schoolroom. Despite the crumbs and mud scuffs lingering on the floor—and an unfortunate spot near the door where
someone had spilled an entire cup of cider—her eyes lingered
lovingly over it all. The walls bedecked with student drawings,
now made brilliant with watercolor paints under Lilac's tutelage. They'd even made frames out of some leftover lumber. The
desks and benches were back in neat rows, and the bookshelves
fixed to the side walls housed what meager library she had so
far. Hopefully someday they would be full.

So many had given so much for this school to happen. Families had given of their time and labor to build it, some donating
extra lumber when the materials needed had exceeded the sum
they'd raised last year. The shiny potbellied stove in the center
of the building had been generously gifted by the Jorgensens.
The windowpanes were from the Youngs, along with the sturdy
wooden door. Behind her desk, which was crafted by Jesse, hung
a beautiful world map from the Caldwells, along with framed
blackboards, again thanks to Jesse and William.

And most precious of all, the notes handed shyly to her by

many of her students tonight, still lying unread on her desk. Del ran her fingers over them, then opened one.

Dear Miss Nielsen, you are the best teacher ever. Thank you for making school fun. Love, Josie Jeffers

Del smiled, a lump in her throat. She unfolded another.

Miss Nielsen, thank you for helping my family. I hope you never leave our school. I love you. Bethany Ann Kinsley

Tears pricked in earnest now. Del gathered the notes and stuffed them in her satchel. She shouldn't read them all now, not with her family waiting for her out in the cold.

"Some program, Miss Nielsen."

Del whirled around. RJ stood near the stove, hands in the pockets of his overcoat.

"RJ." She laid a hand against her chest, her heart thudding more from his presence than startlement. "I thought you'd left."

"Nope." He just stood there for a moment, surveying the room as she had. "You did a fine job tonight."

"So did you, on this building." Del gestured about her. "It's more beautiful than I'd dreamed."

"I'm glad you like it." His gaze warmed, resting on her face with a tenderness that made her stomach flip.

"I'm afraid I have to go." Del forced herself to reach for her coat, though everything in her wanted to stay, to talk to him, to—to touch him. *Delphinium Nielsen, what has come over you?* "My sisters have been waiting for me too long out in the wagon."

"They're gone. I asked Lark if I could drive you home."

Del stilled, her coat half on. "You did?" A trembling began in her middle. "Why?"

"Because I got a telegram from your brother today."

"Anders?" Her gaze swung to his face. "Is something wrong?"

"I guess that depends on you." He stepped closer, jamming his hands deeper into his pockets. "I—well, I asked his permission to court his sister. And he gave it." His Adam's apple convulsed.

Del gripped the chair behind her, so weak did her legs go. She looked up at him, the stiffness of his shoulders, the tremble in his jaw—why, he was as nervous as she was.

Her heart melted. She stepped near him and, suddenly bold, slid her hands into his. RJ's pulse thrummed against hers, his palms warm.

"Did he?" She tipped her head to the side. "Funny, I don't believe you've asked mine."

"I mean to." He swallowed again. "I just wanted to do things in the right order."

"Why?"

His brow creased. "Well, my pa always said—"

"No, I mean, why me?" Her cheeks heated, but she wanted to know.

He drew a breath, then pulled away one hand to tuck a stray wisp of hair behind her ear. "I guess because you're a woman I want to work alongside. A woman I trust, who seeks the good of others. Who leans on the Lord and is humble enough to admit when she forgets to." He hesitated, then leaned his head close to hers until their foreheads touched. "And most of all, Delphinium Nielsen, because I'm falling in love with you."

She caught her breath, the words spinning round and round within her until she thought her feet would lift from the ground.

But a sudden thought set them back on earth again. "RJ . . . I want to." *Oh, how I want to.* "But the school . . . by my contract, I'm forbidden to marry as long as I'm teaching. At least through this next term."

"Then it's a good thing I'm not asking you to marry me yet."

His chuckle warmed the air between their bent faces. "Though I might end up hard-pressed to wait until the end of the term."

Closing her eyes, she leaned her forehead against his shoulder. RJ's arms came around her, his chin resting atop her head. The thump of his heart beat against her, and Del let out the breath she had been holding. All at once, it seemed she'd found the place she'd been searching for longer than she knew.

"Does this mean I may drive you home, Miss Nielsen?"

She turned her head to lean her cheek against his shoulder and smiled. "It means I accept your suit, Mr. Easton. And yes, you may drive me home."

The night air hung quietly as they drove to the sod house, hardly a sound across the prairie but the creak of the gig RJ had borrowed from Adam for the night—seeming forethought, though he claimed he hadn't known Anders's answer until near evening's end.

Del pulled her mittened hand from beneath the buffalo robe and held it out to catch one of the sparkles drifting from the sky. "RJ, look." The delicate flake glimmered a moment on her mitten in the swinging lantern light, then faded. "Snow."

He chuckled. "Waited for your school, sure enough."

She tipped her face to the softly falling flakes, their feathery touch on her nose, eyelashes, cheeks. By the time they reached the Nielsen farm, the lantern showed a thickening blanket of white surrounding the soddy.

"I hope it won't be too heavy for you driving back." She took RJ's hand as he helped her dismount.

"Shouldn't be. It's steady but not thick." He drew her to him for a moment, gathering her hands between his. He glanced at the soddy, snug under its mantle of snow, light gleaming from the windows and the sturdy barn nearby. "It's truly remarkable what you ladies have built here already. I never heard of a family of sisters taking on so much. You make a man feel right indolent at times."

"I'd hardly say that." Del traced the lines of his face, gentled in the soft snowlight, eye patch and all. "You know, it was our dream from the start to someday all build homes on this land of ours. We've still got a whole half section we haven't done anything with yet."

"It was always my dream to design and build a home for my family one day," RJ murmured, his lips brushing her hair. "I started a design with Francine, but . . . well, you know what happened there."

"Perhaps you'll get a chance to finish it." And tossing aside any thought of sisters who might be watching at windows, Del lifted her face and kissed her one-eyed soldier in the falling snow.

Epilogue

I thought spring was here to stay.

Del stood in the doorway of the sod house and stared out over the white fields. The grass had thought so too, sending up enough shoots to create a blanket of green welcoming the sun. RJ wouldn't be happy if the snow had dampened his work on their house.

"Close the door. You're letting all the heat out," Lark grumbled from the stove, feeding the hungry flames so she could finish making breakfast.

Del lifted her coat off one of the wooden pegs in a board fixed to the sod wall. "I'll get the milking done. Has the cream been skimmed yet?" There was no school on Saturday, so she didn't have to be on her way to town by seven.

"Not that I know of, but then, I didn't get home until near dark last night."

"How's Climie doing with the boardinghouse?"

"She had eight people for supper last night, all of them sleeping on pallets upstairs. One of the wives took Sythia's place at the Jorgensens' store, since neither she nor Climie have time to work there any longer."

"So you stayed to help her clean up?"

"I did. Tell you about it after milking."

Del followed the near-to-grown Scamp out the door and called for Buttercup, who was already waiting at the back door of the barn. She bellowed a response as Scamp barked and danced in the snow. Starbright, now showing she was carrying a foal, whinnied from the wooden fence.

"I'm glad you all think this snow is wonderful. Lark had just gotten the fieldwork in full swing, and now it will be too wet again." Not that there was that much snow, but an inch or two melting into the ground would quickly make mud. Surely it would be gone by the wedding, though.

Only seven more days. Her middle fluttered at the thought.

In the barn, she hummed as she set down the three-legged stool and wiped any dirt off Buttercup's udder so it wouldn't fall into the bucket. Milk pinged into the bucket as the bovines enjoyed their grain. If one sought peace, a barn in the morning was a good place to find it.

"Thank you, Lord, for this glorious new day in spite of the snow. Lark will grumble about the fieldwork, but the snow will disappear by noon if the sun stays like it is." She was already thinking her coat was a bit warm.

Her mind flew to the wedding. There was still so much to do, including finishing her dress. She and RJ were getting married right after school was out the last week of May. So the wedding would be the first Saturday in June. She hoped the lilacs would be blooming by then since the forsythia would probably be finished. Surely there would be flowers of some kind for Lilac to make her bridal bouquet and decorate the altar.

She let her thoughts wander back to RJ's proposal in February. She had been stuck at Forsythia and Adam's house in a blizzard, unable to get home after school. Thankfully she'd dismissed class early enough to allow all her students to get home safely, but she'd made the mistake of staying after to grade papers. So RJ's romantic plans, she'd later learned, had turned into the two of them eating popcorn by the fire in the Brownsville sitting room while the storm raged outside the windows and Forsythia and Adam put the children to bed.

"Such an odd thing, popcorn." Sitting beside her on the settee, RJ had turned a puffy kernel between his fingers. "A tiny explosion, mostly fluff and air. Yet we down them by the handful."

"Because they're so good." Del snatched the kernel from him and popped it in her mouth, arching a brow at his mock-frown. "You weren't eating it anyway."

"Fair enough." RJ grabbed another handful, then sat sorting through the kernels, looking even more meditative and broody than his eye patch usually rendered him.

Del touched his arm. "Something wrong?"

He shrugged and gave a half grin. "This just isn't quite how I saw the evening going."

Del slipped her hand beneath his arm and squeezed it. "I'm sorry about the dance. But this is nice too, isn't it?"

"It's not so much the dance. It's . . . what I planned to ask you on the drive back from the dance." Abruptly, he dug back into the popcorn bowl and unearthed a tiny box.

Del stared at it, her mind at first a spinning blank. Until RJ slid from the sofa to one knee before her on the sitting room rug, holding one of her hands fast in his. His other hand held the tiny box, now open to show a ring.

And with a faint catch in his voice, he'd asked her if she'd do him the honor of becoming his wife, as long as they both should live.

Smiling and warmed through at the memory, Del stripped the last of the milk from the teats and set the bucket off to the side. The two-month-old bull calf, Buster, bawled from his pen as she hung the stool on the center post. "I'm coming. Your ma has to go out first." Del opened the stanchion and, after staring at her bawling calf, Buttercup backed up and turned to head out the door, followed by Clover, the heifer. By the end of the year, they would have two cows to milk.

Del poured milk into another bucket for the calf, this one set in a frame to keep it from spilling. After half filling the flat pan they set out for their two new barn cats, she carried the bucket outside to the well house and strained the milk.

"Are you counting the days?" Lark asked when Del returned to the soddy.

"Six until school is out and seven until the wedding. After breakfast, I want to head over and see how RJ is doing with the house."

"Do you think he thought to cover it before the snow?"

"I doubt it. There wasn't much warning last night."

Del found her beloved sweeping snow from the floor of their unfinished cabin, thunder on his brow. He and his crew had been hard at work all week building on the other half section of the homestead, just north of the gardens.

"I should've covered the door and windows," RJ said by way of greeting, his glare enough to scare off any woman who didn't know and love him like she did. "How could I be so stupid?"

"Because one doesn't generally expect a snowstorm in late May. And you're not stupid." Del reached up to tug his woolen cap straight and plant a kiss on his chilly cheek. "See, you've got half the floor swept clean already. Let me do the rest, and you can get ready for your crew."

RJ resisted her grip on his broom for a moment, then relinquished it with a sigh. "Was I crazy to try to build this cabin in a week?"

"Well, crazy or not, you've nearly done it." Del set to sweeping the fine powder from the wood floor RJ had spent hours laying. The sod dug from beneath the cabin had gone into the barn walls for Captain, also almost complete.

"I still wish I could have built you the house you deserve. The house I wanted to build."

"Someday." Del stopped sweeping to step close and twine her fingers through his. "One step at a time. Isn't that what we agreed?"

He stared at her, his one eye rebellious, then he softened into a half smile. "I ever tell you I love you, Delphinium Nielsen?"

"Once or twice." She stood on booted tiptoes for his kiss.

The final days of school flew by—truly final for Del, since she wouldn't be allowed to teach anymore once married. The town leaders had already hired a new teacher for the school, a competent and experienced one by the sound of it. And the new schoolhouse was in fine order for next term. Yet her heart ached as she bid her students bittersweet farewells, hugging Bethany Kinsley and Elsie Weber, hearing Timothy's shy thanks, the little ones clinging to her skirts and declaring they'd never love another teacher like her. "Never ever," Josie said.

She knew this new path with RJ was what the Lord had for her, no doubt of that. But, oh, if only she could do both.

RJ drove her home that evening, though she knew he couldn't spare the time from finishing the cabin. His quiet presence and conversation comforted her heart, and when they pulled up at the Nielsen homestead, joyful voices and open arms spilled from the door of the soddy. Anders had arrived, as she knew he would to give her away, but not just Anders—Jonah peered from behind his shoulder, shy-grinned and impossibly tall. Wrapping her arms around her brothers proved the best balm for a tender teacher's heart.

Then it was Friday, the last flurry of preparations, and then—not soon enough, and yet before she was ready—their wedding day dawned.

A pink pearly dawn promised a clear day but hopefully not too hot, though the weather had settled in since the snowstorm the week before. Del helped with chores, glad that she and RJ would still be close by even after today. Lark and Lilac could never manage the entire farm alone. After chores, the sisters finished fixing the sandwiches for the wedding luncheon to be held at the Brownsvilles' home after the late morning ceremony at church.

And then it was time for the dress—a cream-colored lawn with stripes of lavender flowers. The four of them had all worked on it these past weeks—the graceful bodice and full skirt, with lace edging the collar and sleeves, the tiny pearl buttons ordered from Jorgensens' mercantile. Del held up her arms, and her sisters dropped the dress in place. She felt like a princess, especially once Lilac handed her a bouquet of her namesake blossoms and pinned a delicate wreath of wildflowers on her braided-up hair.

It was a simple wedding in the clapboard church, but a sweet one. Surrounded by their friends and family—for RJ's sister and her family made the trip out by train also—they pledged themselves to each other before God and man. And if RJ's voice hoarsened at times when he spoke his vows, the grip of his hands on hers never wavered. Whatever she might leave behind in stepping into this new season, this, her hands joined with this man, was where she belonged.

Hours later, leaving the festivities and feasting behind for their families to complete, Del and RJ drove away in the light gig that was a wedding present from Esmay and George, pulled by Captain. Past the Leah's Garden sign and up the homestead lane in the falling springtime dusk, they veered off before the soddy toward their own section.

Del squeezed her husband's arm, anticipation swirling. She hadn't seen the cabin since RJ finished it.

They drove past the orchard and gardens, and there it was. One and a half stories, its freshly sided walls gleaming against the prairie, windows blinking on either side of the stout wooden door.

"RJ." Del stared. "You even got glass windows."

He shrugged and set the brake, then jumped down, a shy grin creasing his face. "It was the least I could do. You deserve lots more." He motioned to the building. "I figured we could turn this into the kitchen when we build our real house."

"What a grand idea. Still, it'll be like a palace after the soddy." She let him lift her to the ground, his hands lingering on her waist as he looked down into her eyes. Her husband—her mind still whirled at the thought.

He tucked her arm through his, and they walked up to their new home. There were even curtains at the windows. Her sisters must have had a hand in that.

And sweetest of all, a clump of lilacs, just beginning to show purple, by the cabin corner.

Del slanted a glance at RJ. "My sisters let you dig up their biggest lilac?"

"They must like you or something." RJ grinned and pressed the freshly dug dirt around the bush with the toe of his boot.

She brushed the delicate blossoms with her fingertips, their scent waving over them through the dusk like a benediction. "I love it. We'll always know our anniversary is coming by the bursting purple buds."

"As if we'll need to be reminded."

Blooming time, in so many ways. Del drew RJ's face down for another kiss, and then the two of them, arm in arm, stepped into their new home.

Lauraine Snelling is the award-winning author of more than seventy books, fiction and nonfiction, for adults and young adults. Her books have sold more than five million copies. Besides writing books and articles, she teaches at writers' conferences across the country. She and her husband make their home in Tehachapi, California. Learn more at laurainesnelling.com.

Kiersti Giron grew up loving Lauraine's books and had the blessing of being mentored by her as a young writer. Now it is her joy and honor to collaborate with Lauraine on this new series. Kiersti has a passion for history and storytelling and loves writing about reconciliation, healing, and God's story weaving into ours. She lives in California with her husband, their lively young son, and two cats. Learn more at kierstigiron.com.

Sign Up for Lauraine's Newsletter

Keep up to date with Lauraine's news on book releases and events by signing up for her email list at laurainesnelling.com.

More from Lauraine Snelling

After turning the tables on a crooked gambler, Larkspur Nielsen flees her home with her sisters on a wagon train bound for Oregon. Knowing four women will draw unwanted attention, she dons a disguise as a man. But maintaining the ruse is harder than she imagined, as is protecting her sisters from difficult circumstances and eligible young men.

The Seeds of Change
LEAH'S GARDEN #1

You May Also Like . . .

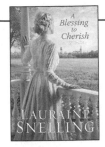

After several years of widowhood and hardship, Ingeborg focuses on the good she's been given while she watches her widowed stepson fall in love once again. But not everything is comfortable for Ingeborg; one of her dearest friendships is changing—and she will have to decide if her settled life is worth more to her than a future she hardly dares to imagine.

A Blessing to Cherish by Lauraine Snelling
laurainesnelling.com

Though her first few months in America were difficult, Nilda Carlson's life now resembles the images that filled her dreams in Norway. But when she spots the man from her terrifying past in town, she worries her new life, and hope for love, is crashing down around her. Did danger follow her across the Atlantic?

A Season of Grace by Lauraine Snelling
<small>Under Northern Skies #3</small>
laurainesnelling.com

New to America, Norwegian immigrant Nilda Carlson is encouraged by her wealthy mentor to better herself and the community of Blackduck. While her ideas to help other immigrants meet resistance, she finds delight in her piano lessons with a handsome schoolteacher. But with a detective digging into her past and a rich dandy vying for her hand, Nilda must decide which future she will choose.

A Song of Joy by Lauraine Snelling
<small>Under Northern Skies #4</small>
laurainesnelling.com

⬦BETHANYHOUSE

More from Bethany House

British spy Levi Masters is captured while investigating a discovery that could give America an upper hand in future conflicts. Village healer Audrey Moreau is drawn to the captive's commitment to honesty and is compelled to help him escape. But when he faces a severe injury, they are forced to decide how far they'll go to ensure the other's safety.

A Healer's Promise by Misty M. Beller
BRIDES OF LAURENT #2
mistymbeller.com

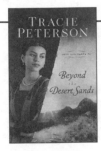

After living an opulent life with her aunt, the last thing Isabella Garcia wants is to celebrate Christmas in a small mining town with her parents. But she's surprised to see how much the town—and an old rival—have changed and how fragile her father's health has become. Faced with many changes, can she sort through her future and who she wants to be?

Beyond the Desert Sands by Tracie Peterson
LOVE ON THE SANTA FE
traciepeterson.com

When three kids go missing from the children's home, Lillian Walsh and Grace Bennet will do all they can to find them. With the future of the children's home in question, and everyone struggling to determine their paths forward, they all begin to realize that sometimes loving well means making difficult choices.

Unfailing Love by Janette Oke and Laurel Oke Logan
WHEN HOPE CALLS #3

❖ BETHANYHOUSE